Taming the Outlaw
by Cindy Gerard

ꕥ ꕔ ꕥ

He hadn't wanted to hurt Peg.

He'd just wanted to kiss her. Just once, for old times' sake. Just once, to see if his memory had been bigger than the reality.

Now he knew. His memory didn't even begin to compare with the real-life perfection of Peg Lathrop's lips. Or her long, lithe body pressed against his like a firebrand. Or the softness of her breasts warm and heavy in his hands.

Well, so much for what he'd wanted, he decided. He'd go for a ride with Peg and her little girl— because he'd promised that he would. Then he'd get out of town. Now that he knew he'd hurt Peg six years ago, he didn't want to hurt her again. And if he stuck around much longer, that's just what he'd do. He'd hurt her because now he knew something else. Something that he hadn't known before.

He wanted more from Peg than a kiss…

Tangled Sheets, Tangled Lies
by Julie Hogan

ᗝ ᗰ ᗡ

'Nothing could stop me from completing this job, I promise you,' Cole said.

Lauren's face creased into a sudden, brillant smile. 'Good. Thank you.' Then she rose fluidly from the chair and held out a hand.

Cole grinned and wrapped his big palm around her warm fingers. 'Congratulations. You just hired the best pair of hands west of the Mississippi.'

'Prove it, Cole. Just prove it.'

His gaze roamed her face, from her famous green eyes down to her famous full lips. 'Oh, I will,' he promised, and wondered how long he was going to be able to keep his secret from Lauren—or keep the best pair of hands west of Mississippi off the most beautiful woman on the planet.

Available in September 2004 from Silhouette Desire

Expecting the Sheikh's Baby
by Kristi Gold
(Dynasties: The Barones)
and
Born To Be Wild
by Anne Marie Winston
(Dynasties: The Barones)

Taming the Outlaw
by Cindy Gerard
and
Tangled Sheets, Tangled Lies
by Julie Hogan

The Cowboy Claims His Lady
by Meagan McKinney
(Montana)
and
Sleeping With Beauty
by Laura Wright

Taming the Outlaw
CINDY GERARD

Tangled Sheets, Tangled Lies
JULIE HOGAN

 **SILHOUETTE®**

Desire™

*Silhouette, Silhouette Desire and Colophon
are registered trademarks of Harlequin Books S.A.,
used under licence.*

*First published in Great Britain 2004
Silhouette Books, Eton House, 18-24 Paradise Road,
Richmond, Surrey TW9 1SR*

The publisher acknowledges the copyright holders of the
individual works as follows:

Taming the Outlaw © Cindy Gerard 2002
Tangled Sheets, Tangled Lies © Julie Hogan 2003

ISBN 0 373 04996 X

51-0904

*Printed and bound in Spain
by Litografia Rosés S.A., Barcelona*

TAMING THE OUTLAW
by
Cindy Gerard

CINDY GERARD

If asked, 'What's your idea of heaven?' Cindy Gerard would say a warm sun, a cool breeze, pan pizza and a good book. If she had to settle for one of the four, she'd opt for the book, with the pizza running a close second. Inspired by the pleasure she's received from the books she's read and her long-time love affair with her husband, Tom, Cindy now creates her own evocative and sensual love stories about compelling characters and complex relationships.

Cindy loves to hear from her readers and invites them to visit her website at www.tlt.com/authors/cgerard.htm

This book is dedicated to Kyle and Eileen Gerard for being you and for the gift of Kayla Marie, sweet child, who owns me, heart and soul.

One

___

When Cutter Reno drifted out of Sundown, Montana, six years ago, he'd always figured he'd be back someday. He had friends here. He had memories here, some good, some not so good. And he supposed, in the overall scheme of things, Sundown came as close to "home" as any place he'd landed in his twenty-six years.

What he hadn't figured on was that when he did finally make an appearance it would be as the grand marshall of the annual Fourth of July parade.

Guess that goes to show how much he knew. He'd never counted on winning back-to-back National PRCA saddle bronc championships, either. And as it turned out, it was the celebrity status of the championships that had prompted his old buddy, Sam Perkins, to track him down and asked him to come back to lead the parade.

He shifted in the saddle and smiled at the faces lining the street. Then he tried not to think about the competitions and the money he was missing out on.

"Half the county will turn out to see you in the parade tomorrow," Sam had told him last night when they'd gotten together at the Dusk to Dawn Bar to catch up. "Why, it's downright huge."

By Sundown, Montana, population four hundred and seventy-three, standards, Cutter supposed it was a pretty big deal. Close as he could figure, it was four blocks long—a new record according to Sam—as it snaked with dogged enthusiasm along the length of Main Street strung with red, white and blue banners. Among the highlights was a twenty-one piece all-school marching band.

"Yeah, we'd a' had twenty-two marchers if Billy Capper hadn't busted his nose in the softball game yesterday when his face connected with Joe Gillman's bat." This from Snake Gibson, a barrel-chested old wrangler who'd joined in on the bull-slinging at the bar last night.

The consensus, over cold longnecks and shelled peanuts, was that since Sundown had beaten neighboring Shueyville in a ninth-inning squeaker, Billy's absence would be missed but not overly mourned.

The band seemed to be holding their own without him, too, Cutter thought, as they sweltered in their red wool uniforms, desperately tried to keep close ranks and belt out a Sousa march. It was a shame they were working so hard, though, because for all their efforts, he was a little embarrassed to discover that all eyes were turned on him.

Well, almost all eyes, Cutter conceded as he spotted a six-year-old memory that should have worked its way out of his system by now. The moment he saw Peg Lathrop, Cutter lost all awareness of the summer sun beating down, burning through his gray-and-black plaid shirt.

The band, the laughter and the cheers from the crowd all faded to background noise as Cutter shifted to autopilot, automatically reining in the big bay gelding when it crow-hopped away from an escaped red balloon. He was only aware of the chestnut-haired woman who moved purposefully along the fringe of the route, avoiding his gaze like she was practicing a religion.

"Ain't he just the cat's meow."

Peg Lathrop crossed her arms beneath her breasts and gave her friend, Krystal Perkins, a tight smile. "Well, you've got the cat part right. What he is, is what he always was—an alley cat with an attitude."

Didn't look like he'd changed a bit, either, Peg decided, watching him wave to the cheering crowd from astride the big gelding the parade committee had arranged for him to ride. With effort, she schooled her gaze away from Cutter Reno's lean rangy angles and slow, seductive grins. Then she told herself that seeing him again didn't hurt. She wasn't angry with him anymore, either. It might have been easier to forgive him, though, if he hadn't known exactly what effect he had on women. Just like he knew exactly what result he was after. Lay 'em and leave 'em.

"Would ya just look at him?" Krystal continued, shaking her head in awe. "Lord above but he's pretty."

Peg had been trying not to look. She straightened her shoulders and scowled at Krystal whose turned-up nose, flashing green eyes and short brown hair had a tendency to make people dismiss her as flighty when in fact she was as grounded as an oak. She was also the most happily married woman Peg knew.

"Sam catches you drooling over Reno like that and you may be looking for an alley to sleep in yourself."

Krystal laughed and hiked her ice-cream-cone-wielding two-year-old son, Grant, higher on her hip. "No crime in lookin' at the package," she said, as Grant smeared chocolate ice cream from his chin to his chest and gave his momma a sticky smile. "As long as the only place I go lookin' for love is with the little guy's daddy here, right baby boy?"

The reference to his father had Grant warming to his current favorite phrase. "Where Daddy go? Where Daddy go?" His brown eyes danced as he bounced on his momma's hip, making a game of it.

"Daddy's on the fire truck, punkin'. You watch. He'll be comin' along pretty soon now. And Momma will just watch that ole alley cat till Daddy gets here, okay?"

Peg snorted. "You make sure you grow up to be like your daddy, Grant." She patted the little boy's back with affection. "Good men like him are hard to find."

And even harder to keep, she thought as her gaze involuntarily sought, then connected with the stunning brilliance of Cutter Reno's slashing smile.

Peg froze the moment their gazes caught and held. As Grant continued to chatter in the background, she felt the warming pleasure in Cutter's summer-blue eyes—and the rabbit-run beat of her heart as it kicked up and thumped her in the chest.

Tearing her gaze away, she gripped her five-year-old daughter's hand tightly in hers and told herself she wasn't running. "Come on, Shell. I see Grampa Jack. Let's go find out if he's got a spot picked out to watch the fireworks tonight."

"But I wanna see the rest of the parade," Shelby protested, planting her tiny scuffed red cowboy boots on the sun-softened asphalt.

Peg looked down at her very own grubby little rainbow. The fine blond hair peeking out beneath her lavender cowboy hat was damp and curling with sweat and escaping in little wisps from twin Annie Oakley braids. Her yellow sunsuit was stained with the same chocolate ice cream as Grant's shirt; her cherub face was pink from the sun and the heat and flushed with excitement. Startlingly blue eyes sparkled with stubborn determination.

"I bet you can see it better from Grampa's shoulders."

Peg knew she'd won the point when Shelby made a beeline for Jack Lathrop who was standing with a group of his cronies at the end of the block.

"Say goodbye to Krystal and Grant," Peg chastised with a shake of her head.

"Bye Krystal. Bye Grant," Shelby called over her shoulder as she loped toward her grandpa.

Peg rolled her eyes then smiled an apology at Krystal. Her smile faded at her friend's speculative frown. "What?"

"Have you decided yet if you're going to see him?" Like her voice, Krystal's eyes were soft.

Peg looked at her sandaled feet, studied the siren-red nail polish on her toes. There was no point in playing coy. Ever since Krystal's husband, Sam, who'd chaired the parade committee, had happily reported that his buddy, Cutter Reno, had agreed to be this year's grand marshall, Krystal had been after her. "Not if I can help it."

Krystal's frown changed from concerned to admonishing.

"Got to go," Peg said before Krystal could launch into a minilecture on why she should talk to Cutter.

"Okay," Krystal conceded at Peg's closed-off look. "No more questions—at least about Cutter, but are we still on for the picnic tonight before the fireworks?"

Peg narrowed her eyes. "Cutter going to be there?"

With her gaze intent on Peg, Krystal nodded.

"Then I'll skip that particular party, thanks."

"Peg—"

"—Don't. Don't say it," Peg cut in, then felt ashamed for snapping. She held up her hand. "Sorry. Just let it go, okay? I've got to deal with this the way I think is best."

Before the conversation escalated into something

she couldn't keep up with, she gave Grant a peck on the cheek and Krystal a one-armed hug. "Maybe I'll see you tonight at the fireworks. Thanks for watching Shell this morning."

Studiously avoiding the cowboy on the horse in the black hat and tight jeans, she threaded her way through the crowd toward the little girl whose hand was linked with the man Peg called Daddy and Shelby called Grandpa. Then she assured herself that Cutter would be gone tomorrow and life, like her heartbeat, would settle back to normal.

Pretty Peggy Lathrop. Man, Cutter thought as he watched her move along the parade route. She always had been a fine sight. Time had only improved on the package of sleek lines and knockout curves. Paint-tight blue jean cutoffs showed off slim hips and long tan legs. A tiny white spaghetti strap tank top hugged a pair of unbelievably lush breasts. The hint of a tanned tummy peeked between the scrap of stretchy cotton and the waistband of those hip-hugging shorts.

As his horse plodded along at parade speed, he did his damnedest to keep a bead on her. Beneath a pale straw Stetson that partially shaded her face, a length of satin straight hair fell to nearly her waist. The July sun glinted off the shining mass, setting off flashes of light like a prairie fire. When he finally got around to checking out the face her hat brim shadowed, he was just as taken as he was with the rest of her—and got pleasantly lost in a sweet summer memory of long-legged Peg.

Pretty little brown-eyed girl.

Never taking his eyes off her, he lifted his hat, re-settled it, and with a smile of pure pleasure, prepared to get sentimentally sappy over the fire of an old flame that had never quite burned itself out. They'd had a little thing six years ago. It had been the summer of his sophomore year in the PRCA. He'd been flying high, still pumped up over being named Rookie of the Year. He'd come home to Sundown a hero then, too. And he'd found little Peg all grown up. When he left town again, he'd left a winner in more ways than one.

Still watching her, he shifted the reins to his left hand, absently rubbed the flat of his palm along his thigh. There was no way she didn't remember. He'd seen it in her eyes in the brief moment when their gazes had connected over the crowd. He'd waited for her to smile for him. Instead, she'd looked away faster than the swish of the gelding's tail.

He was still looking, though. He may have been too busy the past few years for more than fleeting thoughts of those hot summer nights they'd spent together, but he hadn't forgotten. Dew-damp grass. Round July moon. Soft, surrendering sighs. Seeing her again brought all those memories front and center. She'd had an innocence about her back then that had just tangled him up inside, a lack of inhibition that had made him drunk with lust. The taste of her. The sweet, giving heat. *Man, had there been heat.* Enough heat that just seeing her again made him wonder what pretty Peggy was up to these days.

"Cutter—hey, Cutter, over here!"

He whipped his head around, a winning smile in

place as a dozen cameras clicked. He tipped his hat to a little cowboy in tall boots and a big hat who was grinning up at him from the curb as if Cutter held the key to Candyland.

Peg hadn't smiled at him that way. Peg hadn't smiled at all. Her pretty brown eyes had looked right past him while he was still recovering from the punch of pure, spontaneous arousal that had bolted through his body like a summer lightning strike. All flash and fire and electricity.

No. She hadn't smiled. He didn't know quite what to make of that. Everybody smiled for Cutter. Hell. Most women did a lot more than smile. Peg had done a *whole* lot more six years ago. They'd had a good time. At least *he* had. From all indications, she had, too. And now she wouldn't smile for him. He didn't know if that made him feel bad, or mad or just plain puzzled.

Cutter got a line on Peg's straw hat again as she moved easily among the crowd. He caught the smile she gave to a pretty redhead about her age. Scowled as she showed her pearly whites to a gaggle of ranch hands who gaped in awe then panted and groaned in ecstasy as she passed them by.

The booming crack of a cherry bomb sent the bay into a skittering dance that ended up with him snorting and rearing on his hind legs and striking at the air. Cutter settled him with a soft murmur and a strong hand that had the crowd *ahing* in approval just as the band broke into a rousing country rendition of ''God Bless the U.S.A.''

When Cutter looked around, Peg was gone...

without a smile—which, he'd decided, he was going to get from pretty Peggy before he blew back out of town tomorrow.

Everybody smiled for Cutter Reno. Everybody.

''Hey, hey, Peggy Sue. I thought that was you, darlin'.''

The words—laced with amusement and thick with pure, male arrogance—drifted across ten yards of dew-drenched grass and a dome of star-flung sky. Short of walking straight away and pretending she hadn't heard him—a long shot since she'd flinched then frozen like a deer caught in a spotlight the moment she'd heard his voice—Peg had little choice but to square her shoulders, get ahold of herself and face him.

She turned slowly, doing her very best not to react to the picture he made standing there. ''Hey, Cutter.''

The fireworks had ended less than five minutes ago. The scent of sulfur from the pyrotechnical display hung thick on the summer air. Pickups and cars were still jockeying for exit positions down the narrow gravel road that led away from Sundown's baseball park where the fireworks were launched every year. Shelby, thankfully, was on her way to sleep over with Peg's folks. She'd been half-asleep in her grandpa Jack's arms before the last dazzling display had faded to ash.

The man walking toward her had once held her in his arms on a starry night much like this one—when she'd been younger and not as wise and more taken with a rodeo cowboy's heroic charm than she was today.

He still did make a picture, though, she admitted reluctantly. Lone-wolf rugged and utterly male. That was Cutter. From his tall, broad-shouldered frame, to the sinew and muscle of his athletic swagger, to the dark shadows and shadings of his beautifully sculpted face, to the dark brown hair beneath his black Stetson, he was all male, all sex appeal.

In the starlight, he looked almost hard...until he smiled. Unfortunately, when he smiled, it softened that impossibly virile face, warmed those incredibly blue eyes and reminded her...well, it reminded her of too many things. Like how quick he was to laugh, to tease, to drive her wild with the gentle press or the hot possession of a mouth that had the ability to make her want to forget—even want to forgive—how easy it had been for him to walk away from her.

She settled herself with a deep breath, tucked her fingertips into the hip pockets of the jeans she'd changed into for the night's activities and forced herself to meet his gaze.

"You're lookin' good, darlin'," he said as he walked up to meet her then closed in to stop and stand, boot tip to boot tip, in front of her.

He was crowding her. Not to intimidate. Cutter would never attempt to intimidate even though stacking his six feet against her five and a half, it was a given that he could. No, intimidation wasn't in his nature. Touching was, though. Cutter had always been a toucher and he was about a deep breath away from folding her against him into a long, *hello again* hug.

"You, too, Cutter." She backed what she hoped was a casual step away, refusing to let his compliment, or his use of the word *darlin'*, or his intense, steady appraisal undermine her determination to react to him with a need for anything other than distance. She didn't want to be hugged by Cutter Reno. At least she didn't want to admit that she did.

For the longest moment, he didn't say anything. He just stood there, backlit by moonlight, his expression shadowed by his hat brim. She didn't have to see his face to know that he was trying to figure out her reaction.

"I was surprised to see you back in Sundown, Peg," he said carefully. "Thought that after you finished college, you had your mind set for the city— had plans to be an accountant or something, right?"

He was referring to her long-ago pronouncement of getting an accounting degree then partnering up in some urban firm.

"Yeah, well, you know how it goes. Plans change."

When you're five months pregnant, sick and alone, plans change. It's tough to go to class when you're barfing up your breakfast and your heart is breaking because your baby's not going to have a daddy and the man you were foolish enough to fall in love with has forgotten you even existed.

Since she didn't think he'd particularly want to hear about that and since she had no intention of telling him anyway, she shook off the memory and squared her shoulders.

"Not *your* plans, though," she said in a quick, determined attempt to avert the focus to him. "You did exactly what you said you were going to do. An NFR championship. That's quite an accomplishment."

He shrugged and continued to stare as if he were not only trying to see every detail of her face but right through to every detail of her thoughts, as well. "Guess I've been lucky."

She didn't want to like him for his modesty. It took more than luck to get to the top in the PRCA. It took drive, it took guts and, yeah, it took some luck along with a conviction to not let anything stand in the way. Anything like the woman he'd left behind.

"Well," she said, already deeper into a conversation with him than she'd ever wanted to go, "it was a nice thing you did—coming home to grand marshall the parade and all. Sam was over the moon when you agreed to do it."

He smiled. She quickly looked at her boots while her stomach did a little rock and roll and her heart started that damnable rabbit-run beat again.

"I needed a break—and it's kind of fun being back. Nice to touch base, you know? I hadn't seen Sam or some of the other guys...or you—" he hesitated, his voice going soft and low "—since—well, let's just say it's been a while."

"Yeah." She looked up, briefly meeting his gaze. "It's been a while." Six years is a long while but there was no way she was moving toward that watermark with him.

"So...how's your mom, Cutter? Kind of lost track of her since she moved—what's it been? Almost five years now?"

He slung his weight on one hip, crossed his arms over his chest and tucked his hands under his armpits. "Something like that. She's fine. Likes it in Cheyenne, I guess. Anyway, she did last time I talked to her. I don't see her much, though." He gave a small lift of his shoulders. "You know how it is. I'm on the road a lot."

Yeah. She knew. "Well, that's rodeo."

Silence, as thick as the night, as close as the memories of lying in his arms, mingled with the distant sound of laughter and the occasional explosion of a firecracker. She looked toward the sound. Safe sounds. She had to go. She had to go now.

"Well—"

"—So," he said at the same time, cutting her off.

He smiled.

She didn't.

And just when the dead air hanging between them became unbearable, he tilted his head, tried again. "So, what lucky guy coaxed you back to Sundown?" The smile was gone from his voice, an honest curiosity replacing it.

She sniffed, looked past his shoulder toward the city park a few blocks away where Rocky Road, a local country band, was setting up for the dance that would last until midnight.

"Well, let's see, there was a whole raft of them last time I looked."

He chuckled, all soft and low, the sound as intimate as a secret. "I don't doubt it for one little minute. So does that mean you're still footloose and fancy-free?"

About as footloose and fancy-free as a single

mother could be, she thought, biting back the resentment. Not toward Shelby. Shelby was the best thing that had ever happened to her. The resentment she felt was reserved for Cutter, for the choices he'd never been forced to make, the dreams he'd never had to give up. The resentment was for the fact that his voice and his smile told her he'd be pleased as punch to pick up where they'd left off—as long as it was convenient for him.

You're a jerk, Cutter Reno, she thought but swallowed back the barb. It wouldn't do to blame him— he was a man, after all, and experience had pretty much drawn her to the conclusion that it was a condition of the gender. A fair percentage of all men were jerks. They just couldn't seem to help themselves.

"Well, hey, Cutter," she said with a quick nod and an obvious intent to call this conversation closed. "It's been nice talking to you but I've got to go, okay? Randy's going to be wondering where I am." She shouldered past him. "Good to see you."

"Hey, wait." He snagged her arm, spun her back toward him with a good-natured laugh. "Randy? As in, Randy *Bubba* Watkins?" His eyes were crinkled at the corners, no doubt picturing bowlegged, bucktoothed Bubba whose name was the first one that had popped into Peg's head. "You and Bubba? You've got a thing goin'?"

Clearly he wasn't buying it. Which, of course, he was right not to since she and Randy had never been and would never be anything but friends.

"Why not Randy?" She lifted her chin, relying on the premise that the best defense was just that—defense—all the while carefully removing his hand from around her upper arm and working to tamp down the sizzle of heat his touch had sent skittering along her skin. "He's one of the good guys. He's funny. He's kind. And he sticks, you know what I mean?"

The minute her last statement popped out, and sounding way too accusatory, she realized her error. Just as she realized that Cutter understood her point and recognized her anger. He'd neither stuck around nor kept in touch once he'd left her and Sundown behind all those years ago.

He thumbed back his hat; his dark brows lowered over ridiculously thick-lashed eyes. She could see he was warming up to be charitable and that sat just about as well as his arrogance.

"Peg—about that summer—"

"—I wish I could stay and talk, I really do." She cut him off before he made her so mad she'd do something unforgivable, like show him just how much his presence back in Sundown had shaken her. "But I've got to go."

She set out again, walking in long, purposeful strides across the outfield. "You take care now," she added over her shoulder just to make sure he understood that he hadn't rattled her.

Because he had rattled her—and rattled her good—she broke into a fast jog when she had the good luck to spot Randy, who was as surprised as he was pleased when she snagged his hand. Wrapping her arm around his waist, she started chattering cheerfully about the band and the dance he had promised her. And she told herself she wasn't running, that Cutter didn't have the power to make her run. Not toward him. Not away.

Alone, in the dark, Cutter watched and wondered and tried to decide exactly how disappointed he was that Peg had just thrown him the coldest shoulder between here and Bozeman.

Lucky man, he thought about Bubba as he walked toward his truck debating whether or not his night was over or just beginning. Some warm-up drumbeats and a few licks from a bass guitar rumbled across the night from the park.

He thought about his empty room in Sundown's historic old hotel. He thought of pretty Peggy who would be at the dance—with Bubba.

Then he thought, "What the hell."

He fished his keys out of his front jeans pocket and swung up into the cab. As he turned the ignition, he grinned as the words to an old country song came to mind. "If Bubba can dance, I can, too."

Two

"Alley cat," Peg sputtered on her way home from work the next day.

She didn't want to but she couldn't stop thinking about Cutter and the way he'd posed and prowled and strutted his stuff for all the panting little buckle bunnies who had drooled over him at the dance last night.

"Yep. Alley cat tags him in a nutshell," she decided as she turned down the street that led to Krystal's who, in addition to being her best friend, also baby-sat for Shelby while Peg worked at Lathrop's Feed Store where she kept books for her dad.

Too bad she hadn't been able to figure Cutter out six years ago. At eighteen his smiles had said, "You're special." At eighteen, she'd been in love. After all, he'd been daring. A rodeo cowboy. A mysterious breed. A local boy who had returned victorious. And he'd been so beautiful it had made her chest ache.

She let out a deep breath, pressed a closed fist to a spot between her breasts and told herself it wasn't aching now because of him. Now that he was back— victorious again. And even more beautiful.

Face grim, Peg pulled to a stop in front of Krystal's house and killed the engine. Well, he may be back, but this time, there would be no repeat performance of that summer.

She'd been so stupid. The rodeo had been in town for an eight-day run for the Fourth of July holiday then, too. Since she'd had a crush on Cutter when he'd been a senior in high school and she'd been a sophomore, she'd been pretty much a sure thing. He'd known it. He'd played on it. It had taken him five days to talk her out of her virginity.

He'd been good, she remembered as she slipped out of her beat-up old truck then walked up Krystal's front walk that was bordered with valiantly blooming summer flowers. So good. Sweet and attentive. Intense and enduring. He'd taught her about sex. He'd taught her about love. And then he'd taught her about heartache.

He'd left with a promise to call from Salt Lake. She hadn't heard from him or seen him since.

Until yesterday.

"His loss," she breathed on a wind-down sigh as she strolled through the front door and scooped her beautiful little five-year-old tomboy into her arms.

"Him who, Momma?" Shelby asked after a big hug and a squirming wiggle.

"Nobody, cupcake. Nobody."

"Any *nobody* I know?"

Peg met Krystal's bright eyes with a glare meant to silence.

Krystal either wasn't paying attention or chose to ignore the warning. "You can fool some of the people all of th—"

"—Just stop. I'm not trying to fool anybody," she insisted as Shelby slid out of her arms.

Krystal made sure Shelby was back on her tummy on the floor and engrossed in her coloring book. "So that means you were planning on telling me you talked to Cutter last night?" she asked softly.

Peg lifted a shoulder, a failed attempt at indifference. She'd known that someone would have seen them talking just as she'd known the word would get around. Newsworthy or not, the word always got around in Sundown. "So I saw him. So what."

"So—how'd it go?"

Peg crossed to the island counter nestled in the middle of Krystal's cheery yellow kitchen, gave Grant a grinning hello then dug into the perpetually stocked cookie jar. She bit into a crunchy peanut-butter cookie, closed her eyes on a hum of approval and swallowed.

"It didn't *go* anywhere." She touched a finger to the corner of her mouth to catch a crumb and tuck it into her mouth. "We ran into each other after the fireworks. No big deal."

"*Big deal,*" Krystal pointed out unnecessarily. "What did you two talk about?"

Another shrug. "I told him I was involved with someone."

Krystal blinked. "Really? Well, now. That's a pretty tough trick since all you do is work and, oh, yeah...*work*," she added with feeling as she moved to snag a crayon from Grant's pudgy little fist before he ate it. "So who's the lucky guy?"

Peg grinned guiltily. "Randy?"

Krystal let out a hoot of laughter as she wiped Grant's fingers with a towel and handed him a cookie. "So Randy must be, like, on cloud nine, huh?"

"Randy's a pal. And he doesn't know that we have this hot and heavy thing going."

"Must be a lot of fun for him."

Peg sank down on a kitchen chair. "Look. Cutter will be gone soon—if he isn't already—and then we can just forget this whole thing."

"What thing, Momma?" Shelby asked from the floor where she was sprawled on her tummy finishing her masterpiece with crayon and coloring paper.

Peg scowled at Krystal before turning a smile to her daughter. "It's a girl thing, Shell. A *big* girl thing. Hey, is that for me?" she asked, her voice full of hope for Shelby's benefit as she looked at the picture of a cowboy riding a big black horse. Her darling girl had worked so hard to keep the colors between the lines.

"For Grandpa."

"He's going to love it. Next one's mine, though, okay?"

"I'll make another real pretty one."

"Outside," Krystal mouthed over Shelby's head and swung Grant onto her hip.

Peg rolled her eyes, snagged another cookie and reluctantly followed Krystal out onto the backyard deck. She wasn't up for this lecture but it looked like it was going to happen anyway.

The next day was Peg's Thursday off. She planned to spend it like she always did. With Shelby still asleep, she dressed in her chore clothes, figuring on passing the hour between seven and eight mucking out stalls and telling the horses how pretty they were. When Shelby got up, they'd have breakfast then go for their Thursday morning ride.

Carrying her boots, she slipped quietly out the kitchen door and headed down to her little barn. The morning was already July warm, the sun a burning fireball suspended in the stunning blue Montana sky. The air was rich with summer scents: drying grass, ripening hay and the fragrance of wildflowers drifting down from the high meadows.

Nestled against the breath-stealing backdrop of the mountains, her little place didn't look like much. Actually it wasn't even hers, though she thought of it that way. For the time being, she had to be content to rent the house and the three acres that sat on the edge of town from Homer Carmichael. Until she finally wore him down and convinced him to sell it to her, it was the best she could do. When Homer was ready, though, she would be, too. She could afford a contract—if the down payment wasn't too steep—and if that old truck kept running, she thought with a frown and tugged on her boots.

In the meantime, the rent Homer charged was fair; it met her budget and he didn't care what she did to the place in the way of making it her own. Hers and Shelby's.

Rascal, their four-year-old black-and-white border collie, lay in a slant of morning sunlight that filtered in through the open barn door. Dreaming of chasing rabbits, she thought with a smile as his feet fluttered and his tail thumped in his sleep.

Grabbing a grain scoop, she filled a feed bucket with the special blend Jack had mixed up for her. She'd been thinking about her father a lot the last couple of days—not Jack, but her biological father, a man she'd never known. Jack Lathrop was her dad in every way that counted, in every way but blood. She loved him and all the memories of his loving hands and gentle smiles that he'd given her so generously from the time she could remember. And yet, sometimes, she wondered. What was he like? Where was he now?

Thoughtful, she filled Henry's then Bea's feed trough, gave them each an affectionate pat on the rump and dipped the scoop back in the bucket.

"And how are you, you ornery outlaw?" she murmured when Jackpot, the three-year-old gelding she'd brought home just this past month, nickered and pumped his head. "Trying to decide if you want to take a bite out of me or dig into your chow, aren't ya, big guy?" she crooned, filling his trough as well.

Her weakness for a pretty face had gotten her in

trouble again with this guy. Jackpot was a hot-blooded black-and-white paint that her friends, Lee and Ellie Savage, had insisted she accept for her birthday gift last month. Even knowing that the Savage's sole income didn't come from their breeding business, Jackpot was still an extravagant gift.

"I can't," Peg had sputtered, flabbergasted.

"Yes," Lee had said with a grin the day Ellie had invited Peg out to Shiloh Ranch to visit, "you can. I don't have time to mess with him," Lee had added. "But you—with a little TLC and a gentle hand—you just might reform him."

Well. There it was. She'd always been a sucker for an outlaw and now she had one of her very own.

Another outlaw had her thinking about her father again. Cutter showing up back in Sundown had dredged up all kinds of thoughts, all kinds of questions, and resurrected the what-ifs she rarely let herself dwell on. What if she'd known her real father? Would she be different? Would her life be different?

And what about Shelby? What if Shelby knew about Cutter? What if Cutter knew about Shelby?

Scowling, she tossed the grain bucket and scoop back in the bin. She couldn't honestly think that she'd done the wrong thing by keeping it from him all these years, even though Krystal—who was the only person besides her mother and Jack who knew that Cutter was Shelby's father—had lectured her good and long yesterday afternoon about the possibility that it was.

"He has a right, Peg. He has a right to know," Krystal had insisted gently.

Peg hadn't felt one bit gentle. "He has no rights.

Not with Shelby. He lost any right when he left without so much as a long look back. Promise me. Promise me that you and Sam didn't tell him anything about Shelby.''

Of course Krystal had promised. They hadn't told, even though Cutter had fired questions at them like bullets at the picnic, wanting to know all about what she'd been up to. Peg wouldn't let herself—not for a minute—feel wrong about not telling him. Just as it didn't feel wrong that she thought of Jack as her dad.

Snagging the knife she kept tucked on a beam over the tack room door, she cut the twine on a hay bale. Like Cutter, her own biological father had been a rodeo rider. She hadn't even known he existed until she'd come home from college, pregnant and ashamed and needing her mother.

With her arms warm and forgiving around her, Kay Lathrop had told Peg about her blood father then. It had been a gift. An acknowledgment that people made mistakes. That Kay had made one, too, and that her world hadn't ended. In fact, Jack had married her, adopted Peg and they had been her world. Her whole world. Just like Shelby was Peg's.

As she tossed a fat flake of hay into each manger, she thought about the choices she'd made. Tough choices. Now, more than ever, after seeing Cutter again, watching the way he'd flirted and flitted from one woman to another at the dance, knowing the way he lived, chasing the next gold buckle, following the circuit, she was convinced she'd made the right ones. Cutter wasn't daddy or husband material.

Did she feel guilty that she hadn't given him a

chance to be either? Sometimes, she admitted, as she unrolled the water hose, lifted the catch on the faucet and started filling the tanks with fresh water. But guilt didn't override one unalterable fact. She and Shelby were here. And Cutter was long gone. Again. At least, by her calculations, he should have left yesterday. After all, there was nothing keeping him in Sundown and a lot to lead him away. His type always had a reason to ride off into the sunset.

She ignored the little pang of longing that always tagged along behind any thought associated with him as she shut off the water then maneuvered the wheelbarrow over behind the stalls. She picked up the pitchfork, balanced it over the handles of the wheelbarrow. Some things just weren't meant to be.

And that was fine. *She* was fine. The unexpected bite of tears that stung her eyes wasn't anything more than a temporary, knee-jerk yearning for what never could have been.

She sniffed them back, swiped at her eyes with the back of a gloved hand and shook it off. There. Better already.

Forcefully shifting her thoughts from stolen kisses and lean, strong heat to her mom's recipe for blueberry pancakes, she tried to remember whether or not she had the makings in her cupboard. Shelby Lynn dearly loved blueberry pancakes. And it was Shelby Lynn that she had to take care of today and every day.

Cutter was still trying to figure out why he'd just driven into a lane with a mailbox that told him

P. Lathrop lived in the little two-story clapboard house with the sagging front porch and sun-faded gray siding. With his pickup engine idling softly, he sat behind the wheel and couldn't come up with a particularly good answer.

"You should leave it be, Reno," he muttered, as a black-and-white border collie came lumbering up to his truck, tongue lolling and tail wagging.

What point did he plan to make? What good was he up to? Honest truth? None. He should just go. Yet he killed the motor and climbed out of the truck, stretching out the kinks that were his rewards for his fair share of failed eight counts and board-hard motel beds.

He patted the dog's head then followed him to the barn where the doors were open and a bluesy country tune played softly from a radio that was standard equipment in any horse barn he'd ever encountered.

His boot heels crunched through Montana dust until he stopped just inside the wide double-door frame. As his eyes adjusted to the dim interior light, his blood started a slow, mellow simmer at the sight that greeted him there.

No way should she make his blood heat, let alone boil. Not turned out like that. The punch of arousal was hard and strong. So was the kick of reality. He realized with one look how much he still wanted her—and how hard she had it on her own as she worked at mucking out a stall.

He drew another deep breath, knowing he should just turn around and go…but all he could do was stand and stare as she stood in a slant of sunlight.

On her feet were knee-high rubber muck boots. Her shirt—a dust-gray tank top—left her tanned arms bare and those beautiful breasts lost somewhere beneath the sloppy cotton knit. Hanging from her hips was a pair of baggy silk boxer shorts that might have once been siren-red but had faded with many washings and wearings to an anemic pink. The bare, tanned line of leg exposed between boot and shorts was long and coltishly lean. Beneath those ridiculously ugly shorts, her hips were slim, her buttocks tight and high and he could just make out the faint outline of French-cut panties.

He couldn't help but wonder if she was wearing lace under all that utilitarian clothing as his gaze drifted to her hair. She'd tied it up high at the back of her head into a sweeping ponytail that made her look about sixteen years old instead of the twenty-four that he knew her to be. A pretty little scrap of red ribbon held it precariously in place.

That one small concession to her femininity did things to his heart rate he didn't even want to think about and made him realize he had no business poking his nose—or anything else—into Peg Lathrop's homespun little world. She was as off-limits to a guy like him as a nine-to-five job and roots. In some ways, he'd known it six years ago. Well, after seeing her like this, he definitely knew it now. This was a home-and-hearth kind of girl. This was a woman who deserved a lot more than the one-night stand that he grudgingly admitted he might have come out here hoping to charm out of her—for old times' sake. For sentimentality sake.

Hell, for his sake.

He should go. For her sake.

But then she turned around and spotted him—and he'd be damned if he could find a convincing reason to go anywhere.

"Helluva watchdog you've got here, darlin'." He leaned a shoulder against the doorjamb and shoved his hands into his hip pockets. Then he tried to act like his knees didn't feel like putty and his heart wasn't goading him to walk right on over there and kiss her until they fell to the barn floor in a tangled knot of hot, hungry hands and arching bodies.

He wasn't the only one who'd been caught off guard. Those big cinnamon-brown eyes of hers had grown wide before they'd narrowed in what he was pretty sure was anger, not welcome. He didn't want Peg angry with him, which, if he were being totally honest, was another reason he was still in Sundown.

She'd talked a good talk the other night when he'd caught up with her after the fireworks. She'd played it real cool. But there had been a spark of anger in her eyes when she'd faced him and for that, he'd felt guilty. And then at the dance, she'd made damn sure he didn't get within a Texas-two-step of her. Not that he would have poached on Randy's territory, but it hadn't taken long to figure out she'd just been using Randy as a smoke screen. That friendship was the only thing going on between those two, had been obvious from the get-go.

He hadn't pushed it, though, even though he'd wanted to. Yeah, he'd wanted a chance to hold her close in a slow, sultry dance in the moonlight. A chance to feel all that soft, woman heat molded against him. But he'd had no chance. Not with her. Not last night.

He supposed that was another reason why he was here today. Just like he supposed he knew why she wasn't happy with him. He'd told her he loved her that long ago summer and, well, the fact was he had. Hell, he'd fallen a little in love with every pretty girl he'd ever been with. Just not enough to stay.

Peg…Peg had been special, though. Maybe because he'd been her first. Maybe because she'd loved so freely. It had been hard to leave her. But he'd left anyway. Yeah, he'd left her with a shiny gold buckle that he'd won in the rodeo and a promise to call her—which, he was pretty sure, he'd never done.

Until he'd seen her the other night under the stars, he'd never felt near bad enough about running out on her like that. But *she* had. Her eyes had said that she'd felt real bad. And he guessed maybe that was another one of the reasons he'd shown up here today. He still hadn't seen her smile. The way things were stacking up, he had a feeling he wasn't going to anytime soon, either.

''Thought you'd left,'' she said, turning back to her wheelbarrow and filling another pitchfork full of the stuff that a rodeo cowboy considered beneath him to even think about let alone clean out of a stall.

''Well, I was going to, Peg. I truly was, but then I got to thinkin'.''

She tossed a glare over her shoulder that had him scratching his head and grinning.

"Yeah. I know. Imagine that. Me—having a thought."

When she didn't return his smile but turned back to her work instead, he walked into the barn, picked out a stall post that afforded him the best view and leaned against it.

"See, the thing is, what I was thinkin' was that we had a real good thing going that summer, Peg."

She stiffened, straightened, squared her shoulders. When she met his gaze this time, the fire in her eyes could have lit a blowtorch. "And you thought it might be a fine idea if we sort of picked up where we left off before you hit the road again?"

Bull's-eye. He shoved away from the post, grabbed the fork out of her hands—damned if he knew why—and took over her job. "Actually I was remembering how pretty your smile was. And I was thinkin' I was sorry if I was the one who stole it."

He watched her face over a pitchfork full of soiled straw and about three feet of dead silence.

The fire dimmed and she finally smiled, but it wasn't the one he remembered. This smile was brittle and bitter and way too cynical for those petal-soft lips that had once touched his with hunger and need.

"Don't flatter yourself, Cutter. You may fancy yourself a heartbreaker but I promise you, you left mine in one very solid piece."

Well, he didn't know what to think about that. A part of him had kind of hoped he *had* broken her heart—maybe just a little. Just enough to miss him. After all, she'd said she loved him, too.

He scowled, puzzled. So this was how the shoe felt

on the other foot. He couldn't say he much liked the fit. Just like his ego wasn't quite ready to buy her denial. Maybe it was a pride thing. It wasn't easy to think that he'd meant so little to her—whoa—like maybe *his* walking away had told her that *she* had meant so little to him.

It was years too late, but in that moment, he finally understood that her pride came into play here, too.

"Go away, Cutter," she said, trying to reclaim the fork. "I've got work to do—and I'm sure you've got a bronc or a buckle bunny to ride somewhere."

He couldn't even be offended. She pretty much had him tagged, but he held on and there they stood, her glaring and him grinning and totally without a clue how all his good intentions had turned into this little pissing contest over a forkful of smelly horse manure.

"As a matter of fact," he said, warming to the challenge in her eyes and the expanding memory that Peg Lathrop had been as wild a ride as any bronc he'd ever drawn and more fun than a goat rope, "I seem to find myself with a couple of days on my hands."

Well, hell. Where had that come from? He didn't have any free time. He was due to ride somewhere—couldn't think where at the moment—but he knew he was due somewhere tomorrow night.

"I'm happy for you," she said between clenched teeth. "So go do something productive with your time. Learn a skill."

That finally made him laugh. "Damn, I've missed that mouth."

"Yeah, right. That's why you came racing back here after, gosh, only six years."

"I knew it," he said, unable to keep the gloat from his voice. "You're mad as hell. That means you missed me."

"Like a toothache. Now, give me the damn pitchfork."

He held tight when she tugged. "Promise not to use it on me?"

"Unlike some people, I never make promises I don't intend to keep."

He winced. "Ouch. Guess I deserved that."

"And I deserve to be able to eat all the chocolate I want and not have it go to my hips. It's a cruel world."

"Come on, Peg. I'm trying to apolo—"

"Mommy? Mommy, I'm hungry."

Cutter blinked, stopped midapology and whipped his head around to the sound. Then all he could do was stare at a little blond moppet dressed in a soft pink, knee-length nightie, a pair of scruffy red cowboy boots and a head full of baby-fine bed hair.

Mommy?

He was still recovering from that little shock when he turned back to Peg. Her eyes rounded with distress, then darkened with warning just before she let go of the fork and made a beeline for the little girl.

"Hey, baby." Her voice turned as soft as butter. In long, determined strides, she walked to her daughter—*her daughter*—turned her around by her shoulders and herded her back toward the house. "I'm all finished here. How about some pancakes?"

"Blueberry?"

"You bet."

The little girl peeked back around behind her then up at her mother. "Who's that man?"

"He was just asking for directions and now he's moving on." She glared over her shoulder as she said it in a flat-out invitation to leave.

"Did you tell him how to get where he's s'posed to go?" the little girl asked as she walked ahead of her mother.

"Well, I sure tried, honey," Peg said, her voice trailing behind her. "I sure did try to tell him where to go."

Cutter heard every word of the conversation. Some of it even registered—especially the telling him where to go part. But over it all, hung the presence of that little blond-haired girl.

Peg had a child.

Talk about a new wrinkle. She had a little girl. A little girl in a pink nightie and cowboy boots. Red cowboy boots. The picture made him grin—but it faded as his curiosity grew—right along with a little prickle of something that felt suspiciously like irritation.

Well, it wasn't like he'd expected her to pine for him. He rolled a shoulder. Not forever, at any rate.

But a child.

Wreck Grover, a bronc rider from Butte that he partnered up with sometimes, had a little girl. Katie must be about five years old now. Looked to be about the same size as Peg's little one. He stroked a hand over his jaw. *Didn't waste much time forgetting about you, did she, Reno?*

Something about that just didn't set right. Something about it had him watching where they'd walked long after they'd climbed the porch steps and the door had closed behind them. And something made him feel a little uneasy and for some unknown reason, excluded.

Peg was a momma. And last night, she'd let him know that she wasn't attached. The notion of some good-for-nothing smooth-talker laying his hands on her, getting her pregnant then leaving her to fend for herself made him mad as hell.

And he was making a lot of assumptions. Maybe it didn't shake down that way at all. Maybe she'd been married. Maybe they were divorced. Maybe he died.

He cupped his nape then tipped his black Resistol lower on his forehead. And maybe he shouldn't be standing here speculating when it was really none of his business. He'd only driven out here to see if he could get that smile out of her—and maybe a little lovin' for old times' sake. It wasn't like he wanted to make a commitment or anything. Ha. Wouldn't that be a joke?

So why wasn't he laughing?

Slowly, with his fingertips tucked in his back pockets, he walked back out into the sun. The border collie trotted out to greet him, nudging his muzzle against Cutter's leg, begging for a quick pat as he passed him by, heading for the truck. He'd just opened the driver's-side door and was about to hike himself up and in, when he noticed movement on the front porch.

Peg's little girl had slipped back outside. She was standing snug against a porch post, half-hidden, obviously shy as she peeked around the post, her big eyes watchful, her smile tentative and unsure.

He should just drive away.

"How's it goin' today, little blondie?" he asked, instead, one foot on the running board, the other still planted on the ground.

Her giggle was like a bright, shiny penny. "I'm not blondie. I'm Shelby."

"Shelby. Well, now, that's a mighty pretty name for a mighty pretty girl. You're pretty like your momma, did you know that?"

"Yup," she said with the unabashed honesty of a child who was well loved and had his grin stretching wider.

She raised a tiny hand and brushed a swatch of hair back from her face. "You were in the parade. I saw you."

"Did you, now?"

She nodded and dressed in her nightie and bed hair and red boots, came scooting down the steps. "Are you really a sheriff?"

He grinned through a puzzled frown then finally figured out what she was talking about. "Marshall, darlin'. Not sheriff. I was the grand *marshall* of the parade. Nobody in their right mind would ever give me a real badge."

"Why?" she asked, all big round eyes and crumbling smile. "Are you a bad guy?"

He looked at this little girl, at the blue eyes that he'd been trying not to notice and whose bold sweetness tugged at him in a way no child had ever tugged at him before. He thought about her mother who wasn't just mad at him—she didn't much like him, either.

And he'd be damned if he knew how to answer her.

Three

——

"Stupid. Stupid. Stupid," Peg sputtered under her breath as she washed her hands then banged around in the cupboards for the griddle and a mixing bowl. She'd been sniping at Cutter over a pitchfork for pity sake.

"Why didn't you just take out an ad? Cutter Reno Punches All My Hot Buttons."

She braced her palms on the counter, drew a deep breath. Tried to steady herself. And got mad all over again. Darn it. He *did* punch her buttons, but if she was angry with anyone, it ought to be with herself.

Okay. So he'd caught her off guard. He'd been the last—the *very* last—person she'd expected to see today. Why wasn't he gone from Sundown? Why had he come sniffing around out here? And why did her heart skip and stutter and generally send her blood into sizzle mode every time she encountered his handsome, renegade face?

"Because you haven't learned a thing in six years, that's why," she admitted grumpily. Snagging a carton of milk and an egg from the fridge, she added them to the flour mix she'd dumped into the bowl. "And because you panicked."

She whipped a spoon through the pancake mix, blew a stray fall of hair away from her face. She'd panicked because he was still in Sundown kicking up her heartbeat—panicked at the look in his eyes when Shelby had come pattering out to the barn.

Her stomach sank just thinking about it. A thin layer of perspiration broke out across her brow, beaded at the small of her back. Shelby. He'd seen Shelby.

And she'd overreacted. She'd let him see—oh, Lord, had she let him see how desperate she'd been to get Shelby out of his sight? Cutter may be selfish and self-centered, but he wasn't stupid. And the look on his face—had it just been surprise? Or had it been recognition? Had he seen his eyes in the eyes of her daughter? Her daughter who sometimes asked about her daddy?

It's kind of like your friend, Kelly. Some kids just don't have daddies.

But Kelly does have a daddy. He just went away. Did my daddy go away, too?

What do you say to your child who doesn't understand the reason but feels the loss? How do you explain why Grant has a daddy who tucks him in at night and shares a bed with his mommy?

You have Grampa Jack, Shell. Grampa Jack loves you as much as any daddy could. And Gramma Kay loves you. And Krystal and Grant and Sam. And our friends Lee and Ellie? They all love you. But nobody loves you as much as I do, okay?

And nobody did love Shelby as much as she did. Nobody could. It wouldn't be long before her evasive answers wouldn't be enough for her daughter, though. And what would she tell her then?

And why, just because Cutter was in the neighborhood, did she feel a guilt that was neither warranted nor wise? Telling him would come to no good for anyone. She'd always known that. It was just like she'd told Krystal yesterday.

"What do you think would happen if I told him, Kris? He'd just feel guilty and beholden—probably even make a token effort to play the part. But in the long run, he'd leave. Cowboys make an art out of leaving. And Shelby, who loves cowboys, would be left with a broken heart when her cowboy daddy lit out because riding wild horses is more important to him than his child."

Or his child's mother, she thought grimly, as she opened the freezer door, rummaged around and found a package of blueberries she'd frozen last summer. She stuck them in the microwave, punched the touch pads and waited for them to defrost. Hands planted on her hips, she scowled at the revolving glass dish through the windowed door, not liking the part of her that sometimes played with the idea of telling him anyway—just to see him sweat. Just to see him squirm. Just to see him go pale and apologetic and realize that he'd missed his chance with her and with their beautiful daughter.

No. He'd missed his chance with *her* daughter. Shelby was hers, only hers and she wouldn't risk Shelby's precious little heart just to indulge in a little vindictive retribution. She would never put Shelby at risk that way—she'd told Krystal that, too.

"I did him a favor, and you know it. And if I'd told him, you and I both know the only satisfaction *I'd* get is revenge. Admittedly it sounds sweet sometimes, but it's not my style. If it had been, I'd have let Jack drag Cutter back to Sundown six years ago and tie him to a life that would have made him miserable. Then Shelby would have suffered in the process, too."

And she would have suffered, as well, but she hadn't confessed that to Krystal. The look in her friend's eyes had said she didn't have to.

The microwave beeped several times before she had the presence of mind to snap out of her little trance and retrieve the blueberries.

Well, it was all a moot point now anyway. They'd seen the last of Cutter Reno. He should be well on his way out of Sundown by now—which reminded her. Shelby should have washed up and changed by now, too.

"Shelby Lynn," she called over her shoulder as she drained the berries in a colander then started folding them carefully into the batter. "Come on, baby, I'm just about ready to start cookin'. I need you to set the table."

She'd expected to hear Shelby tripping down the

stairs as she hurried to the kitchen, always excited by the prospect of helping out. Instead she heard the front door open then close and then the sound of Shelby's footsteps echoing on the hard wood foyer floor. Mixed with the mini clomp of Shelby's little boots was the faint click of Rascal's paws—and the unmistakable ring of heavier footsteps.

She froze—then spun around so quickly she almost dropped the bowl of pancake batter. She nearly dropped it anyway when she saw what Shelby had in tow.

"This cowboy's hungry, Mom," Shelby said brightly, having clearly decided that the only thing to do about it was feed him.

Cutter, holding his hat in one hand and her daughter's hand in the other, grinned sheepishly from the kitchen door.

"I hope I'm not intruding."

Like hell, she thought and spun back to the counter before she said something she'd be way too sorry for.

Cutter sat at Peg's table looking around the small but homey kitchen with its light blue walls and dark blue curtains. He listened with half an ear to Shelby chatter about Bea, her POA, as she explained proudly but unnecessarily that POA stood for Pony of America—a breed evolved from a cross between a pony and an appaloosa horse. Then she moved on to her favorite TV shows and anything else that popped into her active little mind. All the while, she alternately ate and sneaked bites of her pancake to the border collie who knew he'd hit the gravy train and lay patiently beneath the table.

Well, he thought, as he risked a glance at Peg over his plate, at least *one* of the Lathrop girls was hospitable.

Oh, Peg was trying. Trying hard to be polite. Trying hard to smile at his little jokes. Trying hard to act as if she wouldn't find extreme pleasure seeing him staked bare-ass naked over a bed of cactus under a red-hot sun after a gallon of saltwater had been poured down his throat.

"More pancakes, Cutter?" she asked, all sweetness and light through a strained but determined smile.

"Why, sure thing, Peg. Been a while since I've had any home cookin'. A man would be a fool to turn down any kind of an offer from a pretty woman— especially one who cooks like you do."

Just like a man would be a fool to keep goading her that way. There was fire behind that benign smile. Flames shooting from those spicy-brown eyes. She'd clearly understood that the "cookin'" he'd had in mind had nothing to do with kitchens and everything to do with what they'd once done in the dark with their clothes off.

A man who didn't understand women as well as he did might get to thinking that he wasn't welcome here. But if there was anything Cutter understood, it was broncs and women. And he understood that little Peg still cared about him. She didn't want to. Just like she didn't want to be mad—and there was the rub. If she didn't care, then she wouldn't *be* mad. Both prospects had him wondering and wanting to get just a little better feel for exactly what it was going to take to land in her good graces again.

It didn't make sense that he cared, really. She had her life—that cute little blonde was proof of that—and he had his. It wasn't as if he had the time or the inclination to stick around. Yet here he sat—in the middle of her sunny kitchen, with little green plants sitting on the windowsill over the sink and finger-paint masterpieces papering her ancient refrigerator door. Yep, here he sat, liking what he was seeing and getting fuzzy little pictures of what it would be like to have the right to sit at this table as more than an unwelcome guest.

"Mom and me are goin' ridin' right after breakfast, right, Mom? You should go with us, Cutter," he heard Shelby state as if it were a foregone conclusion just as Peg dropped another pancake on his plate.

He looked up, not into Shelby's eyes but into the eyes of her momma who, he could see by her pointed look, had a real definite opinion of what his response to Shelby's invitation should be.

It was pure orneriness—he couldn't seem to help himself—that had him turning his grin on Shelby as he poured warm maple syrup over his pancake. "Why sure, darlin', if you want me to."

"Shelby, Cutter's a busy man," Peg put in as she turned back to her griddle. She shut off the flame on the burner, but his temperature rose a couple of notches at the sight of what he'd be willing to wager was the sweetest little backside east or west of the Rockies. She'd ditched her work boots and was standing barefoot in the kitchen. There was something powerfully sexy about a barefoot woman—and those baggy silk shorts and that sloppy gray tank top were going to be his undoing yet.

"He doesn't have time to go riding this morning," he heard her add over the haze of sexual heat.

"But he just said he could go."

"He was just being polite, weren't you, Cutter?"

Cutter leaned back in his chair, tilted his head and smiled into eyes that had turned as cold as frost in a Montana winter. "Actually I'm free as a bird."

"See?" Shelby insisted.

"Honey, we don't really have anything for him to ride."

"Jackpot," Shelby said and Cutter could almost hear the "duh."

Peg cleared her throat. "Sweetie, Jackpot's barely green broke. He's not ready to ride yet, you know that."

"But Cutter's a cowboy. He rides wild horses," Shelby insisted. "Don't ya, Cutter?"

Cutter propped his elbow on the table, his chin in his hand and grinned. "Well, I surely have been known to."

"And he can use your old saddle. It used to be Grampa Jack's, didn't it, Mom? But Grampa got me and Mom new saddles for Christmas so now we got an extra one."

A long second passed before Peg's expression transformed from one of backed-into-a-corner acceptance to a you-asked-for-it-you-got-it smile.

"Fine," she said stiffly. "You want to ride a wild horse, you've got one. Just don't say I didn't warn you. Oh, and when we ride, we ride for a couple of hours. I *surely* hope you're up for more than your usual eight seconds.''

Cutter chuckled, low and easy. ''Why, yes, ma'am. I reckon I've got more than eight seconds in me. But then, I guess you already know that, don't you?''

The ice in her gaze melted to fire again in a heart-beat. He felt the burn clear across the table.

''I'll do up the dishes, Shell,'' she said stiffly. ''You go on up and get dressed. Bring your brush down with you, sweetie, and I'll fix your hair.''

''Okay!'' Shelby shot out of the chair and raced toward the stairs. ''Come on, Rascal.'' The dog trot-ted after her like a shadow.

''Let me help you with those,'' Cutter offered—and rather magnanimously, he thought—as he stacked his fork and knife on his plate.

''Sit,'' Peg snapped and rounded on him. ''You just sit right where you are.''

She grabbed his plate, then pointed a fork at him. ''Don't you come into my house,'' she warned him as brilliant color flooded her cheeks and her breath came hard and fast, ''and in front of my daugh-ter...start making your sly sexual innuendoes and... and...''

He snagged her wrist in one hand, relieved her of the plate and fork with his other and set them back on the table. ''And look at you like I want to kiss you?''

With his hand still clamped around her wrist, he stood, walked around the table until he was directly in front of her. And suddenly he did want to kiss her—much more than he wanted to tease her.

She was backing a slow foot away to every step he took toward her until she'd backed as far as she could go. Her hips connected with the counter about the same time as his hips connected with hers. She was shaking her head, but her eyes…her eyes weren't in agreement. And it was her eyes that he chose to believe.

"So, what do you say, Peg? Can I kiss you? Just once? Just to see if it's as good as I remember?"

She wasn't looking at him now. She was looking anywhere but at him. Her pretty cheeks were flaming red. Her eyes were a little wild with panic and denial and a desire that he recognized even if she didn't.

"Just once," he murmured, easing up closer against her, fitting the length of him against the length of her, savoring the contact of lush breasts, long legs.

He released her wrist and because he couldn't stop himself, tangled his fingers in her hair—in the long, silky length of it—and tugged the ribbon free. He'd been wanting to do that, too, ever since he'd seen her in the sunlight in the barn.

Her hair fell into his hands like a waterfall of silk. He gathered it up, brought it to his face, inhaled the Montana morning scent of it, the lustrous weight and the soft womanly fragrance.

"Don't," she whispered, but with little force behind the word, as he tunneled his fingers up to the base of her scalp to cup and caress her head, to tip her face up to his with a gentle pressure of his thumbs beneath her jaw.

"It's okay," he murmured, barely touching his mouth to hers, drowning in the feel of her, the shimmering warmth of her breath quivering against his lips. "It's just a kiss."

He brushed his mouth over hers, softly seeking, gently teasing until seeking and teasing weren't nearly enough.

"Just a kiss," he repeated, opened his mouth firmly over hers—and got hopelessly, unalterably lost.

Sweet heaven. It was just her mouth. Just her warm, wet, wonderfully erotic mouth—and he wanted it. He wanted it open for his tongue. Wanted her willingly inviting him inside. And when, at last, she did, he claimed it as his, wouldn't let her close it to him. Not yet. Not for another million years if he could arrange it.

With his hands bracketing her jaw, he indulged in her, remembered how much he'd missed her, how quickly she could fire him up this way. Good Lord, what she did to him. Even her resistance was sweet as she pressed her hands against his chest and pushed, then knotted them into fists that grasped his shirt and dragged him closer, invited him deeper.

"Sweet, sweet Peggy," he murmured, breaking away long enough to change the angle, heighten the contact as he wedged a leg between her thighs. Sliding his hands down her body, he filled his palms with the delectable curve of her bottom and her mouth with the ebb and flow of his tongue.

She tasted like maple syrup and blueberries and woman. Like hunger and anticipation and the sensual edge of desire. Memories of the girl who had given herself to him so freely joined forces with the blood that had pooled in his groin to coax his hands higher.

The contact of warm flesh on his rough fingers had them both gasping as he tunneled his hands under her shirt. He groaned into her mouth when he found her naked beneath it and skimmed his hands slowly up her ribs until the full weight of her breasts brushed the backs of his knuckles.

He felt her shiver when he grazed the tips of those glorious breasts with his thumbs, felt them peak and, grinding his hips hard against hers, thrust his tongue deeper into her mouth. She sighed into him, opening wider, inviting him deeper still, as he squeezed and caressed and wished to hell there wasn't a little girl about to come tripping down the stairs any minute and expect him to take her for a horseback ride.

''Peg…darlin','' he murmured on a frustrated groan and reluctantly broke the contact of their mouths. Breathing hard, he dragged his hands out from under her shirt and wrapped her tightly in his arms. Then it was his turn to shiver, to draw a shaky breath. ''We…oh, man…we got a little carried away there, baby.''

He felt the moment she came back to herself. Felt the stiffness of her shoulders, the awareness of what they'd just shared hit home.

He was smiling drowsily when she pulled away from him. Until he saw her face.

''Damn you,'' she whispered, barely able to get the words out. ''Damn you for that.''

He'd expected a little anger—at least a token

show—even though he knew that she'd enjoyed it as much as he had.

What he hadn't expected was shame. But that's what she felt, he realized grimly, as her eyes brimmed with tears and the flush desire had painted on her cheeks faded to a ghostly pale.

"Peg?" He touched a hand to her arm. "Hey. It was just a kiss, darlin'."

She jerked away.

"Whoa now, no need for that," he coaxed softly about the same time that he heard widget cowboy boots clumping down the stairs.

He backed a step away and Peg whirled away from him, pressed her hands to her cheeks. And all Cutter could do was stare and wonder about her reaction and why she looked so bruised.

"I'm ready," Shelby announced from the kitchen doorway. She was all decked out in a lavender hat, plaid shirt, blue jeans and, of course, her battered red boots. "Mom…how come you don't have your jeans on?" she asked, sounding put out. "Hurry up, silly."

"Let me…let me just put these dishes in the sink to soak," Peg said, her voice tight and a little shaky.

"I can do that," Cutter said, suddenly feeling like a heel when what he'd wanted to feel was a little more of Peg pressed against him.

"You go get changed," he added, not surprised when she shouldered around him at a fast walk then took the stairs at a trot.

"Come on, Shelby Lynn," she said over her shoulder. "Help me find my riding boots."

Cutter watched the little girl roll her eyes and shrug

her shoulders as if to say, "Moms. They are so scatterbrained." Calling the dog, she trotted along after her mother.

And Cutter was left to smile after them, then frown at the red ribbon in his hand. He resisted the temptation to stuff it in his pocket and laid it on the counter instead. Then he cleared up the table, dumped the dishes in the sink and ran some water over them. Shoving his fingers in his hip pockets, he headed thoughtfully down to the barn to check out the tack situation.

He hadn't wanted to hurt Peg. He'd just wanted to kiss her. Just once for old times' sake. Just once to see if his memory had been bigger than the reality.

Now he knew. His memory didn't even begin to compare with the real live perfection of Peg Lathrop's mouth. Or her long, lithe body pressed against his like a firebrand. Or the softness of her breasts warm and heavy in his hands.

Well, so much for what he'd wanted, he decided, opening what he figured was the tack-room door. He'd go for a ride with them—because he'd promised the little girl that he would. Then he'd get out of Dodge. Now that he knew he'd hurt Peg six years ago, he didn't want to hurt her again. And if he stuck around much longer that's just what he'd do. He'd hurt her because now he knew something else. Something that he hadn't known before. He wanted more from Peg than a kiss—and then she'd want something more from him, too. Peg would want forever. She deserved it, too, but...damn...even if he wanted to, he'd figured out a long time ago that forever was something he just didn't have in him to give.

When Peg worked up the courage to leave the house, she spotted both her sorrel gelding, Henry, and Shelby's POA, Bea, saddled and bridled, their reins looped over a fence rail. Cutter was just leading Jackpot out of the barn.

She made herself breathe deep, tried to forget about what had happened in her kitchen. What she'd *let* happen.

Damn.

Damn. Damn. Damn.

She wasn't even sure how he'd managed it. One minute she'd been laying into him about something he'd said and then the next he'd had her backed up against the sink and was kissing her like there was no tomorrow.

And she'd kissed him back.

That was the worst part. She'd stood there, wanting him to leave her alone, and with one touch of his mouth to hers, she'd been just plain wanting. Wanting him. Naked. Inside her.

Even now, she went all wobbly and weak thinking about his mouth and his tongue. In her mouth. She hadn't even gotten past the shiver when she remembered the feel of his hands—in her hair, on her breasts. And his body pressed up against her. Hard, hot…and ready to take that kiss a whole lot further.

She blew out a breath, flexed her fingers. Shook it off. "That's what you get for living the life of a spinster," she muttered.

And that's what this was all about. This wasn't about Cutter. This was about her physical needs that she'd denied for, well, let's just say a very long time. Okay. Six years to be exact. She could have kicked herself right now for that oversight.

It wasn't that she hadn't had offers. Some of them had even included marriage. None of them had been right. Not for her. Not for Shelby.

"Like Cutter *is* right?" she sputtered under her breath as she neared the barn. No. Cutter was nothing but wrong. He was also too gorgeous for his own good—or obviously for hers.

Well, she was prepared for him now. No more surprises because this time she really did have his number. Alley cat. Love 'em and leave 'em. All she had to do was remember that and not get caught up in his slow, suggestive grins or his hot, hungry looks.

Fortunately he wasn't looking at her when she reached Henry and gathered the reins in her hands. He was very studiously helping Shelby get settled on Bea's back, checking her stirrup length, making sure she had a good handle on the reins.

Averting her gaze, she swung up into the saddle. Then she made a conscious effort not to dwell on the picture the two of them made—Shelby and Cutter—with their heads together, hers adoring, his amused.

"Ready?" he said, never once looking her way.

"It'd probably be best if you led Jackpot away from the barn a bit. If he blows, I'd just as soon he didn't take you through the barn door."

He glanced up then, looking a little encouraged, apparently thinking that she had his welfare in mind.

"I don't have the time or the money to handle a repair bill," she added to make sure she nipped that little notion in the bud.

He ducked his head, shook it, then gathered Jackpot's reins and led him out to the field behind the barn. She kept Shelby beside her and both of them a careful distance away while they waited until Cutter mounted. She really had no idea what the fiery little paint would pull.

Instead of swinging right into the saddle, Cutter took his time inspecting his tack, double-checking the bit, talking softly to the gelding who alternately laid back his ears and flicked them forward as if he were really interested in hearing what the cowboy had to say.

Oh, he was interested all right, Peg thought. Interested in finding the right moment to take a chomp out of Cutter. A part of her relished the possibility and yet her conscience got the best of her. "He's a biter. Watch your back."

Cutter looked up, surprised at her warning. A hopeful grin jacked up one side his mouth.

"Can't afford a vet bill, either," she said, clarifying that she was worried about what would happen to the horse if he bit into tainted meat.

Cutter just shook his head again, tugged down his hat and gathered the reins. He swung up and into the saddle so effortlessly that it took a moment for Peg to realize that Jackpot was still standing there as docile as a kitten. Only his laid-back ears gave away that he was not a happy horse.

"Stay back a bit," Cutter suggested. "Let the two

of us come to an understanding before you crowd him.''

That was just fine with Peg. And Shelby was enough of a cowgirl to understand the importance of following an order. Rascal ran in happy circles around Henry and Bea as they started off at a slow walk several yards behind Cutter and Jackpot.

''Told you he could ride him,'' Shelby said after they'd gone about a tenth of a mile.

Peg smiled for her little cowgirl, working hard to conceal an irritation that had no place in Shelby's world. ''Yeah, punkin', you sure did.''

''I like him. Do you think he likes me?'' her daughter asked with such hope that Peg felt the bend, then the break of her heart. It also reminded her that keeping her cool wasn't really about her unwanted attraction to Cutter. It was about something much more important. It was about her little girl's heart.

''Sure he does, sweetie. What's not to like?'' she added with a lightness she didn't feel and a weight in her chest that made it difficult to draw a deep breath.

Why wouldn't a daddy love his little girl?

She blinked back a sudden mist of tears. Tears of guilt. Of anger. What kind of justice made a mother withhold a father from his daughter to keep from hurting her and in the same breath wonder if her deception might be hurting her more.

Four

"He doesn't much like the bit," Cutter said about Jackpot as the three of them, with Rascal scampering eagerly at their heels, headed toward the barn on their way back from their ride in the foothills.

"He responds much better to leg commands. And he respects authority. You keep that in mind, Peg, and you two will get along just fine."

Cutter glanced at Peg, who acknowledged his advice with a nod. He shook his head, tugged on his hat. They'd ridden the better part of two hours. Two pretty quiet hours—except for Shelby. Peg hadn't had much to say during the whole ride. Now little Shelby Lynn—she was another story altogether, Cutter thought with a grin. Her little-girl chatter and her insatiable curiosity about cowboys and rodeo had tickled the hell out of him.

They'd had a heated debate—one that he'd egged on just to get her going—over who was the best all-around cowboy of all time. She was determined it was Ty Murray. He was pretty much in agreement, but deliberately goaded her by declaring it was Joe Beaver.

"But he don't even ride wild horses," Shelby protested with an exaggerated roll of her eyes that relayed just how wrong she thought he was. "He ropes calves. Little bitty calves. Where's the danger in that is what I'd like to know."

He laughed and defended his position. "Takes a might lot of skill to rope and tie a calf."

She gave a derisive snort. "Yeah, right. Ty could rope a silly little calf if he wanted to. But I bet Joe couldn't ride a bronc—or a bull. You ever ride a bull, Cutter?"

"Do I look *that* stupid?" he asked her with an exaggerated show of horror.

"Well, when you picked Joe Beaver over Ty Murray, it kinda makes me wonder."

He chuckled. "The apple didn't fall too far from *your* tree," he said over Shelby's head to Peg, who seemed to turn a little pale before she found her voice.

"That's my girl." She managed a smile that Cutter noticed didn't hold much humor.

Well, he still didn't know what to make of things. He knew he'd really messed up coming on so hot and heavy in her kitchen earlier. But damn, just being around her seemed to leach the brains right out of his head and into that spot he'd been accused of thinking with far too often to make him proud.

Well, his brain was back in his head where it belonged now and it was telling him he needed to be moving on. Judging by the way Peg was acting, it couldn't be too soon to suit her.

"Whoa, now," he murmured to a suddenly skittish Jackpot when a stalk of bear grass tickled the paint's flank and had him crow-hopping into Shelby's POA. He jerked hard to the right, trying to pull Jackpot around and away from Bea, but the flighty gelding had decided he was good and spooked and wasn't about to be settled down.

Before it was over, Bea had bolted and was heading at a run for the barn. Shelby, he could see, was up to it. She was a natural in the saddle, had a good hold on her reins and her saddle horn as she yelled at Bea to, "Slow down, you goofy pony!"

Peg's gelding was levelheaded but a little fidgety, too, over all the activity. She had him well in hand as Jackpot danced on his back legs and struck out like a kindergartner scared silly in a Halloween haunted house.

Everything was fine. He was in control until Rascal, answering his natural herding instincts, decided he needed to help bring Jackpot to tow and dived in for a quick nip at his heels.

"Rascal, no!" Peg screamed—but too late.

The frenzied paint struck out with a powerful hind hoof, caught Rascal square in the ribs and sent him sailing.

"Damn," Cutter swore, and after several long minutes, finally got Jackpot settled down.

He bailed off and, leading a quivering and heaving

Jackpot, trotted to Rascal's side. Peg was on her knees in the grass beside him.

"Damn," he said again as he went down on one knee. "Where'd he get him?"

Peg looked up through tear-misted eyes. "In the chest. Oh, Cutter, he's barely breathing."

Cutter swiped a hand over his jaw. He glanced over his shoulder and saw that Shelby had seen what happened and was reining Bea back out toward them. He didn't want her to see this.

"Keep him down. Stay with him and try not to let him move," he ordered then he snagged Henry's reins from Peg and swung into her saddle. "I'll get the horses settled and come back for you in my pickup."

"Hurry." A tear tracked down her cheek.

"He'll be fine," he said and wished to hell he knew if he was telling it straight. "He'll be just fine."

Then he cued Henry into a jog and, leading Jackpot by the reins, headed off toward Shelby.

"Come on, Shelby," he said when he met her in the middle of the field. "Let's get these horses settled real quick and then we need to get Rascal to the vet."

"Is he dead?" she wailed, tears pouring down her face. "Did Jackpot kill him?"

"No, darlin'. He's not dead. But he's hurt real bad so we need to be brave and act fast now, are you hearing me?"

Shelby bit her lower lip and nodded as the tears kept flooding down—and Cutter's heart just flat out broke.

"There's my girl. Now you go turn Bea into the paddock and pull off her tack, okay? Then you make sure there's water in the tank while I turn out the other horses. Can you do that for me?''

She nodded and headed for the barn at a fast trot with him right on her heels.

Damn. He hated this. He hated the look on Peg's face. He hated the worry in little Shelby's blue eyes. He hated that that darn little dog may have nipped at his last set of heels.

But most of all, he hated that he was the best thing the two Lathrop girls had going for them at the moment. It didn't say too much about their luck—and less about his opinion of himself than he'd ever care to admit.

When Peg came out of the examining room, they were sitting side by side on the chairs in the veterinary clinic's waiting room. The man and the child. Father and daughter.

In the few moments before Cutter looked up and saw her, the picture the two of them made together burned into Peg's mind in a way that she knew would haunt her forever.

It was a picture she'd never confessed to anyone that she'd imagined before. Many times. In the dark of night. In bed alone. Or when Shelby had been a baby, cutting a tooth, running a temp on a cold, quiet, winter midnight and the rocking chair, a loving hand and her breast had been the only comfort Peg had to offer. In those times, when no one else knew, she would indulge in her fantasies, and wallow in regrets. She would picture them together, wonder at the fit.

She didn't have to wonder any longer. The man

she'd pictured had been younger, leaner, greener. The man who sat with her daughter was more now than he'd been back then. More than Peg had figured he'd ever become.

Cutter's dark head was bent over Shelby's, one big hand stroking her baby girl's downy soft blond hair. His other hand, gentle and scarred and strong, rested carefully and protectively on Shelby's small shoulders. The two of them were oblivious to her standing there watching them. Their blue eyes were locked, his compassionate and comforting, hers worshipful and trusting.

With her heart in her throat, Peg touched trembling fingers to her lips and tried to hold herself together by banding her other arm around her waist. Picturing them together on a long lonely night was one thing. Seeing them together was another. It made her question not only her decision, but also made her question her motives.

Oh, Shelby. What have I done?

"Hey," Cutter said softly when he looked up and saw her standing in the doorway. "How's it going back there?"

Peg forced a smile for Shelby. "Good. It's going good. He's going to be okay."

Shelby shot off the chair and ran to her mother. Peg scooped her up, hugged her hard against her.

"Can we take him home now?"

Peg pressed a kiss to the top of Shelby's head, smelled her sweet little-girl scent—and the faint scent of Cutter's aftershave that made her think of dry fall grass and leather. "Not just yet, cupcake. Rascal's got a couple of broken ribs so he's pretty sore. The doc wants to keep him overnight to make sure nothing else turns up.''

"He could get sicker?'' Shelby wailed.

"No. No, sweetie.'' She ran a comforting hand over her cheek. "That's why he's going to stay here tonight. To make sure that doesn't happen. We can pick him up tomorrow, okay?''

"Okay.'' Shelby's frown deepened. "Darn Jackpot. He was a bad horse.''

"Jackpot was just scared, Shell,'' Cutter said, and Peg watched him stand, unfolding in one smooth, graceful motion and walk over to them. "You ever get scared?''

Shelby was tired and still a little upset. Peg could tell that she was winding up to get just a little cranky. And why not? She'd had a bad scare.

"No,'' Shelby insisted anyway. "I don't get scared, do I, Mom?''

Before she could respond, Cutter did. "What about today? Were you scared when Rascal got hurt?''

Shelby buried her face in her mom's neck rather than admit that she'd been good and scared.

"Well, the way I figure it, you were and now you're mad at Jackpot. Just like Jackpot was scared and he got mad at Rascal for nipping at him. I'm sure Jackpot's sorry.''

While Shelby was thinking that over, Peg was wishing that *she* didn't have so much to think about. Like the fact that she felt grateful to Cutter for his gentle explanation. He'd been careful of Shelby's feelings, recognized that she was acting out her distress. He was a natural, she realized. A natural father.

She closed her eyes as guilt took a deeper gouge out of the hole it had been eating in her stomach ever since he'd shown up in Sundown.

"I don't suppose anyone's hungry but me." Cutter tilted a grin Shelby's way.

On cue, Peg's stomach growled. It had been a long time since breakfast. She hadn't even thought about it until now. She glanced at the wall clock. It was almost one o'clock.

Shelby was still feeling a little pouty. "Not hungry."

"Hmm." Cutter pinched his chin between his thumb and fingers. "And here I was all tuned up for a super-duper double Bozeman burger." He lifted a brow, angled Shelby, who was still hugging her mom, a pointed look.

"And French fries?" Shelby asked into Peg's shirt.

"And a chocolate malt, if you want one," Cutter added and Peg could feel her daughter's cheeks plump up into a grin.

"All right!" Shelby exclaimed, and suddenly having her fill of pouting squirmed out of Peg's arms and ran to Cutter.

He didn't even hesitate when Shelby lifted her arms. He just scooped her up, settled her on his hip and looked expectantly at Peg. "You coming, Mom?"

The fatigue that had set in over Rascal's ordeal regrouped into a panic so profound, it made her tremble. She did not want to do this. She did not want to see this. She did not want to watch her daughter with Cutter and know that she and she alone was responsible for them never being together until now. She did not want to sit beside him on the hour-long trip to Bozeman to get a super-duper double Bozeman burger, fries and a chocolate malt. And agonize over whether she should just tell him.

"Thanks, Cutter, but I...I don't think that's such a good idea."

"It's a *great* idea, Mom! It's been *forever* since we've gone to Bozeman," Shelby wheedled.

Her eyes were bright again. She'd already forgotten her fear for Rascal. And what Cutter was suggesting was a kind and caring way of keeping that fear at bay.

What could she do, what could she say but, "Okay. We go to Bozeman. Satisfied?"

"Yea!" Shelby cried and laughing, wrapped her little arms around Cutter's neck as if she'd been hugging him and loving him her entire life.

Peg looked at her hands, ignored her pounding heart and composed herself. "Well, let's get this show on the road then."

And then she followed them out the door, wishing with everything in her that she was as sure today as she'd been just yesterday of a decision she'd made long ago that had set the course of all their lives.

Cutter sat across from Peg and Shelby in the yellow plastic booth with the red tabletop and salt and pepper shakers shaped like fat little hamburgers and wondered what the hell he was doing with these two *women*.

Sure, one was about as big as a pint of ice cream, but she had a woman's way about her—at least she did with him. He'd never given much thought to kids before, yet little Shelby Lynn Lathrop had wrapped him around her little finger in about the same amount of time it took Joe Beaver to rope and tie a calf.

And then there was the other one.

The other one, looking good enough to eat and as tense as a bull rider's rope, was sitting across from him in the booth. She'd made a great show of working on her burger and fries and occasionally sipping from Shelby's malt, but the truth was she'd hardly eaten a thing.

Okay. So he'd surprised them when he'd stuck his neck out and invited them out for a burger. Hell, he'd surprised himself and was still wondering what on God's green earth had possessed him.

The same thing that had possessed him this morning when he'd headed for her place instead of out of town. Yeah, he'd made a mistake looking up Peg this morning, a bigger mistake kissing her. Then he'd compounded it by going on that ride. Things hadn't been beyond fixing, though, and he hadn't been beyond getting at that point, until Rascal had pulled his stunt. Well, what could he have done then? Just tip his hat, wish them luck with the dog and head on out? No. Wasn't his style.

Then at the vet's he'd gotten in deeper and deeper. That poor little girl. She'd been worried sick. Those big fat tears that had welled then spilled down her cheeks—man. It had just torn him up.

Of course he'd had to comfort her. And when all was well, he'd been so relieved he'd felt like celebrating. Besides, a man had to eat and he *had* been hungry. So had they. The invitation had just popped out. It had been worth it, too—just to see little Shelby perk back up and smile for him.

It was a killer smile. Melted his heart right down to a puddle of mush, that's for sure. Just like looking at her momma did other things to his body that didn't have a thing to do with his heart—at least he didn't think so.

Anyway, that's how he'd ended up still hanging around when he ought to be heading his truck down the highway. That reminded him. He'd seen a pay phone back by the men's room. He needed to cancel a hot date with a wild bronc. He blew out a breath, scratched his head and resettled his hat. He'd just as well have tossed *that* entry fee out a window.

"I gotta make a quick call, Peg, then we can go, okay?"

"Sure," she said.

"Then can we go to the movies, Cutter?" Big blue eyes looked into his with a plea that could have stripped the locks on Fort Knox.

"Shelby Lynn," Peg admonished. "Where are your manners? Cutter was nice enough to drive us here for a burger and now you're trying to take advantage of his kindness."

Cutter couldn't help it. He smiled into those baby blues. He knew he was being played for a sucker and somehow he didn't mind a bit. "You want to see a movie, sugar?"

"Oh, could we, Cutter? It's been *forever* since I got to see a movie."

Cutter sliced Peg a look. She just rolled her eyes and shook her head over her daughter's antics.

"Only if it's okay with your mom."

"As if I really had a say in this," Peg mumbled.

"Yea! We get to go to a movie. We get to go to a movie," Shelby singsonged, happily dipping a French fry into her glob of ketchup then stuffing it into her mouth.

It was dark by the time they turned down Peg's road because after the movie—some silly, sweet little animated adventure about dogs and cats and of all things, pigs—they'd *had* to go out for pizza. Because, well, it had been *forever* since Shelby Lynn had been to her favorite pizza place and because Cutter seemed to be a pushover for anything Shelby set her mind to convincing him that she needed.

Peg looked down on the child who had fallen asleep in her arms before they'd cleared the Bozeman city limits. Her daughter had the face of a baby cherub and the instincts of a grifter suckering in her prey. She smiled in the dark, adjusted Shelby's soft, warm weight and let out a contented sigh—then blinked and brought herself to attention when she realized what had happened.

She'd gotten comfortable. Comfortable with the idea of sitting in the cozy cab of Cutter's truck with Cutter behind the wheel, the radio playing softly, and their daughter asleep in her arms. And it scared her near to death.

She could not get comfortable with Cutter or with these fuzzy little notions about coming clean—just blurting out between a Garth Brooks and a Faith Hill song that Shelby was his child.

She could *not* get comfortable at the thought of the two of them walking into her little house and tucking Shelby into bed—then whispering their way down to her own bedroom and…and—

"—Peg?"

She jerked, blinked and realized that they were parked in her driveway. Cutter had cut the engine. He was staring at her, his eyes questioning across three feet of moonlight-dusted cab.

"I'm sorry," she whispered. "Did you say something?"

"Yeah," he said, looking puzzled. "I said sit tight. I'll come around and get her, carry her into the house for you, okay?"

"No. No," she said abruptly. "I can get her."

But he was already out of the truck. And then he was opening her door. And the next thing she knew, he was sliding his arm under Shelby's shoulders—which just happened to involve brushing against her breasts. And then his other arm was under Shelby's legs—which just happened to involve brushing against her thighs. And his face was just inches from hers in the summer night—which just happened to involve looking at him. At his brilliant blue eyes, his heartbreaker face, his lush, mobile mouth that wasn't smiling as he studied her with a dark, dangerous intensity that stole her breath.

She swallowed hard, worked even harder to keep a coherent thought as her blood took a notion to pound like thunder in her ears.

"I've got her," he said softly, never taking his gaze from hers, lingering with her daughter cradled in his arms and her body wedged beneath them.

So close. He was so close and he smelled so good and the night and the dome light were casting wonderful shadows across his jaw, defining and spotlighting the most intriguing little scar that hooked the left corner of his mouth that she'd never noticed before. Just like she'd never noticed that she could breathe with her heart jammed up in her throat the way it was.

"Peg? You okay?"

"What? Oh. Yeah. Yeah, I'm fine. Have you got her?"

"I've got her," he said, and lifted her baby girl into his arms.

For the longest time, all she could do was sit there. The heat of the July day had faded to a pleasant summer cool. Yet her palms were sweating as she watched Cutter's long, strong body, his effortless stride as he carried Shelby as if she were as fragile as glass, yet as if he'd carried her a hundred times, just like this.

And she didn't know what she was going to do.

He was almost to the porch steps when she realized that the one thing she couldn't do was sit there. She forced herself out of the truck, caught up with and passed him, then opened the front door so he could ease Shelby inside.

"Just put her on the sofa," she said when she'd flipped on the hall light.

"That's silly," he whispered over Shelby's head. "You'll just have to pick her up again and carry her up the stairs. Point me to her room and I'll put her to bed."

Okay. He was right. It made sense. And she could do this. "Top of the stairs. First door on the left."

He headed up the stairs and she stood at the bottom looking up. At a father carrying his daughter to bed.

She couldn't go up there—and she couldn't not go up there.

Cutter had already laid the rag doll that Shelby had turned into in the middle of her little bed by the time she'd trailed them up the stairs. Peg moved around him and tugged off Shelby's boots and socks. Then she carefully stripped down her jeans and peeled off her shirt until she was lying in her little T-shirt and panties dotted with pink flowers.

"She's good for the night," she whispered. She covered her with a sheet then brushed the hair back from her face and pressed a kiss to her brow. "G'night, darling girl," she murmured and trailed the back of her hand across Shelby's cheek.

Then she straightened and backed right into the hard, strong body that stood in silence behind her.

She froze. So did he as his big hands wrapped around her upper arms to steady her. She could feel his solid heat a faint heartbeat away from her back, the soft warmth of his breath feathering at her nape.

And just when her heart told her that he was going to turn her in his arms and take—not ask for—another kiss, he squeezed gently and let his hands drop away.

"She's a sound sleeper, huh?" he said in a hushed voice.

Peg closed her eyes, gathered her wits. "Yeah. She could sleep through a buffalo stampede."

An eternity passed as they stood there in the dark with their heartbeats and their shallow breaths and a soft spill of light shining into the room from the hallway.

"You're a good momma, Peg."

She hugged herself, braced. *Don't ask me. Don't, don't, don't. Please don't ask me.*

The night grew so heavy and so full of the possibility that she actually jumped when he drew a deep breath and touched his hand to her arm.

"I've got to go, okay?"

"Yeah," she said quickly and wondered at the feeling of loss when moments ago she'd thought the only good thing that could happen was that he leave. "Yeah. It's okay."

On stiff legs, she turned and walked out of the room, down the stairs and out onto the porch. She had to get some fresh air. The house suddenly felt stifling and closed in and the air so thick she was drowning in the suffocating, heavy weight of it.

She heard the screen door creak open and shut as Cutter joined her there where she stood with her back to the house and her arms wrapped tightly around her middle. If he touched her, she was lost. If he kissed her, she was gone.

"Peg—"

"—You'd better go."

A long silence passed. She could feel him watching her, sense him studying her.

"Are you afraid of me, Peg?" he asked in a voice that said he hoped not, he really, really hoped not.

It was his honest entreaty that prompted hers. "It's…it's just not a good idea for us…for us to be here. Like this."

Another silence, thick with questions, heavy with the only obvious conclusion. "Because of what it might lead to?"

"Yeah," she admitted quietly. "Because of what it might lead to." She looked over her shoulder at him. "Does it make you happy to know that?"

She hadn't meant to bite the last part out. But she'd never meant to admit her attraction, either, so she figured she was entitled to a little bite.

"It might," he said softly, "if it didn't seem to make you so sad."

She couldn't respond to that. Not without giving more of herself away. She already felt as if she'd stripped to the skin. So she said nothing. Tried to feel nothing.

"Well," he said, sounding sorry and resigned but determined to do as she asked. "Tell Shelby goodbye for me, will you? Tell her—tell her that I think she's quite the little cowgirl."

She nodded into her chest. The apple hadn't fallen too far from the tree, he'd said. What would you do, Cutter, if you knew? If you really knew?

She couldn't look at him. "Sure. I'll tell her. Good-bye, Cutter."

"Yeah," he said and she could feel his thoughtful gaze. "I guess it is."

After a long moment, his booted foot hit the second step. He stopped, drew a deep breath. "Look—it's been good seeing you," he finally said, his voice sounding rusty, as if he was having trouble getting those particular words out—as if there were other words he wanted to say but those were the ones that had come out anyway.

"You, too." She cut him a quick glance, then looked back at the night. At the truck that would be pulling out soon and never return to Sundown again. "Um—thanks for what you did today." She owed him this. "It…it was a nice thing to do for…for Shelby's sake."

He didn't say anything for the longest moment—so long that she couldn't stand it. She looked up at him, at those blue eyes that he'd given to her daughter.

"And what about her momma? Was it a nice thing I did for her, too?"

His eyes were searching. For forgiveness? For encouragement? For what, she didn't know. But it seemed important to him that she wasn't angry with him anymore. And suddenly, it seemed important to her that she wasn't angry anymore, either.

"Yes," she said and found that it wasn't so hard to smile. "It was a nice thing you did for me, too. I appreciated it. All of it."

All of it. Including the kiss. And right or wrong,

foolish or wise, she wanted him to kiss her again. That's why he had to leave. Before he kissed her again because if he kissed her again, she wouldn't want to let him go.

Yet as they stood there, with a soft wind blowing, a night owl calling, and a dusty miller flitting around the porch light, she was sure that he was going to. His gaze sought hers, searched. His hand reached out, touched her cheek, then slowly dropped away. With a long, lingering look, he turned and ambled in his loose-hipped cowboy walk, down the rest of the steps.

"You take care now, you hear?" he said over his shoulder.

She walked to the edge of the porch, hugged a post against her cheek where his hand had been. "I hear, Cutter. I hear."

Then she watched him climb into his truck and drive away.

Five

Cutter thought about driving all night long. Just stopping at the hotel, grabbing his gear and heading out under the big Montana sky. He was in a mood for driving. And Lord knew, he was good at leaving. But he went back to his hotel room, flopped down on the bed instead and folded his arms behind his head.

And he thought about Peg. About how he'd finally gotten the smile he'd been looking for. About how her generous heart had finally forgiven him for sins he should have known he'd committed but had only owned up to today.

He thought about that sweet little blue-eyed girl who didn't have a daddy. And then he made himself think about something else because he did not want to let his thoughts lead him down that road.

That led him right back to pretty Peg again. Soft

mouth. Soft breasts. It had been a long time but he still remembered the taste of her in his mouth. Velvet and silk. Roses and cream. He still remembered the way it felt to be inside her. Tight and pulsing, slick satin heat.

Yeah. He'd gone out there this morning hoping he'd get a little taste of Peg again. And he'd found out that she was a momma.

It had changed things. Kids always changed things. For one thing, it had made her an adult. A kid required that of a person. Made them grow up. Made them give up on their own dreams to cater to things like food and shelter. Money to pay bills.

That's why he'd always avoided any serious relationships. Serious led to responsibility. He wasn't ready for responsibility. He wasn't ready to grow up. Which meant he wasn't ready for Peg. Probably never would be. Hell, he was his old man's son, after all. Wayne Reno hadn't been able to stick around, had he? Cutter couldn't even remember the last time he'd seen him. He'd blow in, blow out, and leave his momma crying.

He rolled to his side, punched the pillow and tucked it under his bent arm. Cutter hated his old man. He hated him because of what he'd done to his mom—and what he'd done to him.

Mostly what he'd done had been to not be there. But when he was, it was even worse. He remembered one time in particular. He'd been six. His dad must have shown up in the middle of the night because he'd just been there that morning when Cutter had gotten up. His momma had had to work so Cutter had stayed with his dad—hoping, as only a child could hope—that there was some love lying behind those eyes that stared at him like he was an ant who'd invaded his private picnic.

"Come on, boy. Let's go git us somethin' to wet our whistle."

Hope. It had grown and swelled. His dad wanted to take him somewhere. Maybe if he was real good, real quiet, he'd see that he was a good boy. He'd want to stay this time.

"Cute kid," the lady behind the bar with the bright red lips and baggy eyes had said.

"That one there?" his dad had glanced over his shoulder at him then laughed into his beer. "Hell, that one there was just an accident—and now him and his momma are like a ball and chain round my lily-white neck, know what I mean?"

Cutter hadn't known what he'd meant, not then. He'd known that he hadn't felt happy anymore and the next day, his dad was gone again. A few years later, he'd finally figured out exactly what good old *Dad* had meant. Just like he'd had a better understanding of why his mom had cried at night.

He sat up abruptly. He hadn't been down that lost highway in a long time. He didn't much like going there now. He checked the clock, dragged a hand through his hair and bolted off the bed. Then he packed his things, checked out and was on the road within fifteen minutes.

And then he just drove. With the windows down and the radio up, he drove and he didn't look back. Not to his childhood. Not to Sundown. Not to pretty

Peggy Lathrop with the beautiful breasts and the strong, giving heart.

Not to the little blue-eyed cowgirl who hadn't had a daddy in *forever*.

"You miss her, don't you?"

Peg shoved her fork around on her plate and looked across the table into the sparkling violet eyes of Ellie Savage. "Yeah. I miss her, but Mom called last night so I got to talk to her."

"And?" Ellie prompted just as someone punched a quarter in the jukebox and an old Brooks and Dunn tune blared out, loud and bouncy.

"And she's having a blast. They went to the zoo yesterday. Sea World tomorrow and Sunday, it's the ocean."

Peg leaned back, looked around. The dinner crowd at the Dusk to Dawn—Sundown's one and only restaurant, bar and youth center all rolled into one—was thinning out. The party people were starting to filter in to belly up to the bar, tip back a few longnecks and wait for the band to start playing.

Ellie waved to John Tyler, one of the local boys, when he walked in the door. John came grinning over to the table to talk with the three of them. Peg smiled, listened with half an ear, and tried not to miss Shelby.

She'd debated about letting Shelby go with her folks for their annual two-week summer trip to visit Jack's brother's family in San Diego. Shelby was only five, after all. But her mom and Jack wanted to take her so badly and Shelby hadn't been to a zoo in *forever*. It was already the end of July and in a little more than three weeks, her baby girl would be starting kindergarten. So, she'd relented. And now she was lonely.

That's why she'd agreed to meet Lee and Ellie here at the Dusk to Dawn for dinner. Shelby had only been gone four days and her little house seemed as empty as a tomb.

"How are you doing with Jackpot?" Lee asked when John moved on over to the bar where a couple of his buddies had lured him over with the promise of buying him a beer.

She didn't look at Jackpot these days without seeing Cutter astride him.

"Fine, actually," she said, quickly drawing herself away from that picture and flashing Lee a smile. "He's really a great horse. It was like you said, he just needed some attention."

She'd been giving him plenty of it, too. With Shelby gone, she'd been spending her evenings in the barn or riding. And Jackpot really was coming along.

Feeling restless, she glanced around the large, open room with its scuffed wood floor, worn-out booths and brass-and-oak bar that looked like it came straight out of an Old West saloon. Then she watched distractedly as the band started setting up in the corner near the dance floor. When her attention returned to the table, Lee and Ellie were grinning at each other and Ellie's hand had disappeared beneath the table.

"You two need to get a room?" Peg teased.

They were little more than newlyweds. The special thing about their relationship was that the two of them had found each other. Lee had come home to Sundown a year ago to take care of Ellie and they'd ended up falling in love.

"We have a secret," Ellie whispered with a pretty blush.

Peg cocked her head. "So...tell."

"We're going to try to have a baby."

Peg looked from Ellie, who was radiant, to Lee, who looked a little green around the gills. She understood why. He was worried. Ellie, for all her exuberance and optimism, was taking a risk trying to get pregnant. While Ellie was one of the most well-adjusted people she knew, Ellie was also epileptic. Peg couldn't begin to comprehend the physical and emotional pain Ellie had endured coming to terms with and living with her condition.

But she did know one thing. Lee Savage was the best thing that had ever happened to her—just like Ellie was the best thing that had happened to him.

"So," Peg said, a little worried for Ellie herself, but determined not to burst her bubble, "trying's half the fun, huh?"

Lee snorted.

Ellie laughed. "I'll say."

They all laughed then and Peg could have cried for the look of love in Lee's eyes when his gaze locked on Ellie's across the table.

"It'll be all right," Ellie whispered.

Lee nodded. Closed his eyes. "It'll be fine," he said at last. "Doc says it will be fine, so it will be."

"Well," Peg said, her eyes twinkling, "guess that means you won't be staying for the dance."

And they didn't. They left shortly after and Peg,

thrilled for her friend's happiness but feeling even more lonely because of it, was left to debate what she was going to do with the rest of her night. She'd just decided she might as well go home when Krystal and Sam walked in.

"Well, lookie, lookie here. Peg, darlin', you out kickin' up your heels tonight?" This from Sam, a big bear of a man who loved his wife, his son and the opportunity to tease, in equal measure.

"Look at her, Krystal," he said tugging on his tan Stetson then making a twirling motion with his finger encouraging Peg to show him all the angles. "She's just as pretty as a picture. Didn't know you owned a dress, Peg. Looks real nice on you, too."

Krystal gave her husband a little shove. "Stow it, you big goon. You've seen Peg in a dress lots of times. At church," she added when he made a big show of crinkling his brows and scratching his head.

"Krystal, sweetheart, a church dress and *that* dress shouldn't even be mentioned in the same sentence. Hot, Peggy. Real hot," he added with a brotherly wink and ambled over to the bar.

Peg rolled her eyes and Krystal grinned. "He's right, you know. You do look pretty hot. Special occasion?"

"Yeah. My good jeans were dirty."

She was starting to feel self-conscious. It was just a dress. Just a pale yellow, gauzy little sundress. She'd fallen in love with it when she'd taken Shelby to the dentist in Bozeman last week. It was short and sassy and buttoned up the front of a bodice that nipped in at her waist and if she tugged just right, didn't show too much cleavage. Or maybe it did, judging from Sam's reaction.

"Is it too much, do you think?"

"Oh, honey," Krystal said with a laugh. "If I had the goods you've got, I'd show off the package, too."

"It's too much," Peg said and started for the door.

Laughing, Krystal grabbed her arm. "Oh, no, you don't. You aren't going anywhere. Now we got us a sitter for the night and Shelby's in California so you and me and Sam are gonna cut loose a little. I know I'm due. So are you.

"Margarita, Danny," she told the bartender as she dragged Peg along with her to the bar. "Two of them. Soon. You're looking at two women who've got some powerful thirsts."

"And a yen to get rowdy?" Sam asked hopefully as he tucked Krystal under one arm and Peg under the other.

His grin was infectious. So was Krystal's mood.

"Why not," Peg decided, feeling a little reckless. She couldn't remember the last time she'd let her hair down, acted anything but the part she'd been cast in as the responsible parent. Yes, it was a part she loved. But every once in a while…every once in a while, she just wanted to have fun. Looked like tonight she was going to get her chance.

She was hot. Her back was damp with perspiration, her hair clung to her temples. She'd danced almost every dance and she was breathless with laughter. The music was country and lively. The crowd was happy and loud. And thanks to the pitcher of margaritas Sam had bought for her and Krystal, little John Tyler didn't look nearly as young as he had an hour ago. She was also starting to remember why she chose not to be much more than a social drinker. The tequila had gone straight to her head.

"How old did you say you were?" she asked with a careful frown as John held her close and the band slowed things down with a ballad.

She felt his smile against her hair where he'd pressed his cheek. "Old enough for what you've got in mind."

She pulled back, grinned. "It's the dress, right?"

"Oh, yeah," he said, grinning back, "the dress definitely did its part, but it's what's *in* the dress that's got me goin'."

It was fun. The flirting, the dancing, even forgetting that she was a mom for a little while and letting herself experience the attraction of a handsome man.

John Tyler was definitely that. He was also what they called jailbait. He couldn't be more than twenty. And even though he was pretty and even though she'd had just enough to drink that she was of a mind to end the long dry spell that had had her acting the fool over Cutter Reno three weeks ago, it wasn't going to end with John Tyler. It wasn't going to end with any of the other cowboys who had offered up a dance— or anything else she might have a need for tonight— either.

Because they weren't right. And, as hard as she'd worked trying to convince herself that she could do it, because Peg wasn't cut from the cloth that thought sex without love was better than nothing at all.

She'd traded her sexuality for motherhood six years ago. And that was fine. Well, it had *been* fine until Cutter had shown up again. It was his fault she was even thinking along those lines. Even knowing that taking up with him would have come to no good, she'd finally admitted to herself that she'd still wanted that cowboy. She'd been all itchy and achy ever since—and angry with herself for having such a loose hold on her hormones. And for letting herself feel a little lonely.

"Why don't you have a girlfriend, John?" she asked, looping her arms around his shoulders, accepting that she had to be content to simply be held for a little while by a warm, hard body and smiled at by a beautiful, interested face. In public. On a dance floor. With all of her clothes on.

"Because I've been waiting for you to notice me."

"Stop it. Truth, now. Why don't you have someone special?"

He shrugged, all cover-boy looks and cowboy charm. "I'm too young and ornery, I guess. I've got to finish school. Get settled somewhere."

"Somewhere that's not Sundown?"

Again, he shrugged. "Who knows. Maybe. In the meantime, what about you? Why don't you have a special guy in your life? And don't say it's because nobody's offered. You've got every single man within shouting distance dropping their jaws just thinking about you."

A loud crash sounded from the corner as a table toppled.

John never missed a beat. "There, see. Another jaw just hit the floor."

She laughed. "You're good for me."

The hand that was warm and strong at her waist squeezed then caressed. "I could be even better."

Oh, he was sweet. And oh, he was tempting—and she could see in his eyes that he was more than teasing. He was tempted, too.

"In another life, handsome," she said wistfully and since she figured she was only so strong she decided it was time to go home. Alone. She hugged him hard then kissed him softly on the cheek. "Thanks."

"For?" He held her hand as she made to pull away.

"For making me remember what it feels like to be a woman. Don't," she added on a laugh when his expression told her he could build on that feeling if she'd just agree to go somewhere dark and alone with him. "Don't even think it."

Then she turned to walk away—and ran right into the solid wall of Cutter Reno's chest.

Cutter had been watching Peg and the cowboy from just inside the door. Watching and scowling and feeling a heat that had less to do with the July night and the crush of partying bodies than it did with seeing that fancy-faced young stud putting the moves on Peg.

"Cutter," she finally said, clearly stunned to see him.

"That would be me."

She looked flustered. And flushed. And like she ought to be lying rumpled in the middle of a bed being made love to—by him—instead of standing in the middle of a room crowded with people.

Her eyes were a melting chocolate-brown. Her skin—and there was a whole hell of a lot of it showing above and below that sexy little excuse of a dress—was just as he remembered. A sweet, honeyed tan, misted with a dewy dampness that had his pulse leaping and his blood pooling to a part of his body that was very happy to see her.

"What…what are you doing here?" she finally asked, raising a hand to her throat where he could see her own pulse fluttering.

He ignored her question, asked one of his own. "Did I interrupt something?" He shot a glare toward the cowboy who had ambled back over to the bar, leaned against it and made a point of keeping an eye on Peg.

She blinked, glanced toward the bar, then back at him with an indignant, "What?"

"The kid? Did I interrupt something between you and junior?"

Oh, boy. He heard the edge of jealousy in his voice, felt the irritation prickle at the back of his neck in a spot right beneath his shirt collar—then he flushed red as a damn rose when she figured it out and laughed at him.

"Wait a minute. In the first place, you didn't tell me what you're doing here." She attempted to tick off her point but missed when she went to slap her index fingers together. "In the second place, what do you care?" She tried again for a check-off gesture.

Missed again. Undaunted, she gave it one more try. "And in the first place—"

"—Whoa now, darlin'. We've already been there," he interrupted with a laugh when it dawned on him that little Peg may have been partying very hardy before he'd wandered into the Dusk to Dawn looking for a beer and the guts to drive on out to her place to see her.

"That may be, but I still don't know what you're doing here."

He squinted down at her, not sure that he knew himself, and decided to play it light and breezy. "Peggy. Darlin'. How much have you had to drink?"

She sniffed and crossed her arms belligerently under her breasts. He damn near fell to his knees when that lush, soft flesh all but spilled out over the top of her dress.

"In the first place—"

His laughter cut her off.

"Okay, okay. So, maybe I've had one too many margaritas," she admitted with a little shrug that drew his undivided attention to the yellow cotton strap that slipped slowly off her left shoulder. "You might even go so far as to say I'm teetering just a little bit toward tipsy."

"Well, now," he drawled and digging deep for casual reached out and tugged her errant strap back into place. "Normally I like that in a woman."

"Well, now," she drawled right back, seemingly unmoved when his fingers lingered on her slender shoulder when it was all he could do to drop his hand

and not haul her flush against him. "I'll just bet you do."

She tried for a scowl but ended up answering his smile. Finally. Then just as fast, she looked away, her hand a little unsteady as she touched it to her hair, telling him that maybe she was a little rattled, too.

"I think maybe I need some air."

So did he. Between the smoke and the noise and her almost dress, he couldn't draw a breath that didn't feel like it was choking him.

Without a word, he took her by the arm and headed for the door. The muffled sound of a classic ballad floated over the heavy boom of the bass and the rumble of good-time laughter and followed them outside. He led her around the building toward the parking lot.

Their silent walk through the parked cars and pickups gave him the opportunity to think about her questions. Tipsy or not, she'd asked some damn good ones. The same ones he was asking himself. Why *was* he here? Why *did* he care? Since he didn't have any good answers, he asked one of his own.

"How's Rascal?"

"He's doing fine." She shot him a considering look that told him the fresh air was doing its job and clearing her head. "And you had a lot of nerve—paying my vet bill before you left town."

Technically he hadn't paid it before he'd left. He'd called the vet from Butte the next day then sent a check. "Yeah, a man could get hard time for pulling a stunt like that."

She stopped, faced him in the dimly lit lot. The summer breeze tugged at her hair. A silken strand caught at the corner of her mouth. "You didn't have to do that," she said softly.

"You could just say thanks." Unable to resist, he hooked a finger on the errant strand. He tugged it away from her face and tucked it behind her ear, his hand lingering longer than it should have before he let it drop away.

He'd felt her shiver, saw her throat work as she swallowed. "I...I could pay you back, too."

"No. You couldn't. Rascal wouldn't have gotten hurt if I hadn't stuck around."

"Oh, Cutter, it wasn't your fau—"

"—Just say thank you, Peg."

She angled her head, accepted that he wasn't budging and finally gave in. "Thank you, Peg."

He tipped back his head, smiled at the blanket of stars and her smart mouth. "Nice night."

"Hmm." She stopped by her old truck. Leaning back against it, her shoulder blades resting on the fender, she watched the sky with him. "Lover's moon."

He'd heard loud silences before. Those moments before the gate flew open and a bronc busted out into the arena, all lightning and strength and outrage. Those moments when a cowboy was down and the crowd sat hushed, waiting for movement, for a sign that everything was going to be okay. Those moments when a man knew that a woman understood what was on his mind.

Lover's moon. They'd made love beneath a moon like this. Hot love. Young love. Wild love.

He met her eyes, saw her searching, seeking, swallowing back a memory and a need he suspected was as strong as his own.

"How's Shelby?" he asked hoarsely.

"Fine." She looked quickly away. "She…she's fine."

He moved a step closer. Close enough to see the pulse skitter just beneath the dew-damp skin at her throat. Close enough to see a tiny, sexy smudge of mascara just below her left eye. Close enough to feel the warmth of her breath feather against his jaw. "Where's Shelby?"

She closed her eyes, was quiet a very long time before looking up and staring at a spot somewhere beyond his shoulder. "In California. With her grandparents."

He studied her face, saw what he'd dreaded, what he'd wanted, what he'd been craving since he'd left her a little over three weeks ago. He didn't know why he hadn't been able to get her out of his head. Was sure that coming back here was a mistake.

She didn't look like a mistake, though. She looked like every man's dream. She looked like a woman he wanted. And as he moved in closer, planted his palms on the fender at either side of her shoulders and caged her in, she looked like a woman who wanted a man.

"You know—I've missed two opportunities to dance with you." He leaned closer, whispered against her temple as he lowered his head. "Once on the Fourth and once…just now…inside. Will you dance with me, Peg?"

Music from the bar filtered softly outside and into the night. A steamy love song, a deep, driving beat.

He wasn't asking her to dance. They both knew what he was asking. And they both knew what other opportunities he'd missed. He could have stayed six years ago. A lot lately, he'd been wondering if maybe he should have. Her next words straightened him out on that notion.

"You shouldn't have come back, Cutter." Her voice was very soft and not at all sure but the moment she said it, he knew she was right. He shouldn't have come back. He'd known it when he'd lain awake every night since they last parted and ached for her. He'd known it when he'd climbed in his truck and headed down the highway to Sundown.

He'd known it and yet, here he was. And now that he was here, he wasn't going anywhere. Not unless she told him to leave. Not now that they were together, beneath the stars of this hot summer night where a distance of six years had shrunken to the few inches of moonlight standing between them.

There was still more she wanted to say. He could see it in so many telling little ways—the pulse that now fluttered like frightened butterfly wings at her throat, the unsteady rise and fall of her breasts, the pretty brown eyes that had grown shiny and a little wild.

"I told myself to stay away," he confessed, watching her eyes as he lowered his head to whisper against her mouth. "I told myself a hundred times that it was a bad idea to come back."

"Very…very bad," she agreed on a hushed murmur as her head fell back and she let his mouth wander.

Summer heat. Woman heat. He felt surrounded by it. Consumed with it. And the wanting to make love to her escalated to need.

"Be bad with me, Peg." The words whispered out on a low growl as he dragged his open mouth along her jaw then bent to that silky spot at the curve of her throat and slid his tongue over her wildly racing pulse. Her skin tasted of salt and seduction and sex. His mind reeled with a hundred ways he wanted to take her.

"Please." He nuzzled a path down her throat, wedged a knee between her thighs, felt her breath catch and her body quiver. An arrow of raw, sexual heat burned a path to his belly. "Be very bad with me."

Six

She wanted to. Oh, she wanted to, Peg admitted as Cutter's big, warm hands spanned her waist and drew her against his hips so she could feel how very, very bad he wanted to be.

And it shocked and excited and embarrassed her to realize that she might have crossed the line from wanting to wanton right then—right there in the Dusk to Dawn parking lot—if the sound of footsteps crunching over gravel and Krystal's concerned, "Peg? You out here, honey?" hadn't brought her to her senses.

She pushed Cutter away, drew a steadying breath.

"Over here, Krystal." She heard the huskiness in her voice, felt Cutter's gaze, dark and hot on her face.

Her heart was still racing when Krystal rounded Peg's truck. She stopped short when she saw Cutter—

looked from him to Peg then back to Cutter again. There was little doubt that she'd figured out exactly what they'd been doing—or about to do.

"Thought that was you I saw walk into the bar," Krystal said, watching Cutter thoughtfully.

"How's it going, Krystal?" Cutter leaned a shoulder against the fender and tucked his hands in his back pockets.

"It's goin' just fine. You?"

One corner of his mouth lifted in a tight smile— more grimace than grin. "Never better."

Again, she glanced from Peg to Cutter then demonstrated why she'd never been known for her subtly. "So, what brings you back to Sundown?"

Cutter locked his gaze on Peg's. It was so hot she felt the sizzle sear her cheeks. "Just a little unfinished business."

Krystal gave Cutter another hard stare and switched her attention to Peg. "You okay?" She looked as if she was trying to decide if this was a good thing or a bad thing, finding the two of them together.

Peg smiled uneasily. "I just needed some air. And now I think I'm going to call it a night. It's…it's getting a little late for me."

Krystal narrowed her eyes. "Can you drive okay?"

"I'm fine," Peg insisted. At least she thought she was. That kiss had been one sobering experience. One sobering, sensual, scary experience.

"I'll make sure she gets home all right," Cutter said, enough challenge in his voice to let Krystal know he didn't appreciate or need her interference.

Krystal stood there, clearly debating whether or not

she should do just that. "It's all right. Really," Peg added and shot Krystal a reassuring smile.

"We'll get your truck home, Peg—but you call me tomorrow, okay?" Krystal said after a long moment.

"Sure."

"You see to it," she heard Krystal say in a hushed voice, "that nothing bad happens to her."

Cutter acknowledged the warning with a nod. "Tell Sam I'll drop by to see him before I leave town again."

"You do that," Krystal said. She was still standing in the middle of the lot when Cutter walked Peg to his truck.

Peg's hands were shaking as she clamped them together in her lap. Her head was clear. She was sober now. Stone-cold sober—had been ever since Cutter had backed her up against her truck and kissed her like he wanted to eat her up in big, gulping bites.

She shivered and flushed hot and cold all at the same time as she glanced at him beside her in his truck's dark interior.

The reality of what was about to happen crept into the night by slow degrees. Did she really know what she was doing bringing this alley cat home with her? Krystal had made it clear that she wondered the same thing. Peg found it interesting that for all of Krystal's attempts to convince her that she should give Cutter another chance, tonight she seemed to have finally understood what Peg had known all along. Cutter didn't play for keeps. Cutter played for the sake of playing. Not out of meanness. He just liked to play.

Which was why she was still puzzled over why he'd come back to play with her.

Sundown was definitely off his regular flight path. She didn't doubt for a minute that he could have found any number of willing and eager partners without altering his course. So, no, she had no idea what had prompted him to come back. Was still trying to recover from the shock of it. And with the fact that she was letting him drive her home.

Her heartbeat quickened as he turned into her driveway. Because she was lonely, that's why, she admitted pragmatically. And because Shelby's absence had driven home a very salient point. She had no life other than the life she lived for her daughter. She'd made that life be enough. She was content for it to be enough. Most of the time. But for one night of that life, she wanted to live it for herself.

Did it make her selfish? Maybe. Did it make her irresponsible? Probably. She couldn't help but think that it also made her human. With human wants and human needs and for one night—*one night*—she was willing to forgive herself for taking what she wanted and damn the consequences.

She would have this night with Cutter Reno. She was entitled. And she was due. She'd use him just the way he intended to use her. For pleasure. For comfort. And, she admitted reluctantly, she'd use him to alleviate a stark, aching loneliness that had crept up on her tonight like a thief and stolen her ability to defend herself against it.

He pulled to a stop in front of her house, killed his lights and climbed out of the cab. Lowering her head to the back of the passenger seat, she closed her eyes and told herself it didn't hurt to know that when he'd gotten what he wanted, he'd be gone.

She would not fall in love with him all over again. Knowing he'd leave. Knowing this time that what had once felt like a promise of forever, was just another love-the-one-you're-with episode in his life.

Yes, he would leave her. But she'd survived the last time and she would survive again. And maybe, just maybe, in the morning, she'd have him out of her system—along with one more reason to confirm that she'd done the right thing by not telling him about Shelby.

Refusing to give in to the guilt or the uncertainty, she lifted her head, turned to see his blue eyes, serious and searching, gaze at her through the open truck window. He was so beautiful. So darkly handsome, so ruggedly male. She wanted to feel his strength over her, pumping into her. She wanted to feel his hands and mouth—everywhere.

This time, she was going to take as much from Cutter Reno as he was going to take from her. This time, her heart wouldn't be on the line because this time, she saw through the tender lies in his eyes that said he loved her.

And this time would have to be enough.

She told herself that the tightening she felt in her chest wasn't heartache. It was anticipation. Excitement. She was entitled. She was entitled to feel like a woman again. And she was woman enough to handle the goodbye.

When he opened her door for her, she drew a deep breath, took his hand and climbed out of the truck.

After bending down to give Rascal the hello pat he begged for and making sure he really was okay, Cutter followed Peg in silence as she walked ahead of him toward her little house.

See to it that nothing bad happens to her. Krystal's words played over and over in his head. Translation: Don't hurt her.

He didn't want to hurt anyone. He especially didn't want to hurt Peg but the closer he got to her door, the deeper it settled that that's exactly what he'd do if he spent the night.

He wished to hell that he didn't have such a big, bad need for her. He wished the gentle sway of her hips as she walked ahead of him didn't undercut his conscience and make him want her more. He wished that any number of women who were both willing and wise to his ways would have been enough to take his mind off this one woman.

Yeah, and he could wish in one hand and spit in the other and the result would be the same. He wanted her. And damn his selfish hide, there wasn't anything he could do to convince himself he wasn't going to have her. Unless she said no.

When she opened the screen door, he reached around her, flattened a palm against the frame above her head and pushed it shut. She turned slowly, leaned back against the door and met his eyes in the moon-drenched night.

He touched a finger to her cheek and searched her

face, her beautiful, wholesome face that he wanted to watch when he made her climax. "You can still say no."

She turned her face to the side. "Is that what you want me to say?"

He drew in a deep breath, then let it out. "Not in a million years."

"Then come inside."

She turned back toward the door. His hand on her arm stopped her.

"Why are you letting this happen?"

A flicker of uncertainty flashed in her eyes and then was gone. "Why are you asking so many questions? Why aren't you kissing me?"

"Because I want you to want this as much as I do." He counted heartbeats and waited for her reply. "Do you want me, Peg?"

She wet her lips with her tongue and nodded.

A fierce clutch of possession curled in his gut. "Say it. Say you want me."

Her eyes were dark. Her breasts rose and fell gently with each tremulous breath she drew. "I want you, Cutter. I've always wanted you."

He didn't need another invitation—he'd been waiting for this one for what seemed like his entire life. To hell with his conscience. It had never stood a chance anyway.

He pressed her into the screen door with his body, covered her mouth with his and took the kiss he'd been craving with a hard, hot assault of open mouth and seeking tongue. She was liquid and lush against him, the soft cushion of her breasts pressing into his chest and driving his hips into action.

She sucked in a sharp breath when he reached between them, his fingers quick and sure as he opened the top button on her dress.

"This dress...has been...driving me...crazy," he growled between hungry kisses and undid another button, shuddering when the soft warmth of her breasts brushed against the back of his knuckles.

"It's...new," she managed to say, sounding breathless and bothered then bent her knee and pressed against his other hand as he worked it beneath her skirt to caress her bare thigh.

"This dress...ought to be...outlawed," he muttered gruffly as he undid two more buttons and filled his palm with the sweet, firm round of her bottom.

"It's...a...oh..." She bit her lip and cried out as he tunneled his hand under the elastic of her high-cut panties and found the heat of her. He ran a finger along the damp cleft between her thighs as she expelled a serrated, "sun...dress."

"This...dress—" he hardly recognized his voice as he worked to free another button "—is comin' off."

Her hands raked through his hair, guiding his head to the breast he had half-bared, then moved to the buttons herself to undo them to her waist with shaking fingers.

With effort, he flattened his palms against the screen door and stiff-armed, pushed away. He wanted to see her. He wanted to see the damage he'd done to her lips that were swollen and wet and open for him. He wanted to see the sexual haze in her eyes as she let her head loll against the screen and watched him with anticipation and an impatience that made his mouth go dry.

He wanted to see those beautiful breasts, exposed to the moonlight where her dress fell open to her waist and the thin cotton straps slipped off her shoulders. She looked ravaged and willing and so ripe he groaned with the rush of desire that knotted in his groin.

"You are so unbelievably beautiful," he murmured and looked his fill. She wasn't wearing a bra. She hadn't worn anything but those thin, lacy panties that, even now, drove him crazy just thinking about sliding them down her hips.

Her breasts were pale and round, the weight of them heavy and firm. Her aureoles were a dark, dusky brown, her nipples delicate little velvet peaks.

"Touch me."

Those two whispered words damn near drove him over the edge. He reached out, traced a finger around an erect nipple and felt a tremor eddy through her.

"Like this?"

She closed her eyes, moaned softly when he rolled her nipple between his finger and his thumb.

"Tell me what else you want," he demanded, even as he reached up under her skirt and drew her panties down her legs.

She clutched his shoulders to keep from falling. "Your mouth. I want your mouth."

He dragged her against him then bent her over his arm and lowered his mouth to her breast. Nothing tasted like her. Nothing. He'd never forgotten the feel of her in his mouth, didn't know how he'd lived this long without grazing his teeth along the silk and honey of her skin. Without the salvation that he'd never known he'd been seeking as he suckled and licked and feasted on the heat her answering hunger ignited.

He had planned to seduce her slowly. He had planned to lay her down and love her in the comfort of her bed. He hadn't planned to take her against the wall with the finesse of a water buffalo. But she did things to his plans. Things he didn't seem to have any control over.

Before he knew it, he was reaching for his belt buckle. With his mouth at her throat, he somehow managed to get it open and his zipper down. "My pocket," he said on a guttural growl, surprised that he even had the presence of mind to think about her protection.

He didn't want to use a condom. He didn't want anything between them but skin and heat. But he'd conditioned himself long ago to take care of business and he wasn't going to let his guard down now.

Between the two of them, they managed to get him suited up before he burst with the need to be inside her. He lifted her in his arms, pressed her back against the screen door and with his hands under her bottom, urged her legs around his hips.

"Open your eyes," he commanded and guided himself to the sweet, wet opening that invited him with the sensuous buck of her hips. "I want to see your eyes when I come inside you."

"Hurry," she demanded and when she was looking deep into his eyes, he drove into her.

She drew in a sharp breath; he lost his completely. She was so tight, so sweetly swollen as she took him in—all of him—and held him deep.

He felt something give at her back, heard the muffled rip of the screen ripping and shifted their weight until her back was pressed against the clapboard siding. With his hands on her hips and her eyes locked on his, he moved inside her. Slowly at first because the pleasure was so sharp and so pure he was afraid it would be all over before he'd had his fill of her. He wanted it to last. This deep, drugging sensation of drowning in her, this union of body that veered dangerously close to body and soul.

"Cutter," she whispered his name on a gasping little hitch and knotted her hands in his hair. "Cutter. Please. Oh, please, please—"

He slanted his mouth over hers, swallowing her plea, giving her what they both wanted. With a hard, driving rhythm, he pumped into her body. Clutching her hips to draw her closer, he deepened the contact, extended the pleasure that built and swelled with each deep stroke, with each silken glide.

"Come with me," he demanded, slamming into her. "Come. With. Me."

He felt her peak, and he was gone. His release ripped through him like a lightning strike—all fire and flash and an electric pleasure so fiercely intense that it hurled him over the edge and into free fall. He was lost somewhere in oblivion, riding on the rich, wild aftershocks as she clenched like a velvet fist around him, cried out, and with a shattered sob, flew over the top with him.

Heart hammering, head spinning, he held her hard against him, sweat slicked, artlessly wasted and hung to lucidity by a thin thread of conscious thought that kept him on his feet. He wasn't sure how long he stood there, buried inside her, flattening her against the wall, keeping them both from falling. He was drained, depleted, yet he felt stronger and more centered than he'd felt in years. Maybe six years.

The thought finally sobered him. He was putting way too much importance to something that was merely a hot bout of mind-blowing sex.

Yet when he roused himself enough to lift his head from her neck and look at her face, it wasn't just the sex that he thought about. It was the look of her. Kitten soft and totally vulnerable. Her eyes were closed, her hair falling across her face where his hands—or had it been her hands—had tangled.

With one arm banded around her waist and still buried inside her, he brushed the hair from her eyes. She made a soft sound…of exhaustion, or satisfaction, or discomfort, or maybe all three…and opened her eyes.

"Hi," he said, and touching his lips to the corner of her mouth, fully expected her to call him everything but a child of God for using her so roughly.

A crooked little smile tilted one corner of her mouth before her head fell forward against his shoulder. "Hi? That's the best you can do?"

He chuckled and hugged her hard, amazed at the depth of her giving. "I believe I just *did* the best I can do. And considering I'm still on my feet, I don't think I'd be complaining if I were you—although, Lord, Peg, I didn't mean to be so rough with you.''

''No complaints.'' She raised her head, smiling now, like a very contented, very sexy cat. ''But just once Cutter—just once I'd like this to happen in a bed.''

He started getting hard again at the memories that marched front and center. Back then he'd made love to her in the grass, in the back of his truck, on a blanket beneath the stars—but never in a bed.

''Invite me in,'' he whispered, nuzzling his nose against hers, then kissing her eyelids that had fallen closed yet again. ''I'll make it up to you.''

She looped her arms over his shoulders and snuggled close. ''You're assuming that one of us is still physically able to climb the stairs.''

''Baby…I'd crawl if I had to, to get in your bed.''

He felt her smile against his throat. ''There's something very appealing about that picture.''

''You want an appealing picture?'' He caressed her cheek with his palm, arrested by the look of her—all lush and languid and thoroughly loved. ''You ought to be standing where I am.''

''There you go again—making an assumption that I can stand.'' She yawned hugely. ''I don't think I could get my legs under me if my life depended on it.''

''You don't need to stand…or walk…or crawl. Just hold on.''

Her eyes flew open. She gasped then laughed and tightened her hold when he started moving and juggling and balancing on one foot then the other. "What…are you doing?"

"Getting out of these boots and pants."

She shrieked and wrapped her arms tighter around his neck when he almost dropped her. "Wouldn't it be easier to just put me down?"

He grunted as he finally managed to toe off both boots and shuck his jeans and shorts. "Easier, maybe. But not nearly as much fun. Besides. I don't want to put you down. Can you get the door? My hands seem to be…full." Of her. Of her smooth bare bottom and her slim, sexy weight.

She reached behind them, managed to get both the screen door—which looked like it had been rammed by a very mad bull—and the front door open. She laughed again when he stubbed his toe on a bootjack just inside the door and swore roundly.

"You think that's funny, huh?" He nuzzled the silky spot just beneath her ear as he climbed the stairs, her arms still looped around his neck and her legs still wrapped around his waist.

"I was laughing *with* you."

When he reached her room, he dumped her unceremoniously in the middle of her bed. "Let's see if you find this funny." He flicked on a bedside lamp and sat down beside her.

Watching her face, he combed his hands through the long tangle of her hair. She reached for him, started unbuttoning his shirt.

"You are so beautiful."

She actually blushed. Color spread downward to paint everything from her cheeks to her pretty breasts with a soft, rosy flush. "You're kind of pretty yourself," she said.

He found her sudden shyness endearing. Just like he found her body irresistible.

"Bronc riders aren't pretty," he insisted, cupping one of those beautiful breasts in his palm. He stroked a thumbnail over her nipple, watched it pearl.

She covered his hand with hers, pressing it deeper against her. "Handsome, then?"

"I can live with that." His smile faded when she looked up at him through eyes that had grown slumberous and dark.

He shrugged out of his shirt. "Your turn," he said and went to work on getting her the rest of the way out of her dress.

When she was finally lying there, completely naked, openly vulnerable, he laid a hand over her abdomen. She moved her hips, ever so slightly. He watched, fascinated as gooseflesh broke out across her skin.

"Cold?"

Eyes on his, she shook her head. "I am so *not* cold."

Her stomach muscles clenched beneath his palm and he moved his hand lower, pressing the heel against her pubic bone. "And soft. You are so, so soft."

She reached for him. "And you are so, so hard. Again," she added with a smile that was both seductive and shy.

"And well, we *are* in a bed," he put in philosophically as he stretched out beside her.

"Hmm. There is that." She turned on her side, ran her hand along his shoulder, down his chest and lower, slinging her long, silky leg over his hip. "And then there's this." She caressed him with her soft hand until he thought he'd die from the pleasure.

"Only one problem that I can see," she murmured, nibbling little kisses along his throat.

He gasped, then groaned through clenched teeth. "Problem?"

"The big guy is underdressed for the occasion."

"Wha? Oh, damn." He drew in a resigned breath, settled himself and grinned at her. "Don't go 'way."

Peg wasn't going anywhere. She'd made herself that promise. She wasn't going to the past and she wasn't going to the future. She was going to stay mired right here in the moment, with this beautiful man who even now pressed her into the bed with a hot, hard, claim of a kiss before he rose, gloriously aroused and unashamedly naked.

"I'll be right back," he promised and headed down the stairs.

But as she lay in the dark, listened to his footsteps on the stairs, to the front door creak open then shut, the past intruded whether she wanted it to or not. Through her open bedroom window, she heard him swear softly and pictured him walking barefoot and bare naked across the gravel. She listened to the sound of his truck door open, then close. Only when she didn't hear the sound of an engine firing, did she let out the breath she'd been holding and believe him.

He *was* coming back. He wasn't leaving. At least not right away.

And because she felt too much relief, she reminded herself what this was all about. This was about sex. It was about pleasure. It was about a temporary relief from a loneliness that had settled marrow deep.

None of it was about love.

The hot tears she blinked back when he walked back into the room, dropped his duffel on the floor and a stack of condoms on the nightstand, had nothing to do with love.

The way his eyes looked deep and long into hers when he entered her, moved inside her…nothing to do with love. The careful way he held her through the night, drawing her back against him when she made the slightest move to condition herself to distance…not one single thing to do with love.

And it wasn't love, deep and true, helpless and hopeless, that made her rise at dawn and, wrapped in his shirt, sit in the rocker in the corner of the room and memorize the way he looked, asleep in her bed.

Seven

Cutter was used to waking up to the smell of stale motel rooms and open boxes of leftover pizza. So he figured he must have been dreaming because what he smelled when he woke to daylight and a soft breeze whispering across his bare back was the farthest thing from stale. He burrowed deeper into the pillow, smelled clean, line-dried sheets, a hint of roses, and, could it be? He rolled to his back, sniffed the air and sighed in contentment. Freshly baked cookies.

With a stretch as huge as his satisfaction, he opened his eyes, squinted at the sunlight and got hard, thinking about the night he'd spent in Peg's bed. A bed he could happily spend the next five to seven hundred years in with her.

The thought sobered him like a bucket of cold water.

He was in some kind of trouble, here. He scrubbed a hand over his stubbled jaw, then craned his neck around to the nightstand where a scattering of destroyed foil packets obscured his view of the clock. He lifted his head, let it drop again. Eight-fifteen. He should be on the road. Hell, he should have beat it out of here last night.

But last night he hadn't been able to get enough of her. He ran his hand along the length of an erection that said he still hadn't gotten his fill.

Yeah, Reno. You're in double big trouble.

With a grim set of his mouth, he pried himself out of her bed, snagged his jeans from the floor where he'd dropped them and dragged them on. Carefully zipping to half-mast, he looked for his shirt, gave up when he couldn't find it and barefoot, followed his nose down the stairs.

He'd say good morning. He'd say thanks. Then he'd say goodbye. Before things got too sticky. Before he got too comfortable. Before either of them got to thinking that what was happening between them was something worth thinking about for the long haul. Cutter didn't do long haul. Not when it came to relationships. Not even when it came to Peg.

So, yeah. It was best to be moving on. But then he stepped into her kitchen. And then he spotted his shirt.

His mouth went dry; his jeans became instantly, unbearably tight. And that's when he decided he wasn't going anywhere. Not just yet anyway.

She was making cookies, all right. In her bare feet, with her long smooth legs peeking out beneath the tails of his shirt that hung on her like a tent. The burgundy plaid had never looked so good.

She stood with her back to him, the radio playing softly. She was moving her hips to the music, humming prettily and scooping cookie dough onto a baking sheet that sat on the kitchen counter. He glanced at the oven. The dial was set at 375 degrees. He figured he'd just spiked up to about 950.

She'd piled her hair on top of her head in a loose, untidy little knot that left her neck bare—except for the stray tendrils trailing like silky fringe at her nape and at her temples and when she turned, drifted over her left eye.

"Good morning," she said when she saw him. There were questions in her eyes, but she quickly shielded them and turned back to her cookie dough.

"Good Lord," he managed to say in a fractured croak that had her turning back to face him. "You look…edible."

She smiled, a kind of surprised, mouthwatering, sexy little pleased-with-herself smile when her gaze dropped from his face to the solid ridge pushing against his half-done fly.

"And you look…happy to see me."

He couldn't even be embarrassed, or apologetic. He was too stunned. Too full of feelings he didn't want to analyze, too aroused to consider anything but how he was going to get her out of his shirt. His shirt, that she was barely wearing with both the top and the bottom three buttons undone.

"Did I wake you?" She looked suddenly shy again when he leaned a bare shoulder against the doorjamb and tucked his hands under his armpits to keep from reaching for her. He wanted to look a little longer before he ravaged her.

"I smelled the cookies."

"I just took a batch out of the oven. Sugar cookies," she added, wiping her hands on a towel then slinging it over her shoulder. "You like them?"

He liked damn near everything about this moment. The look of her. The fact that her eyes danced with an edgy expectancy that said she hadn't quite had her fill of him, either.

He pushed away from the door, and because he couldn't not, he walked toward her. "Well, I guess the proof is in the tasting."

"It hit me this morning after I'd done chores and showered that I'd promised to bake cookies for the Friends of the Library bake sale this afternoon." She turned to scoop another ball of dough onto her spoon, then roll it in a sugar and cinnamon mix before smashing it with a fork on a cookie sheet. "I'm making a double batch so help yourself."

"Oh…" He lowered his mouth to her nape and wrapped his arms around her waist. "I intend to."

When he pulled her against him, she leaned back into him, sighed dreamily. He spread his hands wide over her abdomen, loving the feel of nothing but warm flesh and smooth skin beneath his shirt. Not even panties, he realized with a low groan as her little bottom snuggled right up and nestled against his arousal.

"Well, I'd say *you're* fully rested," she observed dryly.

It was one of the things he liked about her most. Her sense of humor. Her willingness to go with the moment, give in to the feeling and to what made them both feel good.

"I don't know…" He nuzzled a spot that was soft as silk just beneath her ear, found a warm, heavy breast and squeezed gently. "You worked me over pretty good last night."

"What's the matter, cowboy? Was the ride a little too rough for you?"

He smiled against her neck. She smelled of soap from her shower and cookie dough and just about the best of everything he'd ever smelled. "The *ride*, was just the way I like it. But I need to refuel."

She turned in his arms. Kissed him softly. "How's that for starters?"

"Umm. Not bad. You taste like your cookies."

"Couldn't resist. They're best when they're warm out of the oven."

"Wrong." He backed her up to the counter, then lifted her and sat her on its cold surface. "They're best before they're baked. I'm a sucker for cookie dough."

She looped her arms over his shoulders, grinned. "I always figured you for a dough boy."

He laughed. "Such a smart mouth." He kissed her, slow and deep and thorough. "Such a *sweet* mouth." Then he kissed her again. "Only one thing I can think of that might be sweeter."

He dipped a finger in the cookie dough. Brought it to his mouth. "Good." He licked his finger thoroughly, all the while watching her face. "But no comparison to you. Hmm. Let's try this.'' Again, he dipped a finger in the dough, then rolled it in the sugar and cinnamon mix.

''Getting closer,'' he said and made a production of licking his finger clean, while her face flamed and his other hand stroked her bare leg, his thumb riding tantalizingly close to the juncture where hip met thigh. ''But I think we can do better.''

''Better? Um...Cutter...'' His name feathered out on a shaky little breath when he went to work on the buttons of his shirt and laid it open.

He loved the view, loved more, the idea of pleasuring her.

''Cutter...what are you...doing?''

''Shh. I'm not done with my taste test yet.'' Making a place for himself between her thighs, he dipped his finger back into the dough.

''Taste test?'' she managed to say on a husky little whisper when he very slowly and very methodically frosted her right nipple with the sugar and butter-rich dough.

''Taste test.'' He heard the gruffness in his voice, wasn't able to take his eyes off the pretty mess he'd just made of her. ''To see...Lord, that's pretty.'' He stopped, drew in a shuddering breath, bent to her breast and gave it one more try. ''To see if I...can come up with...a combination that's even...sweeter.

''Be still,'' he commanded softly when she squirmed.

She caught her breath on a fractured little hitch as his tongue swirled over her nipple.

''Cutter—''

"Shh." Snagging her wrists, he pulled them above her head and pinned them against the cupboard door. "I need to concentrate. And I need to be…thorough. Very," he murmured as he nibbled and licked his way around her nipple, "very…thorough."

"Cutter." It was more groan than protest this time, a beautifully embarrassed and achingly aroused sound that urged him on to more.

"Gettin' there." Watching his handiwork, he frosted her left nipple. He licked her once, wetting her skin, went back for more when she arched and pressed against him. But he wasn't finished with her yet. He was so not finished.

Pinching a finger full of the sugar and cinnamon mix, he sprinkled it over her breast that was wet from his mouth, sticky with dough until she sparkled and quivered in the sunlight slicing in through the window.

Her eyes were slumberous and dark when she tugged her hands free, cupped his face in her palms and pressed her breast to his mouth.

It was all he could do to keep from devouring her, had to make himself be gentle as he nipped and sucked and tasted the sweetest, softest heat, until tasting wasn't enough for either of them.

She was whimpering when he lifted her off the counter, carried her upstairs and laid her back in bed. And pleasured her some more.

With his hands. With his mouth. With everything he had in him, he made love to her. She cried his name, clutched at his shoulders when he lifted her hips, tilted her to his mouth and finally tasted the very sweetest part of her.

Only after he'd tumbled her over that edge where she was destroyed by sensation, dazed by spent desire, did he move back up her body, sheath himself in her clenching warmth and find his own shattering release.

And only when she lay sleeping beside him, and he watched her—couldn't stop watching her—did he realize that this time, this time, it was going to be hard as hell to walk away.

Careful, so as not to wake her, he made himself ease out of her bed. He stood there beside it for a very long time, watching her breathe, watching the soft flutter of her closed eyelids as she drifted on a dream and snuggled deeper into the tangled sheets.

On a long, deep breath, he turned, headed for the shower. It took a long time to wash away her scent. Longer still to rinse away the wanting to crawl right back in her bed and lose himself in all that womanly heat. And not just for the sex—although the sex with Peg was like nothing he'd ever experienced before or since that long lost summer. He just wanted to hold her. Be something more to her, more for her. Something, he admitted, as he toweled himself dry, he wasn't cut out to be.

When he'd pulled on clean jeans and wandered into little Shelby's bedroom, it took longer still to drag his gaze away from the pictures on the dresser. There must have been a dozen of them of Peg and that little girl with the flyaway blond hair and eyes the same color blue that he faced every morning in the mirror.

Panic. Elation. Anger. Denial. Every emotion that had been prowling around the edge of his consciousness since the first time he'd seen that precious child jockeyed for shape and form and substance. He resisted everything but the denial. Assured himself he had no ownership here. Even less long-term interest.

And yet he stood there, seeing too much, maybe even wanting too much before he finally turned, packed his bag and carried it out to his truck.

When Peg woke up and didn't see his duffel on the floor by the bed, she knew Cutter was gone. It didn't stop her from walking straight to the window, brushing back the curtain and confirming it. Her truck was there—Krystal and Sam had made good on their promise to deliver it. When she didn't see Cutter's truck in the driveway, however, she reminded herself she was not going to let it hurt this time.

She dressed mechanically, combed her hair and finished baking her cookies. Then she walked out to the barn, hating herself for the weakness that had tears stinging behind her eyes. And for the knee-jerk urge she'd been fighting to track him down and beg him to stay.

She wouldn't do that to him.

More important, she wouldn't do it to herself.

She walked over to Jackpot's stall, absently stroked his hip and wished Shelby was home. She missed her. She missed her baby girl. The ache in her chest and the tears that started leaking down her cheeks had everything to do with missing her—nothing to do with Cutter.

"Rascal, come here boy," she whispered, then indulged herself in something she hadn't let herself do since the first time Cutter Reno had turned his back and walked away. She sat down in the middle of the barn floor, wrapped her arms around Rascal's warm, silky neck and bawled like a baby.

She'd pretty much gotten it out of her system when she heard a vehicle pull into the driveway. She wiped her eyes, got up to look out the door and felt her heart skip. *Cutter.*

He was back. Too much hope. Too much joy. It danced through her blood and made her realize how truly pathetic she was. And how angry she was with herself for letting him get to her this way.

She quickly combed her fingers through her hair then hunted around in the tack room for the pair of sunglasses that she knew—she *prayed*—she'd left there yesterday.

She was not a woman who cried willingly or often. And when she did, the aftermath was not pretty. Her eyes, when she'd met them in the cloudy tack room mirror, were puffy and red—so was her nose—not to mention her lips. They'd swelled up like they'd been bee-stung.

"Peg? Peg, where are you?"

She sent a thank-you skyward when she found the glasses, slipped them on and on a bracing breath, answered him.

"In the barn."

Then she made herself busy in Jackpot's stall with a currycomb. She was brushing like a machine when she heard him slip inside.

"Hey," he said when he spotted her.

"Hey yourself," she tossed brightly over her shoulder. Too brightly evidently, because he was suddenly behind her. He touched a hand to her hair.

"What's up?"

It wasn't a casual what's up. It was tender and concerned, like he could tell she'd been crying when that was the last thing she wanted him to see. Just like the last thing she wanted was Cutter being tender and concerned. Aloof and casual, she could handle. But not this.

"Just thought I'd give the outlaw here a little TLC," she hedged then prayed he'd walk away so she wouldn't have to face him.

"Peg?" he said after a long moment.

"Know what?" she said breezily and shouldered past him with her head down so he couldn't see her puffy face. "I forgot about running those cookies into town. I'd better get them in there before—"

His hand on her arm stopped her. He turned her slowly toward him.

She kept her head down, fussed with the bristles in the brush. She wouldn't look at him. She couldn't.

"You thought I'd left." His words were dead cold, dead serious, dead-on.

"No—no...I—" She tried to turn away again. Again, he stopped her.

"Yes. You did. You thought I'd left. I wouldn't do that to you. I wouldn't leave, Peg—not without saying goodbye."

She stood statue still, her head down, her lower lip starting to tremble as he spread his broad palm along her jaw, edged his thumb under her chin and forced her to lift her head and look at him.

He searched her face for the longest time before he reached over, tugged off her glasses.

"Damn," he said. "I'm sorry."

She finally found her voice and surprised them both with the bite in it. "You think this is about you?" She laughed, then touched trembling fingers to her lips, pinched her eyes shut. "Shelby," she insisted. "I just got to missing Shelby. So stop looking at me like that. Stop looking at me period. I'm a mess."

"You're a beautiful mess." He pulled her into his arms.

Because it felt so good there, she pushed away. "You can lighten up on the sweet talk, Cutter. You got what you came for. And so did I. I got exactly what I wanted from you."

Bitterness. She heard it, hated it but she let it hang there, along with the lie, until the heat and the hardness in his voice fractured the silence.

"And what was that, Peg? What exactly was it that we both wanted?"

"Sex," she said bluntly. "That's all this is about. And it was great." And she wasn't. She wasn't great. She was miserable and she could hardly believe she'd said those words, that she'd lied right through them, even thrown in a convincingly tired breath for good measure.

But hey, never let it be said that she wasn't a fast learner. Cutter had just taught her another good, hard lesson. He still had way too much ability to hurt her. She wasn't going to let it happen. Not again.

"Look, Cutter. Don't turn this into something it's not, okay? We both knew going into this that you were just passing some time. Well, it worked out fine because so was I."

His eyes turned hard as he watched her. "Passing time."

"What else would you call it?" Misery built to anger as he stood there and acted as if she was the one breaking the rules when it was his game they were playing. It had always been his game. The one that ended with him riding off into the sunset and left her standing here missing him.

Well, not this time. She couldn't stop herself from baiting him. "Or was I reading you wrong? Do you have plans to stay this time?"

He had nothing, *nothing,* to say to that. And because he'd been offered the chance and rejected it, it hurt that much more.

"You don't have a very high opinion of me, do you?"

"I don't have an opinion, either way," she said, as the fight slowly fizzled out of her.

"Oh, I think you do. I want to hear it."

"No," she said quietly, "you don't. Look, I've got to deliver those cookies." She pushed past him and all but ran toward the house.

Cutter stood there and watched her go.

Sex. It was all about sex, she said. He worked his jaw, feeling hollow and angry and for one of the few times in his life, hating—really hating—the man he'd become. The man who had made her cry and then run away.

She wanted him gone. She'd made that clear enough. Fine. He'd leave. It was probably for the best anyway since it didn't appear as if there was going to be a good end to this conversation no matter what kind of a spin he put on it. Besides, he didn't feel much like spinning. And she was right. He was leaving. He always left.

Face grim, he walked back to his truck, reached over the tailgate and snagged the roll of screen that he'd driven into town and picked up at the hardware store. He'd managed to round up a wire cutter, rip the old screen off the door and cut the new to size by the time Peg headed out the front door, a plastic container of cookies in hand.

She stopped short when she saw him there, rolling up the old screen that they'd destroyed last night.

"Oh. Oh," she said again and he saw in her face that she'd just put it together that when he'd left, it had been to go to town to buy the replacement screen. When her face flushed red, he knew she was also thinking about how it had gotten broken.

"You...you don't have to do that."

"I broke it. I'll fix it." He started tacking it in place.

She didn't seem to know where to look, or what to do.

He knew, though. He knew just what to do and if his heart slammed a little with the decision, he'd just have to deal with it.

"I'll be gone when you get back from town," he said and turned to face her. "Being that I got what I came for and all."

Her gaze shot to his. He watched as his angry words settled, as she digested. And he waited. He waited for her to say she was sorry, she hadn't meant what she'd said earlier, she didn't want him to go.

"Oh… Well, then…"

He stared at her very beautiful but very bruised expression and felt like he'd just beat up a kitten.

Dammit. It didn't have to be this way. He could have stayed. He'd wanted to stay. At least he'd wanted to stay a little while longer. But he knew when he wasn't wanted—just like he knew when it was time to hit the road.

"You take care of yourself, Peg."

"Sure," she said quickly. Just like she smiled too quickly. Those big brown eyes searched his face one last time, before she looked away. "Sure, Cutter. I always do."

Then she walked to her truck and tore out of the driveway.

And for the first time in his life, Cutter knew what it felt like to be on the receiving end of a bad good-bye.

He couldn't say he liked it much.

Couldn't say he liked it much at all.

But it was for the best. He didn't want to stick around until Shelby came home next week. He didn't want to see those blue eyes smile at him and face a truth he wasn't yet ready to accept let alone deal with.

He couldn't say why he headed in the direction he did when he left Peg and Sundown behind. He should have gone south. There was big money and important points to be won as he chased another invitation to the NFR. But after eight hours on the road, he pulled up in front of a little tan house flanked by blooming red rosebushes and tidy green shrubs.

It looked homey and well loved. A nice place to live. Good, Cutter thought, as he walked up the steps and lifted the shiny brass knocker. He was happy for the woman who opened the door with a dish towel in her hand.

She blinked once then started crying through her smile. "Cutter."

He slipped off his hat. "Hi, Mom."

For the second time that day, he felt guilt over this new talent he seemed to have developed for making strong women cry.

It was late that night and he wasn't yet ready to bed down in the room she always kept ready for him. Just in case he came home.

She was so glad he'd come home that it made him feel guiltier still for the months that had passed since he'd last made the trip. And then it had made him feel good when she'd happily fussed over cooking him supper and he'd made her laugh over his stories of the rodeo.

They'd moved into the living room, him nursing a beer that she also kept stocked just in case, and her with a cup of tea. He could see that she was tired. Just like he knew she would never admit it. Because he was finally home, she wanted every minute she could squeeze out of their time together.

"What was it like? Having him use you and then leave you?"

Anna Reno looked stricken at first, both in surprise and at the bluntness of his question. He felt the shock of it, too, hadn't known it had been prowling away back there, looking for an opening to break out.

"I'm sorry, Mom." Pain mixed with the shock on her face. "I shouldn't have asked. It's none of my business."

But then, in that way she had of reaching for strength and understanding his need, she squared her shoulders and she told him. She told him exactly what it was like.

"It was like being nothing. Less than nothing. Like constantly being asked if I wanted to go for a ride and then being left waiting by the side of a long, dusty road with no water, no direction and the sun going down."

He sat beside her on the sofa, propped his elbows on his wide spread knees and stared at his clasped hands. Is that how Peg felt? When he left her—is that how she felt?

"It took a while," she continued softly. "To understand that the fault was his, not mine."

His head snapped up. He frowned at this woman who deserved so much more than she'd ever gotten out of life and out of the man who had made a vow to love and to cherish. "Yours? You actually thought it was *your* fault that he was such a bastard?"

She touched his face, love shining in her eyes over his defense of her. "I thought it was my fault that I couldn't make him a better man. I'd had hopes, Cutter. I...I loved him once. It's not easy for a woman to give up on love. But there came a time when I finally realized it wasn't him I was trying to hold on to as much as it was the idea of loving him.''

Restless, he stood, walked to the window. ''I hate him for what he was. And for what he wasn't.''

She was quiet for so long that his heart had firmly set up residence in his throat and his hands had grown damp and clammy.

''And you're afraid you'll turn out just like him.''

He clenched his fists, closed his eyes, stunned yet not surprised by her perception. Somehow, it made it harder to say the words—to break the news that he had turned into one more disappointment for her. ''I already have.''

He pulled out the picture then. The one he'd lifted from Shelby's room. The one he'd stuffed in his shirt pocket and hadn't let himself look at but had committed to memory.

He turned back to his mother, handed her the photograph, watched her face as she studied it, ran her thumb across it lovingly.

''So,'' she said, tears swimming in her eyes when she looked up at him, ''you're a daddy.''

''Yeah.'' He felt his heart thud with the weight of admitting it for the first time out loud. ''I'm a daddy.''

The emotions he'd refused to deal with since first laying eyes on Shelby hit him with a sucker punch that nearly sent him to his knees.

''I don't want to be like him,'' he said and heard the anger and the anguish and, oh, God, felt the biting sting of tears.

He dragged a hand roughly through his hair. ''I've

already lost her first five years, Mom. Five years,'' he ground out, defeated and angered by the truth it. ''Why? Because I am like him…and her mother knows it.''

He sank back down on the sofa, buried his head in his hands. He resisted for only a moment before he let her pull him into her arms, let himself cling to her, let himself feel the anger and the shame and the guilt of it all. And the fear. Oh, yeah. There was fear. A child. He had a child. A beautiful, bright, thriving child who didn't even know she had a daddy.

He didn't know the first thing about responsibility. Didn't know the first thing about what it took to grow up, to own up, to be what she needed him to be.

''Tell me about her,'' his mother said gently. She brushed the hair back from his forehead, wiped her thumb across tears that wet his cheeks. ''Tell me about both of them. Then tell me what you're going to do.''

Eight

$\mathbf{P}$eg and Shelby and Peg's mom were sitting on the swing on Jack and Kay's front porch. It was Friday afternoon. Peg had hopped in her truck and raced over from the feed store the minute Kay had called to tell her they were home from San Diego.

"I can't get over how big you've gotten in just two weeks. I swear, you've grown an inch!" Peg exclaimed, as she hugged Shelby then set her back so she could look at her. They'd had supper, the dishes were done and she still couldn't stop looking at her— or touching her. "Must be all that California sunshine."

"Or the gallons of ice cream Grampa Jack couldn't resist buying for her," Kay offered dryly, smiling, too, as she watched her daughter and wondered at the subtle change in her.

"How're things with you, honey?" Kay asked casually.

Peg looked at her mom. At her pretty brown hair that she wore short and sleek, at her trim figure and golden tan. At her brown eyes that were watchful and all seeing and she knew she'd done a lousy job concealing her feelings.

Peg looked away, grabbed Shelby and hugged her until she giggled. "I'm great now that my baby's back home. Did you miss me? Even a little? Or were you having too much fun?"

"I didn't get homesick, did I, Gramma? Not once."

"Well, I got homesick for you." Shelby gave Peg a hug that told her everything she wanted to know. She'd missed her mom.

"What do you say we head for home and get you unpacked? Rascal and Bea have been watching for you for a week now."

"Okay." Shelby bounced out of the swing to go look for her duffel. "Grampa Jack and Gramma Kay are sure gonna miss me, though, aren't you?"

Kay grinned then tried to look properly disappointed. "Absolutely, sweetheart. But we'll be okay."

The screen door slammed behind Shelby. "She's quite the girl," Kay said as she watched her go.

Peg smiled, nodded, then clasping her hands together around her updrawn knees, stared down the quiet street.

"What's wrong, Peggy?" Kay asked, her eyes gentle, her intuition, as always, tuned in to Peg's feelings.

"Nothing. Nothing's wrong." Peg glanced at her

mother then away. ''I…I just didn't realize how much I was going to miss her, is all.'' She smiled for good measure.

Kay watched in supportive silence, waited for Peg to give it up.

''Oh, Mom,'' she said at last and lowered her forehead to her knees. She would not cry for him. Not again. She shot off the swing, leaned against a porch post. ''I'm so stupid.''

''You are a lot of things, honey, but stupid isn't one of them.''

''If I'm so smart, then why did I spend last weekend with Cutter?''

Kay was quiet for a long time before Peg heard her rise, poke her head in the door and ask Jack to keep Shelby occupied for a few minutes. Then she walked back to her daughter and without a shred of judgment in her eyes, encouraged her to tell her all about it.

It was a full week later and after ten o'clock on Monday night when Peg's phone rang. She'd already turned in but she wasn't asleep. She'd been trying to lose herself in a mystery and wasn't having a bit of luck doing it.

She picked up her portable phone from her nightstand midway through the second ring—figuring it was Krystal or her mom or something equally routine.

''Hello.''

''Hey.''

Everything inside of her went still at that one word uttered in Cutter's whiskey-and-honey voice. She'd have recognized it in her sleep. She'd dreamed of it too many nights to make her sane.

"Joe?" she said, because she was miserable enough and felt just ornery enough for paybacks. "Is that you, honey?"

"Cute, Peg. Real cute."

She could hear the fatigue in his voice along with a clatter of background noise as neither of them said anything at all. She clung to the receiver and told herself to hang up. To do the smart thing and just hang up the phone. Instead she pulled her knees to her chest and clung to the silence, her heart pounding, her eyes closed tightly shut.

"So," he said finally, "how's it going?"

"Fine," she squeaked out, cleared her throat and tried again, her mind racing. Why had he called? Why hadn't he called sooner? Why was she stupid enough to care? "It's going fine. You?" she asked because she couldn't stand the disquieting silence that followed but couldn't make herself break the connection.

He sighed heavily. She heard laughter in the background along with a shout for more beer while country music blared loud and strong. He was in a bar, partying, no doubt, and with his judgment clouded by beer, must have decided it was a good idea to call her.

Yet he didn't sound as if he'd been drinking when he asked, "Shelby get back from California?"

Her heart picked up another beat. She willed it to settle down. "Yeah. Last week."

"Had a good time, did she?"

Another double beat. It was not guilt. She would

not feel guilty that he was asking about his daughter and didn't even know it. "Yeah. She had a great time. Cutter, what's on your mind?"

He was quiet for so long she wanted to jump through the line and drag a response out of him. Then it was fear, not indecision that sent her pulse rate rocketing.

"Is something wrong? Oh, Cutter…are you hurt?"

"No," he said, finally. "Nothing's wrong. And I'm fine. Won the go-round tonight," he said, almost distractedly, as if he just wanted to fill space, to keep her on the line.

"Well…congratula—"

"—I want to see you again," he cut in—more demand than statement. More growl than request. When she just sat there, speechless, he tried again. Softer this time. "Please, Peg. I want to see you."

She couldn't find her voice. Wasn't altogether sure that was a bad thing because she honestly didn't know what she'd say if he pressed her. Oh, she knew what she should say. Forget it. I don't want to be your port in a storm. I don't want to be your flavor of the month.

I don't want you to hurt me again and tempt me to tell you about Shelby.

Before she could say no, don't come, don't call, his voice came back on the line. "Just…just think about it, okay?"

Thinking was what got her into trouble. Thinking maybe she meant more to him than a good time. Thinking that maybe, just maybe there was something more on his mind than another round of hot sex and a fast goodbye.

"Look, Peg...I've got to go. The guys dragged me down to this bar to celebrate and they're getting restless. I'll call you. Tomorrow. I'll call you tomorrow night, okay?"

The line went dead. And she was left alone in her bed to wonder at the absurdness of her hope and at the resilience of her heart that might not survive another hit from Cutter Reno.

She had her answer the next night. She could live through darn near anything. But it got harder. It got so much harder because as it turned out, he did the one thing she knew she could count on. He didn't call.

Foolishly she'd waited by the phone until almost eleven o'clock. Calling herself ten times an idiot, she'd finally gone to bed—disgusted with herself for wanting him to call, angry with him for planting the seed that he'd really intended to follow up on his promise in the first place.

Nothing had changed. Nothing would change. It was just like she'd told her mom. She didn't understand this attraction she felt for him. She didn't understand this need. It didn't make any sense. It could come to no good. Not for her. Not for Shelby. Cutter was all for Cutter. His wants. His needs. His broncs.

Anger finally gave way to grim acceptance. She drifted off to sleep after midnight, promising herself she was never going to fall for the promises in his voice or in his eyes or in the way he made love to her. Not ever again.

She wasn't sure how long she'd slept when something woke her. She was instantly awake, painfully alert, her heart pounding, her eyes wide as she looked at the clock on her nightstand. Two-fifteen.

"You should lock your door."

She bolted up in bed, the scream dying on her throat when she recognized the shadow in her bedroom doorway. Tall, lean and broad shouldered, he walked on silent steps across the room, turned on her bedside light.

She dragged the hair out of her eyes, hiked herself up in bed. He looked exhausted. Like he'd driven through hell to get here. To get to her. She shook her head. Begged him with her eyes not to make her want him this way again. Not to make her hope—even as she felt his arms wrap around her, draw her close and kiss her like he'd die if he didn't taste her now. Right now.

His eyes were closed, his fingers shaking when he pulled away, pressed his forehead to hers and touched a hand to her hair.

"You…you said you'd call," she whispered inanely.

"I lied."

"You…you shouldn't be here." Already his hands were roaming her back, bunching up her sleep shirt, tugging it over her head.

"I couldn't stay away."

She caught her breath on a gasp as he bent his dark head to her breast, nuzzled, adored, indulged.

"Shelby—" she protested as he laid her down then

went to work on the snaps on his shirt.

"—Is sound asleep."

She whimpered when his bare chest pressed against her breasts. Naked heat, muscled and lean. "She… she can't find you here…in my bed."

"She won't. She won't. Shush. Shush now, let me love you. I can't…I can't stand not loving you."

"Cutter," she groaned his name, dug her fingers into his shoulders as he entered her, long and strong and deep. "Oh, Lord, Cutter."

He hiked himself up on his elbows, pushed the hair away from her face. Cupping her head in his big hands, he watched her face as he penetrated and withdrew, penetrated and withdrew. His eyes were dark, his soul bled through them. "It's not just sex. It's *never* been just sex," he ground out even as he shuddered and fought to hold back his release. "Say it. Tell me it's not just sex."

She was drowning in sensation, lost in a love so strong she couldn't, no matter how vulnerable it made her, continue with the lie. "It's not just sex. It was never just sex. Never."

She clenched her teeth to keep from crying out as he swept her over the edge and held her there—suspended somewhere between sweet heaven and fiery hell. And then she was flying, soaring like a rocket, flaming like a star as he took her to that place where nothing but him mattered, nothing but them made sense. And nothing but reason—lost the moment he'd crushed his mouth over hers—could have kept her from taking the ride.

* * *

Cutter winced, shifted painfully to a sitting position and blinked at the blue eyes peeking through his driver's-side pickup window. Shelby grinned when he glared at her, pressed her nose against the glass and a little *tap, tap, tap* with her finger that must have woke him up.

He dragged his hands through his hair, rolled down his window and shook himself awake.

"Who are you?"

He got the giggle he wanted. "I'm Shelby, silly."

"Shelby Silly. I don't know any Shelby Silly. I know a Shelby Lynn Lathrop, but she wears this pair of scruffy old red boots. You got any red boots?"

She clamped on to the door handle and grunting comically with the effort, lifted one tiny foot shod in bruised red leather and a broken-down heel up to window level. "See?"

"Well, I'll be darned. It is you."

"Yup. It's me," she said all cheerful and bright and happy to have that cleared up. "Hi."

He smiled. "Hi yourself, blondie," he said forgetting about his kinks and his aches and his pains and the fact that he'd crawled out of her mother's warm bed at 4:00 a.m. to insure that Shelby didn't find him there and get the wrong idea. Like maybe he was there because he belonged there, or because he planned on staying.

He hadn't planned on going to her bed. Honest to God, he hadn't. But he'd pulled up, dead tired and dead wrong about what he was going to do. It hadn't been just her bed that had beckoned him. It had been everything. The little house that she'd made a home.

The arms that felt sheltering and warm. The child that she had yet to tell him was his.

He didn't blame her. Couldn't blame her. What reason had he ever given her for thinking she could trust him to be anything but heartache—for her or for Shelby.

He still hadn't sorted everything out in his head. That's why he was here now—he needed to do some sorting with Peg. Some sorting and some talking and some explaining—only he wasn't yet sure he had the guts to do it.

"My mom's still sleepin'," his daughter said, still hanging on the door, her little feet perched on his running board. "Boy, is she gonna be surprised when she sees you."

"Good surprised or bad surprised?" he asked, playing devil's advocate.

"Oh, good," she said with utter confidence. "I told her just last week that I wished you'd come see us again and now you're here. How 'bout that?"

Yeah, he thought, watching this child that was his and falling a little deeper into something he suspected ran very close to love, *how 'bout that*.

"How about we surprise her," he suggested, "and make her breakfast?"

"Cool." Shelby jumped down from the truck. "But we got to hurry 'cause she's gotta go to work and I gotta go to Krystal's. Did you know I start school next week?"

"High school?" he teased as he shouldered open the door and crawled out of the cab.

"Kindergarten, silly, 'cause, duh, I'm only five."

"Oh, yeah? How long have you been five?"

Even before she told him, he knew it had been since April. April 2 to be exact, she informed him.

"That means I missed your birthday." Like he'd missed all of her birthdays, a thought he tried not to dwell on because it made this hollow little ache settle and weigh like lead.

"Do you usually get presents on your birthday?"

No dummy, this child. She regarded him with curious and hopeful eyes. "Lots."

"Well, then you probably don't need this one." He reached behind the seat and pulled out a brightly wrapped package.

"Wow!" She plopped down right there in the driveway and tore into it.

He hunkered down beside her, watching with a guarded hopefulness that told him her reaction meant more to him than he'd ever thought.

"Oh, wow!" she cried again when she pulled out a pair of shiny new red boots. "Just what I always wanted! Oh, thank you, Cutter!" Then she launched herself into his arms, complete joy, absolute trust.

He was still recovering from the jolt of it, from the unequaled pleasure of his daughter's warm little body snuggled against his, when she ran off like a shot, forgetting all about him as she sailed into the house and clamored up the stairs.

"Mom! Mom!" she cried. He winced, knowing Peg was going to have a rude awakening after a very short night of sleep. "Guess who's here! And look what he brought me."

He'd missed so much, he thought, as he walked

slowly up the front porch steps. Rascal came trotting out of the barn, his tail sailing high in a friendly wag.

"Hey, boy." He bent down to scratch him behind the ears. Then he sat down on the steps and waited to be invited inside.

The sound of Peg stirring, of Shelby's giggles had him looking toward the distance for absolution and the capability to not be angry with Peg.

He'd missed so much.

He'd missed so damn much.

Peg sat at her little kitchen table while Shelby tromped around in her new red boots and Cutter— who seemed to fill her tiny kitchen with his presence—stood at the stove flipping eggs.

How had this happened? She lowered her head to her hands. How had she let this happen again?

It's not just sex. It's never been just sex. Say it. Say it isn't just sex.

Cutter's raggedly whispered words played back in her mind as she ate the eggs he'd cooked for her and drank the juice he'd poured. She watched as he slipped another piece of bread into the toaster because Shelby had wanted one.

What did he want?

The look on his face as he sat down across from her and watched her over his coffee mug told her he wasn't sure himself—that he was a long way from figuring out the answer to that question.

"I have to go to work," she said, refusing to let something that looked desperately like need in him, achingly like vulnerability, convince her there was anything but convenience behind his unexpected visit.

"I know," he said.

"And I get to go to Krystal's," Shelby piped up as she munched on her toast. "What do you get to do today, Cutter?"

He looked at Peg over the steam rising from his coffee cup. "I guess I get to wait for you."

Do I get to wait for you, his eyes asked. *Can* I wait for you?

Peg rose, set her plate and glass in the sink. "Feel free to use the shower and catch up on your sleep…on the sofa," she added. She did not want to work all day with a picture of him sleeping in her bed hovering in her mind. "You must have driven half the night to get here."

"Yeah," he said. "I did." Unspoken was the, *"And I'd do it again."*

That was the part she didn't want to think about because that was the part that made her do stupid things—like think he might be thinking about staying.

It's not just the sex.

"Come on, Shell," she said, hearing the desperation in her voice and not caring. "We need to get rockin' or I'm going to be late. Run upstairs and get your backpack, okay, baby?"

"I'll take care of the dishes," Cutter said and she just stopped for a moment and stared.

"What are you doing here, Cutter?" she whispered when Shelby had scooted out of earshot.

"I just wanted to see you." He reached for her, pulled her slowly into his arms.

She pressed her palms against his chest, met his eyes. "And?"

He let her go. Turned and stared out the window. After a long moment he faced her again, leaned a hip against the counter. "And I wanted to talk."

Her eyes asked what she couldn't put into words.

"About us."

She was scared stiff by the probing look on his face, unable to stall the panic that his next words confirmed she had every reason to feel.

"You. Me. And Shelby."

She could hardly breathe and yet she'd known, somehow she'd known that Shelby was the reason he'd come back.

"She's mine, Peg," he said and she watched, stunned, as he worked his jaw and fought to hang on to his emotions. "I know she's mine."

She closed her eyes, resigned and somehow relieved before the panic kicked in double-time. "She doesn't know. She doesn't know. Cutter, please… please—"

"—Don't hurt her? You think I'd *hurt* her?" His voice rose to a dark demand.

She warned him with a look to keep it down.

"You think I'd intentionally hurt her?"

She walked to the table, gripped the back of a chair with unsteady hands. "Every time you drove away."

Her quiet certainty hardened his gaze and set his jaw working.

"Every time you drove away because your rodeo was more important to you than she was—you would hurt her."

She stared at her hands, at the knuckles that had gone white, then made herself look at him. She was determined to make him understand—even at the cost of her pride.

"I can take it. Watching you leave. Knowing you won't be back until and unless it suits you. I can take it, Cutter. She couldn't. She…just couldn't."

He crossed his arms over his chest, looking angry and belligerent and guilty. Mostly guilty. It was the guilt—an admission that she was right, that he would always leave—that helped drive her point home.

"Please—if you care about her…" She watched the tension that set his mouth in a grim, hard line and stayed the course. "If you care about her, be gone when we get home tonight."

Aching—heart deep, soul deep—she turned and walked away, disappointed but not surprised when he didn't try to stop her.

It was two weeks before Peg heard from him again. As luck would have it, Shelby was on a sleepover with her friend, Marty, when she came home from work on a Friday night and found him—just sitting there in his truck in her driveway.

When she thought her legs wouldn't buckle, she got out of her truck. Her arms loaded with a sack of groceries, she walked over to where he was parked. Rascal was sitting on the seat in the cab with him, looking happy and smug and totally in love.

Which she wasn't. Even though she ached just looking at him. Even though she'd wanted and wished and prayed that he was someone she could count on, that maybe he could change. But two weeks was a long time and it told a pretty clear story. Six years told an even bigger one.

When she'd asked him to leave, he'd done it. No argument. No plea for understanding. No phone calls asking for the same. If he really wanted her, if he really wanted Shelby, he would fight for them.

Instead he'd just walked away.

And now he was back. She didn't know what it meant. Couldn't let herself wonder—couldn't stop herself from asking.

She gathered herself, felt the fatigue and the wanting and refused to give in to either. "Why do you keep doing this, Cutter? Why do you keep showing up here?"

He opened the truck door, got out and relieved her of the groceries. "Because I can't stay away," he said bluntly and headed for her porch.

Peg stared after him, then getting ahold of her senses, coaxed Rascal out of Cutter's truck and shut the door behind him.

"What does that mean?" she demanded, catching up to him as he pulled open her front door.

"Don't you ever lock anything?" he snarled, his anger flashing, white-hot and without warning. "Don't you know that anybody could just waltz into your house, take what they want? Hurt you if they wanted? Hurt Shelby? What's wrong with you?"

"Hold it!" she snapped, an outrage as alive as she'd ever felt boiling up and taking over. "Just—"

"—And why don't you have a decent watchdog?" he demanded, rounding on her. He gestured toward the door in disgust. "He doesn't even bark, for Pete's sake. What good is he?"

She flashed on a picture of Rascal gazing adoringly at Cutter, his big hand stroking his coat with affection.

"What right do you have?" she shot back and grabbed at the sack of groceries. "What right do you have…showing up here whenever the spirit moves you and laying into me about how I manage my life? Give me those." She reached for the sack but he refused to let go. "And go away. Just go away!"

"You don't want me to go." His blue eyes were stormy and more than a little steamed. "You just don't know what to do with me now that I'm here."

She tugged, angry beyond belief because he was right. He was so right. The sack ripped. Oranges and apples and little boxes of juice and tins of vegetables flew all over the floor.

"Dammit! And damn you."

"You don't think I am? You don't think that I'm as damned as the devil?" he roared and bent down beside her where she'd dropped to hands and knees to frantically gather her spilled fruit and get away from him. Just get away from him.

"I can't stop thinking about you," he confessed, sounding tortured and confused and beside himself with frustration. "I can't stop thinking about Shelby."

She steeled herself against the torment in his voice. "Yeah, well, that's your problem, not mine."

She cried out when he grabbed her arms and pulled her up against him. "I'm making it your problem."

He hated this, she realized. Hated that he hadn't

been able to stay away. That he'd come all this way and she was fighting him instead of falling into his arms.

She hated it, too. Hated the hurt he caused every time he left her. Hated the guilt she felt over keeping him from Shelby—hated more that every time he left, he proved that she'd been right to do it.

She started crying then. And she hated herself for that, too. But once she started, she couldn't stop. All the anger, all the indecision, all the years of guilt and loneliness and sense of betrayal burst from somewhere deep inside where she'd hidden the pain, denied its existence.

"Aw, damn. Peg. Don't. Sweetheart, don't. Please don't cry."

He cradled her against him, there on his knees on the floor, with apples and oranges tumbling around them.

"It hurts, Cutter," she cried, clinging to him. "It hurts. I can't do this. Don't. Don't do this to me anymore."

The breath that soughed out was unsteady and deep. "I don't want to hurt you. I never wanted to hurt you. Never."

He stood then, picked her up with him and carried her to the sofa where he sat down. Then he held her. Just held her while she clung to him and cursed him and cried.

Nine

Making love didn't solve anything. But it felt good when they'd both felt so bad. So they ended up in her bed again, where they could lose themselves in pleasure and forget the pain they caused each other.

And somehow, in the midnight hour, with both of them stripped to the skin and vulnerable, it made it easier for Cutter to say those things to her. Those things he needed to say.

He knew she was awake. As he lay there in the dark with her warm and snug and silent beside him, he knew. Just like he knew it was up to him to either begin or end this thing between them. *Begin or end.* He was starting to think that the "b" word wasn't as threatening as it had once been. Yeah, it still scared him, but it had a better ring to it lately. A better ring than the other one. The one that was so short and so concise and so unalterably final. The one he'd been so good at using all his life.

"I'm sorry," he said, stroking a hand along her bare hip. "I'm sorry I wasn't there for you."

He was glad she didn't pretend that she didn't know what he was talking about. Doubly glad that she, too, was ready to talk.

"I didn't give you a chance to be there for me."

She began to pull away, to distance herself, but he held her fast, held her close.

"Why didn't you tell me?" The anger was there, he couldn't stop it even though he knew she didn't deserve it. "No. Wait. That wasn't fair. I know why. Because I was a self-centered, selfish, sonofabitch who didn't have a clue. That's more than enough reason."

He felt her relax then turn into him. "Jack wanted to go get you."

He snorted, squeezed her hip. "I'll just bet he did. Why didn't you let him?"

She thought about it for a moment as she trailed her fingers up and down the length of his arm. "Because I didn't see any point in both of us being miserable."

Yeah. He would have been miserable. Miserable to live with, miserable to stomach. And he would have made her miserable, too.

He turned to his side, reversing their positions, pressing her to her back. Propping himself up on an elbow, he watched his hand as he spread his fingers wide over her flat abdomen. He could span the breadth of her from hip point to hip point with his fingers. Suddenly he wanted to know everything that he'd been so sure he'd never want to know. Suddenly he wished he could have seen her, her belly swollen with the child he had put there.

"Was it hard? Were you sick? Was it…did it hurt you a lot?" He leaned down, pressed a kiss to the firm, resilient flesh and silken skin that had harbored their daughter. "You're so small, Peg."

She told him then. With his cheek against her abdomen and her hands threading lightly through his hair, she told him about the morning sickness, about the labor, about the joy of seeing that squished little red face bawling into the world like a summer storm.

He was quiet for a long time, thinking about it. Regretting that he'd missed it. Honestly not knowing what he'd have done if he'd known—and hating himself even more because of his selfishness.

He lifted his head, and she smiled at him. "Do you want to see pictures?" At his horrified look, she laughed. "*Baby* pictures, not delivery pictures. Are you green, Reno?"

He hugged her then kissed her—because of her strong and forgiving heart—and he realized in that moment that his feelings for her ran deep. Deeper than he'd ever let them run before. So deep it scared him. So deep he couldn't talk, couldn't think for the force of them.

"Peg," he said, filled to bursting with words he didn't know how to say. Words that would mean little to her since he hadn't figured out what they meant for either of them. So he kissed her, just kissed her, instead.

She smiled then eased, beautifully naked, out of bed. "I'll be right back," she said and slipped into his shirt.

She came back a few minutes later with a tray of fruit and some granola bars—they'd somehow managed to skip supper—and an armful of photo albums.

Then they sat cross-legged on the bed until three in the morning, and he'd gotten to meet his baby daughter. Grinning and toothless. Drooling and adorable. There were several pictures of her on a springy rocking horse. Even at two, she'd worn her trademark red boots. He smiled over dozens of pictures of her on Bea. Pictures of her in nothing but the bathtub and bubbles.

Did all fathers feel this way? he wondered. Did all fathers feel this pressure near to bursting in their chests as they looked at something they had been a part of making? Something that was someone so special it brought a stinging pressure to the back of his eyes?

"I didn't trust you not to hurt her, Cutter." Her soft confession brought his head up from the images of his daughter. "I'm sorry."

"No. You were right." He didn't like it much but he was solid in the admission. "It was all about me back then. I wasn't man enough. I wasn't good enough. Not for her. Not for you."

Her eyes misted. She looked away.

"I'm not sure I'm man enough yet," he confessed and felt his heart sink when her silence told him that she wasn't sure of him, either.

"I don't lock my doors," she said, her eyes fierce

and true, "but I'd die for her, Cutter. I'd die before I let anyone hurt her. That's why I didn't tell you. That's why I don't know if I ever would have told you."

He understood. He understood perfectly what she was telling him now and couldn't fault her for it. "I won't hurt her. And I won't hurt you. Ever. Not ever again."

She wanted to believe him. Her eyes shimmered with that want. But her heart, battered and bruised from the scars he'd put there, wasn't ready to let her.

"I want to be with her. I won't tell her," he said quickly when panic made her face go pale. "I promise. I won't tell her I'm her daddy. Not until—not unless," he amended, "you say the word. I just want to be with her, Peg. And I want to be with you."

She looked down, gathered the pictures and folded the albums shut. "Rodeo is your life. It's your livelihood."

She didn't have to say the rest of it. He knew the rest of it all too well. Rodeo was also the road. Long, empty stretches of it. And rodeo had taken its toll on more relationships than he could count.

Not for the first time, he felt stirrings of doubt. He didn't know the first thing about building a relationship that didn't start with the intent to leave already factored in. But he did know one thing. He didn't want to leave this woman. When he was with her, he never wanted to leave—yet somehow, the reality was that he always did. And he didn't know what to do about that, either.

"Just…just don't say no, okay? Peg…" He shifted,

set the albums aside and took her hands in his. "Just…can we give it a try? Can we see if we can make something work between us?"

"Sure, Cutter," she said after a long moment but her sad smile told him she gave it no hope at all. Because she knew him. She knew what he was and she knew that leaving was what he did best.

He kissed her then, tried to tell her without words that he didn't want to stand on that track record any longer. Wasn't near as proud of it as he'd once been—but neither was he sure what lay beneath this new leaf he wanted to turn over.

As he laid her down and loved her, he tried to forget that he was his father's son. He tried to lose himself in her warmth and forget that he was the farthest thing from a sure thing that a man could ever be.

And as she took him in, became one with him, he realized that for the first time in his life—for Peg, for Shelby, maybe even for himself—he wanted to be more. He wanted to be the surest, steadiest thing in their lives. He wanted it bad. As bad as he'd ever wanted anything.

Even knowing that, even as he raced over the edge where there was nothing but him, nothing but her, nothing that mattered but them, he'd be damned if he knew if he had it in him not to let them all down.

"Cutter!" Shelby cried at ten o'clock that morning when Peg had collected her from Marty's and brought her home. "Mom, Cutter's here!" she said through a bubbly laugh when Peg pulled her truck into the driveway and parked it by Cutter's.

Peg had barely cut the engine when Shelby had her seat belt unfastened and was scrambling out the door.

Cutter unfolded himself from the porch steps where he'd been sitting—all grins and good looks—as Shelby ran up the steps and launched herself into his arms like a rocket.

"Whoa, there, cowgirl." He laughed as he hugged her.

Peg felt the hot sting of love behind her eyes and met Cutter's gaze over their daughter's flyaway blond hair. Her smile was bittersweet as Shelby chattered and quizzed and snatched his hat off his head and set it on her own.

"When did you get here? How long are you stayin'? Did you win last week? Krystal and Sam get the PRCA News so they tell me how you did but they didn't get it yet this week so I've been wonderin' and wonderin'."

"You ever hear about the cat that got done in by curiosity?" Peg asked her daughter as she joined them on the porch.

Cutter just laughed when Shelby launched into another round of questions. "How 'bout I fill you in while we ride?"

"Really? We're goin' ridin'?" She looked from Cutter to Peg, excitement glittering in her eyes. "Are we goin' ridin'?"

"Mighty fine day," Cutter said, his eyes dancing. "Be a shame to waste it."

So, of course, they went riding. And it only made

sense to pack a picnic lunch—because Shelby hadn't been on a picnic in *forever*. For that matter, neither had Peg and she'd found herself humming as she'd prepared sandwiches, feeling happier and more hopeful than she'd ever remembered feeling. Maybe she was deluding herself but for this one day, she didn't care.

Was it so crazy to think he meant what he said? That he wanted to be with them? That he wanted to make something work between them? She didn't have any answers. She didn't think he did, either.

And later that night, after Shelby had taken her bath then conned Cutter into reading her a story, was it insane to think something had already started to happen?

He hadn't heard her walk quietly down the stairs after her shower. He wasn't aware that she stood there in the soft light watching them snuggle together on one end of the sofa. The book was forgotten; Shelby was curled up on Cutter's lap, sleeping the sleep of angels.

Peg's chest filled with a hope she'd refused to let herself feel as she watched his dark head bent over their child. The hands that held Shelby were so big yet infinitely gentle as he held her close. Tears misted Peg's eyes as he drew a deep breath and pressed a kiss to the top of Shelby's head.

"Sweet little girl," he murmured into the silk of her baby-fine hair. "You just may make a daddy out of me yet."

That's you, Shell, she thought, awash with a swell

of love and longing for both of them. *A low-down, sneaky little daddy maker.*

She swallowed the lump in her throat and walked toward them, these two people who meant the world to her. "You want me to take her?" she asked quietly.

He didn't respond for a long moment. When he raised his head and met her gaze, she could see she wasn't the only one moved by the moment. "She's so beautiful, Peg. It's still hard to believe I could have had a part in making someone this unbelievably perfect."

His voice was gruff with emotion, his eyes suspiciously bright.

If she hadn't already been in love with him, she would have fallen right then. Alley cat or not. This rodeo-loving, woman-leaving man was so deep under her skin she could no longer draw a breath that wasn't filled with him. Couldn't form a thought that didn't start with him. End with him.

"She loves you." It was an offering, a gift she could no longer withhold although he would have to have been blind to have missed it.

"I don't ever want to make her sorry for that. I don't ever want to make *you* sorry for that."

It was bittersweet, this love she felt. He was trying so hard to be what he needed to be for both her and Shelby. And yet it was so apparent that he still had his own doubts about fulfilling that need. And because he had doubts, she understood that her own reservations were still founded in reality.

''Then don't,'' she said simply. ''Don't ever make us sorry.''

The blue eyes that met hers were as tortured as they were beautiful. She felt his panic, recognized his fear. This talk of trying, this whisper of the promise of commitment was uncertain ground for him. He was as afraid that he'd fail as she was.

Why, Cutter? What are you so afraid of? And why hadn't she yet worked up the courage to ask him?

It wasn't just rodeo. It was more. There was an emptiness in his eyes as he rose and carried Shelby up to bed. There was a desperation in his kisses when he took her to bed later and loved her.

Just like there was a sadness in her heart when he woke her at midnight to kiss her goodbye and promise to call her the very first chance he got.

For a long time after she heard his engine fire and the crunch of gravel beneath his tires had faded to a memory, she lay awake in her bed that felt empty and cold. And she tried not to think how like a ghost he was. How he'd come to her so often in the night, and leave her the same way. Needy and wanting, restless and seeking.

What are you missing, Cutter? What do you need that we can't give you? And what's it going to take to finally make you stay?

''Are you sure you know what you're doing?''

The chill in the air had as much to do with the edge in Krystal's voice as it did with the cool evening temperature. Even this early in September, nighttime brought the reminder that winter was only a couple of months away.

"As sure as I am of anything these days," Peg said and double-checked the contents of the suitcase she was in the process of packing.

"I just don't want you setting yourself up for a big fall."

Peg refolded one of Shelby's sweaters, laid it in the suitcase and sat down on her bed beside Krystal. "This is *so not* the song you were singing in July."

Krystal tucked her leg up under her and fussed with the throw pillow she hugged to her lap. "Yeah, well, maybe I was singing the wrong tune."

"And maybe you should stop worrying that what you said had any influence on the decisions I've made about Cutter."

"Thanks. I think," Krystal said with a crooked grin. "Nice to know you value my sage advice."

"What I value is your friendship. What I value is knowing that you care."

"I just don't want to see you hurt. Not by him. Not again."

"She loves him, Kris," Peg said simply. "Shelby loves him to death. And he loves her. I can't keep them apart. Not anymore."

It had been three weeks since they'd seen Cutter. He'd called almost every night. To talk to her. To talk to Shelby. And last night, he'd called begging them to come to him.

"Say yes, Peg. Please. Say you'll come. You and Shelby. We'll make it a long weekend. I've got to see you but this is a key competition. I can't miss it.

Please. You'll love Dallas." He'd gotten a little quiet then before he'd finally confessed, "I want you to see me ride."

From that point on she'd been lost. He'd already arranged for airfare. All they had to do was get to Missoula to catch the flight. Krystal was here to take them.

"And what about you?" Krystal asked, bringing Peg back to the moment.

"*What* about me?" Peg rose and zipped up her luggage.

"Shelby loves him—do you love him, too?"

Her hands stilled momentarily then got busy lifting the bag from the bed to the floor. "Are you going to refuse to drive us to the airport if I say I do?"

Krystal rose, too. She came around the bed and hugged her. "Nope. I'm just gonna say take care, kid. Don't let him hurt you."

Peg hugged her back. "Well, if he does, it'll be my fault, won't it, for letting myself get in this deep." She pulled back, gave Krystal a bracing smile. "Now come on. I've got a plane ride to get keyed up for. Lord, I hope it's not one of those puddle jumpers that's held together with rubber bands and duct tape. I do not want to embarrass myself by getting sick."

"You won't get sick. You'll enjoy every minute of it. So will Shell."

And they did—puddle jumper and all. They switched planes at Denver and made the rest of the trip on a jumbo jet that was almost as fascinating as the look on the face of the cowboy that met them in the Dallas terminal.

"Cutter!" Shelby cried when she spotted him, all lean smiling male and more handsome than any man had a right to be.

"Hey, blondie." She launched herself at him. "How's my best girl?" Laughing, he scooped her up in his arms and hugged her against him—all the while telling Peg with a long, hungry look how much he wanted to find someplace where he could show her how much he'd missed her.

"And how's my other best girl?" he asked as he walked toward her.

"Fine," Peg managed to say as he set Shelby on the floor beside him.

He held on to Shelby's hand, never taking his gaze off Peg. "I'm gonna kiss your momma now, Shell. That all right with you?"

"Sure, sure, sure. Just get it over with so we can get to the rodeo."

They were both smiling as he moved in close, touched his other hand to her hair. "Hi," he whispered.

"Hi," she whispered back just before he found her mouth with his and gave her the softest, sweetest, most lonesome kiss she'd ever tasted in her life.

"I've missed you." He pressed his forehead to hers, sighed in contentment.

She felt young and foolish and in love and not caring that anybody within eyeshot knew it. Anybody within eyeshot happened to take the shape of a bow-legged cowboy with a toothy grin and an Adam's apple that bobbed nervously while his face turned three shades of red.

"Ah, Cutter…" The Oklahoma drawl was as warm as sunshine on a cloudless day. "We got to be gittin' if we're gonna make the first go-round. Ma'am," he added and flushed red all over again when Peg smiled at him over Cutter's shoulder.

"That would be Burt," Cutter said, drawing reluctantly away and tucking Peg under his shoulder. "Burt Winslow, Peg Lathrop. And this cute little blonde with the bright red boots is Shelby Lynn."

"Hey, Burt," Peg said.

"You're a bronc rider," Shelby said, clearly in heaven, surrounded by cowboys. "I saw your picture in the PRCA News."

"Hey, there, little Shelby." Burt's Adam's apple bounced with every word he said. "You ready to see the rodeo?"

"You bet!"

"Why don't you go on ahead with Shelby and see about catching the luggage, Burt." Cutter handed him the claim stubs Peg had dug out of her purse. "We'll catch up in a sec.

"She's okay with him," Cutter assured Peg when she cast a worried look toward her daughter, who happily trotted along toward the luggage carousel, hand in hand with the lanky cowboy. "But I'm not gonna be okay until I do this."

He pulled her with him to a corner on the other side of the flight monitors and backed her up against the wall. "Sorry. This is as much privacy as I can arrange—at the moment." And then he kissed her— like she'd been aching to be kissed, like he couldn't draw another breath until he got it out of his system, or got the taste of her into his.

"We're…creating…a…spectacle," she said between the assault of his hungry mouth and busy, busy hands.

"Don't care," he growled as he dived in for another kiss that turned her knees to noodles, sent her heart rate into overdrive and her mind into a mush that didn't care anymore, either.

They were both breathing hard by the time he lifted his head then buried his face in her neck and held her close against him. For the longest time, he said nothing. He just held her—as if she were the anchor holding him steady in a storm determined to sweep him out to sea.

"Cutter…" She touched a hand to his hair. "Are you okay?"

"I am now." He pulled away, smiled at her. "Come on. Let's go see if Shelby's talked Burt's leg off yet."

Peg hadn't seen Cutter ride since that summer six years ago. Sure, you couldn't live in Montana without catching the occasional rodeo on TNN or ESPN or sometimes even some local TV coverage. And yes, she'd caught snippets of his competitions a time or two on TV. Shelby, after all, was a rodeo junkie. But Peg had watched with reluctance and she'd watched with resentment and it hadn't been the same.

In person, from the VIP seats he'd arranged for her and Shelby alongside Tracy Grover, Wreck Grover's wife, and their little girl, Katie, Peg saw Cutter and the sport he loved in a whole new light.

He was something to watch, this defending National Finals Saddle Bronc Champion. He was something to be reckoned with. And above all else, he was a man in his element. A man who knew his job and loved it.

The crowd loved him, too. So did the media—and the women. For three nights running, the hordes of lush and lively buckle bunnies who vied for his attention had sent the occasional daggered look her way.

"Whoa-ho," Tracy said with a huge grin as she dug into a tub of popcorn. "If looks could kill, you'd have been dead ten times tonight alone."

Tracy was a petite little blonde, a veteran of the rodeo life and as much a fan as Shelby. Peg had liked her immediately when they'd met the day before yesterday. It had also helped that Katie and Shelby had become fast friends.

"You sure those looks aren't directed *your* way? Wreck's a fine-looking man."

"Oh, no, sweetie. Those women know not to go poaching anywhere near my territory. I may be little, but I fight dirty. Besides, Wreck's as true-blue as they come. He also knows I'd kill him real slow and painful-like if he ever so much as poked a toe outside his own pasture.

"Nope. Those daggers are definitely meant for you. Cutter's little bunnies aren't used to getting cut out of the herd and, honey, since he made that trip back to Sundown in July, he hasn't given a one of 'em the time of day. Not that he ever really had much time for them anyway. Katie June, you put that down. How many times have I told you that you do *not* pick up anything from the floor? You don't know where the boots have been that might have stepped on it first.''

Peg grinned then returned the glare of a redheaded woman in paint-tight jeans and knee-high boots. ''If he didn't date them then why are they so upset with me?''

''Well…until you, they at least thought there was reason to hope. Cutter's never brought anyone with him before,'' she added on a meaningful note. ''Not even once.''

The crowd cheered as the team-roping competition heated up. Peg leaned back in the seat, thinking about what Tracy had said, surprised by the information. ''How long have you and Wreck been together?''

Tracy laughed. ''Since dirt. We grew up—both of us—as rodeo brats. My daddy has a stock contracting company and Wreck's daddy was a pickup man for years. Guess you could say rodeo's in our blood.''

''Where's home?''

''When we get there, it's Stephensville.''

''Texas?'' Shelby piped up, suddenly tuning into the conversation. ''That's where Ty's from.''

''Yep. We're neighbors.''

''Ty's the best,'' Shelby said adoringly, '''Course, that's only after Cutter. And Wreck and Burt.''

''Girl's got good taste—and tact, too,'' Tracy added with a grin.

''Not to mention that she's fickle,'' Peg added

with a smile. ''Ty Murray was the man until Cutter showed up.''

''How about you,'' Tracy added pointedly. ''You fickle, too?''

Before Peg could figure out how to respond to that, Tracy rushed on. ''None of my business, I know. But the thing is, we go way back—Cutter and Wreck and me. I just…I just want you to know that you're capable of hurting him. And sweet as you are—if you hurt him, I'd have to hurt you. I just wanted you to know that.'' Then Tracy smiled and hugged her.

Peg was dumbfounded. *She* was capable of hurting *him?*

It was a thought that had never, not in a million years, crossed her mind. She was stunned by the prospect. Shaken by the possibility. And by the time the night's events were over and they were working their way through the crowd to head back to their hotel room, she was starting to wonder if all this time—all this time—the heart that was most vulnerable had actually been his.

Ten

It was late. They were back at the hotel and it was their last night together before Peg and Shelby caught their flight to Missoula in the morning and Cutter headed for Houston. Shelby was bunking with Katie in Tracy and Wreck's set of rooms—the girls had wanted to giggle away their final night together. Peg, just out of the shower and wearing a short midnight-blue gown, was standing in the doorway of the adjoining rooms Cutter had booked for them when he walked out of his own shower, a towel slung low around his hips.

He was so deep in thought as he sat down on the edge of the bed that he wasn't aware she was watching him. His hair was damp; his face was hard. Her heart hurt at the look of him—at both the beauty and the pain. The beauty was there, always there, for anyone to see. The pain, he rarely let anyone witness. The pain, she realized now, was something she had never recognized in him.

She recognized it now. It wasn't physical, although his body had taken a beating. It always took a beating in competition, even a successful competition as this one had been.

As he lay back on the bed, stared at the ceiling, she saw the weight of another pain so clearly now and wondered why she hadn't seen it sooner. Because he'd never let her—because even *he* hadn't come to terms with the source of it. But most of all, because she'd been so afraid of the pain he was going to cause her and Shelby, she'd never realized he was struggling with his own.

Earlier tonight, Tracy had made her stop and think and realize that there was more than rodeo that made Cutter run.

You have the capability to hurt him.

Like he was hurting now.

Lonely.

The man was lonely and he didn't know what to do about it. She wasn't sure that she did, either, but as she walked into his bedroom, she was determined to figure out a way.

He turned his head when he heard her, hid his feelings behind a brilliant smile.

"Scoot up," she said. "And roll over. I'll give you a back rub you'll never forget."

"A man would have to be crazy to turn down an offer like that." He ditched the towel and did as she asked, until he was lying spread-eagle on his stomach.

She was the one who was crazy. Crazy in love. And crazy because it had taken her this long to figure out that he was in love with her, too. Just as she'd figured out that he was scared with the knowledge of it. Didn't trust himself to know how to handle it.

He groaned into the bedspread when she straddled his hips and started working on the knotted muscles in his neck. "You have magic hands. Why don't I turn over so you can work your magic on some other very needy parts of my poor beat-up body."

It would be so easy to go there with him. To lose herself in his arms, to let him show her what he couldn't find the courage to tell her. She leaned down, pressed a kiss between his shoulder blades. "Later, cowboy. Right now, just lie still and let me do this for you."

His skin was hot, his muscles tense. "Don't move. I'll be right back."

She slid off the bed, walked into her room. When she found her body lotion, she returned and settled over his hips again.

"Whoa—that's cold." He shivered when she squeezed a line of lotion down his back.

"It'll warm up."

"And it smells—cripes, Peg—it smells like flowers. You're gonna have me smelling like a girl."

"Just so you smell like *my* girl."

His snort was muffled in the bedcovers. "Lucky for you, you've got such great hands or I wouldn't put up with your lip—or your lotion."

"Lucky for me," she said on a smile and worked on a stubborn knot under his shoulder blade.

She watched her hands move over his broad back, felt the strength of the muscle beneath his skin, hesitated over a scar here, another one there—reminders of the risk of a sport that claimed many casualties. The physical evidence was obvious. It was the other scars she wanted to find and soothe tonight—the ones that had nothing to do with riding broncs.

He was relaxed now; she could feel the subtle softening of all that firm muscle. His breath had slowed to an even, restful cadence.

"Where's home for you now, Cutter?"

Her question surprised him—it surprised her. She hadn't known that was where she was going to start. It also reminded her just how much about him she didn't know. The sum total of their relationship to date had been a long-lost summer love affair and a handful of days and nights together since July—some of them fighting, most of them making love—and hundreds of long-distance phone calls. Conversation had been limited to Shelby, to rodeo, to the weather, to how much they missed each other. They never talked about the future, never talked about the past. And it was the past that Peg suspected held the key to whatever future they might have.

The way Cutter's muscles momentarily tensed before he made himself relax again said he was more than surprised by her question. He wasn't comfortable with it and the doors it might open.

Finally he moved a shoulder. "There's a motel in Denver that holds the same room for me every time I blow into town. Does that count?"

He tried to make light of it but she knew that light

was a far cry from what he was feeling. *Lonely.* It was in his voice—just as it had been in his eyes before he'd seen her watching him.

He wasn't the only cowboy who carried everything they owned in their rigging bag along with their saddle and a duffel that they threw in the back of their truck. He wasn't the only cowboy who didn't have a home to go back to. But he was *her* cowboy and she needed him to open up to her.

"Have you seen your mom lately?" she asked, slipping off his back and stretching out beside him. She pressed herself against all his hard heat and propping her head on her hand, continued to stroke his back in a slow, circular caress, keeping that all-important connection.

He crossed his arms in front of him then rested his forehead on his stacked hands. "A couple of months ago. She's doing good." He drew in a long breath, let it out. And fell silent.

"I remember her," she said softly. "I always felt bad for her. She seemed so…sad."

His eyes were closed but she saw the muscle in his jaw tighten, felt his body tense as well.

"What happened?" she pressed as she maintained the contact of her hand on his back. "With her and your dad? I don't ever remember seeing him."

Another silence, one she was afraid he'd withdraw into and leave them exactly where they were.

"What happened is that he's a sonofabitch."

That much she'd suspected so it was little more than she'd had before. "Do you ever see him?"

"Nope."

End of discussion. Door closed.

She wanted more but after several tense, silent moments, it became clear she wasn't going to get more. And maybe that was for the best. Maybe it should be up to him now.

"Wanna play a game?"

One corner of his mouth crawled up into a grin that had her smiling in spite of herself. "Thought you'd never ask."

"Not *that* kind of game. Pay attention. What am I spelling?" With the tip of her finger, she drew a letter on his back.

"Sex."

She popped him on the shoulder. "Sex does *not* start with *I*. Now be serious."

"Okay. *I*."

"That was a gimme. Now guess the rest."

With light, deliberate strokes she spelled another word.

"Love." His throat worked as he swallowed. He wasn't smiling anymore.

She spelled yet one more word.

"You," he said on a hoarse whisper and started turning toward her.

"Not yet." She pushed him back to his stomach. "There's more."

"Home," he said when she'd finished.

Her eyes were swimming with tears when he turned to her and repeated the rest of the words she had spelled on his back. "Home is here with me."

Eyes locked on hers, he drew her into his arms and kissed her—like he was coming home, like he was craving home, like he was starting to believe that maybe he had found home for the first time in his life.

The next morning, he put her and Shelby on the plane.

And Peg waited. A full three weeks passed—without a word from him, without a call from him—before she accepted that she'd scared him off. Her talk of love, her talk of home hadn't opened the door to their future. It had slammed it in her face.

She would have hurt for him—if she hadn't been so busy wanting to hate him for the hurt he'd caused Shelby. Wanting to hate him for refusing the love she'd offered because he'd been too much of a coward to accept it.

She loved him. Cutter had been running from those words for three weeks. Running and denying and telling himself he was doing everyone involved a favor by making the break hard and clean.

He'd hit three more rodeos since then. Had cinched his fourth invitation to the National Finals in Vegas in December—even had a good shot at another championship. Seven years ago, when he'd thrown his hat into the ring, he would have been the happiest man on earth if he'd known he would be this successful.

Seven years ago, he'd measured success by day money and points, by hard rides and good times. As little as four months ago he'd used the same yardstick.

Now he didn't know. Now the victories felt hollow. The nights—always long—were haunted. With thoughts of her. Of losing himself in her eyes. Of losing himself in the eyes of his daughter.

She loved him—or thought she did. They both loved him. And that's the part he couldn't handle. That's the part he couldn't trust.

"You know, Reno, that pretty face of yours has gotten as long as the highway between here and Galveston and I, for one, am getting damn sick of lookin' at it."

Cutter glanced across the booth into the scowling face of Tracy Grover. They were at some truck stop on some highway on the way to another rodeo. He didn't remember the name of the place, didn't care. Everything had started to blur since Dallas.

"If you're so tired of looking at it, why did you ask me to breakfast? Never mind. Don't answer that. Where's Wreck and Katie, anyway?"

"Sleepin' in," she said, "and don't change the subject."

"I didn't know there was a subject."

"For a smart man, you sure pull some dumb stunts."

"Eat your breakfast, Trac—it'll give you something to chew on other than me." He shoveled a forkful of scrambled eggs into his mouth and swallowed in stubborn silence.

"Go after her."

He froze, braced the edges of his palms on the booth top, then leaned back and stared out the window where a fleet of semis lined up to fill their tanks.

"You're entitled, Cutter. You're entitled to something good. So is Peg. Now for God's sake, be a man and go after it.''

He whipped his head around, glared at his friend. The compassion in her eyes took the bite out of her words.

''Be a man. Be the man she needs,'' she said, then slipped out of the booth and walked away.

It was close to midnight and three days later when Cutter pulled into Peg's driveway. He cut the engine and sat there. Exhausted. Exhilarated. Scared to death that he'd blow what would undoubtedly be his last chance with her. Even more scared that before he got the chance to tell her what she deserved to hear, she'd tell him to hit the road or go to hell or drop dead. She was more than entitled.

The house was dark. And when he walked up the porch steps to let himself quietly inside, the door that was never locked was locked against him. He pressed his forehead to the frame, closed his eyes and for the first time, considered that there might be no bridges left to burn.

He also considered leaving, saving them both another round of pain.

Be a man. Be the man she needs.

Tracy was right. He owed Peg more than an explanation and he wasn't leaving until he'd at least given her that.

Knowing it would be a waste of time to try the back door—no one could make a statement like Peg—he went right for the side of the house directly below her upstairs bedroom window. It took his pickup and the long ladder that he found in the barn, but he finally managed to reach the window, cut the screen, and with the help of a long-handled screwdriver, ease the window open. His booted foot had just hit the floor when her bedside light flicked on.

He whipped his head around—and drowned in the look of her, soft and sleep tousled, wary and wounded from all the distrust he'd fostered.

"Trust you to miss the point of a locked door."

He watched her face carefully. "I've missed a lot of things since Dallas."

She dragged the hair back from her face with both hands. "If this is another hit and run, Cutter, I'll pass—thanks, anyway."

Bruised. She looked bruised and weary and as distant as the rodeo in Texas that he'd skipped to get here.

"I don't blame you," he said, holding his hat in his hands to keep himself from reaching for her. "I don't blame you for hating me."

She turned her face away, shook her head. "If only it was as simple as that."

She looked so vulnerable—this strong woman who showed no fear. He'd done that to her. He wanted to make it right.

Taking a chance, he crossed the room and sat down on the edge of the bed. She watched him warily as he memorized the cinnamon-brown of her eyes, the chestnut sheen of her hair, the silky skin that still held the hint of a summer tan. He wanted to touch her so badly he ached with it. Wanted to feel her pliant warmth against him, ease them both over the line where there was nothing but ragged heartbeats, blazing body heat and hard, mindless loving.

But he couldn't get by on that alone anymore. She needed more from him. He'd finally realized that he needed more, too.

"When I left Sundown eight years ago," he said carefully, "it was because I wanted to be someone. And I wanted to get away from my mom's sad eyes."

He paused, not looking at her now, but at a frayed tear in the knee of his jeans. "I hate myself for that— for leaving her alone. I hate that I've run from sad eyes ever since."

This was harder than he'd thought. Saying the words. Laying out his failures.

"I wanted to be better than my old man." He shook his head, smiled without humor. "The only part he'd played in my life had been an accident of biology yet I wanted to show *him* what I was made of. That I was worth ten of him."

Another deep breath. He looked toward the window, to the midnight sky, then back at her. "It took you—it took loving you to make me realize I'd turned out just like him. It took Shelby to make me see— really see—how like him I was."

"Cutter—"

"No. Let me get this out. I'm not good with words. Not important words. I love you, Peg. Those are important words. You were entitled to hear them long ago."

It was so easy, and it felt so right to finally say it. And such a relief to stop fighting it, as he'd been fighting it since that summer so long ago.

He loved her. He let himself just slide into the feeling, like slipping into a comfortable pair of boots, or a pair of soft, worn jeans or into her when she was wet and hot and ready for him. Easy. Natural. Right. And suddenly the rest of the words just came to him.

"There is nothing about you that I don't love. I love the way you look, the way you laugh, the way you love—both Shelby and me—with every single part of yourself."

Her eyes were closed now, her head down as she clutched the sheet in her hands.

"I love the way you kiss...the way you look at me when you take me deep inside."

A small sob escaped her and then she was in his arms. He didn't know who moved first, he only knew that he was finally holding her, feeling her heart beat against his, burying his face in the sweet scent of her hair.

"You've made me think about things," he whispered, bracketing her face in his hands so she was forced to look at him, to see him as the man who loved her. "Things like home. I've been afraid of believing in that, too, but I've finally figured it out. You did that. You made me see that home *is* you. It's not a place. It's a feeling. It's a pair of red cowboy boots."

She laughed then and he wiped the tears away from her cheeks with his thumbs. "It's a heart that I trust to be true. I've run away all my life—because I couldn't trust the feeling. Couldn't count on something I'd never had—didn't think I deserved."

"You run away from us again," she said between

tears, "I swear…I swear I'll hunt you down and drag you back here by your pride and joy."

He pressed his forehead to hers then matched the promise in his words with the promise in his eyes. "I'm not running anywhere. Not ever again."

He kissed her then, long and deep and laid her back on the bed.

"You're not him, Cutter." She searched his eyes with love and conviction. "You're not your father. You just thought you should be."

Cupping his face in her hands, she laid his final fear to rest—the one he hadn't known he'd harbored until she voiced it. "And I'm not him, either. I'm not going to leave you. I'm never going to leave you like he did."

She lifted her head, touched her mouth to his. Soft and tender. Wild and sweet. She seduced him with the nip of her teeth, the sweep of her tongue, until they were tearing at his clothes and dragging her nightshirt over her head.

"I love you," he whispered and let her take him. Let her push him to his back beneath her and own him. Let her bend over him, tease him with the sweep of her hair across his skin, tempt him with the brush of her nipple against his open mouth, destroy him with the clench of her silken heat sinking over him, around him.

He gasped, bucked beneath her, dug his hands into her hips as she rode him to an end that left him breathless and spent and in awe of her capacity for giving.

He buried a hand in her hair, fought for air. "I love you."

"I know," she whispered against his shoulder, limp and wasted and secure. "I know."

Epilogue

Two months later, Cutter stood on the winner's platform at Thomas Mac in Las Vegas and accepted his third National Finals Saddle Bronc Championship Award.

Among the seventeen thousand fans that cheered from the stands were Sam and Krystal Perkins, Wreck and Tracy Grover. On one side of Peg were Jack and Kay Lathrop. On the other was Anna Reno, who blinked back happy tears for her son—and for the pure and amazing joy of holding her granddaughter on her lap.

"That's my daddy," Shelby said to anyone who would listen. "And he won that buckle just for me, didn't he, Gramma Anna!"

Later, after the celebration had wound down, Peg watched from the bed as Cutter, stripped down to his bare feet and new jeans, picked up a sleeping Shelby and transferred her from their bed to the one in the second room of their suite.

"She's had quite a day," he said as he stretched out beside her again and crossed his hands behind his head.

"We all have. It's been a wild ten days."

She studied his face, loving the look of him, relaxed and weary and content. "What are you thinking?"

He turned his head, smiled. "I was wondering how you'd feel about being married to a circuit cowboy."

She glanced at the wide gold band on the ring finger of her left hand, the one he'd put there at a small family service Thanksgiving weekend. "Circuit cowboy?"

"I love rodeo, Peg—but I don't need it to be my life anymore. I don't want to be on the road away from you and Shell."

"So you're thinking of pulling out of the big competitions—just work the Montana circuit?"

He shrugged. "Seems like a good compromise. I'd be home all week—rodeo on weekends. The money won't be the same, but I figure if I partner up with Lee Savage like he's suggested—"

"Whoa." Peg came up on an elbow. "Lee wants you to be a partner in his horse business?"

"Well, he's approached me, yeah. Said he'd like to get into bucking stock. Figured I'd be the man to know what to look for."

"But where does the partnership come in? Doesn't that usually require some investment?"

He grinned and rolled to his side, facing her. "You know, there are advantages to living out of a truck or a seedy old motel room for eight years. No mortgage, no utility payments. I've been lucky, Peg. I've put a little money by."

Before she could say anything else, he rose, dug around in his duffel and pulled out some papers. He tossed them on the bed.

She looked at him, looked at them.

"It's the deed to your house—along with twelve hundred acres I was able to convince Homer to part with. I know it's not much—not by Montana standards, mostly scrub grass, but there's water."

She went pale, pressed a hand to her chest. "You bought it? The house? And…twelve hundred acres?"

"What? You don't want it?"

She flew to her knees, threw herself at him, hugged him madly. "I love you."

He held her to his chest and didn't figure on ever letting her go again. This woman—this woman was everything to him and he planned to spend the rest of his life paying her back for what she'd done for him.

She'd made him into a man.

She'd made him a daddy.

She'd brought him home. Home—where he planned to stay for *forever*.

* * * * *

TANGLED SHEETS, TANGLED LIES

by
Julie Hogan

JULIE HOGAN

discovered romance novels at the age of ten and spent her youthful summers tearing through one book after another, when she should have been doing chores at her parents' orchard. Luckily, in spite of a checkered past, all that summer reading paid off. After ten years in the rat race, Julie gave up her career as an internet marketing executive and, with her English degree clutched in her fist, finally realised her dream of writing her own romance novels. Julie shares a quiet southern California home with her true-to-life hero husband, Jud, who inspires both her writing and her life, and two bad-tempered cats who rule the neighbourhood with an iron claw. In her writing, Julie loves bringing funny and engaging characters to life, then putting them through the wringer until they realise that love is the only true path to happiness. The only thing Julie enjoys more than reading and writing romances is hearing from readers who share her mania. You can write to her at julie@juliehogan.com

This is for my parents, who, when I was an impressionable pre-teen, were far too indulgent and bought me far too many books with far too adult themes. If Jud and I turn out to be a fraction of the parents you are, I will consider us a smashing success. I love you both.

This for my critique partners past and present. Laura Wright, Julie Ganis, Tami Goveia, Patty Chung—you will never again be able to say you haven't made a huge difference in someone's life. And to the new La-La Sisterhood: Beth, Corinne, Doris, Teresa and Chandra—thank you for taking me into your fold. You have put the light and laughter back into this caper for me.

This is for my mentor and steadfast coach, Barbara Ankrum. Your success speaks for itself, but you know I have to say it anyway: your ability to give is extraordinary, your desire to enrich others is tireless, and your talent for writing transcends the exceptional. I am beyond fortunate to be able to call you my friend.

And finally, this is for my husband, Jud, who believed in me, enouraged me cajoled me, lovingly menaced me and supported me utterly in my journey to becoming a writer. You make me laugh when I don't want to, let me cry when I should and are the most ardent, die-hard fan. You are the very air that I am privileged to breath. I love you with my whole heart.

One

When Cole Travis first drove into the town of Valle Verde, he felt like he'd taken a step back in time.

There were no sidewalks flanking what appeared to be the main street, just well-traveled dirt paths with weeds and wildflowers growing as best they could in tufts alongside it. A group of young boys walked together, pushing each other and talking and laughing loud enough for Cole to hear them through the open window of his truck. A woman pushed a baby stroller with grocery bags piled in the bottom and a few men sat outside the hardware store.

It was quiet and peaceful and kind of pretty. And it made him feel like he was the only person within a hundred miles who had a problem.

He pulled up beside the gas pumps at an old-fashioned filling station, turned the key and waited for the groaning, wheezing pile of bolts and sheet metal that was posing as a truck to shudder and rattle to a stop. Cole had purchased the truck from one of his contractors just before leaving Seattle two weeks earlier and the man had laughingly called its idiosyncrasies "features." One very special feature, he'd said, was that the truck didn't stop until it felt like it.

Cole sighed. Because he intended to be flying home at the end of this journey, he'd wanted a vehicle he could junk when the time came. And he'd certainly gotten what he asked for in this jalopy.

Just then, another image out of the past appeared at Cole's window. A gas station attendant. "Fill 'er up?" the young man asked.

"Sure." Cole opened the door with a loud creak and stepped onto the clean pavement. "You know where I can get a local paper?"

The boy jerked his head toward the office. "You can take mine. I'm done with it. It's on the desk."

Cole took his time walking to the office. He'd been cramped up in the truck for most of the morning during the long drive from San Clemente to San Diego. Unfortunately, he hadn't found what he was looking for in San Clemente, nor had he found it in Laguna Beach before that. But it didn't really matter because regardless of how long it took or what he had to do, he was going to find his son, take him home and try as hard as he could to make up for all the time they'd lost.

As he gathered up the newspaper, he saw a map of Valle Verde thumbtacked to the wall. He pulled a piece of paper out of his back pocket and checked the address of the place he needed to go, located it on the map, then headed back to the truck.

After he paid for the gas, he pulled back out onto the main road. Well, at least now he knew where to find them. Only one small detail remained: how to approach them so they wouldn't suspect his real motive, so they wouldn't know that he might change their lives forever.

A small, neat park loomed up on the right side of the road and Cole pulled into it and turned off the truck, then reached into his bag and pulled out five thick file folders that represented his private investigator's work. They felt heavy in his hands. He'd had five chances to find his child. Three remained.

As he opened the top folder, his gut churned with anger at his ex-wife. In fact, ever since he'd learned that Kelly had been pregnant with his son when she'd left him five years earlier, he'd been swinging wildly between feeling furious and hopeful, anxious and sad.

It was almost a month ago now that Kelly's brother had called to tell him that Kelly had died—*and* that she'd confided something terrible to him just before dying. She'd not only been carrying Cole's child when she'd left him, but she'd abandoned the baby in the hospital's nursery. Worst of all, Kelly's brother had no idea what had happened to the boy, nor the name of the hospital.

Cole closed his eyes and pushed his anger into a small, tight corner of himself. He had to stay focused. His first two disappointing dead ends in San Clemente and Laguna had taught him that showing up and laying the facts out on the table didn't work. Once the people discovered why Cole was there, they treated him with open suspicion and distrust. Now he knew to reveal as little as possible until he could determine the facts for himself.

He reached for the newspaper and flipped to the classified page. Maybe he could get a job here, blend into the community for a week or two. Then when he met the people he was here to find, he would just seem like another newcomer to town rather than a man on a desperate mission.

A sudden gust of wind whispered through the truck's open windows, rustling the newspaper in Cole's hands. He flattened the paper against the truck's steering wheel to steady it, then ran a finger down the Help Wanted column. Halfway down the page, he stopped suddenly, grabbed a pen out of the truck's ashtray and drew a circle around a large ad.

And then Cole Travis smiled for the first time in weeks.

Lauren Simpson took another sip of the killer coffee they served at Uncle Bill's Café and smiled across the silver-flecked Formica table at her son who was running on a zillion gigawatts of syrup-induced energy.

"Read it again, Mommy. Read it again!"

Underneath the table, she stretched out her long legs and propped her feet up on the vibrant aqua Naugahyde bench across from her and let out a quiet sigh. At four years old, Jem's capacity for repetition was truly infinite.

"Pllleeaasssee?" Jem Simpson's powder-blue eyes danced with mischief as he shot her a "c'mon, Mom" grin.

She had to admit she was a sucker for that look, one that was designed to melt a mother's heart while getting her to agree to anything. She smiled as she picked up Valle Verde's local newspaper and read the Help Wanted ad out loud for the dozenth time.

"Wanted—A man who can do it all to remodel our home and barn. Must be a good carpenter, electrician and plumber. If interested, please apply in person at the Simpson's on Agua Dulce Road.''

Her son grinned up at her. ''You think someone'll come today?''

''Lord, I hope so.'' She stuffed the newspaper back into her tote as she sent a quick prayer to the gods of home repair. More than anything in the world, they needed a really handy handyman to help restore their old house and get their big, beautiful barn ready for public use in just six weeks. But the ad had been running for a few days and so far, no nibbles.

Lauren put aside her worries and smiled at her son. ''If we don't, pal, it's just going to be you, me, a hammer and one of the biggest first-aid kits we can find.''

She put money down on the table to pay for their breakfast and eyeballed the decimated pancakes on Jem's plate. ''You didn't eat much. Why don't you go ask Uncle Bill if he'll box up some new pancakes for you?''

''Okay.'' He slid his agile young body along the bench seat and picked up his plate. Lauren watched as he balanced it carefully on the way up to the counter, then saw Bill laugh at the mess Jem had made of the pancakes just like he had every Saturday morning since they'd moved to this little town just two months ago.

Even though it was fairly close to a large city—if you could call San Diego large—Valle Verde really was a warm, friendly place, she thought as she looked out the window at the slow, sweet pace of the main street. Kids rode their bikes down the middle of the road, moms walked to the store, women gossiped outside the beauty parlor and businesses put out simple, carved wood shingles with their names on them. From her vantage point she could see Johnny's Pump and Tune, the

What's Shakin' Chicken Pie Shop, Gordy's U Pic It We Pac It Grocery and the Top of the Valley Hardware. And soon, just a few blocks away, a new shingle would sway in the warm summer wind of northern San Diego County: Simpson's Gems, the Best Little Antique Store in the Southland.

Lauren put a few more dollars on the table to pay for the boxed-up pancakes, then grabbed her tote and went to fetch her son. She let him finish the longwinded story he was telling the counter full of diners about how they were looking for a handyman and how he was going to help because he was really good with tools—she smiled at that because it had taken her all morning to put the can opener back together after Jem had "fixed" it. Then, when he was done, she grabbed his sticky hand, said her goodbyes and stepped out into the pleasant, early-summer morning.

Jem chattered nonstop as they walked the two blocks home. She wondered to herself if she'd been the same way at his age. Probably not, considering that there hadn't been a soul around to listen to her. But that was *her* childhood—a childhood spent in one cold, awful foster home after another, a childhood Lauren wished she didn't have to remember but couldn't forget no matter how hard she tried. And *this,* she thought as they walked down the shady main street lined with eucalyptus trees, this wonderful, peaceful existence was going to be what Jem remembered about his childhood, no matter what she had to do to protect that.

She looked down at his tousled brown curls as he stopped to pick up a particularly grimy rock and stuck it in his pocket. Always gathering things, he was a bit like her in that way, although they shared no blood. But because she'd been his foster mother since he was abandoned as a baby and now she was his official adoptive mother, she realized this particular behavior could have been learned from her.

After all, she'd been collecting things as long as she could remember, long before she took Jem in and made good on the most important of her childhood pledges. And now that she'd retired from her grueling and time-consuming modeling career, she was going to fulfill another of her pledges and trot out all her precious things and open an antique store.

Jem slipped his hand back into hers as their house came into view and tugged to get her attention. "Look, Mommy," he said in a loud whisper.

Lauren followed the boy's gaze and automatically slowed her steps. There, standing on the front porch of their grand, gorgeous, dilapidated, falling-down Victorian house was a man, leaning casually against the main beam that held up the ornate overhang. He was staring up at the house's eaves, his back to them. She took in the long length of him—his broad shoulders encased in a snug black T-shirt, down his sleekly muscled back, to his sculpted behind and his long, denim-clad legs—and swallowed thickly.

Holy cow. If she were looking for a *man* instead of a handyman, she wouldn't have had to look any further. But she wasn't. Two hundred and twenty-one days ago, she'd made herself a promise: no men for one year. It was the only way she'd been able to think of to reset her own personal Jerk-O-Meter and establish some good sense when it came to men. Her sanity—and, more importantly, the happiness of her child—depended on it.

As they approached, the stranger turned his head slightly, just enough for her to see a shock of sandy-colored, wind-tossed hair falling over his forehead and a sharp, confident profile so chiseled it should be etched in bronze and placed in the window of an art gallery. A disconcerting heat rushed through her as she watched him lift one hand to grasp a beam above his head and the muscles in his forearm and bicep bunched and flexed as he tested its strength. Oh, my, she thought, this guy really did have a body that went on for days, maybe even weeks. And for her that was saying something. In her former business she'd seen a lot of beautiful male bodies—not to mention some inflated, appalling male egos to match.

She slowed their steps further and worked to reclaim her composure as she took in the unfamiliar, battered truck with Washington State plates parked alongside the house. Whoever he was, she was sure it would be a mistake to bound up the steps with her face far too flushed for the cool morning temperatures, looking like a cheerleader stalking the captain of the football team.

Jem pulled on her hand. "Mom, do you think it's him?" he said in a childish, hissing stage whisper.

And apparently it was loud enough for the man to hear because he turned around and smiled, revealing dazzling white teeth and lagoon-blue eyes that contrasted sharply with his wind- and sun-bronzed skin. Lauren's breath hitched, then released in one long rush.

She tightened her hold on her son's hand as the stranger reached behind him and pulled a newspaper out of the back pocket of his just-snug-enough Levi's. Don't worry, she told herself soothingly, he's probably new in town and looking for directions. Just because he had the classifieds didn't mean he was answering their ad. *Please don't be answering our ad. You're far too distracting to be our handyman.*

"Can I help you?" she asked as she and Jem walked

up the steps, carefully avoiding the two broken ones near the bottom.

The man looked at Jem with a certain bewilderment, like someone looks at a person they're sure they've met but can't quite place. Then he turned and fixed his gaze on her. Their eyes locked and held, pulling her into a strange, thrilling vortex that made her feel as if she was still strapped into the Tilt-O-Whirl Jem had made her ride at the county fair last weekend.

"Maybe you can," he said finally, and the spell was broken. "But I'm sure I can help you."

"You *are* the man!" Jem exclaimed.

The stranger cocked his head to the side and the corners of his firm, sensual mouth tipped into the beginnings of a smile.

"He means—" Lauren began.

But the man just smiled at Jem and said, "I think I know what he means," with a hint of laughter in his voice. Then he unfolded the newspaper and as he did, she saw their ad circled in red ink. "I'm here for the job you advertised."

Wasn't that just her luck? She'd been expecting a nice, graying old man with dentures, not some godlike creature who, with a simple smile, was stirring up something inside her that was better left undisturbed. Something that felt like it might be putting her yearlong hiatus from men in peril.

She sighed inwardly and told herself she'd just have to keep that commitment at the top of her To Do list. She was convinced that in just one hundred and forty-four more days, her instinct for men would be refreshed—not that her instinct had ever been all that finely honed to start with, but that wasn't the point. For now, she'd simply have to get rid of this stranger who had been dropped on her porch by fate to tempt her.

The man in question waved the newspaper with a flick of his wrist. "Unless the position's already been filled."

She thought about lying for a half a second, but there was a light in his blue eyes that made it impossible for her to manufacture a fib on the fly. "No, it hasn't. But—"

"That's great." His voice was calm, his gaze steady, his smile sure. "Because I can start immediately."

Not on your life, she thought, certain that the hordes of very safe and very unattractive grandpa types would be descending on her house any minute. "Actually," she said, seizing what she hoped would be a successful thanks-but-no-thanks tactic, "I'm really looking for someone local." She glanced pointedly toward the side yard and his truck. "And I can see you're from out of state."

"Yes, ma'am. Seattle area." His gaze never strayed from hers. "That's where I've been most recently anyway. Did some good work up there."

"Then I'd be happy to take your resume. But like I said, I'm giving the first crack at the job to someone local." Sounds good, sounds reasonable, she thought as she watched the giant oak tree that swayed gently in her front yard cast captivating shadows on his handsome, confident face.

"I've got to warn you," he said as he leaned against the post. He crossed his powerful arms in a way that let her know he had no intention of just tucking his tail and slinking away. "You're not going to find anyone better than me."

Any red-blooded woman with a good pair of eyes

could see that, but Lauren wasn't the type to acquiesce so quickly. "I guess I won't really know for sure until I see the rest of the applicants. But I'll be happy to review your resume and call you for an interview if you'd like."

The stranger's smile widened, softening his features and giving the impression that he could be trusted with the contents of Fort Knox. Then he pushed away from the post and walked toward her and Jem with animal grace. "Don't have a resume." He leaned on the final word, like a resume was an item required only by mere mortal men. "Or a phone number, either. I'm really just passing through, looking for a few months' honest work before I get on my way."

Oh, *passing through,* Lauren thought. That meant she wasn't going to be bumping into his charming grin— and all the other troubling attributes that were attached to that grin—around town. She breathed a little sigh of relief. Or was it regret? No, no, no, she chastised herself. It was relief.

As she tried to figure out what it was going to take to get this magnetic man on his way to the next town, Jem, clearly thinking he'd been silent long enough, piped up with, "Can you fix houses?"

The man hunkered down in front of her son, straining the denim that was stretched tight across his legs, and stared into her son's eager eyes. "What's your name?"

Jem smiled at the man in the guileless way that only children have the luxury of and said, "I'm Jem Simpson."

"It's nice to meet you, Jem. I'm Cole Travis, and the fact is, I can fix anything." His voice was deep and filled with the promise of his words—and something else that had Lauren reaching over instinctively to put her hand on Jem's slim shoulder. After all, it wouldn't be the first time a man had tried to get to her through kindness to her son.

The man glanced up at her then, his eyes darkening as he quite openly studied her, but not in the way men usually did when they recognized her as one of the models in the Boudoir Lingerie catalog. No, Cole Travis was looking deeper than that, and it made her feel restless and excited—and a little bit annoyed.

Cole looked back at Jem and jerked his head in her direction. "Is this your mother, Jem?"

The boy nodded and smiled wider. "Her name's Lauren." But he pronounced it as he always did which made it sound like "Woe-when."

"Lauren," she said. "Lauren Simpson." She hesitated a moment, then reached out her hand.

Cole Travis straightened, then took her hand in his own. His fingers felt like sandpaper as they slid roughly against hers. Lauren stared down at their intertwined hands and felt her control slipping a tiny notch. Warm, rough and electric, his gentle grip seemed to pour pure energy into her body.

It must be all that coffee she'd had at breakfast, she thought suddenly as she pulled her hand away and took one involuntary step back. "It's been nice meeting you, Mr. Travis," she said, shoving her tingling hand into the pocket of her jeans and forcing a wobbly smile to her lips. "But as I said, I'll have to interview some local tradesmen before I decide."

He shrugged. "Suit yourself. But I promise you, you won't find anyone better."

"Can you fix the swing?" Jem asked as he ran over to the creaky old wooden swing that was hanging precariously on its chain at the end of the porch.

"Sure could," Cole said as he walked over and tested the swing's chains with a gentle tug. He looked back at Lauren. "Tell you what," he said. "I'll give you a free sample. What harm is there in that?"

Lauren frowned. She wasn't sure, but something about that slow, lazy smile was giving her the strangest feeling that he was making the decisions, like he was making the rules.

"And Jem can help," Cole said and the boy's face lit up like the night skies on the Fourth of July.

Her son glanced over at her with that same guaranteed-to-work grin, an unspoken plea to let him help beaming at her like a floodlight.

Common sense warred with her need to get Cole Travis as far away as possible. She was uncomfortable around him, and not just because the way he looked at her made her feel like her knees were made of rubber.

On the other hand, she did need a thousand and one things done around here and unless she wanted to miss the beginning of the summer tourist season in just under two months, she couldn't afford to lose any more time. So what if she was attracted to him? she thought, mentally cracking the whip on her awakening hormones. Getting her business up and running was Priority One, dammit, and she wasn't going to let her simple attraction to this man stand in her way. In no time at all, he would cease to be a temptation. She was sure of it. Absolutely sure…

Cole Travis leaned his head back and laughed at something Jem had said. Low, deep and heartfelt, the mere sound of it sent a shiver of pure, unalloyed longing careening through her.

She mentally shook it off, then reminded herself that if, for some unlikely reason, his appeal did fail to wane, certainly she could get a grip long enough to find The Old Man of Valle Verde—couldn't she?

She wrapped her familiar control around her like a superhero's cape before she spoke. "I'll tell *you* what. I'll give you an hour. If the swing's fixed before the hour's up, I'll hire you for the weekend."

Cole Travis hesitated only a moment before that lazy smile appeared and he said, "You've got a deal."

She nodded, then looked back at Jem, who was now grinning from ear to ear, clearly anticipating his own participation in Cole's work. "As for you, young man, didn't you promise you'd help me clean that train wreck you call a bedroom?"

Her son's expression went from sixty to zero in one second. He looked down at his feet and nodded, his voice holding about as much enthusiasm as if he were going to the guillotine. "Uh-huh," he said.

"When you've finished," she said, softening her tone, "we'll come and check Mr. Travis's progress." She slanted a look at Cole. "Then we'll see how good he really is."

Amusement—and something else she couldn't put her finger on—flickered in the eyes that met her gaze. His voice was soft and almost sensual when he spoke. "I think you'll like what you see."

Too late for that, she mused, then checked herself mentally. Lauren gave him a smooth nod, turned the key in the ancient lock on the front door and waited for Jem to precede her inside. Hopefully that gray-haired old man would show up soon, she prayed as she followed her dejected son, and then she could get started on the things that really mattered: making a house and business that would sustain her and Jem for the rest of their lives.

Cole watched as Lauren let the rickety screen door close with a wheezing clatter behind her. He made a mental note to fix the screen door next. He breathed in deeply, noticing how the sweet, citrusy scent of her lingered—as did the vision of her tossing her deep, dark-red mane of hair and sashaying away in a flurry of perfectly shaped behind and long, long legs. She reminded him of a glamorous 1940s-era pinup girl he'd fallen in love with as a boy when he'd seen her on a calendar in his grandfather's garage.

And Jem—whether it turned out the boy was Cole's son or not—was an inquisitive, engaging child who obviously adored Lauren, and she him. But while something about the boy might look familiar, it wouldn't help for Cole to start imagining the boy as his own. If Cole had learned anything while he'd investigated the previous two leads, it was that until he knew for certain, it would be best to avoid any attachment.

To either of them.

But as he walked down to his truck, he still couldn't help remembering how Lauren had looked a few minutes before. She'd gotten all feisty, crossing her arms, forcing up those amazing breasts that just about every red-blooded male in America had dreamed of at least once.

Lauren Simpson was one of the world's most beautiful lingerie models, with absurdly full lips and dark green eyes that slanted up at the corners and teased men from the printed page. But that wasn't what had surprised him. What had surprised him was that she was also smart, confident and incredibly spirited for a woman he'd assumed would be as one-dimensional as she appeared in print.

And that was not to say that he hadn't noticed her actual *dimensions,* too.

He wiped beads of sweat from his forehead. Why in the hell was he so hot? He looked up at the sky, expecting to see that the reason for the heat pouring through his body was just the sun, blazing overhead. But it was still midmorning, and the feeble, pale sun was still lying low in the eastern sky. He couldn't deny it. Lauren Simpson was making him sweat. And he didn't like that fact one bit.

He'd come here with one thing in mind, Cole reminded himself as he grabbed a toolbox and threw the necessary tools into it with a clatter, and he wasn't going to stray from it. To get what he wanted, he needed this job. And he'd do a lot better work if his mind wasn't filled with images of her in the silky, flimsy, barely there stuff she wore in that damned catalog.

He cursed under his breath as he grabbed a hacksaw. Knowing just what she looked like under her harmless frayed jeans and blue T-shirt wasn't going to help him find out what he needed to know. Nor would it help him to stay focused on finding what had been taken from him, prove it was his and head home.

Toolbox filled, he walked back to the house and took the swing down. In less than twenty minutes, he'd filled the damaged holes where the threads had been stripped, drilled new holes for a stronger chain he'd found in his truck, attached the chain with sturdier bolts and hung the swing back up.

He sat down to test the swing's strength and was surprised by the satisfaction he'd taken in performing the simple task. Obviously it had been too long since he'd put his hands to actual labor. He sized up the front of the house and made a mental list of what needed to be done with an eye trained by over fifteen years in the construction business. The roof leaked, the porch boards were warped, the paint was peeling, the windows needed glazing—and that was just what he could see from where he sat.

He sighed as he got up and pulled a big, flathead screwdriver out of his toolbox. He was seriously over-qualified for this job, he thought as he began to unscrew the screen door's hinges. But Lauren would never know that. At least not until it was time for her to know.

Suddenly, Jem peeked around the doorsill, his smile shy. "Whatcha doin'?" the boy asked as he inched his small frame outside the house.

An odd turbulence rocked through Cole as he remembered his own fascination with tools and construction when he was a boy. "I'm fixing the screen door," Cole said as he pulled the wooden frame away from its moorings and leaned it up against the house. "If you've finished cleaning your room, why don't you go get your mom to come check out the swing. It's fixed."

Jem spun on his heel and ran back into the house. "Mom! Mom! The swing's fixed. C'mon!"

The boy's enthusiasm tugged at Cole's heart, but he continued working until he saw Lauren appear in the doorway, her son pulling her hand. She was smiling that cool, composed smile he'd seen so many times in print. She'd put an old-fashioned apron on over her jeans and top, but she still managed to look like the picture of a very sexy housewife who was meeting her man at the door.

And he'd be damned if he didn't want to be that man for one crazy second.

"You're finished already?" she asked as she stepped out onto the wide porch.

Cole nodded as he moved aside to let her past. But when she squeezed by, she lightly brushed one curvy hip against his thigh, making the heat in his veins spike dangerously. He felt as much as heard her sharp intake of breath, then saw her glance at him from wide, surprised eyes.

"You first, Mom," the boy said, pulling them from the undertow created from their simple contact.

Lauren moved away from Cole quickly, then lowered herself into the swing gingerly and gracefully, crossed those long, lovely legs, then patted the space next to her for Jem to sit down. The boy plopped down enthusiastically and Cole noticed Lauren wince as she looked above her head to see if it would fall from the rafters at the impact.

"Awesome," Jem said as he perched at the edge of the swing and dangled his legs.

Lauren looked at Cole and repeated, "Awesome," then put her arm around her son and smiled down at him. Cole felt like a boulder the size of Cleveland had settled in his stomach as he watched them but he quickly shuttered his expression as she looked up at him, her exotic green eyes troubled.

"Thank you, Mr. Travis," she said, her voice wrapping itself around his name so sweetly he almost felt like she'd reached out and touched him. "We've wanted to use this swing every day since we moved in." Her smile wavered and she lifted her chin a fraction. "I'll hire you for the weekend. But I still intend to conduct interviews and I'll still need to see your references."

The stubborn tilt of her chin warned him to tread lightly. "You interview everyone you can find," he said as he turned and began to remove the hinges from the screen door. "I'll just keep working until you find someone who can do the job as fast and as well as I can." He paused, then glanced over his shoulder at her. "Or until you don't."

Two

By four o'clock the next afternoon, Lauren was so frustrated she wanted to cry. She peered over the top of the dog-eared, grease-stained piece of paper at the two pot-bellied brothers sitting on her antique settee who were, unfortunately, only the latest marchers in the parade of inexperienced candidates who'd come to apply for her job. But these brothers were different. While the others had been merely amusingly underqualified, these two were downright offensive.

From the moment she'd answered the door fifteen minutes earlier, she'd felt their oily gazes as distinctly as if they were touching her. Luckily, only a few minutes after they'd arrived, Cole had come in to change the lock on her front door. And though it pained her to admit it, having him there was reassuring.

As she pretended to read the Beer Boys's list of references, she glanced over at Cole. He was entirely too sure of himself—and probably getting a good laugh out of this, she thought, her gaze lingering on him for a moment as he worked with graceful efficiency. Sitting before her was graphic proof that Cole Travis was the best man for the job. And let's face it, she told herself, when it came to everything she was looking for in a man…er, *handy*man, these two lumps weren't even in the same galaxy as Cole.

Suddenly, as if he could hear her thoughts, Cole looked over at the brothers and a deep frown settled in between his brows. Even in profile, his posture and demeanor were intense, ready.

In spite of a little voice inside her that tried to assure her with, "I can take care of myself, I always have!" she felt a warm sense of ease settling over her as she lowered the paper.

"So, ummm…" She looked back down at their "resume." "Bobby, Johnny." She looked up at them. "All the people you have listed as references seem to have the same last name as you do."

They grinned at each other, displaying crooked teeth yellowed, she assumed, by chewing tobacco. "Yeah. We been working around our daddy's place all our lives."

"I see," she said as an image from *Deliverance* flashed through her mind. She glanced at Cole again before trudging on with the interview. "And what kind of work do you know how to do?"

"We can do anything you want us to do," Bobby said. Beside him, Johnny wiggled his eyebrows at her and added suggestively, "And then some."

And even as the meaning behind his words sank into her consciousness, she saw Cole shoot to his feet, a muscle working in his jaw like a two-ton piston. When he spoke, there was a dangerous timbre to his voice. "I think the lady is asking if you understand the most basic things about construction. Like repairing lath and plaster walls?" Their expressions were blank. "Or glazing windows? Replacing tongue-and-groove flooring?" Their faces were as unresponsive as monks in a deep trance. "How about something simple, like hanging and taping drywall?"

After several long moments of silence, Lauren heard Cole make an impatient noise that sounded almost like a snort before going back to work on the lock, now with a little more vigor. Annoyance at Cole's interference warred with amusement at the idiocy written on the Beer Boys's faces as they exchanged nervous glances.

"Who's he?" Bobby asked, looking over one sloped shoulder at Cole.

"I'm the interim handyman," Cole said in a loud growl.

The brothers went cross-eyed as they struggled with the word "interim."

"He's doing the job temporarily," she interpreted.

"Oh," they said in unison. "Okay."

She stood up. "Well, I think I've got all the information I'll need. I'll call you if you get the job." *Or if you're the last men on earth, whichever comes first.*

Moments later, Lauren watched the two men amble out the front door and wondered how one little town could have so many inept handymen. Her hopes for getting Simpson's Gems ready on time were beginning to wane.

If she wanted the job done she was going to have to hire Mr. Tempting. She knew it, but it still bothered her—because hell, *he* still bothered her. But as she turned to face Cole, the words, "you're hired," died before they could be uttered. His thunderous expression was enough to stop her cold.

"What were you thinking?" he demanded, his lips drawn into a tight line.

For a moment, Lauren could only stare. What was his problem? "What are you talking about?"

"Those two, that's what. What were you thinking inviting those two losers into your house?"

Her temper flared up then, and she narrowed her eyes and straightened up to her full five foot nine. "Thinking? I was *thinking* of hiring a handyman, Mr. Travis."

"The name's Cole," he said, a muscle jumping at his jawline. "And if you were really looking for a handyman, you would have seen that there's one standing in your living room right now."

"I think I made it clear that I'd be interviewing before I made a decision. And I don't require your help with the interviews, by the way."

Cole's laugh held not a single ounce of humor. "Well, it sure looked like you needed help with those two."

Lauren planted her fists on her hips. "I was handling it fine, *Cole*. Believe me, I've been handling that type for a long time."

"It sure didn't look that way to me."

Pure, unmitigated exasperation made her blurt out, "Then maybe you shouldn't be looking." She took a deep breath before she spoke again, cooling her voice by at least twenty degrees. "Besides, don't you have work to do?"

His eyebrow arched up, questioning her. "Are you saying I've got the job?"

Cole watched Lauren's straight white teeth bite softly into her lush lower lip, the mere sight of which sent a streak of heat whooshing through him so fast, he felt like he was a match and she was the striking plate.

Several long tense moments hung between them before she said, "I have several other people coming today."

"Really?" He leaned his shoulder against the doorframe with an ease that he didn't come anywhere near feeling. "Another high school boy, like the one this morning? Or," he said with a twist of his head toward the porch, "more victims of inbreeding like those two?"

She let out a little hiss of annoyance. "I have a very qualified man coming any minute." She tipped her chin up in a way that he now recognized as a sign of stubbornness. "And I'd appreciate it if you weren't underfoot when he gets here."

Underfoot? He'd never been underfoot in his life. Granted, he *had* stepped over the line with his spontaneous interview of the two liquored up, would-be handymen. But what she didn't know was that he'd heard them talking about her as they'd gotten out of their truck. And what he'd overheard had been enough to make him grab the first project he could find and head inside.

If he hadn't been there, how far would those beer-soaked pinheads have taken their drunken ramblings? It didn't really matter, of course. The fact was that he *had* been here when they'd undressed her with their eyes and he'd seen her reaction. And that's when he knew he had to get this job for another reason: whether Lauren liked it or not, he was going to make sure nothing happened to her or to Jem—at least until he found out what he needed to know.

Cole put his own anger on ice, knelt down and began

to put his tools away. "How long are you gonna keep this up?"

"Until the pool of applicants is exhausted," she said, her worn-down voice lacking the conviction of her words.

"They looked pretty exhausted to me." He tossed her the new keys to the house and she caught them handily. "C'mon, Lauren, you know I'm the best man for you."

As her eyes darkened and her lips parted in surprise, Cole felt another flash of heat pass between them for the briefest moment. Just a moment, but long enough for him to glimpse a vision of her beneath him, her moan of pleasure, her long legs tangled with his—and then she composed her face into that damned serene expression she'd obviously developed for the cameras long ago and the image was gone.

"You really do have the most awful ego, Cole." She shook her head in wonder and the action spilled her dark hair around her bare shoulders in a fluid drape.

Although he had a sudden urge to reach out and touch that silky mass of hair, he managed to dredge up a laid-back smile, the one he used when he told one of his subcontractors that their bid was out of line with reality. "Thank you. One of my many strong suits, I assure you."

She was smiling, but as her chin tipped up again in defiance, he realized just how much he was enjoying their sparring. He was still anticipating her return volley when the doorbell chimed with a sad, mournful *clunk*. He put the doorbell on his mental list of projects and reached for the crystal knob.

"The next man must be here," he said, smiling. "I'll get it."

"Don't you dare!" She swept down on him, grabbing his hand where it was wrapped around the doorknob.

And then she froze right there, practically holding his hand. Searing heat bulleted up his arm as he breathed deeply of the sweet scent of her, but he, too, seemed incapable of movement.

Finally, after what seemed like a hundred years of silence stretched out between them, he managed to rally his vocal chords. "Lauren," he said, "let me be a gentleman."

"You, Mr. Travis," she said as she let go, "are no gentleman." She was smiling again, but he saw her eyes burning with the same fire that continued to rage inside him.

With a Herculean effort, he turned away from her, opened the door—and saw a nervous, pimpled teenager, his baseball cap turned backward, his baggy jeans hanging low on his hips.

Cole smiled widely. "Good afternoon," he said, relief filling him at the certainty that he was one step closer to the job. He turned to Lauren. "I believe your next applicant is here." Then he leaned toward her and said in a whisper, "And I think it's going to be okay to leave you alone with this one."

By the time the sun had begun to hang low in the mottled-orange western sky, Lauren was at the end of her rope. And it had been a surprisingly short trip.

She stood up and showed her final applicant to the door. "Thank you for coming by," she said as she shook yet another teenage boy's slim, soft hand.

"Thank you, Miz Simpson," and his voice was so uneven she thought it must've changed just last week.

As the eminently unqualified boy walked down the

driveway, she saw Cole working on shoring up the ramshackle barn doors in the dim light of dusk. Her pulse sped up as he turned around, and gave her a half smile that had "why on earth are you making this so hard?" written all over it.

Why, indeed, she thought to herself as she watched Cole turn and lift one of the huge doors off its hinges and carry it inside the barn. The references he'd slipped under her door before he'd left the previous night had checked out beautifully. The four people she'd called had been so rhapsodic in their praise, she'd thought perhaps he'd written their scripts himself. But even if that were so, she'd already seen what he could do. He was a good worker, and he was fast. At the rate he was going, he could have the barn and the house fixed up in plenty of time for her grand opening, then he'd fire up his beater of a truck, scoot out of town and her life would return to normal.

Or at least what she imagined was normal, she thought as she turned to go back into the house. After all, she was only just starting to get her life back together after her highly publicized breakup with Miles Landon, the man who'd finally broken her Jerk-O-Meter—not to mention her heart—with his betrayal.

Lauren sat down on the antique sofa she'd bought for a song at a tag sale in Maine and pulled her legs up beneath her. The broken heart was her own fault, of course. Growing up as she had, she'd always been wary of close relationships, but when she'd met Miles, the lure of his personality and magnetism had been undeniable. Like an idiot, she'd let her guard down and taken the chance. And then, predictably, it had all gone to hell.

Miles was a Rock Star—with a capital *R* and a capital

S—and even though he'd been on the road or in the studio much of the time, she'd thought they'd loved each other. Then, two hundred and twenty-two days ago, while standing in line at the grocery store, Lauren had read all about Miles's infidelity in *People.* She'd found out in a glossy, two-page spread that Miles, who was supposed to be recording in London, was living right there in Hollywood with a wispy, redheaded A-list actress.

That was Day One of Lauren's yearlong sabbatical from men. Three hundred and sixty-five days of no distractions, of peace and quiet to spend with her son, building a new life and a thriving business.

Lauren straightened and gazed out at her front yard that lay beyond the living room's ancient leaded glass windows. Where in heaven's name had her control gone? Where was that familiar, dependable control that had practically been her shadow since she was about Jem's age, living a chaotic life in home number five with that hardhearted alcoholic couple? Her experience with them had been awful, but it had taught her to be pleasant, even-tempered and totally in control, no matter what life threw at her.

Don't get too close and don't rely on anyone. Those were her rules. Unfortunately, she'd broken them not only for Miles, but also for a few other handpicked jokers—and she'd lived to regret it. Oh, they'd all seemed normal at first but each and every one had turned out to be jerks or philanderers, and one had been struggling with his sexual identity. When she was twenty, it was a photographer; at twenty-one, she'd taken a chance on a much older magazine editor; at twenty-three, it'd been a fashion designer and a professional baseball player; then, at twenty-five, the coup de grâce, Miles.

And now there was Cole Travis. She had to hire him, even though when he smiled at her, or argued with her, or basically stood within ten feet of her, she felt so damned powerless she wanted to run into the streets screaming. He was a man who threatened everything she'd worked so hard to reconstruct—and he was a man who was leaving in six weeks, she reminded herself sternly, and she'd best remember that every time she got her priorities mixed up.

It was time to get some real advice, she thought as she grabbed her car keys, got in her enormous, brand-new SUV and drove to pick Jem up from his playgroup at the Bouchard's house a few blocks away.

As she strapped the seat belt over him, she asked, "You want to go check the sign with me before we go home, honey?"

"Yeah!" he said, clapping his hands.

She smiled and tousled his unruly mop of hair. Never in her life had anyone supported her eccentricities the way her son did. And this quirk of hers, in particular, was a pretty hard one to swallow.

Lauren looked for signs. Not the mystical, "Ooh, I think that's a sign!" kind of sign, but actual, real signs that bore messages for the masses. In the course of her life, she'd found them at shopping malls, car dealerships, churches, restaurants, high schools and civic centers. Sometimes they were old-fashioned signs that were changed manually by a human being and sometimes they were electronic signs that were changed every day—which made things so much easier because some of the most important decisions in her life had been resolved by signs.

In fact, the reason she'd known that they had to settle in Valle Verde was that the local ice-cream shop, the

Frosty King, had a nice, old-style sign. And the first day they'd driven into town, it had had a message that read, *Put Down UR Baggage. Home Is Just Where U R.* Underneath it had said, *Double Dips, 99 Cents,* and she and Jem had taken advantage of both pieces of advice. And when they were done with their ice cream, they'd driven straight to the real estate office.

"Can I have a Rainbow Bar, Mom?"

Lauren signaled and made a left turn onto the main street. "You haven't even eaten dinner yet, mister." She looked over at his crestfallen expression and chuckled. *What an actor.*

As they approached the Frosty King, the familiar fluttering in her stomach revved up. When she went to look for a sign, she usually knew what she wanted it to say. But today, she had no idea. She told herself she wanted it to say, *Don't Give Up,* but deep down in her bones she knew it was more like, *The Answer Is Right Under UR Nose.*

Suddenly the sign came into view and her heart sank and soared simultaneously at its advice. *Don't Waste UR Energy,* it read. *Take The Path Of Least Resistance.*

She stopped the car on the road's graveled shoulder and gripped the steering wheel so tightly she thought it would snap in two. Was Cole Travis the path of least resistance?

Jem peered out the windshield, then looked over at her for an explanation. "What's it say, Mommy?"

"It says," she answered, her eyes still fixed on the huge red-and-white sign, "that we have found our handyman."

As she prepared dinner that night, Lauren sighed and sliced the three-inch high lump she'd baked in her new bread machine. She was still trying to expand her very small cooking repertoire and the loaf was a bit flat, but she'd improve. The sign had said as much a few weeks back when she was deciding whether to hire a full-time housekeeper. *Do It URself,* it had said. *Pride Is In The Accomplishment.*

She smiled as she threw the bread in a basket, then called Jem and her future handyman—who she'd asked to stay for dinner—to come inside. In five minutes, the three of them were gathered around her big, nineteenth-century farmhouse table.

Cole had changed into a clean denim shirt and his collar lay open at the neck, revealing only some of the dark-golden curls that lay beneath it. She tore her gaze away but not before her pulse had kicked up to a hot, salsa rhythm. What was it about this guy? she thought as she continued to fill her son's plate and her own. A denim shirt and a peek at his chest hair was all it took to raise her blood pressure? *Get a grip, Lauren.*

As they passed the food around and Jem chattered away, she noticed that Cole asked questions and answered them in language her son could understand— something Miles had never quite mastered—and she wondered with a sudden flash of concern if her son might grow attached to Cole. Jem hadn't mentioned Miles in ages, so maybe not, but she added it to her growing list of things to worry about anyway. She'd just have to make sure that attachment didn't happen. And she'd start by making sure she didn't get too close to Cole herself even though just having the man at her dinner table was making her feel melty in all the wrong places.

Cole hefted a forkful of the very tasty but very lumpy potatoes and, as he chewed, thought about how much his mother would love to pass on a few bits of potato lore to Lauren. But that wouldn't happen because his mother was never going to meet Lauren, he reminded himself. And he'd do well to remember that before he complicated this thing further.

The dinner passed quickly in a buzz of companionable chatter, mostly stemming from Jem. Cole was amazed by how the smallest things in Jem's day—catching a pollywog, finding a really nice stick to hit rocks with, rolling lemons from their tree down the street—took on a mythic quality in the boy's retelling.

But as the narration went on, Cole couldn't help but reflect on his own life—and what might have been if Kelly hadn't left him one rainy Seattle morning with nothing but an envelope full of divorce papers to show for their marriage. If things had been different, he thought as the familiar tension tightened inside him, perhaps they, too, could have brought up a child like this.

The possibility that Jem might be his son overwhelmed Cole for a moment but he snapped out of it quickly when the boy's face lit up in rediscovery of something that he'd forgotten.

"I found a snail shell by that big tree!" He fixed his excited gaze on Cole. "Wanna see it?"

"Sure I would," Cole said as he laid his napkin beside his plate.

Lauren reached over and touched her son's arm and her hair, that silky curtain that kept tempting Cole to bury his hands in it, swept forward over her cheek. "Why don't you bring it downstairs in a few minutes, honey. Cole and I have something to discuss."

"'Kay," he said, slipping out of his chair and running up the stairs.

When Cole followed her to the living room, Lauren sat down where she had earlier when she'd interviewed the Brothers Grim, so Cole took a seat on the fancy old couch across from her. His curiosity about what she wanted to discuss pricked at his mind, but an alarming amount of his concentration was caught up with the sinful way her low-slung jeans hugged her curves.

Lauren twisted her slender hands together before folding them in her lap. "I'd like to hire you," she said in a rush of breath.

The ever-present spring inside him relaxed a bit and a wide grin spread across his face. "No!" he said with mock surprise. "And with so many other qualified candidates?"

She delivered a quelling look, then spoke again. "In addition to the work on the house, the barn must be completely renovated in six weeks, with the fixtures built, display cases installed and security system operational. If I don't open at the start of the Summer Festival, I'll miss the biggest influx of tourists for the entire year." She looked up at him, a tentative smile peeking through her mask of worry. "I'd like for you to take the job, Cole. You're very talented."

He almost said, "I'd like to show you just how talented I am," but instead dipped his chin to hide a smile and waited patiently for the "but" he could hear in her voice.

Her expression took on an earnest hue before she said, "Cole, I need to know right now if you can commit to completing this job. From the little you've told me about yourself, it seems that you are the type of man who may wake up one day and, for whatever reason, decide to take off."

Even though there was no way she could know who

he really was, the idea that he, Cole Travis, the Rock of Gibraltar, was having his level of commitment questioned made him more than a little crazy. An awful bitterness he'd thought long since rested in peace began to smolder within him. But since nothing of his current situation was her fault, he buried it and answered her civilly. "Nothing could stop me from completing this job," he said. "I promise you."

Her face creased into a sudden, brilliant smile. "Good. Thank you." She sounded relieved, which made him almost feel bad about what he wasn't telling her about himself. And what he still had to say.

"Now." He leaned forward and planted his forearms on his thighs. "About room and board."

As he'd expected, her smile faded to a faint shadow. What he hadn't expected was the slight but unmistakable blush that rushed in to stain her smooth cheeks. "Room and board?" she repeated weakly.

"The hotel I stayed in last night is the closest one I can afford. And it's forty miles of winding country road from here. I'll be able to start earlier and finish later if I stay here. I'd be willing to take something off my pay, of course, since you'll be cooking for me."

Her lips parted as surprise touched every feature on her beautiful face. "You *did* taste my cooking tonight, didn't you?"

He tore his gaze from her sweet, bow-shaped mouth, nodded soberly and went on. "I worked out a simple plan while I was in the barn today. I'll need to use a bathroom in the house for a week or so while I build your customer washroom, but I can fix up the loft as a bedroom right away."

She kept trying to get a word in, making her look like a cute little guppy.

"Don't you have a wife at home who might object to this plan?"

He shook his head. "No wife."

"And you want to sleep in my *barn*." It was a statement, but she sounded as if she'd run out of arguments.

Even though he shrugged like he didn't care one way or the other, the truth was he suddenly realized it felt like his whole life was hinging on this one conversation. "Only if you want me to finish this job on time."

Her eyes narrowed. "That sounds like blackmail."

"I call it practical," he said, shrugging with a nonchalance he didn't feel. "But it's your choice."

She looked around the room, from the cracked floorboards to the broken newel post to the fading paint. He tried not to feel satisfaction in the fact that she really had no choice at all. Finally, she looked at him and said, "Okay," infusing her voice with none of the word's meaning. "You can sleep in the barn." Then she rose fluidly from the chair, held out a hand and smiled at him unsteadily.

He grinned, came to his feet and wrapped his big palm around her warm fingers. "Congratulations, you just hired the best pair of hands west of the Mississippi."

She rolled her eyes at his cocksure statement. "Prove it, Cole. Just prove it."

His gaze roamed her face, from her famous green eyes down to her famous full lips, and couldn't help himself. "Oh, I will," he promised and wondered how long he was going to be able to keep his secret from Lauren—or keep the best pair of hands west of the Mississippi off the most beautiful woman on the planet.

Three

Lauren sat at her kitchen table, balancing the phone between her shoulder and ear as she stifled a yawn and fiddled with her cup of cooled coffee. Her friend and former agent, Sherry Buchanan, was going into hyper-drive as she told Lauren about the sheer hell that her retirement was putting the Boudoir Lingerie folks through.

Truth be told, Lauren couldn't have cared less. They'd had her dangling on a string since she was eighteen, standing around in her underwear in bizarre locations, working fifteen-hour days and waking up in the dark for indecently early calls that had made it almost impossible to care for her child. She'd earned a lot of money working as Boudoir's lead model—enough to sustain her and Jem for a lifetime if she was careful. But she'd done her share by being part of the reason that the catalog could now call itself one of the world's premiere fashion outlets.

"I told them I'd ask, sweetie," Sherry was saying over the Monday-morning din of her busy office. "Would you please come back just for the fall season?"

As a cool morning breeze floated in the kitchen window, bringing with it the clean, country scents of the summer morning, Lauren laughed. She wasn't leaving this small-town paradise for the fall season—or any other season, for that matter. "Jem is loving it here, Sherry. And if you remember, one of the reasons I quit was Boudoir's habit of making motherhood about as convenient as being an international spy."

The older woman laughed, making Lauren smile. When Lauren had run away at sixteen, Sherry—who at the time already had two grown children—had discovered her in a shopping mall talent search. And since then, she'd been more of a mother to Lauren than anyone else ever had.

"Okay, honey," Sherry said. "I'll tell them you considered it very carefully and that you decline." The sound of Sherry shuffling through the heaps of headshots on her desk rustled through the phone before she asked, "Hey, how's your handyman search going?"

Lauren stared down into the inky-brown liquid in her cup and remembered how Cole had looked last night sitting on her antique settee. With his natural handsomeness and well-muscled frame, he should've looked silly there amongst the faded cabbage roses and ornate woodwork. But he hadn't looked silly at all. He'd been as cool as could be, like he'd spent many an evening chatting in a fancy old parlor.

She pushed the vision out of her mind. "I'll tell you about it if you stop working and shut your door for two minutes.'' She kept her tone deliberately mysterious to tempt her workaholic friend into taking a break.

The rustling stopped abruptly, and then Lauren heard the sound of a door shutting noisily. Sherry, who was a closet devotee of romance novels, sounded breathless when she said, ''Do tell.''

Lauren frowned. How could she describe Cole? Gorgeous, charming, good with kids, a drifter? ''Well, you'd love him. If he was a model instead of a handyman, you'd have his headshot on your wall in nothing flat. And if he was a few years older, I'm sure you'd be working overtime to get him into your bed.''

''Oh, *really?* Is he available?''

Lauren realized in that moment that she had no idea if he was available, or even why he'd landed in Valle Verde. The last thing she needed was to get all chummy and personal with him.

''I don't know if he's available, Sher. Sounds like he moves around a lot,'' she said as she stood and walked across the kitchen and the cool, hard floor under her feet sent a shiver up her bare legs. ''I guess he's available if you don't mind being a camp follower. Or getting your heart broken.''

''Uh-oh.''

''What?''

''Nothing. I just thought I heard the distinct sound of you emerging from your post-Miles cocoon ahead of schedule.''

Lauren almost dropped her cup. ''What on earth are you talking about?''

''I'm saying that it's high time you ditched your silly rule about avoiding men. And it sounds like your handyman might be just the one to help you celebrate its demise.''

"Not a chance." *And I'll just keep repeating that mantra every time I see him and those seductive blue eyes of his.*

Sherry just laughed. "All right, all right. Have it your way." She paused for a moment. "And if you *do* have it your way, don't spare me the details."

Lauren laughed. "I miss you, you crazy old broad."

"Right back atcha, sweetie. Tell Jem his Grandma Sherry misses our Sunday dinners and that I can't wait to see him. And you, get to work on that handyman!"

"I have no intention of working on my handyman— Hello? Hello?" she said before she realized she was talking to dead air. Shaking her head, she walked to the opposite wall to hang up the phone, then stopped in her tracks. Her heart skipped a few beats, then picked up where it left off in triple time as she stared in utter dismay at her worst nightmare: Cole, standing in the living room not ten feet away from the kitchen door, his big, callused hands easing a pane of glass from her beautiful, rattling old windows. He stopped what he was doing long enough to turn and smile at her, his eyes sparkling with amusement.

Lauren's mind pumped feverishly as she tried to recall exactly what she'd just said. "How long have you been standing there, Cole?"

His smile grew wide. "A long, long time."

She felt a furious blush rush straight up to the roots of her hair. *Dammit.* "That was my agent…I mean, my friend on the phone," she said, flustered, struggling to find a way to get the hell out of this gracefully. *Dammit, dammit.*

"Agent? Oh, that's right, you're a model," he said, as he returned to his task, placing the loosened panes on a cloth he'd laid at the base of the window. "Didn't I read somewhere that you'd retired?"

Lauren stared at his back, dumfounded. Until that moment, she hadn't been sure he knew who she was. And now, even though most of the western world knew what she looked like in her underwear, the knowledge that *he did* made her feel strangely exposed—naked even though she was fully clothed. She crossed her arms over her chest guardedly before saying, "Somehow, I can't imagine you reading the tabloids, Cole, but those are the only publications I can think of that report such useless trivia."

He turned around, one brow arched. "I believe I read that in the *Wall Street Journal,* actually. The reporter seemed to think your retirement might affect the stock price of Boudoir's parent company."

She'd read that load of tripe, too. "In a year," she said with a shrug, "no one will remember my name, I assure you."

"Your name, maybe. But *you* I think they'll remember." As he spoke, his gaze never strayed from her face for a second.

The intensity in his blue topaz eyes sent a wild tribal dance into full swing in her stomach, but she couldn't seem to look away. The good news was that his attention had been effectively diverted from the phone conversation during which she was horrifyingly sure she'd said something about "working on her handyman." The bad news was she was beginning to think that something about her handyman was working on her.

Finally she mustered herself and blurted out, "Don't you have a barn to repair or a toilet to install?"

He grinned at her. "I just went on a break."

Exasperated, she looked at her watch. "At ten in the morning?"

"Yep," he said, laughing, then he dragged a hand through his ruffled hair, leaned up against the dark wood of the mantel and crossed his arms. "So, about your retirement…"

Lauren watched each of his movements slide gracefully into the next and felt oddly lost—and more than a little confused by the way this man was beginning to turn her inside out.

She knew she should just turn around and leave, but as usual, her damn stubbornness wouldn't let her walk away. "All right, yes, I'm retired."

"You seem a bit young for retirement," he said. "What made you decide to do it now?"

Even as she wondered why he'd care, she knew this information was nothing he couldn't find out if he really wanted to know. So, like so many times during her career, she went into press release mode. Only the best part about this press release was that the information was one hundred percent true. "I wanted to spend more time with my son. He'll be five years old in August and he'll start school in September. It just happens to also be the perfect time and place to start the business I've always dreamed of."

"Antiques?"

She nodded, smiling. "I've always loved antiques."

"A symptom of your privileged childhood?"

Just like that, she felt the smile drain from her face, only to be replaced by a chilly sensation that made her rub her arms for warmth. Apparently, he *had* been reading the tabloids, only he couldn't know her real history, since she and Sherry had made up a fictitious background for her long ago. "Loving parents," the story went. "Professionals, old-blood New England, killed in a tragic accident that left her alone in the world, ready to make her way." If he only knew…

Suddenly, Lauren realized she would be crazy to reveal any grisly details to this man, now or any other time. So she put on her best "I'm the boss" smile and said, "I think break time's over, Cole. For both of us."

And then she did walk away.

Cole plunked down his tray laden with a chili dog, French fries and jumbo Blue Raspberry Sir Slushy and slid into the booth. He looked across the bright red Frosty King table at Jem and smiled. Cole enjoyed the boy's intelligence and enthusiasm more than he could have imagined and, much to his discomfort, he enjoyed exactly the same traits in the boy's mother, too.

He stared down into the murky, turquoise depths of his slushy, then looked up into Lauren's sexy, tilty, tempting green eyes. He swallowed hard and poured on a smile he hoped wouldn't betray his thoughts. "Looks good. By the way, do you think it's possible to have a heart attack at thirty-two?"

The carefree warmth of her laugh rippled over him. He realized it was the first one he'd heard from her, aside from when she'd been talking on the phone that morning. He smiled again, though whether at the memory of what he'd heard her say during that conversation or in response to her honeyed laughter, he didn't know.

"Hey, thanks for the invite tonight. After this morning, I thought I might be sharing a brown paper bag dinner with the moths and june bugs on the porch swing."

She flushed a bit but quickly waved it off. "It was Jem's doing." She put an arm around her son. "This is

Monday and on Monday night Jem gets to choose what's for dinner.'' She looked down at her son's chili-smeared face. He smiled back at her and pure bliss radiated from his grin. "It's never much of a mystery what he's going to choose," she said as her son snuggled up against her, leaving a big streak of chili down the side of her T-shirt.

"Hey," Cole said, pointing to the stain. "You got a…"

Lauren glanced down at it, then shrugged and picked up her burger. "Comes with the territory," she said, tipping her head toward her son.

Cole realized as he sat there in the middle of this small-town burger joint that Lauren looked both strangely out of place and exactly where she should be. Tall, exotic and beautiful, every eye in the place was on her and yet she was totally unaffected and completely natural. In fact, she seemed almost entirely unaware that there was a world beyond their table.

And there most definitely was—a world populated, he noticed with irritation, with men who were very aware of Lauren. Cole looked across the table and knew that any man who had eyes would be gawking, too. She looked so incredible it made something inside him ache, even in her tan overall shorts, clunky wooden-soled clogs, a light-bluish T-shirt—now with a sticky, dark smudge on it—and very little makeup. He tried not to, but he took great satisfaction in the fact that she was sitting with *him*.

Lauren glanced at Cole's food, then looked back up at him. "Do you want something else?"

"No, no. This is great." And to demonstrate, he picked up the chili dog and attacked it with enthusiasm. If he had a heart attack, so be it. He'd go out happy, with ketchup on his fingers and French fries on his mind.

Laughing, she said, "It's your funeral."

As he took another bite, she picked up a fry with her long, graceful fingers and dabbed it in a circle of ketchup. When she looked up at him with a conspiratorial smile before joyfully devouring the fry, he found his desire to end the mystery that had transformed his life warring with a new and unwelcome glimmer of guilt.

"I thought models only ate food suitable for Peter Rabbit's lunch box," he said, trying to distract himself from the million unanswered questions rattling around in his mind like so many noisy marbles. "They're going to drum you out of the ranks," he said, gesturing to the two thousand-calorie meal she was working on.

She smiled with her dripping cheeseburger halfway to that enticing mouth of hers. "I gratefully accept the discharge." Then she took a big bite and closed her eyes in sheer delight.

He chuckled at her theatrics. "I'm guessing you didn't get to eat a lot of cheeseburgers while you were working?"

"Nary a one," she said, grinning. "It was not exactly the glamorous life it's made out to be." She devoured three French fries at once, then took a sip of her extra-large chocolate shake. "You can't believe some of the things I did to get junk food," she began. "One time…"

With sparkling eyes and plenty of embarrassed laughter, she told him a story about sneaking pizzas onto a photo shoot when she was still a teenager. As she mimicked the shoot's stylist who berated her for trying to sabotage the other models' perpetual diets, Cole realized that she was charming him, damn her, and that she was beginning to infect his normally pessimistic view of the world with her pure energy.

"Anyway, we should talk about what still has to be done to get ready for the opening," she said, interrupting his thoughts.

As he watched, she slipped the red straw between her lips and sucked down her shake. He felt his jeans grow snug and he shifted uncomfortably in his seat.

Why didn't they turn on the air-conditioning in this restaurant? he thought, taking a deep, fortifying breath to get his mind back in the game. "Well, since you're already zoned to turn your residential unit into a commercial unit, as I see it, all I have to do is get the permits, then gut the barn, construct interior walls, wire it, plumb it, install heating and air and security systems, insulate it, lay flooring, finish the carpentry and the walls and paint the whole thing." He held another fry aloft as he said, "That sound about right?"

Her brow wrinkled as she tipped her chin down slightly and looked up at him with those eyes that could trap a man's soul. "I hope I'm not setting an unrealistic timeline, Cole. Do you think all that can be done?"

Her voice was so sincere and hopeful, he felt like a jerk for giving in—even for a second—to his attraction to her. *Get it together, Travis. You're not some fan with a crush. You have a purpose here.*

"With a charge account at the hardware store and my truckload of tools, I think we'll be fine as long as the inspectors don't hold me up," he said and the relieved smile she rewarded him with made him want to do whatever it took to leave her with Simpson's Gems exactly as she'd dreamed of it. After all, when he did leave, he just might be taking something infinitely more important with him. And if he did, he knew he was likely going to feel the weight of her pain for the rest of his life.

"I've sketched out what I want the interior to look like. I'm not an artist, so no laughing," she warned as she pulled several crisply folded pages out of her overalls and handed them to him. "Hopefully, it's enough to give you the idea. I want Simpson's Gems to be sort of homey and comfortable, not tacky or craft-showy."

Cole pulled his gaze from hers and flipped through the pages neatly crammed with notes and freehand drawings. The drawings were good and they helped him form a mental picture of the store's interior, as well as the permits and supplies he'd need.

When he was done, he folded the pages up and put them in his shirt pocket, then looked over at Jem. "If it's okay with your mom, I can think of a few things you can pitch in on, if you want."

Jem's face lit up, and Cole felt a stinging in his chest when he thought how he himself probably looked much the same when he was a boy and wanted to help his father. Nothing had made him feel closer to his dad than the simple act of holding a two-by-four while his father sawed it into lengths. They'd had some of the best talks of their lives while working together like that. Maybe, just maybe, it would be the same for him and his own son someday.

"Can I, Mom?" the boy asked, turning his appeal to Lauren.

Not surprisingly, she resorted to the famous and time-honored motherly term, "We'll see," but the boy's enthusiasm dimmed only a little, so perhaps "we'll see" usually turned out to mean "yes" around the Simpson house.

"I know you'll be busy getting ready for the opening, but I'll probably need your help from time to time as well," Cole said to Lauren.

"No problem," she said as she wrapped up the remainder of her meal. "I'm at your service." As soon as the words were out of her mouth, she looked up at him, her eyes wide, a pretty stain touching her cheeks.

He smiled even though that damn flame flared up again. "Now that's an offer I wouldn't dream of refusing."

She tried to frown at him, but a slight smile played about her lips. "You know what I meant," she said and reached over to smack him lightly on the arm.

"Yeah," he said, laughing and rubbing his arm where her fingertips had just brushed him. "But I prefer it the way I heard it."

In the way that was now becoming familiar, she rolled her eyes at his nerve, making him smile even as he realized he didn't want anything about her to become familiar.

"So how much work do you still have to do before your opening?" he asked in an effort to steer them back to safer territory.

"I have about fifty crates in the storage shed behind the barn that I need to unpack and inventory. I'm excited to do it—some of this stuff I haven't seen in six years. Then after I unpack it, I'll need to clean up each piece and check the current prices online."

Cole smiled at the enthusiasm in her voice. "Where's your inventory coming from? Are you selling family heirlooms?"

"Hardly."

A certain stiffness in her voice made his head snap up. The passion he'd seen written on her every movement and word moments before had clouded and obscured, making it impossible to understand the meaning behind her simple statement. In spite of himself, he was curious to learn what was really going on behind that very expressive and very beautiful face.

"If I had family heirlooms," she went on, "I'd be happy to sell them. But these are things I've just acquired over the years."

Jem looked up from where he was carefully coloring a picture of Superman with dozens of felt pens. "What's an airwoom?"

"It's something that's handed down from grandparents to parents, and from parents to children," Lauren answered.

Jem seemed to consider this for a moment before he said, "Oh." Then he addressed Cole, his tone matter-of-fact. "Mom doesn't have airwooms. She just has me. And Grandma Sherry." He leveled his gaze on Cole, his expression serious. "And I'm 'dopted. You know what that is?"

Something felt as if it was constricting Cole's throat, like he was wearing a dress shirt that was many sizes too small. "Adopted? I think so, Jem. But maybe you can explain it to me."

"Well," the boy said, returning to his coloring, "my mom and dad couldn't take care of me. Then I got *my* mom. And now I'm Jem Simpson," he finished proudly as his mother leaned down to plant a noisy kiss in his messy curls.

As Cole watched the interplay between Lauren and Jem, the spring inside him twisted tighter and tighter. His voice sounded strange in his own ears when he said, "You were lucky to have found each other, then."

Lauren looked up at him and smiled, her eyes glossy

with a sheen of tears. "Yes, we were." He tamped down another pang of guilt and smiled back at her.

Just then, Jem finished coloring his picture of Superman and handed it to Lauren. She admired it at great length, pointing out things she particularly liked. "Looks like another masterpiece for the refrigerator," she pronounced.

"Oh, Mom," Jem protested, even as he banged his heels against the chair, clearly pleased by her praise. Lauren laughed as she carefully put the drawing into her tote bag.

"Can you catch fish?" Jem asked Cole with that out of the blue subject change thing children did so well.

"Sure can."

"Mom and me fished once," he said, looking at his mother. "'Member?"

With an exaggerated shudder, she nodded, glanced over at Cole and uttered a single tortured word. "Worms."

Jem and Cole looked at one another. Cole shrugged and said, simply, "Girls." Then they laughed together, one the uninhibited giggle of a child, the other a low, deep chuckle of a man.

Lauren tipped her chin up and crossed her arms. "Laugh all you want. Worms are disgusting. I wouldn't touch one again if my life depended on it."

"Maybe we'll all go sometime. I'll bait all the hooks, I promise," Cole said, then instantly wished he could take the offer back. After he straightened out this mess he would probably never see Lauren Simpson again. Besides, if just a few months ago, someone had told him he'd be sitting in a dive called the Frosty King in the backcountry of San Diego, drinking a Sir Slushy and promising to go fishing with a beautiful woman and her son, he'd have told them to seek help.

"I got sinkers in my box," Jem said, his voice full of anticipation for the future fishing trip. "Someone dropped 'em by the creek…" The rest of his words were lost as he began digging furiously in his backpack.

Cole caught Lauren's eye and raised his eyebrows in question.

"Jem likes to keep all his most important things with him," she said, smiling. "He used to keep them all in his pockets, which was pretty hard on the washing machine." Jem emerged from his search with a small wooden cigar box. "Now he keeps them all in his box." She shrugged. "I guess I've taught him a few bad habits." She ruffled his hair and called him a packrat in a very fond voice as he opened the box like it held the Holy Grail.

He pulled out one thing after another and told Cole the origin of it, then reverently put it back in the box. Cole saw a parade of nuts and bolts, string, shells, marbles, rocks, nails, baseball cards, plastic frogs, buttons and pens before Jem finally lifted out a thin bracelet made of turquoise and amber beads.

Cole froze. He held his breath as the bracelet dangled from the boy's small hand. A little oval charm hung from it, with the inscribed initials "K.T." still clearly visible. "When my old mom and dad left, they forgot this."

Somewhere, deep in the haze of Cole's mind, he heard the unemotional tone of Jem's voice. Cole struggled to keep an interested and cheerful expression on his face even as the spring within him tightened beyond endurance, then snapped, leaving behind a horrible pain, anger and sadness to find a place to dwell inside him as best it could.

There was no mistake. Sitting across the table from him, clutching the bracelet Cole had given Kelly on her twenty-fifth birthday, was his son.

Four

Cole sat in the barn's loft with his head in his hands. Through the open windows, he heard the night sounds all around him—crickets chirping, the wind whistling softly through the trees, the frogs croaking on the banks of the creek that ran behind the barn. The glow from the warehouse light overhead poured a pool of bright white onto the abandoned building plans strewn across the table he'd fashioned out of sawhorses and plywood.

Jem was his son, he thought, staring with unseeing eyes at the pages before him. Just a few hours earlier, he'd watched the boy across the expanse of the Frosty King table and felt as if a giant band were tightening painfully around his chest. Just like in a movie where the noise and hubbub surrounding the actors recedes, there was suddenly only him and Jem—and an overwhelming sense of love and disbelief. He'd wanted to leap across the table and say, "I'm your dad. I didn't leave you. I'll never leave you." But he couldn't.

Thanks to his ex-wife's deception, he'd already missed the first four years of the boy's life. If he didn't want to miss more, he was going to have to watch his step. So instead, with his heart in his throat and bursts of anger at his ex-wife popping like firecrackers in his blood, he'd listened as the boy had discussed the contents of his box.

Jem was his son. And the woman who had been seated next to him, helping him to remember all the details of where he'd found his treasures, was the only mother he'd ever known. The little boy loved Lauren. Cole could see that plainly.

The thought of her banged at his mind mercilessly as he looked at her neat, hand-drawn sketches for the antique store. For the first time since he'd learned that he had a son, he wondered how he would be able to take the boy from the woman who had always been a mother to him. It had simply not occurred to Cole that when he finally found his son, the boy would be living in a happy, loving home with a nurturing mother. And it was both a blessing and a curse, he thought now as he reached into his duffel bag for his cell phone and punched in the speed dial for his attorney and best friend, Doug Sherman.

"Hello?" came the sleepy greeting.

"I found him," Cole said. The words were simple, but it seemed as if he'd had to pry them out of his very soul.

"Well, I'll be damned," a now very awake Doug replied. Then, with caution in his voice, he added, "Are you sure?"

"The proof just fell into my lap tonight," Cole said, then quickly explained about the bracelet.

"I've got to tell you," Doug said as the crackle of him digging into his ever-present pack of Marlboros sounded through the phone, "I thought I knew Kelly pretty well. Hell, I was the best man at your wedding, but I still would never have guessed she'd do something like this."

Cole gripped the phone. "I may never understand it. All I can do is get back what she took from me." He took a deep breath. "You know what, Doug? I almost feel sorry for Kelly. Now that she's…" No matter how angry he was, it was still hard for him to say it. "Now that she's dead, she's never going to see what a great kid he turned out to be."

"I wonder if she even saw him before she ran out of that hospital and left him." Doug paused for a moment. "Wait, I'm practically his uncle and I don't even know his name."

"Jem." Cole could hear the fondness in his own voice. "I can't believe I didn't see it right away, but he looks so much like my dad. Same eyes, same hands," he said, momentarily overcome by the vision of Jem meeting his grandparents.

"So it turned out to be the Boudoir girl?"

Cole brushed aside a sudden pang of annoyance that someone like Lauren would be summed up in such a way. "Lauren Simpson, yes."

"It must be your lucky day. You found your son and one of the most beautiful women in the world—and you have them both under one roof."

"It's not like that," he said quickly, then chuckled in spite of himself. "But damn if I haven't been having that exact same thought."

"Yeah, well, life's tough all over, buddy," Doug said with mock commiseration. "And speaking of which, you might want to kick in a few extra clams to give my investigator a bonus. Since Kelly never told the hospital your name—or her own real name, for that matter—it's amazing he was able to dig up the case."

The smile died on Cole's lips as he looked down at the file with "Simpson" written in bold, black letters. It was just a stroke of luck that Lauren's ad had run the day he'd arrived and that he was the perfect man for the job. More than perfect, in fact. He was probably the only man in the whole county that could get the job done in the amount of time Lauren had left. But still, he thought with a grim smile, he should just be grateful that he hadn't had to get a job at the Tea Garden Nursery or the Frosty King to try to get close to her.

"Well, buddy, congratulations," Doug said. "I'll file the papers tomorrow and give you a long overdue cigar when you get home."

Cole looked out the window and saw lights shining in the upstairs windows of Lauren's house. *Papers. Damn.*

"After we file," his friend continued, "it won't be long before things start to happen."

Yeah, like Lauren would be notified and then she'd not only know who he was, but what he wanted here. His gut tightened. He wasn't going to take the chance that this woman, too, would take off with his child and disappear. She certainly had the means. He wasn't about to give her the motive.

"Hold on a minute," Cole said, then explained his situation and his handyman ploy. "Don't do anything yet, Doug. Give me a few days."

"We really should get started, man. The courts won't

consider a bracelet to be irrefutable evidence. We'll need DNA tests—''

"It's more complicated than that," Cole said, cutting off what he knew was going to be a boring, lawyerly treatise.

There was a long silence at the other end of the phone. "More complicated than DNA tests?"

"Look, Doug, I'm not in control of much in this situation, but I am in control of when she finds out that I'm not just the friggin' handyman."

His friend let out a short laugh. "Hey, I don't blame you for wanting to spend a little time with one of the world's most gorgeous women. I'm envious, truly. But he's your son, Cole."

"Believe me, I get that," he said and could hear the irritation in his own voice. "I just want to give him some time to get to know me before all hell breaks loose."

Cole *was* Jem's father, but Lauren had always been his mother, Cole thought to himself as he looked down at a photo that had fallen from a file folder. It looked like it had been ripped from the pages of *People* magazine and showed Lauren and Jem walking hand in hand on a Southern California beach. "I want to wait on this," he told Doug firmly. "Give me two weeks. Then you can file the papers."

As he hung up, he tucked the photo back into the file right behind the copies of the adoption papers that officially—and supposedly, irrevocably—made Jem Lauren Simpson's son.

Just two weeks, he thought. Already it didn't seem as if it would be long enough to find out everything he'd missed in Jem's life, to spend enough time with the boy so that when the inevitable happened, Cole and

Jem would no longer be strangers to each other. He grabbed the phone to call Doug back when he remembered that he'd also just signed up for fourteen nights of lying up here in his loft, wide awake and thinking about the beautiful woman sleeping just a hundred yards away.

He chucked the phone back into his duffel. How was he going to stay so close to her for so long and still resist this attraction? How was he going to pretend like she hadn't already gotten under his skin? Right now, he wasn't even sure how he would stand two weeks of worrying about how and if he could take Jem away from her. But he'd have to.

He'd just have to focus on the job. He certainly wouldn't be here long enough to remodel the barn into the store that she dreamed of, but he was going to do his damnedest. At the very least, she deserved that in exchange for what a wonderful mother she'd obviously been to his son. Hell, maybe when he got back to Seattle he'd send one of his crews down to finish up the project properly. But even if he built her the Taj Majal, he knew he'd never be able to temper the disaster that he was going to bring to her life. And yet, he simply couldn't see any other way.

Cole drove an angry fist onto the table and the vibration caused his drafting pencil to skitter off one end of the shaky surface. He leaned down to snatch the pencil off the floor, then banged his head on the bottom of the plywood table on the way back up. "Damn!" he roared.

"Cole? You okay?" Lauren called from the bottom of the loft's stairs.

"Damn," he repeated with considerably less volume as he shoved the investigator's files back into his duffel. "It's nothing," he said. "Just got a splinter."

Silence reigned at the bottom of the stairs for a moment, then, "No one hollers like that over a splinter. I'm coming up."

That's all I need, Cole thought, cursing as he kicked his bag under the table. A splinter was nothing compared to having her near—in his bedroom of all places—and knowing she was the most untouchable woman in the world.

As she clumped up the rickety wooden stairs in her noisy clogs, he searched for the finger that had been harpooned by a splinter earlier in the day. By the time she appeared at the top of the steps, his heart was pounding as hard and as loud as a marching band's drum corps, though whether from guilt, frustration or pure animal attraction he couldn't possibly have said.

"Really, it's okay," he told her as he stood up and buried his hand deep into the pocket of his jeans.

She laughed. "Men. Such babies. Let me see that."

As she came toward him with her hair pulled back into a thick ponytail, wearing her inexplicably erotic overalls and a clean white T-shirt that hugged her wicked curves, he actually took a step back. For God's sake, didn't this woman know not to come to a man's room after dark?

Obviously not, he mused as she planted her hands on her hips, showing no sign that she knew the direction of his thoughts. "C'mon," she said, giving him a smile that made him want to give her anything she asked for. "I have a four-year-old child. I'm an expert splinter extractor."

Why did she have to be so nice to him? And right when he was planning to do something so horrible that he wouldn't blame her if she hired a hit man to retaliate? Guilt as thick as tar poured through him as he reluctantly withdrew his hand and showed it to her. She reached out to take his fingertips in hers and the contact with her cool, smooth skin made him pull in a sharp breath.

She glanced up at the sound. "That bad, huh?"

"Not bad at all," he said, his jaw tight with frustration.

Cole nearly groaned as she pinned his arm against her body to keep it still as she examined his hand. Her firm, slightly upturned breasts rested lightly on his arm, driving him crazy and making him feel as if he was being branded by the contact. He was going to be *looking* to get splinters after this, he thought crazily. Then she touched his swollen fingertip gently and he did groan as the heat from their closeness and her touch reached its inevitable boiling point.

She looked up at him, and he noticed her eyes had become deep, fiery pools of emerald. Insistent, indecent thoughts of taking her in his arms and pulling her down onto his bed crowded his mind, making it hard to think rationally. He felt hypnotized, unable to look away as her expression evolved from troubled to sensual—and his own body temperature underwent its own evolution: from hot as a pizza oven to hot as hell itself.

Two weeks, he thought. *Two long weeks.*

Thankfully, at that moment, she dropped his arm as if it had grown too heavy to bear, broke from the clutches of their eye contact and stepped away from him.

"You're right," she said in an odd voice. "It's not that bad." She dipped her hands into the pockets of her short, sexy overalls. "There's a first-aid kit in the kitchen. You can bandage that up in the morning if you want."

Cole watched her fidget as she spoke and knew, suddenly, that she'd felt it, too. That heat, that terrible and tempting desire. *Dammit.* Her initial response to him had been so cool, he'd been counting on her to keep him in check. He looked at his watch. "It's late. Are those fries you stole from me keeping you up?"

She looked confused for a moment, then her gaze jerked up to his and, with her eyes twinkling in renewed amusement, she said, "I'm surprised you noticed, considering you were busy gulping down the rest of my chocolate shake." It was true, so he kept quiet. She smiled in smug victory, then continued. "I really just came up to see if you needed anything." She looked around. "Sheets, pillows?"

Sheets, pillows? Hell, what he needed was her, in his arms, in his bed. "Nope. I excavated one of your beds from your storage shed after dinner. Thanks for the loan," he said as he fished the key to the shed out of his pocket and handed it to her, being careful not to touch. "And I bought sheets today in town." He swept a hand over the newly made bed, its white sheets tucked in, its quilt and matching pillows fluffed.

She glanced at the bed and then looked away quickly, like she was looking into the sun. "Well," she said, her smile dimming the barest fraction, "it looks like you're all set then." She hesitated, as if she wanted to say something else, but after a moment she appeared to dismiss it and said, "Good night, Cole," instead and turned and departed in a blur of thick auburn hair and that clean, citrusy scent that seemed to always cling to her skin.

Yeah, right, he thought. Good night. Try *torturous* night.

He went over to the window and stared down as she

walked across the lawn with that hypnotic feminine sway, her hair dancing with silvery highlights under the pale light of the moon. When she'd almost reached the house, she paused and looked up at her wide front porch. Then, after a long moment, she trotted up the steps and sat down on the porch swing, kicked off her shoes and began to rock back and forth.

Regret sidled in and took up permanent, viruslike residence inside him. He knew that the web of lies he was creating was, without a doubt, going to become more and more tangled. He also knew that he was going to take his son away from here. It was the right thing, the only thing. And yet the lines between what was right and what was wrong were blurring with every minute he spent with Lauren.

Time seemed to slow down as he watched her propel the creaking swing by pushing her feet against the porch's rough boards. He thought about how he'd fixed that swing with his own hands just a few days before. He thought about how it now held Lauren as she sat under the infiniteness of the stars and the night sky and its moonlight. And he thought about the fact that he'd never felt an attraction quite like this before.

And then he thought about how very hard it was going to be to keep his eye on the ball.

What was that?

Lauren's pulse jumped and her body tensed. She lay very still, waiting to see if she'd hear that strange *creak* again. A moment went by. Nothing.

She'd just begun to drift off to sleep after what seemed like hours of lying there thinking about Cole and their disturbing contact in the barn tonight and about how she'd reacted—overreacted, really—to

standing there with him in such close proximity to a
bed. But that mysterious creaking sound from points
unknown had quickly put all thoughts of Cole on the
back burner. She looked at the clock. Half past midnight.

Maybe it was Jem. Maybe he'd gotten up to go to
the bathroom or to get a drink, she thought hopefully,
lifting her head, listening more intently.

But what if it was a prowler? Her throat went dry.
No, she reminded herself, this wasn't L.A. In the two
months she'd lived here, the worst crime she'd heard
about was somebody tipping one of Roger Jenkins's
cows. In fact, it had been so peaceful here that after a
month or so, she'd stopped bothering to lock her doors
most of the time like the rest of the locals.

More than likely, what she'd heard was far worse
than a prowler—it could be *rats*. Please, she begged
silently, don't let it be rats. This poor old house has
been enough trouble already.

Creak! She sat bolt upright in her bed, her gaze dart-
ing from her bedroom door to the window. If it was a
prowler, she could call for Cole. His lights were still
on.

Wait a second, she thought as she threw back the
covers and fought to control her thudding heart. She
didn't need a man to help her. She'd been on her own
for a long, long time. Her first and only job was to
protect her son, and she could damn well take care of
that herself.

She slipped off the bed, her breath shallow, her fortifying pep talk evaporating like mist. Taking care not
to make any noise, she left the room and crept down
the hall. She peeked into Jem's open doorway. He was
there, fine, sleeping soundly. She grabbed his baseball
bat, eased his door closed, then tiptoed down the stairs.

Her heart was beating a feverish tap dance in her chest, but it still managed to pick up speed when a faint light began to glow from the direction of the kitchen. An intruder for sure, she thought—or one very talented rat. She smiled grimly at her own whimsy, then moved silently toward the kitchen with the heavy bat digging into her bare right shoulder.

As she rounded the corner, she peeked into the kitchen. The light she'd seen was coming from the open refrigerator. Gingerly, she took one step inside the kitchen. She squinted and just made out the shadow of someone hunkered down in front of her fridge.

Blood pounded in her ears as she swallowed a lump of bitter fear. What should she do? she thought wildly as she heard the intruder poking through a crisper drawer. While the plastic produce bags crinkled, she envisioned her hungry prowler, half-starved and weakened by fatigue.

She made her decision quickly. Adrenaline whooshed through her as she readjusted her sweaty grip on the bat. Then she approached the fridge, weapon held high. "Move and I'll crack your head open," she said in the most intimidating voice she could muster.

What happened next, happened fast, like she was caught in a tornado. Bologna flew, mayo fell and Lauren squeezed her eyes closed and swung the bat hard. She hit something and a stinging vibration ran straight up to her shoulders. She gasped as an angry voice yelled, "Christ!" and the single word shuddered off the kitchen walls, as out of place in this peaceful after-midnight world as a shout in a library.

The intruder yanked the bat easily from her grasp. She snapped her eyes open as it clattered noisily across the kitchen floor. *This is no rat.* The thought barely registered before her intruder rushed her like a linebacker and ran her up against the edge of the counter, then lifted her up onto it effortlessly.

Then she saw who'd been skulking around her kitchen. And what she saw didn't help her heart slow down one bit.

Cole Travis.

His nose a scant inch from hers, he glared at her with a look she was sure was meant to scorch her right down to her marrow. It almost worked.

"What were you trying to do?" he demanded as he used his hands to bracket her in place on the cold counter. "Knock me unconscious?" He loomed before her like an avenging dark angel. "You're lucky I caught the bat before you cracked my skull open!"

Fear, adrenaline, shock—and a healthy portion of desire and need—united in a crescendo of sensation that was making Lauren's body vibrate. She pulled her head back until it touched the kitchen cabinet and struggled to assemble her scattered thoughts into a rational pattern. Unfortunately, they wouldn't get organized, so she spoke up anyway. "What were *you* thinking, Cole?" She pushed at his bare chest and tried ineffectually to dislodge him from between her knees. "You scared the hell out of me! I thought you were a rat."

She tried to ignore the heat of his breath, the press of his strong body against hers as his muscled—and completely naked—chest contracted under her hands. For a moment she was spellbound by the sight of her own fingers, intertwined with the dark-golden curls sprinkled like glittery dust on his powerful chest. She swallowed thickly and forced her gaze back up to his.

One of his brows arched up and an errant lock of his wheat-colored hair fell down over his eyes. "You brought a baseball bat for a rat?" His gaze swept over her then, from bare shoulder to barely covered thigh and it felt exactly like he was dragging a fingertip over her quivering skin.

"A girl can't be too careful these days," she muttered as frustration and confusion swept through her. "You never know when some half-naked rat's gonna jump on you and pin you against the cabinets in your own kitchen." She tried to shimmy away from him, but the movement only served to intensify the contact of their bodies and send her silk chemise skimming up her thighs.

"Whoa, whoa," he said as he thwarted her feeble attempts at freedom. "You're not going anywhere." His voice was calm, but his expression was clouded, his breathing irregular.

"The hell I'm not," she said as she tried to concentrate. She knew she should put out this spark that was making her respond to him, to his nearness, to his pure male scent. She knew she should be angry that he'd sneaked into her house. Certainly she should be annoyed that he was holding her here on the cold, hard counter against her will. But how anger and arousal got so mixed up inside her, she didn't think she'd ever figure out.

He leaned in closer, too close, and a lazy grin spread over his features. "How do I know I can trust you?" he whispered and the sound of it shivered straight up her spine.

His lips were mere inches from hers, and her double-crossing body was on fire. She instinctively reached out and touched a scar on his chin she hadn't noticed before. "You don't," she whispered. "You can't."

And those were the last words she uttered before their lips met and they came together in a single moment of pure insanity.

Five

Lauren couldn't tell who moved first. All she knew was that by the time their lips touched, her limbs felt warm and soft, like a candle that had been burning far too long. He felt so good, tasted so good. She gave herself over to the sensation, wrapping her arms around his neck and opening her mouth on a quiet sigh, which instantly took the kiss to a new and more dangerous level.

He groaned as he tangled his fingers in her hair, pulling her closer. And even as her mind screamed that this was wrong, stupid, careless and rash, her body pitched and soared. She was suddenly alive, like something inside her had been waiting for this moment to happen.

She arched up against the hard, uncompromising wall of his chest, giving as good as she got. His lips left her mouth and scorched a path of absolute bliss down her neck. But it wasn't until his hand slid over her shoulder and skipped lightly across one aching, tender breast that a shudder of pure desire passed through her that was unlike anything she'd ever felt before.

And then, with a soft but violent curse, he released her and stepped back, raking his hands through his hair. Without even seeing his face, she knew what was in his eyes, what he must be thinking. Because she was thinking it, too.

That wasn't supposed to happen.

She scolded herself as she smoothed down her chemise, crossed her legs, and wrapped her arms around herself in one quick, clumsy movement. But even with the protection of distance between them, she could still feel the velvety warmth of Cole's lips, the hungry urgency of his tongue as it met hers, the whisper of his breath on her neck as he burned a path to the hollow of her throat. *Damn, damn, damn.* She was the biggest fool this side of Foolsville.

Cole backed up farther before he looked at her, but when his gaze finally met hers, she saw that his eyes had darkened almost to the point of blackness.

I did it again, she groaned inwardly as she kept her gaze averted from his naked chest and arms with care. *I made another mistake. And this one was a whopper. Groping in the near darkness of the kitchen with the handyman, for chrissakes.*

But then again, the whole point of the "no men for one year" abstinence program was to take a step back, not live the life of Mother Teresa. So what if she was attracted to Cole Travis? So what if he made her bones melt and her senses take flight? That didn't mean she had to act on it.

To paraphrase another careless, reckless woman, "tomorrow was another day.'' Day two hundred and twenty-four, to be precise.

Lauren was no actress, but she put on her most devil-may-care smile, shrugged casually and said, ''Sorry. That shouldn't have happened. Heat of the moment, I guess.''

But he didn't even crack that lazy smile of his. Instead, the fire in his eyes crackled and burned and she'd be damned if she couldn't almost feel flames lick at her very core.

''I should be apologizing,'' he said finally. ''It was my fault.''

But he didn't look a bit sorry and she had to resist the urge to fan herself with her hand to cool down. Good Lord, no man had ever looked at her like that. Note to self, she thought: Must keep Cole Travis at arm's length if I am going to get through the next six weeks.

She smiled gamely and waved his words away. She had to get the hell out of here. ''Enough mea culpas,'' she said with forced lightness. ''We both just went a little crazy.''

''Just a little?'' he said with a short laugh that had nothing to do with humor.

She shrugged again, but felt the relentless drumming of her heart quicken another dozen beats at his words. ''So, I guess I'll leave you and the bologna alone so you can have your midnight snack,'' she said, sliding off the counter.

He looked down at the sandwich makings as if he'd never seen them before. ''Sorry I…frightened you,'' he said as he straightened and gave her a look that made her shiver in remembrance. ''If you promise to start locking your doors, I'll promise to keep my midnight cravings under control.''

She wanted to tell him not to, to tell him that if his midnight craving was ever for her, come on in. But instead she simply said good-night and hightailed it out of there while she still had the threads of her resolve in her grasp. And all the while, she could feel his hot gaze stroking her retreating, cowardly back.

As Lauren headed upstairs, she considered giving herself a lecture, but she lacked the energy. She'd been swept away, that was all, floating on a wave of desire powerful enough to drown her. She was just going to have to work harder to stay as far away from him as possible. They'd have meals together and they'd work together when it was necessary. There was no reason for anything more.

As she gratefully slipped beneath her cool sheets, she thought about the dream fairies she'd made up to help Jem fall asleep. And just to be on the safe side, when she flipped off her bedside lamp, she sent the fairies a quick wish for dreams about anything but her handyman.

Cole pounded nail after nail into the boards that were forming the interior walls of the barn, his mind blissfully numbed by the activity.

Thwack, thwack.

The busier he stayed, the better off he'd be. Even though it was only eight o'clock in the morning, sweat was already dripping down his face and trickling down his back. He wiped at the salty drops on his forehead with the back of his hand, then set another galvanized nail and drew back his hammer.

Thwack, thwack, thwack.

After what happened last night, numbing his mind
with work was his only hope at sanity. He certainly
wasn't going to gain any control over his three-alarm-
fire libido with Lauren Simpson moseying around looking like she'd just walked off a page of that stupid catalog. He frowned as he laid another crossbeam in place
and set the nail.

Thwack, thwack, thwack.

In his present state of mind, it didn't even seem to
matter if, like today, she was wearing khaki shorts and
a T-shirt or if she was wearing something that could
short circuit him like that, that…*scrap* of fabric she was
wearing last night. It was all driving him nuts.

Really, what the hell was he supposed to do when
she attacked him in the kitchen at midnight with ninety-
nine percent of her soft, cool skin exposed and the rest
covered in thin, smooth, pink polka dot silk? he thought
darkly as he pulled out another nail and prepared to
annihilate it.

Thwack, thwack—damn!

Excruciating pain made him drop the hammer with a
loud *thunk* as vibrant stars of agony danced wickedly
in his vision for a moment. He gripped the throbbing
thumb that he'd just hit with a hammer that was going
fifty miles an hour and waited impatiently for the ache
to pass.

The last time he'd hit his thumb with a hammer, he'd
been a green sixteen-year-old day laborer. He sat down
on a stack of lumber and surveyed the damage to his
hand. Lauren Simpson seemed to be able to do something to him that no woman had ever done—she made
him feel clumsy and confused—as if he was that teenage boy again.

The worst part, of course, was that he was as responsible as she was for what had happened last night. Perhaps even more so. After all, he was the only one who knew what was at stake here.

But he hadn't been able to help himself. Her soft, sweet lips moving against his had been pure sin. Teasing, giving, taking. And her response had made him think she was as warm and willing as he was.

Then, when he'd pulled away, she'd waved it off as if it was some amusing bit of fun, nothing to be worried about, nothing to try to explain. But even so, there'd been something about her indifference he didn't quite buy.

He dragged a hand across his forehead, then stood up and got back to work. No matter how blasé she was, what happened last night had certainly meant something to him. It meant he was going to have to stay far, far away from her. It would only confuse matters if the sparks from last night were fanned to life. Hell, if either one of them so much as whispered near those sparks, they'd probably start an inferno neither of them was prepared to extinguish.

Cole turned his head to catch a cool wind that flowed through the open barn doors, carrying with it the familiar scents of sawdust and freshly milled wood. He closed his eyes, pulled in a deep breath and reminded himself once again why he was here.

His son.

And with the image of Jem fixed firmly in his mind, he picked another board out of the pile, checked it for straightness, then set it up to become a part of the framework of Simpson's Gems.

The sun was setting slowly, like a pat of butter melting in a frying pan. And after a long day of work and worry, Lauren welcomed the early-evening breeze that came with the sunset as she labored to fire up her new barbecue.

Labor *was* the word for it, she thought as she wiped at her brow, because despite her very best efforts, the barbecue refused to fire up. On a frustrated sigh, she restacked her tumble of charcoal briquettes into a pyramid that would make an Egyptian proud, hosed the structure down liberally with lighter fluid, then held out a long fireplace match with a shaky hand.

Flames shot up out of the kettle-shaped barbecue like a flambéed Cherries Jubilee, making Lauren jump away and yelp as she smacked into something very hard. And that something, she realized with a glance over her shoulder and a quickening of her pulse, was a worried-looking Cole.

"We've got to stop meeting like this," he said with a frown as she spun around in the arms that had instinctively rushed to steady her moments before.

She tipped her head back to look at him, squinting against the orange-red frame of the setting sun that haloed him. "Well, at least I got it started."

"And almost everything else within twenty feet." He reached down and gently dragged a thumb across her forehead. "Charcoal smudge," he said and showed her his blackened thumb to prove it. "Would you like some help?"

Lauren stamped out a tiny, insurgent voice that said, *Yes, please,* and shook her head. "No, thanks. I can do it." She backed out of his arms and began to search for the long fork that she could use to poke at the briquettes. It was here a second ago, she thought. "What did I do with—"

"This?" he asked with a grin, pulling her prized

1950s-era Danish Modern barbecue tools out from behind his back. "Call me old-fashioned, but where I come from, the barbecue is man's territory." Then, without her blessing, he proceeded to expertly arrange the now barely smoldering charcoal, tipped a match to it, and leaned down to blow on it until it caught.

Carpentry, drafting, kissing and now barbecuing. Did the man have to be good at everything? But still, she mused, watching him appreciatively as he leaned down to blow on the fire, she had to admit she liked having him around. If for nothing else, just to enjoy the view, she thought as she took in the plain white T-shirt stretched tight over his David-esque shoulders and his worn jeans doing something similar to his bum, making his backside look as if it was carved from a single piece of marble.

She sighed at what a flop she was at keeping her resolutions in place. She'd just spent all day listening to the rhythm of Cole's hammering and telling herself that last night was an anomaly. *What a crock.*

"Hamburgers and hot dogs okay with you?" she asked.

"Perfect." He looked around. "It's just us tonight?"

She stomped the life out of the little sparkler that went off inside her at the thought of being alone with Cole. Thank goodness Jem would be home from his day camp soon. "Jem'll be home—"

She stopped and turned at the sound of a car pulling up the driveway. Lauren smiled and waved at Tracey Williams, one of her big circle of fellow Valle Verde moms, as she swung her Chevy around the driveway.

Jem's happy grin was clearly visible through the mirage of Tracey's dusty window that had "Wash me, please," scraped onto it. Lauren walked over and helped Jem to unhook his seat belt and get out of the truck.

He yelled goodbye to Tracey and her daughter as he ran over to Cole, waving some pages he had clutched in his hand. She saw Cole smiling as he watched the boy approach.

Lauren stuck her head inside the truck and thanked Tracey quickly, hoping to forestall any probing questions about Cole. She was certain her new, happily married friends would make something of nothing if she gave them half a chance. She was right, because Tracey winked and said, "No problem, anytime," with sheer mischief twinkling in her eyes as she looked past Lauren.

It wasn't until Tracey had left and Lauren was on her way to the kitchen to get the fixings for dinner that it hit her. A man, a woman, a little boy and a barbecue. To the untrained eye, it might look as if they were a family. But they weren't a family and she told herself sternly that she'd do well to remember that whenever she started to feel all squishy and warm about it.

When she returned, Cole and Jem looked up at her and she smiled at how they'd done it at almost exactly the same time, in almost exactly the same way. She shook her head at them and laughed. "I'll bet that's the same look the caveman and cavekids gave the cavewoman when she showed up with the grub."

Cole laughed. "And the expression you had on earlier when you couldn't get the barbecue started is probably exactly what the caveman saw when he came home and found that dinner wasn't ready because the woman was still rubbing sticks together."

She tried to hide her amusement. "Why, Cole. What a Neanderthal thing to say."

He merely smiled and said, "Ugga bugga," which caused Jem to run around the yard shouting "ugga bugga" while he rubbed two sticks together.

The music of the stream, the twittering birds and the wind in the trees played all around them as they prepared dinner side by side, then sat at the picnic table with Jem and shared their meal. It wasn't until later, when Lauren returned from putting her son to bed, that she remembered that being alone with Cole was a test she didn't want to take.

Twilight shimmered overhead as she handed him one of the steaming cups of coffee she'd brought from the kitchen and sat down next to him. "If that cake isn't too manhandled, maybe we can still have a slice," she said, gesturing with her mug. "I made it myself."

Cole remembered how he was as a child, anxious for the meal to end so he could have dessert. Judging by the job his son had done on this cake, a sweet tooth must run in the family. "He really demolished it, didn't he?" he said, laughing as he served them each a squarish piece.

Lauren laughed, too, a pretty sound that meshed seamlessly with the night sounds around them. "I guess I should have insisted he eat it with a fork, huh?"

Cole shook his head. "Wouldn't have mattered. That's just how boys are."

"You sound pretty knowledgeable on the subject," she said as she brought the stoneware mug to her lips. "Do you have kids?"

That bullet had come out of nowhere and nicked him. *Shake it off, Cole. She doesn't know.* "Three brothers."

Her eyes widened over the rim of her cup. "Send your mother my condolences."

"Hey!" he said, laughing. "We weren't that bad."

"Uh-huh. What's the worst thing you ever did?" she asked, taking a bite of her cake.

When she'd gone inside earlier, she'd pulled her hair back into a clip, but one strand of it had already fallen down to frame her face. He had a crazy urge to reach out, pull her into his arms and tuck it behind her ear, but he knew that touching her would be a very bad idea. That could only lead to trouble.

"Worst thing I ever did? Now that's hard," he said evasively as he tapped his chin with one finger in a parody of searching his memory. "It really depends on which class of crime you're interested in. Simple crimes of personal assault on one another? Or crimes that would land us in detention, crimes punishable by doing time in juvenile hall, crimes punishable by death—"

"Stop, stop," she said, laughing at his silliness.

"Okay, worst thing I ever did…I dared my kid brother to ride his tricycle down a hill."

"That's not so bad."

"Yeah, but on the other side of that hill was a car, backing out of a driveway."

"That wasn't your fault. You couldn't know it was there."

"Didn't matter," he said, shrugging. "I was the one that called the double-dog dare."

She smiled at the childish phrase. "What happened?"

"I ran home so fast I thought my lungs would burst."

"And he was okay, right?"

"Yep. Has a scar that runs all the way up inside his nose to remind me, though." He paused. "Which he does at every opportunity."

She laughed and said, "What does he do now?"

"He owns a performance bike shop. He can ride circles around me."

This was a good night, he thought as she laughed and teased him about karmic justice. The warm weather, the sprinkle of stars overhead, the beautiful woman sitting across the table—if he took a step back and looked at it, he would swear he'd just stepped into a fairy tale.

But this particular fairy tale was his life. And he'd be damned if he wasn't going to enjoy it while it lasted.

"All right, how about you?" he asked. "Any skeletons in your closet?"

"Too many," she said simply as she smoothed the tablecloth which was ruffling and snapping in the breeze.

"Well?" he prompted. "Care to share with the group?"

"I *have* done a couple of things I'm not very proud of to get some of my antiques," she admitted with a grin that said she wasn't ashamed at all.

"Spill one."

She hesitated, a blush blooming slowly on her cheeks. "Once, at a tag sale in this little town in Arkansas, I actually got into a…well, a scuffle with this older woman over a very special item."

"How old was she?"

"Oh," she said, twisting her coffee cup innocently, "maybe pushing eighty."

"What?"

"But she was really spry!" she insisted. "She almost wrestled me to the ground for the thing."

"And what was this valuable item?"

"A toaster."

He waited a moment to see if she was kidding. She

wasn't. "You got into a fistfight with an octogenarian over a toaster?"

She nodded enthusiastically. "It was worth it. It's my favorite vintage toaster. And it has a great story. That's what's so cool about antiques. They all have little histories of their own."

"Oh, I gotta hear this," he said, draining his coffee cup. "Tell me this toaster's story."

"Well, it was still in its original box and it was beautiful. The chrome was shiny and the design was perfect Art Deco. Taped to the top of the box was a card," she said, warming to her story. "It was a wedding gift. It had the date at the top—August 1, 1936—and the card was from the bride's aunt saying how proud and happy she was that her niece had found her love."

"That's very sweet," he said with a wry grin as he tried to follow why she'd fight for this piece of someone else's history. "I wonder why she never used it."

"It doesn't matter. She kept it all those years, don't you see? With the card. From her aunt. It's perfectly preserved history." She cocked her head to one side as if to say, *don't you get it, you bonehead?* "And now I'm a part of its history, too."

He paused for a moment as he tried to understand. Maybe it was a *really* great toaster. "So, is it toasting some pretty good bread after all these years?"

Her lips parted in shock. "I don't *use* it, Cole! It's too special."

He laughed out loud at the sheer horror on her face. "You're a mystery, Lauren Simpson," he said, shaking his head. "But I'll give you this—you're never boring." Then without thinking, he did the inconceivable: he reached out and tucked that damn strand of hair behind her ear.

She went very still, almost as if she'd stopped breathing, and a look of what he was sure was longing crossed over her features. Then it disappeared.

"Mystery, huh?" she said as she stood and began to gather up the remains of dinner. "Good. I like that."

He stood to help, too, and in no time at all, they had everything packed neatly into two baskets. When Lauren stooped to pick up the baskets, he rushed to help her. "Let me do that," he said, and reached down for them.

As his hands brushed hers on the wicker handles, she glanced up quickly. "I've got it, thanks. I'll see you in the morning, Cole."

"Good night, Lauren." He started to go, then turned back. "Oh, and I promise, no midnight snacks tonight."

She looked up at him, her eyes wide, and even in the darkness he could see the unmistakable pink stain on her cheeks. "Then I'll know for sure it's a rat if I hear anything," she said with a slow smile.

She was stunning, even more than usual in the glow of the moonlight. But it was more than her looks, he thought. It was the woman herself.

He gritted his teeth in frustration when she turned away and the image of her in the scrap of nothing she wore to bed tumbled through his mind. No matter how hungry he got, he promised himself, tonight he wasn't going to budge from his room until the sun came up.

Lauren woke up with an extra dose of energy pumping through her veins the next morning. After she'd left Cole last night, she'd been buzzing for hours, running on the sheer momentum of the evening she'd just spent with him, talking like friends—though, heaven help her, she knew she wanted to be anything *but* his friend. Finally, sometime after midnight, she'd fallen into an exhausted sleep.

Now, this morning, life seemed more interesting, the sun seemed brighter, and the day ahead seemed like an adventure. Which was probably why she'd bounced out of bed, made pancakes, dropped Jem off at Camp Tumbleweed, got a cup of coffee from Uncle Bill's and took the long way home—the way that took her by the Frosty King.

Look Not 4 Blessings & They Will Find U.

This sign was beginning to misbehave, she thought as she stopped at the side of the road for a moment. But maybe it wasn't the sign's fault that the message was so cryptic. Maybe it was because for the first time in her life, she was looking for answers when she really didn't even know the questions.

She pulled back onto the road and headed for home. She had a lot of work to do today. Not looking for blessings would be an easy task to take on.

Lauren turned into her driveway and slowed, surprised to see an unfamiliar Ford parked beside Cole's beater of a truck. Who could be visiting so early on a Wednesday morning, she wondered. Then she saw Lisa Walker, her social worker and savior, stepping out of the Ford.

Lauren pulled to a stop and jumped out. "Lisa!"

The short, dark-haired woman who'd helped her to find, foster and then adopt Jem smiled as she walked toward Lauren. They hugged each other fiercely, then Lisa stepped back. "I'm sorry for not calling, I—"

"Are you kidding?" Lauren said with a broad smile. "I just wish I'd known you were coming. I dropped Jem off at camp a few minutes ago. He's going to be so sorry he didn't get to see you."

"Maybe next time." Lisa's smile wobbled, then died. "I have some news I wanted to tell you and I didn't want to do it over the phone."

Lauren's own smile ebbed. "That sounds serious."

"It could be."

A trickle of fear curled through her. "What is it?"

Lisa reached out and took her hand. "Lauren, Jem's father is looking for him."

Six

In an instant, all of Lauren's energy drained out of her with the force of a spring flood. Lisa followed her into the kitchen and they sat down at the table. Lauren's head felt thick, her mind slow.

She tried to brush away the cobwebs of panic that were keeping her from focusing. "How can this happen?" she asked the woman who'd championed her and vouched for her in the adoption hearings. "I mean, the people whose names are on his birth certificate don't even exist."

Lisa shook her head. "According to our original research, Jem's mother gave the hospital false names. But when I received the call from our legal people yesterday, they said a private investigator had turned up Jem's case as a possible match for his client."

Lauren's throat felt constricted when she tried to speak. "Who's the client? Do you know his name?"

Lisa's expression was sympathetic when she shook her head again. "We don't know. It's been filed without naming the alleged father."

Father. How could he even call himself that after abandoning his child? Her heart squeezed with anger and fear. If this man could prove that he was really Jem's father, he would have rights. Perhaps stronger rights than her own. And if there was a father, could that mean that Jem's mother wasn't far behind?

A curtain of sheer blackness swept across her heart at the thought that someone might try to take Jem away from her—especially parents who had cared so little for him that they'd abandoned him just hours after his birth.

Oh, no. No one was going to take her child away from her. She'd fight to her dying breath to prevent it. But first, she had to concentrate, make plans.

She looked up into Lisa's kind gaze. "What can I do?"

Lisa stayed for most of the morning. They made a pot of coffee, sat at the kitchen table and strategized. There was a chance that it was a fishing expedition, that it would turn out to be nothing. But there was also a possibility that the investigator had done his job well. If this man—or "John Doe," as they were calling him—could prove that there was a reasonable chance he was Jem's father, the court could order tests. In any case, Lauren would have rights. Meanwhile, she would have to sit tight and wait to see what the man could come up with as irrefutable proof.

By the time they finished talking, Lauren felt calmer, more confident. They began to talk about other things, like Jem's camp, Lisa's work and the plans for the store.

And that's why Lisa's next comment seemed completely random and almost laughable.

"Too bad you don't have a husband," she said.

Lauren finished rinsing out their cups and set them in the drainer. "Too bad for who?"

"For you, of course. If you were married, it would be much harder for them to take Jem away from you."

Lauren turned around and gaped at her. "I thought you said they wouldn't be able to take him away. Legally, I'm his mother, you said."

"You are, but you remember the fight we had during the adoption. The law still frowns on single-parent homes. I'm just saying that if this guy's married, he might have a strong case that he provides the more stable home."

The pace of Lauren's heartbeat sped up to five thousand rpm. "Lisa—"

Lisa shrugged sheepishly. "I'm not saying it's impossible this way, I'm just saying that it would be a helluva lot easier. Besides, being married is great."

Lauren rolled her eyes and turned back to the sink. "How would you know? You're single, too."

"I know," Lisa said, laughing. "But at least I want to be married."

A half hour later, they walked out to Lisa's car together and Lauren gave her a tight hug. "You know, you give public servants a good name."

Lisa smiled. "And you give legs-up-to-here fashion models a good name."

"Call me as soon as you hear something, okay?" Lauren said, trying to sound upbeat, but now that her strong shoulder was leaving, she was starting to feel frightened and worried all over again.

"You know I will, honey." Lisa started her car.

"Kiss that son of yours for me. And don't worry. You're not in this alone."

She knew that was true and yet, somehow, she'd never felt so alone in her life. As Lauren watched her friend drive away in a flurry of gravel and dust, she remembered Lisa's comment about marriage and a little rain cloud hovered over her heart.

Marriage? She'd never been further from marriage. She hadn't even had a date in over seven months. And if you didn't count that reckless incident in the kitchen with Cole the other night, she hadn't even really been tempted. Her moratorium on men simply forbade it.

Mr. Right was probably out there somewhere, but there was no way he was going to just show up with a diamond ring and a marriage proposal today. Nope, even if it were a solution, she'd simply have to find another way. Because losing her son was simply not an option.

Cole watched as the dark-haired woman's car tooled down the road, turned right and disappeared from view. Then he looked back toward Lauren.

She stood straight as a flagpole, her face a mask of worry. When she turned and walked slowly toward the stream that ran along the back of the property, he fought an urge to go to her that was so strong he thought he might have to nail his shoes to the new barn floor to keep himself in place.

He told himself that he was only concerned about her because he didn't want Jem's mother to be sad or worried if he could do anything about it. But all the while, he had to force down the feelings of protectiveness that were running rampant through him. He wasn't the knight in shining armor type, especially not about a woman he was trying—and failing miserably—to care nothing about.

But by the time she'd walked around the side of the house and out of sight, Cole had made his decision. He followed her, then stopped when he saw her standing at the base of an old oak behind the house. Her head was tipped back and she was looking up into the sun-dappled leaves. He followed her gaze and noticed, for the first time, an enormous, ornate Victorian-style tree house wedged between the gnarled branches.

She touched the wooden steps nailed to the side of the trunk for a moment. Then, to his surprise, she began to climb. He held his breath as she put one sure foot after another, her sensual, smoothly muscled arms and legs pulling her higher into the tree with feline grace.

Keep your eye on the ball, Cole.

When she disappeared inside the white structure, he walked to the foot of the tree. He was just getting ready to call up to her when he heard the soft, muffled sound of her tears. And, like most men, the sound of tears struck terror in his heart. *Damn.*

"Lauren?" he called.

The sound stopped, followed by two big sniffles, and then Lauren peeked over the edge of the tree house, wiping her cheeks with the back of her hand. His jaw set tight when he saw fresh tears trembling on her eyelashes like droplets shimmering at the tip of an icicle during the spring thaw.

"Are you okay?"

She nodded mutely, but then immediately pulled away from the edge and out of his sight. Fine, it looked like he'd just have to go to her, then. He put a foot on the first step, grabbed another one for a handhold and sighed.

He climbed up quickly, then pulled himself into the structure which smelled slightly of damp, fallen leaves and fresh paint. It was roomy inside, but he still had to sit so close that his legs brushed up against hers. Her eyes were downcast, and he only had to move a few inches to put his fingertips under her chin and tip her gaze up to his. "Tell me what's wrong."

Her eyes held a look of despair when she gave a very feminine response in a very small voice. "It's nothing."

With his fingers still beneath her chin, he used his thumb to wipe away a tear that was glistening on her cheek. He raised a skeptical brow.

She let out one of those cute hiccough sounds women make when they try to stop crying. When she smiled, it was a little wobbly at the corners. "Okay. Something's wrong."

"I thought as much," he said with a grin and pulled her into his arms, tucking her head under his chin with one hand and stroking her hair with the other. She resisted slightly, then relaxed into him as a fresh batch of tears shook her. "Just let it go," he whispered into her hair and tried not to notice its clean lemony scent.

Gradually, her tears subsided, but he held her in his arms for a long moment more. She seemed small, making him want to shield her from whatever threat was beating down her door. They stayed like that, with the hum of the meandering stream blending effortlessly with the sound of her breathing as it became more regular.

Finally, he pulled away to look at her. "Can I help?"

Instantly, her eyes swam with fresh tears. "No, you can't. Unless you're a lawyer."

Faint alarm bells began to clang in his mind, as if

they came from a siren many miles away. "Why do you need a lawyer?"

In a rush of grief stricken words and another gush of tears, she said, "Because someone's trying to take my son away from me."

Guilt as heavy and sobering as a battering ram punched him square in the chest even as he pulled her close again.

Dammit. How could she know? His mind was spinning like a child's frenzied top, but he forced himself to focus as her tears burned themselves out. When he pulled away again, she was chewing on her lower lip.

"Who's trying to take him away?" he asked, both dreading the answer and knowing with certainty what she was about to say.

Her watery gaze shifted to the tiny window. "A man who says he's Jem's father."

Doug. That son of a bitch. He'd filed the papers without Cole's go-ahead. But if that was so, why didn't she know *he* was Jem's father?

And even as he itched to jump out of this tree and get on the phone with that Judas of a best friend of his, he looked deep inside himself for the right thing to say. "I wish I could do something to help you," he said, and when he heard his own words, he realized that he truly meant them and that he was also the last person in the world who could help her with this problem. After all, he *was* her problem.

She reached up and touched his cheek. It was a simple gesture, but it seemed to charge the very air about them with electricity. Her eyes gleamed with a spark of gratitude, and another arrow of guilt struck him with a ping of pain, this time much closer to his heart.

"Thank you, Cole," she said. "It means so much just to know that you would if you could."

Ping!

He nodded in acknowledgment. After a long moment, he reluctantly let her go and watched as she leaned back against the tree house's rough wall.

"Okay, Rapunzel," he said with as much lightness as he could dredge up. "You ready to come down from your tower?"

A faint light sparked in her liquid emerald eyes, softening the pain that had been there earlier. "Why'd you call me that?"

He smiled. "You seemed lonely up here, like Rapunzel."

"I'm not lonely anymore," she said with a smile. "But I think I'll stay up here a little longer. You're welcome to stay, too, if you want."

There was nothing he wanted more at that moment than to stay up here and make her smile until she forgot her troubles, but he knew he was crumbling with every breath he took and every doe-eyed look she gave him. "I should get back to work," he said with a wink. "My boss is a real slave driver."

She was still smiling when Cole turned and began to climb down. As he headed back to the barn, he struggled to recall the rest of *Rapunzel*. When he remembered that the prince was blinded by his desires until the princess helped him to see, he felt as if he'd just been socked in the stomach by Jack's hungry giant.

Dammit, Doug, he thought as he took the loft stairs two at a time. *I'm going to throttle you for this, pal.*

Four hours later, a fresh wave of anxiety was choking Lauren as Cole pulled her SUV into a space marked with logs in the parking lot of Jem's preschool day camp, Camp Tumbleweed.

"Thanks for driving," she said as she fumbled with the door handle. *Why couldn't she figure anything out in this stupid car?* "If the counselor had just told me what the problem was, I wouldn't be so nervous, I swear."

"Don't worry." Cole flipped the button that unlocked the doors. "We'll get it straightened out."

The rich scents of pine and oak filled the air, but she hardly noticed it as they walked quickly to the office of the head counselor. Thank God Cole had insisted on driving her when he'd seen her run out of the house. When she'd gotten off the phone, her hands had started to shake so badly she couldn't even manage her keys.

The second Cole and Lauren entered the office, Jem jumped up and ran to his mother with the speed of a rabbit being chased by a coyote. He was so fast, in fact, that she barely had time to see that his chin was covered by a heavy gauze bandage and his cheeks were streaked with tears, which renewed themselves once he was in her arms.

"What happened to him?" Lauren asked the counselor in a tightly controlled voice as she soothed her son, stroking his hair as his little body shook with tragic sobs.

"Well," the thin, flustered man said, "the boys were playing Monkey Bar Wars. You know, where they—"

"We know what Monkey Bar Wars are," Cole said, his voice even and firm.

The counselor paused and eyed Cole before he continued. "Even though the other boys were older, Jem wanted to play." He sighed loudly. "He was doing well until he got walloped on the chin by another boy's boot."

Ohmigod. She held her son slightly away from her and reached out to take the bandage off but Jem winced, so she pulled her hand away.

Cole came over and hunkered down beside them. He gave the boy an easy smile. "Got your first battle wound, eh?"

Jem looked down at his feet and sniffled. He nodded.

"I got my first one at about your age, too," Cole said. "Right here." He pointed to his chin, which sported a white, jagged scar—the same scar, Lauren realized suddenly, that she'd traced with her fingertip just a few nights before.

Jem looked up at Cole and studied the scar. The boy sounded solemn when he asked, "What'd you do?"

"Well, it wasn't nearly as good as what happened to you. I was playing with one of my brothers and he catapulted me into a dresser drawer."

Her son considered this, then asked, "What's a cat-typull?"

"We'll explain it later, honey," Lauren said. "Right now, we need to go to the Emergency Clinic so Dr. Linblade can take a look at you." She knew he'd be fine, but she wanted to see their own doctor to be sure.

The harried counselor piped up. "I think that's a very good idea."

"Let's go, honey," she said.

As they walked to the door, Jem turned around and told the counselor, "See you tomorrow, Mr. Ott."

"It's swim school tomorrow, Jem. Don't forget to bring your bathing suit."

"'Kay," he said as he slipped his hand into hers.

What a day this was turning out to be. Thank goodness Cole had been there with his cool head. He'd really pulled her keister out of the fire today. And she'd never—

She'd never let a man comfort her in her life, she realized as she turned back to look at him in surprise. She'd never even wanted to. And she'd let this man do it twice. In one day.

"Is Co' coming?" Jem asked as she opened the door.

She raised her brow at Cole in silent question and he said, "I'll meet you two outside in a second. I just want to ask…" he glanced at the counselor's name badge, "Todd a few questions."

"All right," she said even as she wondered what he could possibly be asking Camp Tumbleweed's top man. She closed the door behind her and said to Jem, "You think Dr. Linblade will let you pick a toy out of the goody drawer?"

"Only if I'm good," he said seriously and she laughed for the first time all day.

When Cole came out, she regarded him with curiosity. "Everything okay?"

The beginnings of a smile tipped the corners of his mouth. "Everything's great," he said, then he picked Jem up and gently hoisted him onto his shoulders. "Did you know that the hero of the battle always gets carried off the battlefield?"

"Am I the hero?" Jem asked breathlessly.

"What do you think?"

As she followed them to the car, she smiled at Cole's attempts to cheer her son. Battles, medals, parades, hero's welcomes. By the time they got to the doctor's office, Jem was convinced he'd just done the most courageous thing of his young life.

She couldn't have been more relieved when their own

doctor examined him and pronounced that he was fine. As it turned out though, he did need three stitches, which he bore stoically as they watched. Cole's expression was almost as tortured as hers when Dr. Linblade gave Jem a local anesthetic, then stitched up his chin.

Jem earned his toy, then they all went home and had ice cream for dinner. While her son called his Grandma Sherry and babbled the whole grisly story, she asked Cole what he'd said to Todd when he'd stayed behind in the office.

His expression grew mysterious. "It's a surprise."

"Is it a surprise that's going to have me looking for a new preschool tomorrow morning?"

"Of course not. But don't be shocked when Jem comes home tomorrow and tells you about the parade the four- and five-year-old group had in his honor."

Her mouth dropped open.

"Oh, and make sure to admire the medal they're going to give him, too."

When she got done laughing, she talked to Sherry for a few minutes, then put an exhausted Jem to bed early.

She looked down at him as he slept, clutching the stuffed lion—"for courage," Cole had told him when he'd helped him pick out the toy. Her son's thick, tawny lashes swept his cheeks, a faint smile dwelled on his mouth.

When she was a young girl and she'd made herself a promise to take in a foster child, she'd wanted to do it for purely selfish reasons. Now that she was living that dream, she knew it had become so much more.

She wanted to prevent just one child's life from becoming a lonely, frightening, touch-and-go experience. She wanted to make sure that no one—especially other children—made fun of one foster child's hopeless situation, that the whole world would know how much that child was loved. To make sure, in fact, that *her* child was so loved that if he ever got sick, he would have a crowd standing by, waiting for news of his recovery.

She thought back to Cole's expression when the doctor took his first stitch. The blood had drained from his face, making him look pale and dizzy, but he'd watched every move the doctor had made right alongside her. She found the memory very comforting.

Someday, he was going to make a great father.

Lauren was so startled by that thought, she gasped. Cole would make a great father, she repeated to herself.

Too bad you don't have a husband, Lisa had said. *If you were married, it would be much harder to take Jem away from you.*

She couldn't. No, she couldn't even think of that prospect. It was too emotionally dangerous for her and too much to ask of Cole. She ran her shaking hands through her hair and glanced at the door. But what if—

What if she could convince Cole to marry her? Just long enough to fight for Jem. If he would, theirs would be as stable a home as any absentee birth father could produce. But could they make it look like they were in love?

No, no. How would she ever be able curb her attraction to him? They'd have to live in the same house, possibly share the same—

She shook her head to cast out the image. If she did get into a bogus marriage to keep her son, she would have to be able to walk away without looking back when it was all over. The way she felt about Cole, that sounded impossible. She already had a feeling she was going to be thinking about him for a long, long time after he left.

She looked down at her peaceful, slumbering son and thought about the way Jem was with Cole. He really liked him. And Cole was great with Jem.

She impatiently pulled her racing thoughts together as she tucked the blanket around Jem. She had little choice. She closed the door behind her with a soft *snick* and went back downstairs.

Cole was in the living room, thumbing through a catalog of store fixtures. He looked up at her and gave her a smile so devastating, it almost melted her resolve. "You know, some of these display cases need extra wiring—"

"Cole," she said with deceptive calm as she slipped the catalog from his hands and pulled a chair over. When she sat down facing him, her bare knees just touched his denim-covered ones. She leaned forward and said, "Do you remember earlier when you said you wished you could do something to help me?"

A smile remained on his handsome face, but his blue eyes turned a shade grayer, like the sea when the sun fades at the end of the day. "Yes, of course."

"Well, I think I found a way you can." Her mind was a wild knot of hope and fear, but she had to do it. "Cole," she said. "Will you marry me?"

Seven

For one long, breathtaking moment, Cole simply stared at her. He was sure he'd heard her wrong. "Could you repeat that?"

She watched his eyes and never moved from her perch at the edge of her chair. "I asked if you'd marry me."

So he *had* heard her right. After a day filled with frenzied events, a dazed smile was the only response he seemed capable of.

Her face was full of strength, her eyes shining with determination. "I need a husband."

"May I ask why?" he said carefully.

She nodded again. "If I had a husband, it would be much more difficult for anyone to take my son from me."

Cole stared in mute shock as the tangled web of the past weeks wrapped around what was left of his mind.

"I know this must sound strange," she said as she sat back and folded her hands in her lap. "And I know this is a lot to ask. But you wanted to know if you could help."

"There's got to be a better solution," he said, finally finding his voice and willing her to come up with another idea. *Immediately.* "Have you thought about—"

"I've thought about everything. Trust me, Cole, I wouldn't go to these lengths if I hadn't. It would be very temporary. You won't have to do anything."

Won't have to do anything? How about burning in hell for an eternity? *That* was something. He had to talk her out of this. But before he could, she jumped in again with words that made his heart both soar and ache.

"Jem likes you, Cole. And you—" she hesitated only a heartbeat, "you're a natural with kids."

"Lauren, I—"

She put one finger to his lips and her whispery touch only served to rattle him more. "I promise this marriage will only have to last as long as it takes to make sure there's no danger of losing Jem. In fact, you can still leave when you're done with the store. I'll just say my husband is working on a job out of town."

My husband. This was crazy!

The expression in her extraordinary eyes grew bright, overwhelming, like when a policeman shines a flashlight in your face at a traffic stop. "I need you, Cole. Probably more than I've ever needed anyone." She laughed, but it was more melancholy than mirthful. "And when you know me better, you'll understand how meaningful that really is."

When she met his gaze again, both her eyes and her voice were softer, but her determination had multiplied.

"I'm afraid I don't have a lot to offer you in return. I only have the business. But I'm willing to negotiate."

He ran a hand through his hair. "Lauren, even if I could do this, I wouldn't take any part of your business."

But he *couldn't* do this for her, no matter how much he wanted to ease her pain, quiet her mind, and protect her home. There were obvious reasons why, but his nightmare marriage to Kelly was a factor, too.

For Cole, marriage would never, ever be an option again. He'd learned the hard way that no matter how well he thought he knew someone, there was no guarantee they wouldn't someday drag him through an emotional minefield and leave him there, buried under a barrage of lies.

Nope, there was no way he was going to sign up for another tour of marriage. And to do it under this cloud of deception? No way.

She'd fallen silent and he watched as the expression on her face shifted from hopeful to uncertain.

Lord, if only he could turn back the clock. He could show up on the doorstep waving his copy of Jem's birth certificate, put his cards on the table and do this thing right. But instead he was stuck, forever and for all time, stuck with the chaos he'd created here.

A junkyard of broken-down emotions flowed through him when he said, "Lauren, I'm sorry. I can't marry you. I was married once. I'm not doing it again."

He watched as her determination dimmed, then flickered out. It was evident in her posture, in the fading light in her eyes. He felt like a Grade A jerk.

"I understand," she said finally. "I knew it was a lot to ask of someone who has no stake in this at all."

Ping! Another arrow hit its mark. If she only knew

how much he really did have at stake, she'd probably maim him in ways he didn't even want to think about. "Maybe I can help some other way—"

She shook her head. "Don't worry about it. I'll just have to figure something else out. I have some friends in L.A. I know someone will…" She looked over his shoulder and her words trailed off, but only moments later, he saw the light of determination reignite in her eyes.

Someone will what? he thought with alarm. Marry her? Someone from Los Angeles?

He narrowed his eyes. He could just picture the guy. Probably some pretty boy who used more hair gel and spent more time getting ready in the morning than she did.

He looked at Lauren closely. There it was. Tenacity, stubbornness. *Oh, hell, no.* There was no way he was going to let some other guy stroll in here, set up camp and play father to his child—or play husband to her, either.

Damn stubborn woman. She couldn't know it, but she'd just lit the fuse of his "protect what's yours" instinct.

"I'll do it." He said the words quickly, without giving himself any more time to think.

Her gaze snapped back to his. "What?"

"I said I'll do it."

A smile tipped the corners of her mouth. "Why?"

"Because I want to—" He floundered. He simply couldn't bring himself to use the word "help." "Because I want to," he said finally.

Then the most amazing thing happened. She jumped into his lap, threw her arms around him and squeezed him like an anaconda. "Oh, Cole," she said, her breath sweet and warm against his neck. ''You're the most wonderful man.''

''No, I'm really not,'' he said dryly as he tried to ignore the pressure of her bottom against his thighs, the feel of her in his arms. He tried to think of something, anything besides her soft curves pressing against him. Baseball, he thought. Traffic school. Monster truck pulls.

Mercifully, she got up from his lap and sat back down across from him. ''And what do you want in return?''

He looked at her as the question rushed him from all sides. What he wanted from Lauren Simpson was not PG-rated and he definitely wasn't going to ask for it.

''I'll let you know if I think of something,'' he muttered, knowing that even though this marriage was only temporary, only for show, he was still doing the craziest thing he'd ever done in his life. He couldn't even begin to think about the legal consequences. And after the threats he'd heaped on his attorney and ex-best friend on the phone earlier today, Cole would be surprised if he could even get Doug to return his calls. At least the little weasel had confessed to overstepping his bounds when he'd filed the papers. Not that it mattered. There wasn't anything Doug could do now to erase the damage he'd done.

As he watched Lauren stand up and pace the room while she made wedding plans, he realized that in a few days, he'd legally be a part of his son's life for the first time. But at what cost? While he certainly didn't want to hurt Lauren, his need to protect his son came first.

How was he going to deal with his attraction to her? And what was going to happen after they tied their flimsy knot?

He rubbed his forehead with an agitated hand. He had

a tremendous amount of work to do on the store, so resisting temptation during the daylight hours might be doable. But, oh Lord, he thought with a sigh, how in the hell was he going to keep from touching his "wife" after the sun went down?

Cole's heart was pounding.

"Lauren, will you have this man as your lawful wedded husband..."

He looked to his left and saw the beautiful stranger who was about to become his wife. Her silken voice wrapped around the words, "I will," then she looked up at him with those soft green, grateful eyes rimmed with dark, thick lashes and it was his turn again.

"Do you have the rings?" the justice of the peace asked.

Cole nodded at the man stiffly, then reached into his pocket and withdrew the matching set of antique platinum bands Lauren had given him that morning. What was he *doing?* he thought for the hundredth time as he fumbled with the rings. And why didn't someone have the decency to turn on the air-conditioning in here?

"Please join hands and repeat after me."

Cole took Lauren's left hand in his, held the delicate ring suspended over the glossy fingernail on her fourth finger.

"I, Cole, take you, Lauren, as my wedded wife, to have and to hold from this day forward..."

He listened and responded dutifully, but after a moment he began to feel something strange happening in his chest, as if someone was dancing a soft-shoe right in the center of it.

"To love and to cherish." *Tap, tap, tap, slide.* "'Til death do us part." *Tap, tap, tap, slide.*

He slipped the ring onto her finger and felt her hand tremble in his. He squeezed her fingertips to reassure her and when she squeezed back, he felt something inside him stretch painfully tight.

It didn't seem possible, he thought with wonder, but in spite of the circumstances, in spite of the lies and that they were virtually strangers and the fact that he'd decided long ago never to be married again, this wedding was making him sweat more than the wedding he and Kelly had had all those years before.

Lauren's chin had a way of quivering when she cried, so she was concentrating very hard on holding back tears when she repeated the appropriate words, slipped the thick platinum band on Cole's finger and turned back to the justice of the peace. Only a few more words and the deed would be done.

"By the authority vested in me by the state of California," the man said, "I pronounce this couple to be husband and wife."

Her chin quivered, her eyes burned. She blinked hard and looked at the man who stood beside her.

Her husband.

He smelled divine, like spice and sunshine, and was even more breathtaking than usual in a wickedly well-fitted dark Italian summer wool suit and deep-indigo shirt that made his eyes look almost otherworldly. She wondered briefly where he'd gotten it on such short notice, then forgot all about it when she saw his lips curve into a devilish smile.

"You may," the justice of the peace began, but Cole was already leaning down to her, his intention crystal clear. "Kiss the bride," the man finished with a chuckle.

Her eyes widened and she started to tell Cole this

part wasn't necessary but it was too late. Right there, in front of her son and Sherry and Lisa and a witness whose name she'd already forgotten, he took her in his arms, brushed her parted, pliant lips with his own, then deepened the kiss, pulling her body tightly against his. She shivered deeply, vaguely heard her mind say "no" even as her hands telegraphed "yes" by reaching up to his shoulders, sliding across the back of his neck, then buried themselves in that thick, unruly hair.

Oh, my, she thought. This was going to be much more difficult than she'd anticipated.

Cole pulled back slightly and the flash of heat in his eyes was unmistakable. Lauren opened her mouth to say something but when Cole looked down at her parted lips, she found she'd completely lost track of her thoughts.

Luckily, her attention was drawn away in that moment by an audible sigh that came from the vicinity of Sherry. Lauren looked over and saw her almost-Mom beaming as proudly as if this were the love match of the century.

"I have a special wedding surprise for you two," Sherry said with a quick glance at Jem who'd long ago gotten bored with the ceremony and was absorbed in telling Lisa about his stitches and showing off his hero's medal.

"That's really not necessary, Sherry," Lauren said, stepping away from Cole and sneaking a peek at the justice of the peace. "You know this marriage isn't real," she added in a whisper.

"Of course it's necessary." She looked at Cole, back to Lauren and then, in a low, conspiratorial whisper, said, "You know the trip Jem and I have been planning? The week at Disneyland? Now, I know it wasn't supposed to happen until next month,'' she said with a coy smile. ''But I've arranged some time off to take him a little early.''

Lauren narrowed her eyes and lowered her voice threateningly. ''*How* early?''

''We're leaving today,'' Sherry said with a satisfied grin.

Lauren's stomach clenched, and she chanced a quick sideways look at Cole. After what they'd been through today, she wasn't surprised to see the healthy hue of his skin had faded to a grayish tone. She was surprised, though, to see that his eyes betrayed the same alarm she was feeling.

Lisa and Jem chose that moment to start asking about lunch, so Lauren didn't get a chance to protest Sherry's offer until they got home. Unfortunately, by then Sherry had already shared her plan with Jem, who wasted no time in retrieving all his stuffed Mickey and Simba and Tarzan toys from his room so he could rehearse his stay at Disneyland on the living room floor.

As they watched Jem and Cole discuss whether Simba and Tarzan lived in the same neighborhood, Sherry shot Lauren a smug smile, patted her hand and whispered, ''I just know you and Cole are going to enjoy your honeymoon.''

Two hours later, while Lauren stood outside her house with Sherry and Lisa as they prepared to leave, another bombshell exploded in her face.

''Lauren, I have to hand it to you,'' Sherry said as she put Jem's Scooby Doo suitcase into her Mercedes. ''When you bailed out on your abstinence program, you really went for the hard stuff. That is one gorgeous hunk of man.''

Lauren flushed as she glanced over to where Cole and Jem were practicing throwing the Wiffle ball in the front yard. Looking at Cole was like looking into the sun—mesmerizing, but very dangerous. Not too long from now, she thought, prying her eyes away, she and Cole were going to be alone together. And then her wavering self-control was going to be the only thing standing between her and the terrible temptation to wave the white flag and surrender to him.

"The important thing," Lauren said, shaking off her mental meanderings, "is that he's a warm body who turns this place into a two-parent home."

"Honey, that's what I'd call a *hot* body," Lisa said, grinning. "I sure envy you sleeping with that every night."

Lauren's heart danced a crazy mambo in her chest. "I'm not going to sleep with him!"

Lisa's smile faded. "If this all comes to a head, Lauren, you can bet someone's going to come around to check on the fitness of your home. And I'm just saying you better know which drawer he puts his socks in."

Lauren worked to breathe rhythmically as she brushed away the image of Cole in her room—and in her bed. "This is just a…" She hesitated. "Temporary arrangement, not a marriage. He lives in the barn. That's where he stays."

Lisa studied her. "That's too big a risk—"

"And a ridiculous waste of what I predict is going to be the best sex of your life," Sherry added.

"Sherry!" Lauren hissed. "Not so loud." She eyed Lisa, then asked, "Are you serious about this?"

Lisa nodded solemnly. "And it isn't just here at home, Lauren. You're going to have to make sure the people in this community know you as a couple, too. If anyone even suspects that this is a sham, you'll be in worse shape than you were before.''

''And hey,'' her traitor of a former agent said with a wink at Lisa, ''if this is just an *arrangement,* you shouldn't have any trouble keeping your paws to yourself.''

The two women laughed, then dummied up when they saw Cole and Jem heading toward them. Lauren felt her whole body grow absurdly warm as she watched Cole, his tie loose and his sleeves rolled up, his gait relaxed. If this was just temporary, she thought, then how come she could burst into flames just looking at him?

Lisa gave hugs and kisses all around, then took off at her usual hurried pace. Minutes later, Cole gave Jem a high five and a hug, then, in a serious tone, asked Sherry if he could speak to her alone for a moment.

As they walked away, Lauren gathered her son in her arms and told him how much she'd miss him, how much she loved him. He gave her the requested kiss and hug, but he was over-the-moon excited about meeting Mickey Mouse, so after a few minutes of squirming, she put him in the Mercedes, then buckled him up and closed the door.

Cole helped Sherry into the car before coming to stand close beside Lauren. As the car pulled away, Jem waved wildly through the glass. It made her heart hurt to be separated from him, especially now that the earth was quaking under her feet. But his happy expression reassured her that she was doing the right thing.

''He's going to have a great time,'' Cole said. ''Oh, and I gave Sherry my pager number so she'll be able to get us anytime.''

Us. Lauren smiled. She'd gotten lucky in finding him

to marry her. After all, he hardly knew them and he was already doing thoughtful things for her little family.

Without thinking, she reached out and took his hand. Beneath her fingertips, he felt solid, warm. "Cole, I want to thank you for what you did today."

He smiled down at her and squeezed her hand. "My pleasure, Mrs. Travis."

He was teasing, but the low, husky tone of his voice brought back visions of that night in the kitchen—Cole between her thighs, her hands on his naked, built-like-a-Mack-truck chest, his lips drinking from hers. Oh, no. She wasn't ready to be alone with him. Not yet. So she turned to him and said as casually as she could manage, "You know what I've heard is the very best way to celebrate a wedding night?"

His eyes darkened to a sensuous smoky blue before he said slowly, "Well, I've got a pretty good idea—"

"Bowling," she said quickly before he could finish.

He looked surprised for the barest moment, then he chuckled and the sound moved sinuously from his body to hers. "When I get through with you at the bowling alley, you are going to wish you asked for something else."

I already do, she thought. *I already do.*

Cole leaned back in the hard fiberglass chair and took a sip of beer. By now the wedding ceremony and Jem's unexpected departure with Sherry seemed as if it had occurred in a surreal dream. He'd been suspicious at first, thought that maybe Sherry and Lauren were planning to hide the boy from the phantom "father" who'd prompted the investigation into Jem's parentage. But after having a brief talk with Sherry, Cole's suspicions were put to rest. They'd be home in a week, and that meant that Cole had seven days in which to find a way to tell Lauren who he really was. And then, he thought as he took another slug of beer, he'd have to deal with the price of his deception.

But that was for another day. For now, like almost every other man at Herbie's Rock-n-Bowl, he noticed with annoyance, he was occupied with just one thing: watching Lauren stand at the foul line of lane number twelve, waggling her superior posterior as she prepared to launch the ball.

He looked around and took stock. Maybe twenty-two other people in the place, fifteen of them men. Of those, at least five had already been put on a leash by their wives. That left less than ten that he'd have to personally acquaint with the fact that Lauren was married. To him.

Not that it was necessary, of course. On their walk over to Herbie's, Lauren had told him that the community of Valle Verde was about to meet them as a couple. And the big emphasis she put on Travis every time she said her name—Lauren *Travis*—was pretty much taking care of that goal.

He looked over at her now and saw her dilly-dallying before she threw the ball—aiming, planning, then aiming again—and he wondered why hearing her refer to herself as his wife didn't scare the hell out of him like it should. Probably because he knew it was temporary but maybe, just maybe, he thought as he sat back and enjoyed the scenery, it was because Lauren Travis was the best show in town.

She'd changed into baggy white pants and a bright pink sleeveless sweater that hugged her narrow back lovingly and bared her athletic shoulders and her tanned, toned arms. It wasn't an overly sexy getup, but something about her smoldered anyway—something that let him know a trip wire was about to be activated inside him, something that let him know he was being pushed to his personal limit.

But so far tonight, they were having nothing but fun—even though after their first couple of frames, Lauren had gotten serious and declared a bowling war. All she wanted was to win just one frame. "Is that too much to ask?" she'd demanded.

He'd assured her it wasn't, but two full games later she had yet to achieve her goal—and Cole was getting hungry. "Lauren, honey? As much as I love watching you run around and fling that ball every which way, I feel it's my duty to tell you that your husband's starving."

She shot him a mock glare. "Well, *my husband's* just gonna have to wait a sec," she said as she turned to face the lane again. "And if you don't like it, you can come on over here and share your wealth of bowling knowledge."

It was easy to see that if she threw the ball from where she stood, she was going to send it on a slow, diagonal trip to gutterballdom. He sighed as he put down his beer, then stood and walked toward her.

He came up behind her and slipped his arms around her waist. "Why didn't you say so, my sweet?" he asked and smiled at the perverse joy he got from tossing out the endearment for the benefit of all the men within earshot. "We could have been finished hours ago."

She turned her head to retort and she was so close it would have been child's play to swoop in and steal a kiss. And it would've been a damn good time to amplify the kiss he'd given her at the courthouse with all those incredibly interested bystanders standing around.

But just then her soft lips parted, and a warning shot sounded in Cole's brain reminding him that this marriage of theirs was an act and nothing more. So, with regret and a bit of difficulty, he turned her toward the lane again.

Her back was pressed up against his chest, and he could feel her heart beating hard against him—or was that his heart beating against her? He couldn't quite tell, so he took a deep breath, tried to ignore their perfect fit—her back to his chest, her bottom to his throbbing groin—and explained how to use the arrows on the lane. Then with one arm wrapped around her slim waist and the other holding her wrist, he helped her aim for the arrow as she drew her arm back and let it rip.

And…*s-t-r-i-k-e!*

Anyone watching would've thought she'd just bowled a perfect three hundred, for Pete's sake. She jumped, she whooped, she high-fived anyone who dared come near.

Then after she'd done a victory lap, she came back to him and threw herself into his arms and kissed him— and it was a very different kiss from the one they'd shared that morning. This kiss was a bolt from the blue, a kiss filled with fire, a kiss that quickly rocketed into something that, in spite of himself, had him wrapping his arms around her, pulling her closer, taking more, molding her around the hand he held at the small of her back.

As he tasted her, he was only vaguely aware of where they were and all the interested eyes on them. Time itself seemed to pass as if it were in no hurry, like pouring syrup from a bottle. Finally, she pulled away, but slowly, like someone was making her do it.

Her eyes were wide and jungle-green as she cleared

her throat and said, "That…I was, uhh…just trying to make this whole marriage thing look kosher for the on-lookers."

"Well, Mrs. Travis," he drawled, then dipped his head to steal one more quick kiss. "You've certainly convinced me." And while he really was just playing along with her game, he still couldn't help but marvel at how easily "Mrs. Travis" had just rolled off his tongue.

A pink stain spread across her cheeks as she stumbled and stammered. Finally, she got out, "Well, thanks for the lesson, Cole."

A blaze of desire streaked through him when he thought of all the things he'd like to teach her, but he buried it and pretended to misunderstand her. "Don't be so hard on yourself. I think you were doing all right—" He stopped short, then acted like he'd just that moment understood what she'd meant. "Oh! You mean the *bowling* lesson…."

Her flush darkened to the approximate shade of her hot pink sweater before she rushed out with, "Of course!" then, "Jeez, Cole. Your ego…"

She let her words trail off as they turned and headed for Herbie's Pizza and Pasta Bowl at the back of the alley where they ordered a wedding-night dinner consisting of a large pepperoni with thin crust and a pitcher of beer.

"That was great," she said, her voice cheery, her moment of embarrassment apparently forgotten as they slid into a booth upholstered in a furry green fabric. A tacky lamp hung over their table and by its dim light he could see her lips were still swollen from their kiss and that little tendrils of her hair had escaped the pony-tail and were dipping down over one cheek. "I think that I should get a trophy for that," she said, smiling. She was a fast learner, though, because when he started to retort, she narrowed her eyes and added, "For the strike, that is."

Chalk one up in Lauren's column, he thought to himself before he said, "Okay, I'll have a trophy made up. What do you think?" he asked agreeably. "'Cutest Preparation at the Foul Line'? 'Best Butt at the Rock-n-Bowl'?"

A little smile began to get the best of her even as she tried to look put out, crossing her arms under her full, firm breasts—the same ones that had been pressed up against him just minutes ago as they kissed in front of Herbie's entire Saturday night crowd. Well, at least Valle Verde was clear that she was off the market—at least for now, he thought with a frown.

He poured beer from the pitcher into two frosted pint glasses, handed her one and held his up in a toast. "To..." To what? he asked himself. To weeks and weeks of untold torture being married to a woman I can't touch? Yeah, why not. Didn't he deserve such a fate, after all? "To us," he said finally and tipped his glass against hers.

"To you," she said, smiling, "for being my knight in shining armor."

He blew on his arm, then pretended to polish it like it was armor and she laughed at his pantomime. Lord, he liked to make her laugh. He watched her eyes sparkling like something expensive in a jewelry store window and tried not to think about what was going to happen when she found out how tarnished his armor really was.

"You know, Cole," she said after taking a respectable slug of her beer, "I think I did very well tonight considering I've never bowled in my life."

"Seriously, never? My God, bowling was practically religion in my hometown. My family used to go every Friday night. You know, forced togetherness. I'm sure your family did something similar, right?"

Lauren felt a familiar band tighten around her heart. There it was. After he'd shared about his brothers the night of the barbecue, she knew it would happen eventually. It was normal for people to talk about their pasts, their families. After all, he was from one of those warm, loving families that told warm, toasty stories about each other. And now he was going to want to know about her warm, wonderful—and very fictional—family, too.

"Don't tell me you never got roped into togetherness time with your family." He looked at her over his glass and prompted her. "Movies? Picnics? Weekends at the lake?"

Do I tell him the truth? she wondered as a bubble gum snapping teenage waitress dropped off their pizza, momentarily distracting him. Do I *want* to tell him? She wavered, then decided to ignore it. Maybe he'd let it go.

"Wow," he said. "That look on your face says miniature golf to me." He shuddered. "The worst."

So much for him letting it go, she thought, and took a deep, fortifying breath. "Actually, it was nothing."

"What do you mean?" he asked as he loaded pizza onto a plate for her. "How did you manage to escape?"

Aw, hell, what was the point of hiding it from him? With Jem's father poking around, her past was going to get dug up anyway. Besides, now that she was out of the limelight, the reason for secrecy was obsolete. Cole was going to find out—she might as well be the one to tell him.

"I don't have any of those experiences to share because I grew up in foster homes," she said, keeping her voice intentionally flat.

"After your parents died, right." His expression was sweet, regretful. "I forgot about that. I'm sorry."

She'd never confided in a man like this, ever, and it tugged at her somewhere she didn't want to be tugged. "No, I always lived in foster homes. All my life. Dozens of them. Until I ran away at sixteen. Sherry and I invented that story about my parents to cover up that I was a runaway from the foster care system."

Something passed across his face for a second, something dark and disapproving, and it kept moving and transforming until only a shadow of it remained. But she could still see it in the set of his jaw, the slight crease in his forehead, the tightening of his lips.

Her pulse jumped and shook. She was confused by his response and wished fervently that this uncomfortable moment would end so they could move on.

"Lauren," he said, his voice tight, the shadow of disapproval blooming anew in his expression. "Why the hell would you lie about something like that?"

The accusation in both his words and his tone sent her hackles up like a feral cat's. It was absolutely, positively, the last thing she expected to hear him say. "Why are you acting like I lied to *you*, Cole?" she asked, trying to control the tremor in her voice. "This has nothing to do with you."

He ignored her question as soundly as she had his. "Why would you of all people want Jem to grow up thinking that being a foster kid is something to be ashamed of?"

Her temper soared in direct proportion to the plummeting of her patience. Sure, he'd done her a huge favor today, but that didn't mean he had an open invitation to begin criticizing her, especially about something that was none of his business. But she'd been a fool to think that she could let her guard down and confide in him without being judged. After all, people had been judging her since before she could hold a rattle, for God's sake. Had she learned nothing at all in twenty-six years?

"Listen, Cole," she said as she scooted out of that tattered slime-green booth with as much dignity as she could rally. "I think I've had just about all the fun I can stand. You have yourself a good night."

And then she walked out of the noisy bowling alley and left him with two pairs of rented bowling shoes to return, a full pitcher of beer to drink and a pizza that had grown ice-cold.

Eight

The persistent clamor of the heavy resin bowling balls crashing into the hapless pins faded into the recesses of Cole's mind as he watched Lauren walk away. In her haste, the now-familiar swaying thing she did with her hips without even trying was barely discernable. With one tiny portion of his mind, he thought about how he loved to watch her move while the rest of his mind was fully occupied with resisting the almost irresistible urge to put his fist right through Herbie's cheap, sticky tabletop.

Could that have gone any worse? he asked himself, groaning silently. No—wait, yes. He could have made her cry. That would have been the cherry on top, he thought grimly and called himself a dozen different kinds of fool.

But, really, the most awful part of what had just happened was that he wasn't even mad at Lauren. She'd done whatever it was she had to do to get through what sounded like a really tough childhood. Then she'd not only made something of her life, she'd adopted Jem and was helping him make something of his. Cole slunk a little lower on the green bench seat and knew with certainty that he was the biggest jerk in ten counties.

Nope, it hadn't been Lauren at all. He was angry with another woman who'd lied to him, another woman who'd run away with something he didn't even know to look for, who, for reasons he might never understand, had abandoned their son. He was angry with Kelly, a person with whom he could never resolve those things, so he'd taken it out on Lauren.

But for Cole, knowing what had come over him didn't make jumping all over her any more defensible— and right when she was looking a bit like a baby bird about to take its first test flight. He had no idea why, but she'd been nervous about what she was telling him, he could see that plainly in her eyes, in the way she'd played with her beer glass and, most tellingly, in the fact that the normally ravenous Lauren hadn't eaten a single bite of her pizza.

Damn. He thought about the day—their wedding, Jem leaving with Sherry, bowling, laughing with her, kissing her, the feeling of her in his arms. Of all the dim-witted, hotheaded—

As his God-fearing mother still said on so many occasions, he really could be a horse's hindquarters sometimes. And now he was going to have to go after Lauren and take his lumps. He deserved them. If he was lucky, they might even absolve him.

Cole left a twenty on the table to cover the check, stuffed another ten spot into one of their bowling shoes and chucked both pair across the counter on his way to the door. He had to catch up to her and apologize. Because only then would he know if he'd be moving from the barn to the doghouse on his wedding night.

The moon was full and lit the short walk home like a beacon. There was no sign of her anywhere on the two blocks he covered on the main drag, so he quickened his pace. It wasn't until he turned onto her street and saw the lights from her house shimmering like a mirage through the thick trees that he was sure he could make her out, cruising up her driveway on those long, gorgeous legs of hers at a breakneck speed.

"Lauren," he called out, his voice sounding unnatural and loud in the relative peace of the small town.

She broke into a little jog, not even glancing over her shoulder.

"Lauren, wait," he called again. He had to give it to her, he thought as she made it to the bottom of the porch steps. She was determined.

But so was he.

Lauren felt like the hounds were nipping at her heels as she took the porch steps two at a time in a doomed attempt to elude him. She had to get inside—to the sanctuary of her home—before Cole caught up to her. Of course, her home wasn't really her sanctuary anymore, because she'd invited him into it and he was making her crazy in every possible way. But tonight of all nights, she simply didn't think she could take any more of his anger, any more of his damning judgments.

It seemed like he made it onto the porch in one giant leap, but she knew that was impossible. It also didn't seem possible that he would come to stand before her, civil and shamefaced. But he did.

"I'm sorry," he said in a low, gentle voice. The night was warm, waiting, still. "I'm so sorry."

"It doesn't matter, Cole," she said quickly, but she knew it did matter. More than it had in a very long time. She'd shown him her scars and dared him to shy away. And he had.

"Yes, it does," he whispered. "It matters to me."

She looked down, shook her head, held her voice steady. "For better or worse, Cole, I've been on my own a long time. I learned not to care what others thought of me. It's how I survived."

"Lauren, honey," he said just exactly as he had at the bowling alley earlier, and the intimacy of it gave her heart an unsolicited twinge. "That wasn't me back there. Hell, I'm not that judgmental bastard."

Her throat was tight with tension. She wanted to believe him, trust him, because…well, dammit, she liked him so much. "What do you want from me, Cole?" she asked, and everything inside her tightened for another assault.

"I want to listen. And I want to know who you are."

Lord, if only she could grant that simple request. But she was sure that if he did know who she really was, he wouldn't like her. And, worse, he wouldn't want her—certainly not in the way she knew she wanted him.

She began to shake her head, saying, "I don't—" but he stopped her, touched her cheek, his eyes glowing with kindness. "Can't you give me a second chance?"

What was happening to her? she thought as instinct had her leaning into his rough palm while warm tears began to burn trails of weakness down her cheeks. Her exhale was shaky.

If only his healthy, happy upbringing didn't make him so uniquely unsuited to understanding her shame-filled, friendless, familyless childhood, the things she'd missed out on, the dysfunctional foster families she'd endured, then maybe...

With one strong finger, Cole caught the next traitorous tear before it could fall and looked at her with a smile so concerned it sent sudden, unwelcome shivers of longing curling through her.

"Pretend I'm an idiot—which should be easy," he said, making her smile a little, "and tell me again." He pulled her into his arms, held her, stroked her back, pressed his lips against the top of her head. "Tell me again so I can rewind the tape and do it right this time."

His compassion was undoing her more thoroughly than his condemnation, she thought with a distant sense of alarm as his warm breath and his slightly spicy, slightly sawdusty and very seductive scent enveloped her, making her soften involuntarily in his arms. Either way, she knew she was seriously in way over her head with this man.

Lauren pulled away and looked at him. The bugs that hovered around the porch light danced behind him as she searched his eyes. She knew there was no way to be sure he wouldn't judge her again, no way to be sure he would accept her with all her warts, but she had to try. She had to try because the one thing she now *was* sure of was that she'd already begun to fall in love with him.

"My parents gave me up as a baby." She looked directly at him, dared him with her gaze to flinch. "*Threw* me away, really. In a train station. Like trash."

His face grew dark again, thunderous and ominous, but this time she knew instinctively that he wasn't angry with her. "Sweetheart," he began and compassion was heavy in his voice.

She held up one shaky hand to stop him. "I didn't

come from a wealthy family, Cole. But I was more than just poor. I was essentially a broken person, like a defective doll no one wanted to play with. My whole life—as a child, as an adult, in my career—I never belonged anywhere. No one ever wanted me. Can you understand that? No one ever wanted me.''

He stood very still for a very long time and she watched very closely, but his expression never did change. It seemed as if the moon had set, the sun had come up, and the stars had returned by the time he spoke.

''You're wrong, you know,'' he said quietly and the anger in his face dissolved before he pulled her back into his arms. His lips hovered above hers, his voice was tender but filled with need. ''*I* want you, Lauren. I've never wanted anyone like I want you.''

As he lowered his head and his lips touched hers sweetly and gently, Lauren felt as if the next time she inhaled, it would be the first time she'd ever breathed in her life. A profound anticipation and deep excitement stirred within her and any vestige of her resolve to keep their relationship simple and safe melted under the heat of that kiss. She wanted him. She wanted to be close to him, and in that moment nothing else mattered.

So on the two hundred and twenty-eighth day of her Year Without Men, Lauren set her commitment aside. She'd thought that she'd needed that sabbatical to protect herself, but now she knew that she'd only needed it to lead her here, to a place where she could learn to trust a man, learn to let him comfort her, learn to let herself need someone like she needed Cole—right down to the very roots of her being.

Sliding one hand over his lower back and slipping the other one up his chest to his neck, she found the place where his unruly hair licked the collar of his shirt and pulled him closer while he kissed her with aching tenderness. And when a groan escaped him, she closed her eyes and exhaled one long, slow, trembling breath.

Her heart hammered hard and insistent as they began to explore each other with curious, pleasure-giving hands. She felt his muscles tense under her exploratory touch, and a wonderful, powerful shiver passed through her.

"Cole," she said, pulling away from their kiss and looking up into those eyes that made anything seem possible. "I want to be with you tonight."

There was no mistaking her meaning. His eyes deepened to a color she'd never seen. When he spoke, his voice was low and intense. "Are you sure, Lauren? It seems like I've wanted you forever, but—"

She brushed her mouth against his to silence him and she melted into his warm soft lips for a moment before she stopped. She heard her breathing in the still night around them, felt the air between them compress as she whispered, "And I want to give you what you want. What we both want."

He hesitated only slightly, and when his mouth descended and crushed against hers, she let out a sigh of longing that she knew now had been bubbling just under the surface since the first day he'd stepped onto her porch.

The touch of his lips, the exploration of his tongue, sent thrilling sensations swirling from her fingertips all the way down to her toes. Feeling as if she wanted to pull him inside her, she arched into his body, her breasts against his chest, her hips against his thighs.

He abandoned their kiss and used his mouth to skim down her neck with a mind-melting intensity. Her head fell back and she let out a sound of pure pleasure as his hands skimmed her body. Touching all the places she'd been dreaming he'd touch every night as she'd tried to sleep.

Suddenly, he pulled away and looked at her with a gaze that sent chills rippling through her. He might not love her, she thought in that moment, but he wanted her and that would have to be enough. He reached down then, lifted her in his arms, pushed open the front door and carried her over the threshold of her home.

As they entered the living room, Cole realized he was adding logs to a raging bonfire that would eventually burn him, but he couldn't stop what was happening. He simply couldn't get enough of her. Funny, smart, sexy, vulnerable—all of it was converging to make this something he couldn't control.

With her still in his arms, he headed for the stairs, then spied the couch, which somehow beckoned him— and was infinitely closer.

Man, you are going to pay for this later, a shrill little angel on one shoulder warned him as he laid her down on the couch, covering her mouth with his own hungrily.

Yeah? Send me the bill, the devil on his other shoulder scoffed as Cole lay down beside her and slipped one hand under the edge of her sweater. Lauren sucked in a sharp breath when his fingers touched her warm, soft skin. God, how he'd wanted to feel her, see if her skin was as smooth and sweet as it looked.

He smiled against her lips. It was.

He wrapped his hand around the slim column of her waist and dragged his thumb across her ribs, just barely brushing the underside of one glorious, firm breast. She made a noise deep in her throat that sounded just like a purr and pushed her body into his hand.

Heat rushed through him, settling low in his body. "Lauren," he groaned, breaking their kiss. "What are you doing to me?"

She put her lips against his again, her sweet breath mingled with his when she answered, "Tell me. Tell me what I'm doing to you."

"You're driving me crazy, that's what," he whispered as his tongue traced the fullness of her lips and his hand roamed freely over the skin he'd dreamed about nightly. She'd been driving him crazy—with her smile, her laughter, her beauty, her sweetness, her love for his son—almost since he'd first laid eyes on her.

They were married in name only. But tonight, she belonged to him and he belonged to her.

Cole crushed her closer, kissing her deeply as a hot ache began to grow to critical proportions inside him. Then she met his tongue with hers and a wild, incredible pleasure surged through him, settling solidly, achingly low in his stomach. The sweet, honeyed taste of her, the electrifying feeling of her under his hands…it was simply overwhelming. He knew he wasn't thinking straight but he did know that no woman had ever made him feel this wild.

He slid his hands down her body, molding every inch of her into every inch of him, pulling her into the fullness straining painfully against his jeans. She moaned into his mouth and the heat rolled down and around and through him again.

She began to pull at his shirt buttons, opening some, fumbling with others. She was in a hurry and that knowledge sent a shiver of pure desire echoing through him. It seemed like it took a lifetime, but once she'd managed the last button, he shrugged off the shirt, then pushed his hand beneath her sweater. "Now it's my turn," he said.

She gave him a slow smile, a little wobbly at the corners, and something that had been tightening inside him contracted further. He tugged her sweater off and pulled away from her to see, at last, what he had been imagining a thousand times a day.

"You're so beautiful," he whispered, mesmerized.

He watched a bad-girl smile spread slowly across her features. Man, what would it be like to wake up every morning to a smile that made so many sinful promises? She pushed him away until he was the one lying on his back on the couch, then she leaned over him and began to unbutton his jeans. He smothered a groan as her fingernails grazed his skin and sent a shuddering ripple of excitement through his body. Then, in a smooth, seductive blur, she stripped his jeans off and shucked the rest of her own clothes. When she stood before him, her eyes filled with a sweet, sexy confidence, a strange and heady brew of desire and tenderness filled him.

Lauren's heart pounded a furious tattoo as she stood there, her body responding to his gaze, silently struggling, begging to be touched. And then he did touch her, reaching out for her, his rough hands cupping her flushed, swollen breasts and a violent shiver passed through her that had nothing to do with the night air on her naked skin. Her every nerve, every muscle seemed to vibrate under the pressure of his touch—just him, just one simple touch, but she found herself straining for breath. All at once, she hoped the moment would go on, hoped it would end, hoped she could survive the intense pleasure that she knew was just beginning.

With a muffled oath, he pulled her back down on top

of him. Their bodies came together—warm, naked, trembling skin against skin—and she felt an indescribable desire pour through her in thick, turbulent waves. The tips of her breasts tingled where they touched the silky hair on his chest, and when he moved his hands down her back, a trail of fire blazed in their wake.

She felt his hands slide down and cup her bottom, pulling her closer, their lips meeting in a frantic search for closeness. The incredible hardness of his arousal pressed against her as his fingers dipped lower, between her legs, and found her, wet and ready. She gasped, her need for him slipping out in little moans against his mouth.

"Lauren," he whispered, his voice frayed with intensity as he rolled her beneath him. "You feel…" His hands began to spread liquid fire over her naked skin, down to her stomach, her hips, her thighs. "…Amazing."

Lowering his head to her tight, aching breasts, Cole drew one sensitive bud into his mouth and the sensation of his tongue, hot and wet, caressing her beaded nipple both bound her and freed her all at once. She cried out, burying her fingers in his hair, arching her back to get closer. He pulled at her gently with his teeth, sending delicious shudders down the length of her and making her whimper in pure bliss. And when he moved to her other breast, she let out a sound of sheer frustration, writhing under his hands.

"Cole, please…" she begged breathlessly, haltingly. "I need…"

Smiling, he moved between her trembling legs, caressing her inner thighs. "What?" His voice was a low, thrilling whisper as he slipped one finger into her heated, throbbing core.

"To feel you." She pushed her hips up against his hands. "Please…"

"Yes," he said, "yes. Wait," and he got up and left her for what seemed like hours but was really just a few long, excruciating moments. She lay there on the couch, saw the light flip on in the room he'd used to change for the wedding, then smiled when she realized what he was doing. When he returned, he sheathed himself, then settled his big body over her and pulled her back into his arms.

Something inside her wound up like a watch spring as he kissed her deeply, then began to enter her slowly, so slowly, and the pressure of him between her legs sent a hot, intense shaking spiraling through her. Slanting her hips up, she pulled him into her, her body accepting him eagerly as he pushed himself inside, inch by glorious inch.

He murmured her name against her cheek and his breath burned hot and uneven as he began to move inside her, slowly and smoothly until, together, they found the sweet, deep rhythm of pleasure. Echoes of pure ecstasy flowed over and through her as they flew, higher and higher, to a height of passion so dizzying, she was almost frightened. She tried to control it, knew that she always had, and yet now, with Cole, that seemed impossible, as if it were completely beyond her power.

Her body began to vibrate, her control slipped further, far beyond her reach, until finally it gave, and she clutched at the couch beneath her, crying out his name as she began hurtling into a stunning, blindingly beautiful place she'd never known existed. He answered her, his voice so raw and primitive, the mere sound of him overwhelmed her.

It was then, right then, held tight in the embrace of

the man she was falling in love with, that she shattered into a million tiny fragments, then fell back together in his arms, safe and complete, and he followed, spilling into her with a groan torn from deep within him.

It was impossible to move, so Lauren lay still as her breathing returned to normal, and enjoyed the wonderfully unfamiliar weight of him upon her. Cole held her in his arms and sprinkled kisses down her temple and ear, his own labored breath fanning warm and sweet against her skin. She knew she should be worried about what would happen next, what would happen during her next breath, but she simply wouldn't do it. Tonight, she was ignoring the lessons of her past, ignoring the fears of the future. Tonight, she was going to be right where she was.

She drew in the spicy scent of him, of their love-making, and tightened her hold, enjoying a sense of contentment she'd never known, a sense of completeness and belonging she never thought she'd experience.

He chuckled then and the sound rumbled through her. "By God," he said. "This couch has got a new chapter in its history now."

She smiled as she remembered trying to explain her love of objects and their stories at their barbecue. "Do you think it'll tell the toaster about it?"

They laughed together and when they did, she realized with a jolt that she'd never laughed after making love before in her life. "Unbelievable," she whispered and heard the awe in her own voice.

He smiled as he rolled off of her and pulled her into his arms. "You can say that again."

Smiling, she rested her cheek against him and mumbled into his strong, muscled chest. "I hope I will. Very soon."

He laughed quietly as he trailed shivers down her back with his fingers, then cupped her bottom with his big hands. "I can guarantee it."

She tipped her head back so she could see him and teased, "Promises, promises."

His smile died by degrees, making her frown for the barest second before he jumped up and swept her into his arms. "I always keep my promises," he said with a sinister smile that made her laugh again. And with that he carried her upstairs like a pirate making off with the kidnapped princess. And that's just what she wanted tonight, she thought as she wrapped her arms around his neck. To live in a fairy tale.

Pushing open the door with his foot, he strode across her bedroom and laid her down on her beautiful antique double wedding ring quilt that she bought from an Amish farmer last year in Pennsylvania.

Then he leaned down over her with a sinful glint in his eyes. "After what we just accomplished down on the couch, I think we can do some serious damage in this much space."

She pulled him down into her arms, then rolled him over and climbed on top of him. His eyes caressed her, warming her and making her feel like the most desirable woman in the world. "You know," she said, reaching down and grazing her fingernails over his chest, "you are worth giving up on my year of celibacy."

He stilled beneath her, then asked, "What?"

"Celibacy. You know, abstinence?" she prodded him playfully, then explained about her now-abandoned plan.

That damn lazy grin of his, the one that had been

sucking her into his vortex since the first day she'd met him, spread silkily over his face. "How much of your year did you complete?"

She hesitated, then thought, why not? "Two hundred and twenty-eight days."

He gave her a wicked grin as his hands slid from her hips to her waist. "Then I think we have some very serious catching up to do."

"Hallelujah," she said, then gasped as his fingers went on the move. "When do we get started?"

"You got a problem with right now?" he said as his hands slid up farther and caressed her sensitive, tingly breasts hungrily.

With a wicked grin of her own, she leaned into his stroking palms, then lifted up slightly, just high enough to slide her body down over him, impaling herself on top of him. He was hard, hot, ready, and with his erection buried deep inside her, she began to move over him in a primal rhythm. "No problem at all," she said on a breathless sigh.

He groaned, his eyes dark with desire, then whispered almost soundlessly as he pulled in a deep breath, "Hallelujah."

Nine

Cole woke slowly, stubbornly refusing to give up the dream he'd been having—the dream of Lauren in his arms, making love with her, hearing her moans of pleasure—until he felt, almost simultaneously, the sting of sunlight on his closed eyelids and the warm, soft pressure of Lauren's curvy backside snuggling up against him.

He smiled and flung an arm over the woman who was both a dream and no illusion. Visions of last night played like a motion picture on the screen of his closed eyes. He pulled her closer against him as he savored the moments and felt a little as if they were floating on her big, comfortable bed, adrift in their own perfect world.

Lord, if only he could find a way to be with her, see her, date her. But when the real world came to find them—which it would soon enough—and she learned who he really was, the possibility of them seeing one another would be gone. Once she learned about all his lies, all the things he hadn't told her, he'd be persona non grata around here.

And up until just yesterday, he'd been willing to bear that cost. It had seemed worth it. But now, things had changed between them—things had changed inside Cole. And no matter the risk, or the loss of this sweet paradise, he knew he had to tell her the truth about himself.

Lauren stirred again. "Cole," she murmured sleepily, sweetly, then burrowed closer.

His body warmed and roused and demanded attention as she pressed into him. Resisting her was impossible, so he didn't even try. He breathed in the lemony scent of her hair as he let his hand roam down the flat plane of her stomach, searching, circling, teasing her until she sighed and stretched and rolled to her back beside him.

"Morning," she said, smiling, her eyelids heavy, her lips as pink as cotton candy, her cheeks flushed.

"Good morning, sweet," he answered, and wasn't even surprised when the endearment popped out his mouth. It seemed natural. Too natural. And that made it even harder to say what he had to say. But she deserved his honesty. "Lauren, there's something I have to say—"

"No," she said, reaching up and touching his lips with her fingertips.

His brows drew together. "What do you mean, 'no'?"

She pulled her hand away with a little smile. "I mean I'm not looking for answers or explanations or excuses. I'm not looking for you to tell me anything right now."

He barely had time to lament how difficult she was

making this for him before her smile deepened and she said, "Cole, I told you about my life and my past. And even though this," she said as she swept his cheek with the back of one slim hand, "is just a fantasy, it feels more…*right* than my life has felt in a long time. I just want to live on this cloud for a while. All right?"

Did she have to look at him like that? With her eyes imploring him to understand? God, how much would he love to be able to sweep his responsibility under the rug for a few days?

She gave him a soft smile, an encouraging smile. "Let's enjoy the week, then we'll bare our souls. Deal?"

He nodded, said, "Okay," even as he wondered at his sudden, irresponsible desire to do…well, to do whatever they wanted to do.

"And that also means no regrets about last night, this morning or anything else, you get me?" she said, shooting him a stern look.

Making love to her was not the regret he was worried about, he thought, then his brain shifted and lasered in on what she'd just said. Last night, this morning…

"This morning? What happened this morning?" he asked.

"Nothing yet," she said with a very devilish smile. "But a girl can hope, can't she?"

So can a man. Images of them lying here together like this every morning rumbled across his mind like a stampede. But the image evaporated as quickly as it came because just then Lauren reached down and began to stroke his thigh. An almost unbearable heat spread through him, pooling in his groin, stretching his desire for her practically to the point of pain.

His quick arousal should have surprised him—especially after last night—but it didn't. Lauren was a woman he wanted like he'd never allowed himself to want anything. She lay beside him, one hand grazing slowly up his thigh to enclose his erection in her warm palm, her other hand trailing over her own breasts teasingly.

"You're doing it again," he said on a groan, pulling her into his arms.

A seductive smile curved her lips. "Doing what?"

"Driving me crazy."

"I am?" she said as she stroked the hard length of him. And as she batted her eyelashes in a play of false innocence, he knew that all he wanted in the world at that moment was to possess her again, to be a part of the power and wonder of being inside her.

Revelations would come soon enough. But for now...

He dipped his head and captured her mouth in a kiss that was both greedy and giving. The softness he found there seduced him like a drug, binding them together, just as it had last night. But this time, he made love to her slowly, until she begged him to give her release, to let her fall from the heights where he held her prisoner.

And when she convulsed around him, crying out her pleasure, the sound of it reached deep inside him and tugged at him in places he hadn't known existed. But then time came to a sweet halt as he toppled over the edge, holding her close as he filled her with one last thrust.

He lay there, holding her while her breathing quieted, stroking her, feeling more replete, more tender than he could ever remember.

She turned her cheek to his chest and her skin felt so incredibly soft against him. She burrowed closer, mumbling something against his skin.

"What's that, sweetheart?"

"Thanks," she said, her cheek still glued to his chest, a smile in her voice, "for playing with me."

He laughed, remembering her words last night when she'd told him she'd always felt like a doll no one wanted to play with. "Anytime," he said as he pulled the quilt up around her shoulders, tucking her in for a bit more sleep before the day—and, eventually, their future—reached in and pulled them apart. "Anytime at all."

And, he thought as he dropped another kiss into her hair and she snuggled against him, he'd be damned if he didn't mean it.

Lauren sat back on her haunches, pulled off a glove, wiped her brow and surveyed her work. It had taken her two hours to staple insulation to *one wall* of her barn. Good Lord, how on earth were they going to finish this on time?

Maybe if she'd been a little more focused, spent a little less time woolgathering about Cole and their love-making, she might have finished sooner. She checked her watch for the dozenth time, saw it wasn't even noon, yanked off her other glove, stood, stretched and yawned. Tonight she was going to need more sleep. Or more coffee. She could sleep some other time, she mused with a frown, like after Cole finished this job and moved on to sunnier pastures. But since that thought only served to stab at her heart with tiny, painful darts, she pushed it away.

The earsplitting whine of a steel blade chewing wood pierced the air, making her look over her shoulder. She saw Cole hunched over the table saw she'd rented for him last week, cutting boards as quickly and efficiently as if he were slicing cheese at a deli counter. Her gaze raked over him, from the Levi's molding his backside to the shirt drawn tight across his back to the muscles in his arms bunching and flexing with each pull on the saw.

Closing her eyes and breathing in the sharp, nutty scent of the freshly ripped boards, Lauren remembered the feel of his sleekly muscled body beneath her touch not so many hours ago. She curled her fingers into her palms to scratch the hands that itched to get at him again.

The sound of the screaming blades quieted and she opened her eyes to see Cole laying the boards out in order, getting ready to create the hardwood floor of her store. As she watched him work, she congratulated herself for stopping the heart to heart he'd almost gotten into this morning. Sure, next Saturday she'd probably still get his "I'm leaving in a few weeks and I don't want to hurt you" speech, but until then she knew that something deep inside her needed this time with him, just a few more days with the man she loved. Lord, he wasn't staying forever, she knew that, but she was going to take what she could get, while she could get it, like a greedy child in a candy store.

"Hey, Bob Vila," she called out to him, forcing a lightness into her voice she wished she could feel. "You ready for a break? Lunch maybe?"

Cole turned around, his gorgeous mug splitting into a wide grin as he glanced at his watch. "At eleven-thirty?" He cocked his head to the side. "Why do I think you have some sort of ulterior motive, Boss?"

"I'm crushed," she said, flushing hotly under her lightweight denim work shirt. *Good Lord, am I that transparent?* "I just don't want the labor inspectors coming down on my head, that's all."

"You *have* been working me a little hard lately," he said, his eyes twinkling with amusement. "I have an idea. Why don't you come over here and help me. Then we can talk in depth about the best way to relax on our break."

Her stomach dipped at his emphasis on the words, "talk in depth." He'd done a bit of that last night, whispering spicy, sensual things to her as he moved inside her. With warm cheeks and warmer insides, she came to sit beside him.

"After this, that is," he said, pulling her close and giving her a mind-melting kiss before releasing her. "By the way, that's all you're getting until lunchtime," he joked, but his eyes told a different story—one that spoke of heat and passion and skin on skin.

"Rationing them out, are you?" Lauren laughed at his grave nod. "I see that the balance of power has shifted."

"You have all the power, sweetheart, I assure you."

She took a breath, trying to calm the disquiet that rioted inside her and focused on helping him with his work. And as she did, she began to get a sense of Cole's skill, watching him work quickly, without wasted movement or fierce bouts of cursing like one of her foster fathers who'd fancied himself a handyman around the apartment.

"You love what you do, don't you, Cole?" she asked as she marked the boards with numbers to keep them in order.

He looked up and gave her his trademark grin. "Yep. And at the end of the day, I have the satisfaction of knowing I've created something from nothing."

As he spoke, he pushed the long tongue and groove edges of two boards together with a flex of his strong arms. When she noticed how perfectly the boards fit together, she couldn't help but be reminded of the perfect fit of their bodies the night before.

By the time they were finished, it really was time for a break. Lauren stood and stretched her back, then sucked in a sharp breath when Cole came up behind her and began to knead her shoulder muscles.

Pure rapture made her sigh at his ministrations before she turned toward him, lifted up on tiptoe and dragged her lips over his. Without warning, he wrapped her tightly in his arms and gave her a long, knee-buckling kiss.

Pulling his lips away a mere inch, he looked down at her with his magnetic gaze. "If you're still worried about those labor inspectors, I have an idea how you can keep them off your tail," he whispered, his eyes twinkling with his teasing words.

His breath had tickled her lips so she dived in for another quickie before saying, "Cole, I won't stoop to bribing my employees."

His eyes widened with playful innocence. "You, Lauren Travis, have a bad-girl's mind."

"I was hoping you'd notice," she said, laughing even as he picked her up in one smooth move, slung her over his shoulder and spanked her while she squealed in surprise.

"Cole, Cole," she yelped and laughed and screamed all at once as she pounded ineffectually at his broad back, feeling a bit like a woodpecker trying to fell a tree. "Put me down...noooo, put me down! Please..."

He stopped, then pulled her back over the front of his shoulder, smiling mischievously as he let her slip slowly, agonizingly down his body. It wasn't until her feet hit the hard wooden subfloor that she felt the evidence of his arousal against her stomach.

Her gaze snapped up to his as her whole body responded to his silent call. Oh, Lord, she thought as she sank into the dark, passionate blue light in his eyes, how was she going to let this man go when the time came?

"Dammit, woman," he said, his voice hoarse, crackling with tension. "I don't care how late I have to stay up to finish my work tonight." He grabbed her hand and headed up the loft stairs. "We're taking that break right now."

They bounded up to the loft, laughing, racing, buttons flying and zippers whirring. But Cole was faster, and when he jumped onto the bed naked as can be, leaned back against the carved wood headboard and said, "Stop!" Lauren instinctively did as she was told.

She'd already managed to peel off her shorts, so she stood before him in her day of the week undies and her work shirt, which was unbuttoned and hanging open. "What?" she asked in exasperation.

"Correct me if I'm wrong," he said, lacing his hands behind his neck as if he had all the time in the world. "But isn't today Monday?"

She put one hand on her hip and said, "Uh, yes. Why?"

"Because your underwear says it's Friday, so I just wanted to be sure."

"Well, I'll tell you what, Cole," she said as she glanced down to confirm his claim, then sauntered up to the side of the bed. "When you start doing the laundry, you can be personally responsible for my underwear matching up with the calendar."

"Laundry, barbecuing, back rubs." His slow grin was filled with seductive intent. "You ask and I'll do."

A whirlwind of ideas rolled into her mind. "Anything?"

He nodded almost imperceptibly as his gaze bathed her with his appreciation, moved over her like a caress. And her body responded in kind. Her skin was tight, her breasts ached and her heart hammered mercilessly as she slipped off her shirt and let it fall to the floor.

Suddenly, he leaned forward and grabbed her hand, pulling her down onto the bed. While this thing between them had an uncertain future, she thought, right now, the present was looking pretty good.

Cole felt a shiver of anticipation as he gazed down at her lying beside him on the bed, clad only in undies and a plain white bra which somehow managed to look like a showcase for a priceless work of art. She was beautiful, all silken skin and smooth muscle and just enough curves in exactly the right places. Perfect. And all his.

He took her wrists gently in one hand and pulled them just above her head, then settled himself beside her. He watched as the laughter in her eyes died and a sultry passion darkened them.

"So, what can I do for you?" he said as he used his free hand to stroke her body, lingering over her breasts, teasing her nipples into tight, pink buds through the thin fabric with his fingertips.

Her hands trapped, she arched into his body in response to his touch. Her tongue darted out to wet her lips and the simple action almost undid him. "Clothes…off," she said in a breathless whisper.

"Done," he murmured as his hand slid down and skillfully unsnapped the front clasp of her bra, freeing her breasts to his gaze, making her gasp. Then he continued down her silken belly, between her legs. She bucked up against his hand, and he lowered his head to capture her mouth just as she let out a soft moan.

Her response made him crazy, sent his blood pounding fast and furious, but he kept a control over himself that he hadn't known was possible. He didn't know why, but he knew he wanted to give her something, do something that would show her just how much he wanted her.

He freed her hands and let his mouth follow the trail he'd blazed moments before, nipping and licking wherever he went. Then, he moved down her belly and farther still, to the soft, sweet place between her thighs.

"Cole," she cried. "I...please—"

"Is that a request?" he asked gently, his hands sliding beneath her, removing her panties and lifting her to him.

"Yes," she moaned. "Oh, yes." And then her fingers tangled in his hair as he moved over her there, her breathless sighs full of passion. She thrashed against the pillow, gasping as he took her higher and higher, her muscles straining and flexing as she lifted her hips off the bed until, finally, crying out, she came apart in his hands.

And he wondered in that brief, wonderful moment if he'd ever get enough of her, knew he wouldn't, knew he alone was responsible for whatever happened when this whole thing came crashing down. But then Lauren moaned his name, her body still shuddering in climax, and he could only feel a wanting of her that bordered on desperation.

In one smooth movement, he ripped open a packet, sheathed himself, then eased himself up to cover her, grasping her hips and slipping inside her. She closed around him, sighing, and when he looked into her face, he saw a passion and abandon that tore him apart.

They moved together as one, their voices rising and falling in a passionate harmony, their rhythm so perfect Cole felt like their very breath was in sync. He strained to hold on, to last forever inside her, feeling like if he did, he could hold on to some precious part of them.

But when she threw her head back and begged him to release her again, he knew he was lost. She cried out, clutching at his shoulders, pushing her hips up and drawing him impossibly farther inside as she convulsed around him. And at that he, too, tumbled over the edge, fast and unrestrained, crying out his release.

The week sped by, feeling more like a day in paradise than five days laughing, talking and working side by side, toiling to get Simpson's Gems ready. And the nights, too, Cole thought. Ah, yes, the long nights with her in his arms, sharing their minds and bodies, giving and receiving the most intense pleasure of his life.

But by Friday night, Cole was jolting back and forth between joy and despair with the velocity of a pinball fresh out of the chute. Now that the week was drawing to a close, he was going to tell her what he should have told her days ago. And then he was going to lose her in the most difficult way possible, just as he'd always known he would. But now, after their week together, it somehow seemed more than he could endure.

This afternoon while they were working, they'd decided that since they'd been eating breakfast out of Donut Hut boxes all week, they'd quit work early and make breakfast food at dinnertime. He looked over at Lauren who'd gone upstairs and changed, emerging dressed for breakfast in her men's-style pajamas with fried eggs embroidered on them, the pant legs rolled up to show her tanned ankles and slippers that were each decorated with another fried egg. In that goofy getup, she shouldn't have looked so sexy. No one should. It just wasn't fair.

"More coffee?" she asked with a *Price is Right* hostess smile on her face, holding aloft a brilliant blue vintage aluminum percolator she'd bought in Bakersfield one hot summer day a few years back. The coffeepot had a story, of course, and he remembered it.

And that scared him out of his damned mind.

"Absolutely," he said, looking away from her and turning back to the stove to begin fishing the poached eggs out of the saucepan. "Then sit down and fasten your seat belt, because you are about to eat my one and only breakfast specialty," he boasted as he spooned hollandaise sauce over the eggs, ham and toasted muffin halves.

Moments later, he set the plate of Eggs Benedict before her with a flourish, offered her a fork, then waited patiently for the praise he knew was coming his way.

And sure enough, after one bite, she rolled her eyes heavenward and moaned her approval. "Ohmigod, you have to teach me how to make this."

He smiled proudly as he settled down in front of his own plate. "Not on your life. It's my secret weapon."

Lauren's features clouded a bit beneath a very slight frown. "Something tells me this isn't your first time making this for a lady in her kitchen."

She looked as startled by what she'd said as he felt hearing it. All week, they'd avoided talking about their past relationships as studiously as they'd avoided talk of the future, but it was all still there between them.

"It's not," he said. "In fact, every so often I still make this for the woman who taught me."

"Oh," she said, smiling weakly, speaking so quietly he almost had to read her lips. Silly girl, he thought. Didn't she know he'd already figured out the nuances of her smiles? That one was a counterfeit, for sure.

"Yeah," he said, savoring another bite—and teasing her—for a moment longer. "Every Mother's Day, actually. My mom loves it."

One fried-egg slipper containing a surprisingly pointy foot connected with his shin. "Ow!" he said, looking up into her innocent eyes.

"What?" she said, hefting another forkful of eggs.

"You know you're going to pay for that," he began, sliding his chair around to her side of the table.

She smiled widely and shook her head. "You keep making these promises, Cole…"

His hands were just reaching for her when the phone rang, shrill and insistent. "I'll get it," he said, dipping his head to take one quick kiss first.

"Hi, Co'." He heard the childish voice of his son beam through the phone like bright sunshine. Even though Cole had spoken to the boy every day since he'd left, today was different because soon, very soon, Jem would know Cole was his dad.

"Hi, kiddo," Cole answered, almost choking on the simple words as the complexity of his predicament hit him anew with the force of a speeding train.

Cole and Jem talked for a few minutes—about Jem's audience with Mickey, about the great places he'd been, about all the junk food his Grandma Sherry had let him eat. When they were finished, Cole told Jem he'd see him tomorrow, then handed the phone to Lauren.

He watched her expression change as she spoke

to her son—interest, laughter, encouragement, love, pride—and found himself smiling when she was smiling, frowning when she was frowning, hopeful when she was hopeful.

Suddenly, Cole couldn't take any more. The whole scene was something he'd never thought to experience, never knew he'd even wanted, and now would never be able to have. He gestured to Lauren that he was going upstairs to shower and change and she nodded her understanding.

When he emerged from the bedroom fifteen minutes later, Lauren was just coming up the stairs.

"He'll be home tomorrow," she said. The glow of happiness on her face was flawless. "I can't wait."

"I miss him, too," he said, then wished he could reel the words back in when she looked up at him, her eyes wide and sincere, and said, "You know, you're so much like a father to him, Cole. It seems so natural for you both."

Cole took one long look at her as a strangling steel band encircled his chest, his temples, his throat, choking him. This was crazy and so was he. He couldn't lie to her again. He had to tell her now. He had to tell her the truth, then watch, helpless, as that glimmer of hope and happiness in her eyes died.

"Lauren, I know you asked me to wait until tomorrow to talk about anything serious, but this can't wait. We have to talk—"

"No!" she said, then laughed at her own fierce reaction. "No home truths until tomorrow. Sorry," she said, shrugging as if to say she couldn't be held responsible for his foolish promises. "But you agreed. And I'm holding you to it."

She was serious. She was seriously going to hold him

to that silly pledge they'd made in the afterglow of their lovemaking. Well, he wasn't just going to sit here and pretend like his mind wasn't preoccupied and his conscience was clear. Cole felt the frustration, the sheer volume of guilt and lies expanding painfully inside him until, finally, it exploded with the force of a ton of dynamite.

"I have to go," he said in a gruff voice as he brushed past her and headed down the stairs two at a time.

"Wait…where?"

"I need some air," he mumbled as he took the last few stairs in a single leap and headed out the door.

Air, hell. What he really needed was her, in his arms, her mouth on his, her soft, husky laughter soothing his senses. But that wasn't gonna happen—and the only person he could blame was himself.

Ten

Lauren stared at the empty staircase, waiting until she heard Cole close the door behind him. When she did, she had the overwhelming sense that she'd just lost a friend, her best friend. No, it was worse than that. When he'd walked out that door, it felt like he'd taken a huge chunk of her heart with him.

A shiver ran through her overheated body as she tipped her forehead against the cool wall. *Why, oh, why did I say that about him being a father to Jem?* Was it because Jem had questioned her five times in ten minutes about whether Cole would be there when he got home tomorrow? Or was it because she'd just had an unspeakably wonderful week with the man who was only supposed to be playing the role of her husband but who had ended up being her friend, her lover, her confidant, her strong shoulder, her…well, her *husband?*

That was it. She'd just spent a week in a fantasy

marriage, a week in the arms of a man that made her laugh, made her think, made her shudder in the most extraordinary ecstasy. *That* was why she'd all but blurted out something she hadn't even known she was thinking. Cole *would* be a wonderful father for Jem, but he'd also be a wonderful husband to her.

Based on his rather abrupt departure, however, that obviously was the furthest thing from his mind. Her heart sank. Cole had accepted her proposal and had married her to help her keep her son, not because he felt anything for her. She was the one who'd had to go and fall in love.

What had once been desire—a crush almost—had turned into so much more. It had turned into love. The kind that when they were together made it seem like the birds sang just for them, that the bunnies danced across the yard just so they could laugh. And, apparently, that pesky little detail called love had tempted her into her careless behavior—because she now knew with a blinding rush of clarity exactly what she wanted. She wanted him to stay and make her and Jem his family. And not just for appearances. For real.

She knew she had to regain control of this situation, and the only way she could think of to do that was to be grateful for what he *had* given them, be satisfied with that gift, and let him go when the time came. But could she? Would she have the strength? Did she even have a choice?

Suddenly, she understood Cole's need to get out of the house. The air inside was thick with questions and restless energy. Perhaps the air outside was fresh and filled with answers. And she did know of one place that might do the trick. She was long overdue for a Double

Dip—and a peek at the sign, if only for confirmation of her mind-boggling stupidity.

She changed out of her pajamas quickly, stuffed some money in her pocket, headed downstairs and pulled her car keys out from under Cole's on the hook by the door. If she'd checked sooner, the Frosty King sign might have told her "not to be hasty," or "look farther afield," or "trust not the damned serpent who winds his charms around your heart." Lauren sighed as she pulled the SUV onto Main Street. Anything that could have warned her not to marry a man she was falling in love with would have been fine and dandy, she thought as she headed out for her reckoning with today's maxim.

Her hands clamped the steering wheel rigidly as she approached the Frosty King and squinted through the windshield. It was eight o'clock, dusk, that terrible time when a driver's pupils had to struggle with the fading light. She slowed, stopped, peered out the window— then dropped her forehead onto the hard plastic of the steering wheel.

Love Is The Triumph Of Imagination Over Intelligence.

Just as she'd thought, she mused as she pulled into a parking space and went inside for something to soothe her bruised spirit. However misguided, she *had* been thinking there might be a future for Cole and her. But that had been wishful thinking, just like the sign said.

Lauren got her order bagged up, then headed home to start her pity party. Wherever Cole had gone, she was sure he wouldn't darken her doorway—at least her bedroom doorway—again tonight. But the sooner they both met reality head-on the better. Right after she established a good sugar buzz, she was going to pack up his things that had, over the course of their week, gotten integrated into her bedroom and move them to the guest room.

And that's how she'd think of him until he completed work on her store and departed for parts unknown. A guest. One that she knew she'd be wishing would return for a long, long time to come.

During the week, Valle Verde basically rolled up their sidewalks by six o'clock, but tonight was Friday and things were hopping—relatively speaking, anyway—so Cole walked around town for a while, trying to put order to his confused mind. But it wasn't too long before he'd seen enough of couples flirting, holding hands, laughing and kissing as they emerged from restaurants, the bakery, the single-screen movie theater and the local bed-and-breakfast. In fact, there were so many couples out tonight, it made him feel as if he was missing the next departure of Noah's Ark.

Thinking maybe a beer would help, he escaped to Herbie's Pizza and Pasta Bowl where he knew he could get a cold one. But considering how agitated he was when he first tipped back his frosty glass, the drink quickly lost its charm. He couldn't stop remembering what it was like to be here the night he and Lauren got married, what it was like to have her throw herself into his arms and kiss him so deeply he'd felt it all the way down to the toes of his boots. He couldn't stop remembering everything he'd learned about her that night and where it had led. And he couldn't stop thinking about how what he'd just done back at the house had probably reinforced her beliefs about herself.

On that grim note, Cole abandoned his beer and ditched Herbie's. As he walked toward the Frosty King, he wondered with every step he took how in the hell he was going to tell Lauren the truth tomorrow, how he was going to face her reaction and how Jem would feel when he learned that Cole was the father he'd always thought hadn't wanted him.

Cole ordered, then, with a weighty sigh, sat down and waited at a bright red Frosty King table—the same exact table where not so long ago he'd learned that Jem was his son. He looked across the empty expanse of table and thought of how Lauren and Jem had sat there side by side, laughing, coloring superhero coloring books. Lord, how could he even consider taking his son away from her? There had to be another way. Some way that he and Lauren could share Jem as easily and effortlessly as if they were neighbors.

He smiled to himself. Having Lauren for a neighbor would be the most distracting, unnerving solution he could imagine. And yet... His smile died away a bit at a time. It *would* be a way for everyone to come out a winner.

He looked outside the window and watched a young man climb a tall ladder and quickly change the Frosty King's huge outdoor sign. It was a possibility, one he wouldn't have even considered a few weeks ago. But if he moved to Valle Verde, Jem wouldn't have to be taken away from Lauren, and Lauren wouldn't feel as if she was losing her son.

His brothers would have to take over the business and he'd have to start fresh here, but he had plenty of money saved. And his family would hate the idea, but they'd understand that he wanted to do what was best for his son. Of course, he couldn't deny that somewhere in the tiny fine print of his plan, he was also going to stick to Lauren like glue and see if, over time, after he'd groveled and charmed her half to death, she might consider dating him.

Cole glanced absently at the boy who'd just put up a new sign and the completed message he'd written there: *Everything Is Possible. Pass The Word.* He looked away, his mind pumping like a fire hose. They'd still have to dissolve this crazy marriage. No matter how amazing their time together had been, he was still strongly opposed to marriage. But they didn't need to be married for them to be just like a family—if only he could get Lauren to someday forgive him for his deception.

He grabbed his take-out bag and headed out of the Frosty King at a jog, already feeling like a ton of weight had been lifted from him. Tomorrow, he wasn't going in to their talk blind—he was going in with a plan.

He was home in record time and up the stairs in seconds, but when he came to her bedroom door he hesitated.

She might be angry or, at the very least, confused by his hasty departure earlier. What would he say? He couldn't share his plan with her, and until they had what he was beginning to think of as their doomsday conversation, he couldn't share anything about himself, except that he'd really, really missed her tonight.

That's when he heard her call out in a voice that was not quite chilly but not quite warm, "If you're a rat, keep walking. There's no cheese in here."

He knew her well enough now to know she'd been smiling when she'd said that. He grinned to himself as he cracked the door, then snaked his hand and the Frosty King bag through the slim opening so she'd see he was armed. "Even rats who come bearing gifts?" he asked through the wood.

Her muffled chuckle gave him a shot of confidence. Pushing the door open a bit farther, he stepped through it. That's when he saw the evidence that she, too, had been to the Frosty King. A half-full shake sat on the nightstand, its sides sweating like a glass of iced tea on a sunny day. Two cardboard pint-size containers lay open before her on the bed, one spoon stuck in each sweet dessert, ready for action. A crumpled white bag with a red-and-yellow crown lay near the trash can. He imagined her trying and failing to score a basket with it and smiled again.

As he approached the bed where she sat cross-legged, she caught him looking at her own private ice cream social and raised an eyebrow that clearly said, "you want to make something of it?"

"Lauren," Cole said, ignoring her challenging look as he sat down beside her. "Tonight, I just had to—"

"It's okay," she answered quietly. "I understand."

He shook his head as he picked up one of her cartons of ice cream and halfheartedly dug out a bite. "No, you couldn't possibly understand, sweetheart," he said. "But you were right. We'll talk tomorrow like we—" He paused as he realized what kind of ice cream he was holding. "Hey, you hate Strawberry Cheesecake ice cream. Why'd you buy this?"

She shrugged. "So I bought your favorite flavor. So what? It doesn't mean anything."

"Then this," he said, opening his own bag and pulling out another carton of strawberry and a carton of her favorite, Peanut Butter Fudge Ribbon, "doesn't mean anything either."

She looked up at him, a slow smile spreading cautiously over her face, first confused, then mystified, then something softer he couldn't name. "That's a coincidence, isn't it?" she said finally.

"I wish that's all it was," he said, but he finished the thought silently—but I know it's so much more.

She considered him for a long moment. "I was going to move your things into the guest room tonight." She hesitated, then said, "Now I'm not sure what to do."

Cole swung his body around and lay down against the huge stack of fluffy white pillows only a woman would bother with. "There'll be time enough tomorrow. Time enough for everything," he said, setting his ice cream on the table before reaching over for hers and doing the same with it.

He pulled her down into his arms and she sighed and rested one hand on his ribs, her cheek against his chest as had already become their custom. Then he tucked her head under his chin and dimmed the light.

"Cole?" she asked him in the semi-darkness, her voice sleepy and content.

"Yes, sweet?"

"Remind me to clean out a drawer for your socks and underwear tomorrow, okay?"

Cole felt a blinding pain in his chest as he stared at the ceiling. After she heard the truth about him, she wouldn't want him or his boxer shorts anywhere near her.

"You got it," he whispered and even though he hadn't asked God for anything since that Turbo 9000 racing bike when he was ten, he found himself praying now that the sign at the Frosty King was right. Maybe, he thought as he stroked her bare, warm arm, everything really was possible.

Lauren puttered around her bedroom, gathering and sorting the dirty laundry and smiling like a loon. The sound of Cole working in the barn floated through the windows she'd opened a few hours ago when they'd finally extricated themselves from the tangled sheets and one another after a long night in each other's arms.

As she filled her huge wicker laundry basket, Lauren thought about the wonderful, erotic experience she'd had in the wee hours when she'd woken to Cole's mouth on her breast, his hand slipping down to feel her already wet and ready for him. And afterward…oh, afterward when he'd taken her to the outer limits of who she was, to the very edge of what she thought she could actually *feel*.

Even now, hours later, she let out a shuddering sigh at the memory, then refocused on her task. If she didn't get the laundry done this morning, she'd never have a full sock drawer by the time Sherry came to inspect— as she'd threatened to do on the phone last night just before Cole had taken off for parts unknown.

He'd come home, though, and with a bagful of her favorite ice cream—a peace offering. She hoisted the basket and headed for the door. Maybe, just maybe, that meant he was thinking of staying. Maybe it meant he was starting to feel something for her and for Jem.

As she walked by the bed, Lauren spotted Cole's duffel bag sticking out from underneath the bedskirt. She smiled and thought about him reaching down and yanking it from under the bed, grabbing a foil packet to protect her, something she'd watched him do a remarkable number of times this week.

She started to scoot it back under the bed with her toe, then decided she may as well look to see if he had any dirty clothes in there. God knew she hadn't done much laundry this week, what with the working and the sweating and the passionate nights together. Now she had to catch up on the chores quickly since Jem would be home soon bearing, no doubt, a Scooby-Doo suitcase jam-packed with dirty clothes.

Thinking about the pleasure she got from taking care of her two men, she smiled to herself as she dropped the basket and knelt down to check the bag. She pulled out some underwear and socks that she promptly chucked into her basket, then found a stash of extra shoelaces, a pair of his jeans and a pile of black T shirts. He must've cornered the market on these damn things, she thought as she held one up to her nose for the briefest moment and inhaled deeply.

The warm, summer scent of him was embedded in the fabric, widening her smile. She put the shirts down, then opened the bag wider to continue her search. She stilled for the barest moment, though, when she saw a cell phone—an item he'd sworn he didn't have the first day they'd met—and a stack of fat manila folders, the top one of which had the word "Simpson" written in heavy black ink on its file tab.

Thoughts zipped through her mind at warp speed. Was it the plans for her barn? No, all of his papers relating to her construction project were in the loft. So what the heck was it? She leaned closer and flipped open the folder.

Then her pulse skittered, tripped—and started again with a fierce, banging rhythm.

There, on top of a harmless-looking stack of papers was a photo of her and Jem that the paparazzi had taken of them last year. A vague, unfocused fear filled her as she turned the page to see what lay beneath it.

Her eyes narrowed, fixating on a thick report of some kind, written on letterhead from a Seattle law firm and addressed to Cole at Travis Brothers Industrial and Residential Construction Company. *Travis Brothers?*

With trembling fingers, she pushed the report aside and saw a variety of other photos, some of her and Jem, some of her from Boudoir, some just of Jem. Now her nerves started to jangle, so she pawed through the remaining papers and notes. What the hell was all this? Her throat tightened up and her muscles tensed as she flipped through more photos and continued her search.

And just as her frustration grew to a pitch that had her gritting her teeth hard, her searching gaze caught on a copy of Jem's birth certificate and a copy of his adoption decree lying there amongst the pictures and papers. Her stomach began to pitch and churn violently as she snatched up the decree and scanned the notes written in Cole's familiar handwriting. "Still possible to void adoption," it said at the top. "Unfit mother?" and "unstable home environment?" were listed like bullet points in one column. Then, "DNA needed to confirm parentage."

The room spun around her—or at least it seemed to. Why would Cole have all this information about her and her son? But she realized quickly that only one man knew, so there was only one way to find out.

Her jaw set, she got to her feet, the decree and the birth certificate clutched in her hand. She headed down the stairs, her sweaty palm slipping on the banister. Once outside, she walked quickly across the driveway to the barn and yanked open the door.

Her voice sounded flat and harsh to her own ears when she called out, "Cole. Where are you?" *And who are you?*

"Hey, where've you been? I thought you'd—" He

stopped, frowned. "What's wrong? Is it Jem?" he asked as he rushed toward her.

With her hands shaking and her temper kept so tightly in check she thought her nerves would snap, Lauren held the birth certificate up like a kryptonite shield. And it seemed to act as one on Cole, who came to a sudden and abrupt stop just about the same time the color drained out of his face.

"Where did you—" He hesitated for a moment, his expression swinging like a pendulum from soft and sorry to hard and heated. He cursed, knifed a hand through his hair. "I wanted to tell you, Lauren. I tried."

Her eyes narrowed. "Tried to tell me what?" she asked, her anger battling ferociously with her fear. "All I know is that you have pictures and documents that don't make sense to me. *What* don't I know?"

"Lauren," he said, coming toward her again, lifting a hand as if to touch her, then letting it fall to his side with a ragged sigh. "I'm Jem's father."

Lauren felt his words as if they were a physical blow. A thousand questions filled her mind, begged to be the first to be answered. But her throat was constricted, too constricted to speak. She felt as if she was choking on her own anger, humiliation and pain.

"I didn't want to tell you like this," he began, but then she found her voice, cut him off.

"How do you know? How can you be sure?"

"He looks so much like my father, but I really *knew* when I saw that bracelet," he said. "It was a gift I gave to my ex-wife...."

The sound of his voice buzzed in her ears as he continued to speak unintelligibly. She remembered their encounter in the tree house and felt a pain in her chest, a weakness in her limbs.

"Why didn't you tell me? Why didn't you tell me right away? Then, maybe…" She stopped, swallowing a lump of pain that made it impossible to go on.

"At first, I couldn't," he said, his face softening. "I didn't want to mess up Jem's life if it turned out I wasn't his father. I had to make sure first. But once I knew, I should have told you. I knew I should and I was going to, this afternoon when we had our talk."

"Cole," she said, her voice quavering, her breathing shallow. "You lied to me all this time, you lived in my home." She paused, mortification coloring her face. "You made love to me. And it was all a lie."

"Not everything was a lie," he said softly, stepping closer.

But she moved away, shaking her head, clasping her hands in front of her to still them. "Don't. It's too late, Cole."

"If you'll just hear me out. I didn't even know I had—"

"And then you married me," she said, cutting him off. She looked at him and felt her chin start to quiver as the tears welled up and floated there at the rim of her eyes, ready to topple at the slightest provocation. "Why?"

"I didn't want to, remember? It was what you wanted."

She stared at him, this beautiful stranger, this lying devil who'd walked in and taken her heart, and the tears fell. "What did you think? That if you married me you could get Jem?" She laughed harshly, hiccoughing back her tears as her anger took center stage. "My God, this is like a scene from one of those late night talk shows—"

The remaining softness in his expression hardened

and disappeared. This time it was Cole who interrupted her, saying, "Listen, Lauren. I told you I never wanted to be married again. But when you asked me to marry you, you didn't care who I was or what I wanted. You just wanted to marry *somebody* so you could start telling your own lies."

Lauren swayed on her feet. By marrying him, she'd done nothing less than harbor the enemy—and imagined herself in love with him. God, she was a fool.

Both of them turned their heads at the sound of a car pulling up the driveway, its horn honking loudly. Lauren stood immobile just inside the barn, standing like a sentinel in front of the door as she and Cole stared at each other. The fact that he'd slipped through her impenetrable filter and made a place for himself in her life shocked her to her core even as she felt the holes in that filter tightening, squeezing him out again.

Now she really didn't care who he was or what he wanted, but she'd be damned if she was going to let him anywhere near her son.

Two heavy doors slammed, then her heart clenched when she heard her baby call out, "Mommy, Co'!" before his voice receded toward the house.

"*My* son is home," she said, her voice surprisingly strong in the face of Cole's inexplicable anger. "And that's where he's going to stay."

Cole started toward her, lifted his hand. "Lauren, you have to hear me out."

But she wasn't quite sure she could take it if he touched her, so she put one hand up in front of her and said the words that she suspected would ring in her mind for a long time to come.

"I trusted you with everything I had. My home, my life, my child…my heart, everything." She stopped to

shake the web of unreality from her mind, then continued. "Even if you can prove you're Jem's father, you
don't deserve to be a part of his life. And, God knows,
he deserves more than you for a father.

"I want you to leave our home immediately, Cole,"
she said, standing as straight and tall as she could under
the circumstances. "Or I swear I'll call the police and
have you arrested for trespassing or murder or mayhem
or whatever it takes."

As his eyes hardened to ice-blue stones and his lips
thinned and whitened, she took a deep breath, promised
her heart she'd look after it later and finished her little
speech. "And then I'll do whatever it takes to keep you
away from us for the rest of our lives."

Eleven

Cole sat at Herbie's elbow-worn, oak wood bar and watched a revolving, 3-D sign featuring a two-foot tall polar bear holding a can of beer. And every time it spun around and that damn bear smiled at him with his big, toothy, mocking bear grin, Cole felt like getting a set of darts and taking potshots at it.

He glared at the sign, polished off his pint, then gestured to the bartender with a tap on the rim of his glass—the universal symbol for "bring me another one, Bub." Same bartender as last night, he noticed. Although the reason for coming to Herbie's the night before seemed like an insignificant blip on the radar compared to how his world had crumbled earlier today.

If it wasn't for Jem, he wouldn't even have stopped here. Instead of being on his way to getting stinking drunk, he'd be in his truck on his way out of town, as far away from Lauren and this mess as he could. But he wouldn't leave. It didn't matter if she followed through on each and every one of the threats she'd just made, he couldn't leave his son. And right now he didn't feel like he could leave her, either.

He spun his empty glass absently. What a fool he was—what a fool he'd been. Cole Travis, Mr. Downright Cynical, holding out an illogical, hidden hope that he'd be able to sit down with Lauren, tell her everything and she'd understand, forgive him and they'd work it all out.

He raked a hand through his hair. Damn, it was easy to blame her. How many times had he tried to tell her the truth? Exactly as many times as she'd refused to let him, that's how many.

Yeah, not communicating had been easier for both of them. But in hindsight, it had been a terrible mistake.

As the bartender dropped a fresh beer in front of him, Cole rubbed his jaw. As mad as he was at Lauren, he knew that the misery he was feeling right now was one hundred and ten percent his own fault.

The door groaned opened behind him and a sliver of fading daylight streaked into the dimness of Herbie's. And even though he'd told himself to stop doing it an hour ago, Cole turned around on his barstool to see if it was Lauren.

It wasn't.

It was Sherry, and she didn't look too happy. *Well, join the damned club.*

"Hello, Jem's father," she said with a grim smile as she slipped onto the stool next to him.

He cast a glance her way and practically growled, "I'm not in the mood for conversation."

That seemed to amuse her immensely because she laughed. "Tough. Could you pass me those peanuts?"

Cole grabbed a bowl of peanuts that was just beyond her reach and didn't try to hide his annoyance as he slid them over to her.

"Thanks." She popped a few in her mouth with one aging, bejeweled hand. "Hey, these are pretty salty."

Cole sighed. "Can I get you a drink? Or are you not planning on staying long?"

"Oh, no, I'm staying," she said, brightening. "I'll have a Cosmopolitan. With a twist."

He signaled to the bartender and ordered her drink, then turned and said, "So, what are you doing here? Bringing my bags and making sure I get out of town?"

"Not at all." Sherry shrugged. "I just thought you might want someone to talk to."

"Why?" he asked, his irritation ratcheting up. "So I can say I really thought I was doing the right thing? So I can say that I lied to Lauren because I wouldn't let my son be taken away from me again?"

Sherry's plucked eyebrows arrowed into perfect arches. "Again?"

He glanced up at her. Apparently, Nosy Nellie wasn't going anywhere until she got the dirt. Fine. If she wanted it, he'd give it to her. Since he had about as much to lose as a snake that had been flattened by a truck, he went ahead and told her about his ex-wife and the bracelet and why he couldn't let Jem slip away again.

"I see," she said, nodding slowly. "So you came to get your kid in a stealth attack. But if that's all you wanted, why did you put that ring on your finger? You didn't need to marry Lauren to get Jem. In fact, when the whole story comes out, you might find that was your biggest mistake."

He glanced at the antique platinum band on his fin-

ger. A mistake. He wanted to believe that, *had* to believe it, in fact. "I honestly don't know why I did it.
I've never met anyone like her. It's the only way to
explain it."

"Sounds like love to me," she said as she lifted her
martini glass by its fragile stem and sipped.

"Whoa, whoa," he said, his blood turning cold at
that idea. "Who said anything about love? I was just
trying to help her out with this marriage thing. Then the
whole situation just spun out of control. I couldn't stop
it."

His muscles tensed as he thought of all the times he
could've stopped it and didn't. All the times he'd made
love to Lauren, knowing he wasn't being fair, wasn't
giving her any more of a choice than his ex-wife had
given him.

"I *didn't* stop it," he corrected himself.

Sherry dropped her chin into her palm. "She's a
steamroller, all right."

He shook his head. "I went willingly enough."

"Sure you did. She's a beautiful, persuasive
woman."

He stared at Sherry over his glass, his jaw tightening.
Lauren had only been trying to protect what was hers,
just as he'd have done five years earlier if given the
chance. "She is beautiful—and persuasive—but that
has nothing to do with it. You and I both know there's
a lot more to her than what people see in that catalog."

Sherry sipped her drink innocently. "Well, for someone who isn't in love, you sure are protective of your
wife."

Cole tossed back the rest of his beer and fumed. He
fumed because he didn't know what love was, wasn't
sure he'd ever known. He cared deeply about Lauren.

Too deeply for his own good. Because in spite of his firm convictions on the subject of marriage, the thought of never hearing anyone call Lauren his wife again made his chest hurt in all the wrong places.

"You're one clever lady, Sherry." She looked over at him so fluttery and surprised, it made him smile. "But no matter how you spin this one, there's nothing possible for me and Lauren. I have nothing to offer her. And she doesn't want me. Hell, she *shouldn't* want me."

"I think you're wrong about that," Sherry said after finishing off her drink. "But don't you think you should find out for sure? Take a chance?"

The answers to those questions were so obvious, he found himself unable to speak. After a moment she apparently decided she'd made her point because she patted him on the arm, grabbed her purse and headed for the door.

He looked around for the bartender, and when he found him, Cole signaled for another beer. While he waited, he noticed a family having dinner together. The father was showing his young son how to twirl spaghetti around a fork, while the mother laughed at the mess they were making.

Longing settled deep inside him at a vision of him and Lauren and Jem as a family. He'd actually been a part of that vision a few times since he'd been here—at the Frosty King, at the barbecue, at Camp Tumbleweed. As he watched them, the itch to have that again, every day of his life, almost overwhelmed him.

He wasn't sure about love. That word made his gut twist into painful knots. But he was sure that Lauren had changed him in some way. And that all he wanted was to go to sleep at night with her in his arms and wake up to her in the morning. And be with her and his son every other minute. But that wasn't reality. He and Lauren weren't ever going to be, and the sooner he learned to deal with that, the better.

The bartender thumped the beer down on the pocked wood. It was Cole's third. Hopefully, it was also the magical brew that was going to dim his need for Lauren, maybe even help him to forget her altogether.

But by the time he'd drained the frosty glass, he finally had to admit to himself that getting Lauren out of his mind was going to be one of the toughest things he'd ever had to do.

Lauren woke with difficulty, but not with as much difficulty as she'd had falling asleep for the past three nights. The smell of coffee wafted up to her, convincing her to sit up and swing her legs over the edge of the bed. She smiled and stretched, knowing that Sherry was already up and about. She'd extended her vacation to stay on for a few days and without her and Jem, Lauren didn't know what she'd have done.

What with missing Cole like crazy, the uncertainty about getting the store done in time for the Summer Festival and waiting for the custody battle for Jem to begin, she needed her family around her for support and a sense of normalcy.

Of course, for the first two days after Cole had left town—a matter of gossip she'd heard through the Valle Verde grapevine—she hadn't been all that successful at carrying on as if everything was normal. She'd worked hard, gone to bed exhausted and slept poorly. She'd thought constantly about how he'd gone without a word—well, without a word to *her* anyway. He had sent Jem a card before he left, writing both, "See you

soon,'' and "Love, Cole,'' something that had both un-
nerved her and ignited a tiny spark of hope within her.
A traitorous, illogical hope that he was coming back.

But that hope had flickered out over the ensuing days,
though her mind dwelled on him constantly. She wanted
to hate him for what he'd done, tried hard to, but still
he remained in her mind, in her heart. His things were
all around her and she found it impossible to move or
touch any of them. His clothes were still in her room,
his tools were still in her barn, his scent still lingered
in her mind, his smile and laugh still gripped her heart.

She wished she understood how he could've shared
some of the most intimate moments of her life and kept
his terrible secret from her day after day. Sherry had
been able to shed a little light on his behavior when
she'd told Lauren about Jem's birth mother and the circumstances surrounding Cole's appearance in Valle
Verde. Of all people, Lauren understood the need to
connect with family. She'd been looking for the same
thing all her life.

But it didn't seem to matter if she was compassionate
or not, clear about his intentions or not. Her heart was
simply breaking a little more every day.

What had happened was for the best. And thinking
he was gone for good would eventually make it easier
to stop missing him. Make her stop wishing she could
be in his arms and laugh with him and make him dinner
and fold his socks and hate him and love him all at
once.

*What a liar I am. I still want him. More than I've
ever wanted anything in my life.*

Lauren stood up and was just beginning to get
dressed when the sound of hammering rat-a-tat-tatted
through the open window like a machine gun, making

her jump. It was louder, more frantic than she remembered from the last few weeks. *Cole. He was back.* It was the only thing she could think—and that thought sent pure adrenaline shooting through her.

She rushed to the window, scolding herself for her excitement even as she looked for him. But she didn't see anything except two big yellow pickup trucks.

She tried to calm her racing heart as she dressed quickly, then ran downstairs and yanked open the front door.

And what she saw made her frown in confusion.

A vaguely familiar man was hauling supplies into the barn. Two more men were just inside the barn, installing drywall. They moved quickly, efficiently, and reminded her very much of Cole. As she walked across the yard, she began to draw the attention of these strangers.

"Hello," one of them called, his grin wide, genuine—and also damnably familiar.

"Beautiful day, isn't it?" said another, pausing in his work to rake his choppy hair out of his eyes with his fingers.

She opened her mouth to respond, but snapped it shut when she saw Cole, leaning against the door of one of the yellow trucks, beaming that lazy smile at her. And even as her bones melted and her remaining anger threatened to evaporate, she noticed that the trucks were painted with the words, Travis Construction.

He *had* come back. And with reinforcements.

She walked straight to him, attempting to quell both her excitement and her fear. "What are you doing here?"

"We're here to finish the job."

Finish what job, she thought wildly. The hatchet job on my heart? "I told you I didn't want you here, Cole," she said. But, in truth, she didn't sound all that convincing even to her own ears.

"Yes, I remember," he said as he stood there. He was close, too close. "And I don't blame you. I wanted to know my child so badly that I did a lot of stupid things. I'm sorry, Lauren. I really am." He shook his head, that lazy grin fading more with each word. "But that's not who I am. *This* is who I am. I know it may not be easy to understand, but I made a commitment to you. And I'm going to finish what I started." He gestured toward the other men. "And I brought my brothers to help me."

With effort, she forced herself to refrain from gawking at the three handsome men who each bore a resemblance to Cole.

So he was here to complete his project. And she—foolish girl that she was—had already let her little spark of hope run rampant. He wasn't here because he wanted her. He was here to honor his promise, clear his plate of old business before he went into round two of the Jem tug-of-war. And those facts had her heart hurting all over again.

She lashed out so he wouldn't notice the hurt she was sure shone in her eyes. "What is it, Cole? Gotta finish the store so you'll look good in front of the judge when the time comes?" Her voice shook slightly when she added, "Well, I can give you the verdict right now. You're not taking Jem from me."

His smile died but his eyes remained intense as he shook his head and said, "I would never take Jem away from his mother."

Her resistance softened as a quiet shiver traveled up her spine. *His mother?* It felt like her heart had opened a crack and a tiny thread was beginning to twist her and

Cole together. Could he be thinking of keeping the fight out of the courts? "What are you saying?"

"Lauren, I don't know yet how this is all going to work. But I'm staying in town, living here, moving here." He sounded resolute, energized. "In fact, I already have."

Despair fell over her like a ten-ton blanket. The last few days had been a horror *without* him here. But with him in town, she was going to have to see him, bump into him, treat him like a neighbor, for God's sake. She simply didn't think she could survive that.

"Excuse me," she said breathlessly, spinning around and heading back into the house.

"Where're you going?" he called after her.

To think. To think and to see the sign, she wanted to say, but her throat was too tight.

It took her two minutes to run into the house, ask Sherry to watch Jem, grab her keys and head back to the car. Then she gunned the engine, maneuvered a clumsy five-point turn, and skidded down the driveway.

But before she turned out onto the street, she let her gaze linger on the rearview mirror where she could see Cole, staring after her with a mix of curiosity and confusion on his handsome face.

Listen 2 UR Heart.

"Listen to my heart?" she asked the sign quietly. If ever she'd encountered an ambiguous sign, this was it. It may as well have said, *Figure It Out For URself.* She couldn't listen to her heart—it was too untrustworthy. Listening to it was like listening to the ramblings of a dreamer.

It was her heart that should have warned her about Cole. Her heart that should have known that she'd been taking a stupid chance, her heart that stood by and waited for the bomb to drop. And when it had dropped, her heart had paid the price.

She peered up at the sign again and read it one more time. *Listen 2 UR Heart.* She sighed. If she *really* listened to her heart, she could hear it telling her that Cole had tried to come clean. That she'd wanted so much to live in their secluded oasis that she'd kept him from confessing.

She'd set herself up, pure and simple. She was the one who'd stormed ahead, doing anything she could think of to keep her son. She'd asked Cole to marry her, when she should have been thinking about what was right for her.

She'd built a wall around herself so long ago she'd assumed she could ignore her initial attraction to Cole. That, of course, had proved impossible. He was too much. Too funny, too giving, too sexy, too generous, too warm. And too patient and loving with Jem.

Jem really deserved a dad like that. A dad like she'd never had.

She took one more look at the sign before heading for home. She loved Cole but since it was clear he was here for Jem and not for her, she'd simply have to keep what was in her heart a secret. There was no sense in humiliating herself further by making Cole say he didn't want her.

Instead, she would use all that love to find a way to share her son with Cole. Because when she really listened to her heart, she heard it say that she owed the man she loved a chance to be a father to his own son.

Twelve

Lauren's resolve to keep her heart and its secrets safe from Cole took its first beating when she pulled into her driveway and saw a Kodak moment unfolding on her porch.

Cole sat on the swing with Jem, the three Travis brothers sat on the wide steps and Sherry leaned against the porch railing drinking coffee. They were all talking, laughing, smiling. As she pulled to a stop, they all turned toward her in an almost choreographed unison. And in that moment, a renegade thought sped through her mind—that's my family. My son, my husband, my brothers-in-law, my almost-Mom. *I finally have a family.*

But that second passed and she woke up to the painful fact that they weren't a family—not hers, anyway. She didn't have a real family, and that knowledge had never made her quite as sad as it did at that moment.

A huge lump formed in her throat as she slid out of the SUV and Jem jumped up and ran to her. They walked back to the porch together, and Lauren listened intently as Jem introduced her to Cole's brothers. Cole's gaze followed her, making her feel hot and tingling when she really wanted to be calm and cool.

But she didn't have much time to dwell on it because just then someone asked to see Jem's tree house and in a flurry of muffled laughter and chatter everyone scattered, and before Lauren could stop them, she and Cole were alone.

Dammit. The members of her little Kodak family were all in cahoots. She straightened to her full height and began to walk past Cole to the front door. She didn't feel ready or strong enough to be alone with him. Not yet.

"Lauren," he said, his voice low but commanding. "What do you say we stop running from each other?"

She came to a halt halfway to the door. She wanted to point out that he was the one who'd left town, but then she knew how hypocritical that would be. She'd been running away her whole life, beginning at age five, continuing through…well, today, she supposed. In fact, she wouldn't even be in this town if she hadn't been running away from what she'd thought of at the time as lost love—something she now knew to be a poor, flimsy imitation of love. Even her abstinence program was a sham, covering up yet more things from which she was scampering away like the fox before the hounds: vulnerability, intimacy, fear of rejection.

She sighed. He was right. It was time to stop. Because she'd never had so much at stake in her whole life.

She turned around. He sat on the porch swing, looking totally at home, propelling himself with the toe of his work boot. It had only been three days since she'd seen him. This morning it had seemed like three years. Now that he was here and the spicy, sunshiny scent of him was wrapping around her, it seemed like three minutes.

Listen 2 UR Heart, she repeated to herself like a mantra. "All right. I'll stop running away if you will."

His smile made his eyes crinkle up at the corners and his voice was low when he asked, "Will you come sit down?"

She hesitated, felt her heart pulling her toward him, her head pulling her away—and went with her heart. "Sure." When she sat down beside him gingerly, she tried not to be thrilled that he was here, right next to her, tried not to be afraid of what was to come.

"Lauren," he began, "I know I should have told you who I was from the first day. But I was afraid. I didn't want to lose Jem again, and that fear made me do some really asinine things."

"Yes, it did," she agreed, but something inside of her sank at his words. How many times did she have to hear that she'd pushed him into something he didn't want? "But I can understand it," she said, swallowing the frustration in her throat. "I don't want to lose him either."

He shook his head. "Neither of us has to lose him. That's why I moved here, so you and I can be his parents."

She stared at him, a breathtaking mixture of hope and uncertainty coursing through her. But she knew better than to guess at the true meaning behind his words. "You moved just so we could both have Jem?"

"He needs us both, Lauren. He loves you so much."

At his words, her chin began to quiver and tears started to pool up inside her eyes, but she refused to let them fall. *Listen 2 UR Heart,* she told herself sternly. "Cole, I have something to tell you, too. I know you didn't abandon him, that you didn't even know you had a son. I was wrong when I said you didn't deserve him. You do. And he deserves you, to be a part of your family."

He put one arm along the back of the swing and touched her hair with his fingertips. He said nothing, and even though a few tears ended up spilling over, she felt like she wanted to sit here with him like this forever.

But she couldn't go up and down the roller coaster with him one more time. Contentment to despair to hope to—what was next? She had to get off the ride. "Oh," she said, punctuating the word with unconcern as best she could. "By the way, as soon as you're ready, we should talk about how to deal with this marriage."

Cole simply couldn't take his eyes off her. There was no denying it anymore. He loved her, loved her fiercely. He'd known it long before he'd left Valle Verde a few days earlier. And he should have known it sooner than that, but he'd been too afraid of giving his heart and having it trampled on again.

But that was the past, and Lauren was his future.

What an odyssey the past few days had been. He'd gone home to Seattle, gotten an earful from his parents who'd sworn they wanted to disown him and adopt Lauren, fired his ex-best friend and attorney, then went to Puget Sound to be alone and do some serious thinking. When he'd returned home, he convinced his brothers to come back down with him to help him move and finish Lauren's construction project.

But he wasn't just here to finish the work on her store

or be near his son. He was here because he loved her and couldn't live without her. He wanted Lauren— every day, every night, every minute in between. And if that meant he had to give up his fears, his cynicism and the safety net he'd constructed around his heart, then that's exactly what he was going to do.

He'd missed her like crazy while he was gone and had been planning on rearranging the heavens if that's what it took to make her say she loved him, too. He wanted to live with her, be her husband, create a family. Because this was where he belonged.

Cole turned toward her so he could see her face when he took what felt like the biggest risk he'd ever taken in his life. She was beautiful, but her eyes were troubled, her smooth brow was beginning to crinkle up with worry.

"I'm not letting you go, Lauren," he said, then took a fortifying breath. "I want to marry you again. This time with our friends and families around us and Jem standing with his parents."

Lauren sat back down in the roller coaster car with a hard thunk. It began its ascent as soon as she gazed into his eyes. Hope springs eternal, someone once said, but she was made of more practical stuff. She was going to have to be absolutely sure she understood before he got any closer. "Cole, I—"

But then he did get closer, kneeling down before her with his broad chest just brushing her knees. "Lauren," he began, and the earnestness in his gaze threatened to snuff out any remaining anger or mistrust she still had for him. "I know I don't deserve you. But I think Jem deserves us both. He deserves a family. We all do."

The coaster climbed higher but it still seemed as if it

was only a matter of time before it fell. "But you *have* a family to offer him, Cole."

"They'll be your family, too," he said, his voice cracking slightly. "If only you can forgive me."

Lauren's heart soared, and she wanted to reach out and reassure him that she had already forgiven him. But she held back, folding her hands into her lap. How could she know why he was really doing this? Was it just for Jem? If only he could love *her,* too, then she would leap into his arms and kiss him until they were both senseless. If only he said the words, it would be a sign that it was all right to let go of her fear and give herself to him.

Cole brought her hand up to his lips, closing his eyes as he brushed a kiss across it, and her last shields against him began to crumble. "I can't imagine one more day without you in my life," he said, then held out a gorgeous antique platinum diamond ring so brilliant, it shone with its own silvered light. Then, his eyes twinkling with teasing, he said, "This was my grandmother's. She got it from her mother who, so the story goes, sewed it into the lining of her petticoat when they came from Oklahoma to Washington in their covered wagon. And now it's yours—if you want it." His eyes softened. "I love you. Say you'll marry me."

And in that moment, all the pain and loneliness and doubt that had filled Lauren's heart for so long drained away, and instead it began to overflow with pleasure and joy. She looked up into his eyes to see the love shining there. He'd already proved himself to her as a man, as a lover, as a father to her child. He'd already made her fall in love with him. And now he'd just offered her as a wedding gift something she'd wished for all her life—a family for herself, a family for their son.

"Say you will," he whispered.

Tears sprang to her eyes and gathered, thick and heavy in her throat, threatening to choke her. "I will. I'll marry you, Cole."

He smiled up at her, twirling the ring between his fingers, his eyes twinkling as brightly as the diamond. "There's one more thing, though," he said. "I haven't heard the magic words yet." Then he mouthed, *I love you* to prompt her.

She laughed, knew the words were in her eyes, but she said them anyway. "I love you, Cole, you big idiot. I've already loved you for a long time."

He reached up to kiss her quickly, then she let out a little yelp when he hauled her to her feet, took her left hand and slipped the beautiful ring into place beside her wedding band with reverence.

Then he took her in his arms and kissed her in a way that was downright sinful. As she melted into him, she suddenly realized that no matter how much she loved him before, she loved him more now—now that he was hers.

He pulled away slightly. "Ready to go tell our family?"

Lauren's heart was riding a new roller coaster now, one that featured loop-di-loops and crazy high speeds. "Our family." She reached up and trailed one finger across his jaw. "You have no idea how ready I am for that."

They walked with their arms draped around each other until they reached the base of the tree.

Cole leaned down and gave her one more kiss before he released her, then yelled up into the green, still branches, "She said yes!"

A loud cheer went up inside the tree house, then the

whole group started piling out like fraternity boys from a telephone booth. Cole's brothers came down first before helping Jem and Sherry.

Jem's expression was lit up like fireworks in the night sky. "Co', Grandma Sherry says you're gonna be my dad!"

"That's right, son," he said, his voice thickening on the final word.

Lauren smiled and squeezed his hand as Jem jumped up and down, then hugged Cole's legs. Then she and her family—her son and her husband and her brothers-in-law and her almost-Mom—all turned toward the house.

And when Lauren walked up the porch stairs with her two men beside her, she knew she'd just gotten her heart's desire.

She knew that she was finally home.

*   *   *   *   *

Your opinion is important to us!

Please take a few moments to share your thoughts with us about Mills & Boon® and Silhouette® books. Your comments will ensure that we continue to deliver books you love to read.

> **To thank you for your input, everyone who replies will be entered into a prize draw to win a year's supply of their favourite series books∗.**

1. There are several different series under the Mills & Boon and Silhouette brands. Please tick the box that most accurately represents your reading habit for each series.

Series	Currently Read (have read within last three months)	Used to Read (but do not read currently)	Do Not Read
Mills & Boon			
Modern Romance™	❏	❏	❏
Sensual Romance™	❏	❏	❏
Blaze™	❏	❏	❏
Tender Romance™	❏	❏	❏
Medical Romance™	❏	❏	❏
Historical Romance™	❏	❏	❏
Silhouette			
Special Edition™	❏	❏	❏
Superromance™	❏	❏	❏
Desire™	❏	❏	❏
Sensation™	❏	❏	❏
Intrigue™	❏	❏	❏

2. Where did you buy this book?

From a supermarket ❏ Through our Reader Service™ ❏
From a bookshop ❏ If so please give us your Club Subscription no.
On the Internet ❏

Other _____ _____/_____

3. Please indicate by number which were the 3 most important factors that made you buy this book. (1 = most important).

The picture on the cover	___	I enjoy this series	___
The author	___	The price	___
The title	___	I borrowed/was given this book	___
The description on the back cover	___	Part of a mini-series	___

Other _____

4. How many Mills & Boon and /or Silhouette books do you buy at one time?

I buy ___ books at one time ❏
I rarely buy a book (less than once a year) ❏

5. How often do you shop for any Mills & Boon and/or Silhouette books?

One or more times a month ❏ A few times per year ❏
Once every 2-3 months ❏ Never ❏

6. How long have you been reading Mills & Boon® and/or Silhouette®?
_____ years

7. What other types of book do you enjoy reading?

Family sagas eg. Maeve Binchy ❏
Classics eg. Jane Austen ❏
Historical sagas eg. Josephine Cox ❏
Crime/Thrillers eg. John Grisham ❏
Romance eg. Danielle Steel ❏
Science Fiction/Fantasy eg. JRR Tolkien ❏
Contemporary Women's fiction eg. Marian Keyes ❏

8. Do you agree with the following statements about Silhouette? Please tick the appropriate boxes.

	Strongly agree	Tend to agree	Neither agree nor disagree	Tend to disagree	Strongly disagree
Silhouette offers great value for money.	❏	❏	❏	❏	❏
With Silhouette I can always find the right type of story to suit my mood.	❏	❏	❏	❏	❏
I read Silhouette books because they offer me an entertaining escape from everyday life.	❏	❏	❏	❏	❏
Silhouette stories have improved or stayed the same standard over the time I have been reading them.	❏	❏	❏	❏	❏

9. Which age bracket do you belong to? Your answers will remain confidential.

❏ 16-24   ❏ 25-34   ❏ 35-49   ❏ 50-64   ❏ 65+

THANK YOU for taking the time to tell us what you think! If you would like to be entered into the **FREE prize draw** to win a year's supply of your favourite series books, please enter your name and address below.

Name: _____

Address: _____

_____

Post Code: _____ Tel: _____

Please send your completed questionnaire to the address below:

READER SURVEY, PO Box 676, Richmond, Surrey, TW9 1WU.

SILHOUETTE®

Desire 2 in 1

are proud to introduce

DYNASTIES:
THE BARONES

Meet the wealthy Barones—caught in a web of danger, deceit and…desire!

Twelve exciting stories in six 2-in-1 volumes:

0904/51a

❖ SILHOUETTE®
Desire 2 in 1

AVAILABLE FROM 17TH SEPTEMBER 2004

MAN IN CONTROL Diana Palmer

Texan Lovers

Since Agent Alexander Cobb had rejected Jodie Clayburn eight years ago they'd been sworn enemies. But now they were working together on a drug-smuggling case and Alexander was finding Jodie hard to resist.

THORN'S CHALLENGE Brenda Jackson

Thorn Westmoreland had wanted a commitment-free affair with Tara Matthews. But he soon found himself striving to win her love. Would she give her heart to this tough tycoon?

❧

SHAMELESS Ann Major

The Country Club

With loan sharks on her trail, Celeste Cavanaugh turned to ex-marine Phillip Westin for help. He was the only man she'd ever loved but she'd broken his heart. Now he wanted her back in return for his help…

DESPERADO DAD Linda Conrad

When Randi Cullen offered refuge to Manuel Sanchez she didn't expect him to be an undercover agent hunting a ruthless killer! She agreed to marriage in order to protect his cover—but then found herself falling in love with him…

❧

BILLIONAIRE BOSS Meagan McKinney

Montana

Kirsten Meadows's boss Seth Morgan was sophisticated, rich, sensual and completely off-limits. But one look at Kirsten and this playboy tycoon knew he wanted to be more than just her boss!

IN BED WITH BEAUTY Katherine Garbera

King of Hearts

Sarah Malcolm needed security in her love life. So why couldn't she keep away from Harris Davidson? He was certainly wealthy, powerful and sexy but he'd also made it clear he had no room in his life for a woman…

SILHOUETTE®

Desire™ 2 in 1

is proud to introduce

DYNASTIES:
THE DANFORTHS

Meet the Danforths—a family of prominence...
tested by scandal, sustained by passion!

Coming Soon!
Twelve thrilling stories in six 2-in-1 volumes:

0105/SH/LC96

GEN/18/RTL5

SILHOUETTE®

Passionate and thrilling
romantic adventures

Sensation™

NIGHT WATCH

Suzanne Brockmann

FREE!

2 Books
and a surprise gift!

We would like to take this opportunity to thank you for reading this Silhouette® book by offering you the chance to take TWO more specially selected titles from the Desire™ series absolutely FREE! We're also making this offer to introduce you to the benefits of the Reader Service™—

- ★ **FREE home delivery**
- ★ **FREE gifts and competitions**
- ★ **FREE monthly Newsletter**
- ★ **Exclusive Reader Service offers**
- ★ **Books available before they're in the shops**

Accepting these FREE books and gift places you under no obligation to buy, you may cancel at any time, even after receiving your free shipment. Simply complete your details below and return the entire page to the address below. You don't even need a stamp!

YES! Please send me 2 free Desire books and a surprise gift. I understand that unless you hear from me. I will receive 3 superb new titles every month for just £4.99 each, postage and packing free. I am under no obligation to purchase any books and may cancel my subscription at any time. The free books and gift will be mine to keep in any case.

D4ZEF

Ms/Mrs/Miss/Mr ....Initials ....

BLOCK CAPITALS PLEASE

Surname ....

Address ....

....

....Postcode ....

Send this whole page to:
UK: FREEPOST CN81, Croydon, CR9 3WZ